The Prophet of Central Park

by P C Burhenne

"Free will is a terrifying gift. No wonder

mankind tries so hard to return it."

Rockefeller Center Sage

THE PROPHET OF CENTRAL PARK

THE PROPHET OF CENTRAL PARK. Copyright © 2024 by Patrick C. Burhenne. Published by Kensie Point Books, Fairfield, CT.

Cover design by Isabel Webre

Library of Congress Control Number: 2024927489

ISBN 979-8-9922935-0-0

Table of Contents

Prologue: January

A possible very near future for the US in which
court decisions make firearms common in public
and a new underground railroad pits pro-choice
and pro-life states against each other.

US News
*In a startling Gallup Poll, more than a third of respondents say they do
not believe their grandchildren will have a United States of America to
reside in. Most participants who identified as conservative cited the "woke
values" of LGBTQ rights and the overreach of the federal government as the
reason for the eventual end to the Union. Those who called themselves
liberal pointed to Supreme Court decisions that promote a society that they
have no desire to reside in, especially in its abandonment of the separation
of church and state.*

"That's the best I can give ya for it, young man."

Saying this, the car dealer rests his hand on the hood of Caleb's pickup,
already taking possession. He wears a sympathetic frown because of the
disappointing offer but Caleb knows the man is lowballing him. Growing
up at the family auction hall has taught Caleb value. The bus leaves in a
little over an hour. He realizes he is trembling, can only imagine the "deer
in the headlights" look on his face.

"So do we have a deal?"

A smirk flashes across the man's face before he catches himself. With
his pencil legs sticking down from his parka, he seems liable to blow over in
the cutting breeze but he is in control. Caleb needs the money to make a
start in New York City. A desperation the man has read. Caleb can almost
cry at being so easily fleeced. He stares out past the lot, back north where
ten miles away the bus depot waits to take him out of Kentucky. He only
knows this town to drive through but, more importantly, no one here knows
him to report the transaction back to his father. The sun has just set and the

thin filigree of clouds look like frost over the weak blue of the sky. He very nearly nods in surrender. Then the words of Psalm 12 play in his mind: "Because the poor are plundered and the needy groan, I will now rise," says the Lord. "I will protect them from those who malign them."

Caleb rolls the new resolve about his lower lip like a pinch of snuff and turns away, pulling out his phone.

"Wait. What, what are you doing?"

"Canceling my ride," Caleb says without looking up. "That ain't near enough."

The car dealer throws his arms out, looks ready to grab Caleb to keep him from leaving. "Hold on, you're here to sell, I'm here to buy. Maybe—"

Caleb turns back finally to cut him off. "You're gonna put eleven plus in the window, get at least ten. I won't take less than half that."

Somehow the man doesn't hear Caleb's heart beating and they settle on forty-eight hundred. Not enough but better and time, now as important as money, is fast running through his fingers. The Uber arrives as the dealer's secretary is notarizing the title transfer. Once in the stranger's car with the extra funds he exhales, a breath broken by relief. Yet he is anxious over his final stop before the depot. With his father an hour's drive away on a house call to a possible consignor, Caleb can see his mother where she is volunteering at the food pantry. She will object to his defiance but he hopes she will hug him one last time.

She is sorting cans into distribution packages with two other ladies and despite the urgency, he stops at the sight of her unguarded ease here which has restored an assurance Caleb forgot she could possess. She seems younger too and with her auburn hair down and her broad smile softening her crow's feet and other lines, she is attractive, though he does not dwell on that inappropriate thought. Then a companion points to him in the doorway and like a shadow falling across her, the timid harried caretaker he knows too well dispatches this former self. If he has any lingering doubts about leaving, the change he brings to her scatters them.

She comes forward so they are several paces from the others. "Caleb, your father's trying to get a hold of you."

He takes her hand. "Mom, I've come to say goodbye."

"What do you mean."

THE PROPHET OF CENTRAL PARK

"I've got a job in New York," he exaggerates. "My bus leaves, well, soon."

Taller than she is, he stares down expectantly. She looks back bewildered.

"How did you get your father to agree?"

"This is my decision, Mom."

At first she is silent as she works through the implication of his answer. Then she shakes her head, her hands, so that he lets go. She begins shaking all over. "No. You need to speak with him. Of course, you do."

"'Speak with him'? Mom, I may as well be a boarder at the homestead. We don't any of us talk anymore."

"We would." She reaches up to take hold of his shoulders. "Everything would be fine if you accepted God's will. Annaliese's death was God's will."

Never far from his thoughts, the ghost of his friend Annaliese accuses him: You'd worship my killer. He almost answers: God didn't kill you—I did. He does say, "I'm not pretending anymore that there's no world outside of Father and the church."

She steps away and despite the wrinkles, this time her face shows the child she must have been, caught in a lie or having broken a cherished figurine. "Your father won't allow this," she says, heading back to the table.

"Mom, he's down by Lexington."

"He canceled that." She has her phone out. "He'll want to speak with you."

It is Caleb's turn to revert to a child terrified before paternal judgment. He leaves.

Outside a mere moment has passed but the night seems firmly in place, a blind for threats everywhere as he gets back in his ride. The bus station is several blocks away. He chafes at the red lights, checking out the rear for his father's dark blue King Cab to rush up on the Uber's bumper. A Coachliner sits next to the squat depot building. CINCINNATI—his first stop—shines like a promise in the destination slot above its windshield. Other travelers are boarding. He is alarmed at how close he cut his arrival as he transfers his bag to the undercarriage storage, hands the driver his ticket. In fact, once seated he endures a nerve-wracking wait for the driver to join them. The rolls of the man's stomach make him struggle to get behind the wheel. He could almost be scratching at a spot on his back where his fingers can't reach. Nevertheless Caleb stifles a cheer for the man when they are pulling out of the station seconds before his father rumbles in.

Without slowing his father turns around in a tight half circle that the truck tires squeal against. The back of the coach blocks where he goes next and Caleb wants to believe that the race-car maneuver is nothing more than frustration at missing his departure. Then the King Cab speeds past. Caleb spots his brother Alfred Jr. in its passenger seat and his brother locks eyes on Caleb. Alfred Sr. doesn't come to a screeching halt in front of the bus as Caleb half expects. Instead he leads them across the bridge into Ohio and onto the river road.

"I've done nothing wrong," Caleb mutters to himself to try to put away his fear. "And I'm not coming back."

For the whole trip to Cincinnati, the King Cab's taillights show out of the night ahead of the bus. Again and again, Caleb makes himself look away and scours his mind for any escape. Perhaps squeezing himself under a seat to hide. Perhaps, if the city traffic helps out, persuading the driver to drop him off a few blocks from the depot. At his most despondent, he considers turning himself over to the posse.

When they can see the highrises of the city's downtown, he approaches the driver.

"Stay in your seat, young man."

Ignoring this Caleb leans close to ask, "Is there a police stand in this station?"

"Why?"

The driver looks at him in quick glances which jiggle the bunting of flesh tucked backward from his chin to low on his neck. Caleb points to the baleful red eyes of the King Cab in front of them.

"My father and brother are in that truck. They're gonna try and stop me going to New York."

"How old are you?"

Caleb is embarrassed to admit, "Twenty-two."

"What are they thinking?"

"That they're saving my immortal soul."

The answer sharpens the concern in the driver's wide eyes. "Oh, Christ."

THE PROPHET OF CENTRAL PARK

"Something like that."

"There's no police stand. The counter has to call for a car." The driver waves a hand at him. "Now go back to your seat."

The passengers close by overhear. Some look up at him with sympathy. Others with suspicion. Back in his place he chides himself for not thinking of the police sooner. Already the bus is slowing for the depot's lot. Then Caleb sighs, not sure how he can describe his situation so the police will take him seriously. No, he challenges himself, My way out goes past Father —It's up to me to take it.

Bringing the coach to a stop, the driver dislodges himself from his cockpit and hops out the door. The riders begin exiting row by row. Caleb is at the back. When his older brother takes up a position below his window, Caleb stares down with all the disgust he can muster. Al Jr. tries to return this but fails, starts watching his feet stomp a two-step against the cold. The truck sits several yards from where people are disembarking. Those lined in the aisle begin grumbling at what the holdup is already. When Caleb stands, he sees that his father is the holdup.

Alfred Ellison Sr. stands in front of the coach door as inspector and guard. At first glance he seems an unlikely obstacle. Spare of build, average in height and strangely underdressed in a tufted, sleeveless orange vest over a green and black flannel shirt, he clearly shows his sixty-seven years in the hollows of the cheeks rising out of his white-speckled bramble beard. But an intensity of will doesn't just radiate from his searching grey eyes, it seems an engine giving off ribbons of vapor that corkscrew off his torso into the sawing wind. Even the physically imposing riders falter a moment then turn aside to not brush against him. Caleb sees also that of course his father is exercising his expanded Second Amendment rights to wear his Smith and Wesson on a hip. As soon as he locates Caleb in the queue, Alfred Sr. steps back to hasten his son to him.

The idea transfixes Caleb right then, one he hadn't truly believed before: I **am** twenty-two and I don't have to go back.

Al Jr. has rejoined their father by the time Caleb reaches the short stairway down. Somebody's dowdy mother is in front of him. His father says over the woman, "This sinful episode ends now."

The fanatic's insistence behind the statement sends the woman scurrying away to the right. As Caleb reaches the asphalt, he fills his lungs to keep his voice from faltering.

"This is my business, Father. Go away."

He turns to follow the dowdy woman but finds the baggage bay doors still closed and the other passengers crowded around them a shocked audience to the confrontation. Briefly wondering where the driver is, he turns back only to have his father seize him by the forearm.

Annaliese yells in his head: Fight for yourself like you didn't fight for me! Caleb throws that arm in an arc upward to break the hold. Caught offguard, his father stuttersteps back then his lips appear out of his whiskers to bellow, "How dare you raise a hand to your father!"

Al Jr. inches forward. "Caleb, you know you're going to obey. Make it easy and get in the truck." He is trying for a voice of reason but it sounds wheedling and scared.

"You two are gonna have to . . . subdue me to get me in that truck. And you'd have to lock me up to keep me in Maynardsville. There's nothing for me there."

"'Nothing'?" Alfred Sr. repeats, a note of care displacing the anger. "Home is your only hope for redemption. I am your only hope for redemption."

Caleb answers with what he knows. "You don't own God."

Alfred Sr. trembles at the rebuke. Then he sets his jaw. "A terrible spirit has taken you over. Al Jr., we must do for Caleb what he can't do for himself." When his oldest son still hangs back, he barks, "Al Jr., with me!"

The driver reappears between them. "I've called the police. Leave now while you can."

Alfred Sr. turns his most withering gaze on the intruder but the man holds.

"Don't interfere in what you don't understand."

"I understand the boy don't want you bothering him. Everyone here's heard. You go through me, that's assault of a public transit employee—three year sentence. Reach for the gun, it goes up. You take him, it's kidnapping."

Al Jr. starts to suggest, "Maybe we should—". His father raises a hand to cut him off and looks past the driver to Caleb.

THE PROPHET OF CENTRAL PARK

"You would discard your family, **your family**, to move to the very heart of depravity in this country?"

"Goodbye, Father."

"Oh, Son, you will soon find yourself wishing for the pods thrown to the pigs."

With that he and Al Jr. leave. Caleb tells the driver, "You're my hero, Sir." The man hunches forward, every fleshy fold aquiver. "I almost shit myself."

No police come so Caleb doesn't know if the driver was bluffing or if he called to cancel them. Caleb takes his bag into the station, buoyed by the high of his deliverance. Soon though, his father's parting reference to the prodigal son gnaws at him. Cincinnati is by far the biggest city he has set foot in. Its skyscrapers loom over one side of the terminal, impersonal steel fortresses. On the opposite side blocks of rundown tenements stretch off and up a steep hill. Occasional shouts rise from these. Other murmurs of discontent. There is a pop that could be a gunshot. He wouldn't want to venture in either direction, fears both would devour him, and where he's going dwarfs this place.

The connecting bus north holds a different driver, an older sullen black man—or African-American, Caleb should probably call him. The hills rolling by become flat parcels of farmland divided by country roads or runoff ditches, borders of single file trees. Solitary points of light wink out of the darkness. Otherwise he could believe the world is deserted. Caleb feels even more alone, an orphan by his own hand.

He considers that he should finally tell his twin sister that he is leaving. His mother and Al Jr. couldn't be trusted to keep his intentions secret, obviously, but Carolyne had enough to worry about with her newborn. That's how he rationalized hiding the move from her anyway. Staring at his phone, he admits the truth: she is the only one who could have persuaded him to stay. Not that she would but she could have. Since childhood they always knew when the other needed them. In her calls of late she kept asking, So what was he planning these days? Obvious invitations to share. Caleb is sure she has heard already from their mother, has probably called the old cell. Caleb puts away the new one.

The transfer in Cleveland to the New York bus takes two hours. Safely seated on the final leg of the journey, he allows himself to sleep, wakes at a rest stop in Pennsylvania. Monstrous snowflakes fall out of the ink void through the spheres of the floodlights, blurring the facilities and other parked vehicles and the travelers hurrying between them so that at first he thinks the scene is the remnant of a dissolving dream. With his destination now a few hours away, panic sets in. The interview he set up holds no guarantees. A world renown auction house is not keeping a job open just because he's run away from home. The apartment he arranged through an emergency relocation helpline is a blank that his imagination fills with awful scenarios. A ghetto location where he fears for his life. A predatory or otherwise untrustworthy roommate. Sidney his name is. He is only a flippant voice on the phone. Right off the bus, Caleb will have to find his way to the place. He has directions but the address is in the borough of Queens. If he doesn't find a job, the city will eat his savings like cotton candy. Was his father right—will New York reduce him to begging for the scraps people feed their animals?

Daybreak is a grey mottled stain seeping westward through the canopy of the storm but the snow stops as they leave the mountains. Once they reach New Jersey an electric sense of being lost threatens to become nausea. Caleb is breathing through his nose, eyes closed, when his cell hums with a text.

It is the roommate Sidney asking, Are you on the 11:20 into Port Authority Bus Station? When Caleb answers, Yes, this Sidney writes back, I'll meet you at the gate so you don't get mugged your first day, LOL. Before Caleb can ask how to recognize him, the other texts, Don't worry— you can't miss me. Caleb begins to breathe normally again. His first glimpse of the Manhattan skyline, immense even at several miles distance, makes him doubly grateful for the welcome party.

When he exits his bus in an upper level of the terminal, the city honks, shouts and calls to him from every direction so that he prays this roommate character keeps his word. Inside the swinging door, there is indeed a character waiting, wearing a chauffeur's cap and holding a handmade sign for "C. Ellison". He asks for proof of ID, his full lips puckered in a frown, then as Caleb reaches for his wallet, the mouth flies into a smile that punctures his chipmunk cheeks. "I'm messing with you. Let me buy you a slice. You gotta be hungry after that trip."

THE PROPHET OF CENTRAL PARK

On the street Caleb stays within an arm's reach of his guide. Sidney is not as tall as he is, just under six feet, and about the same age, and his elastic face is an instant barometer to whatever emotion takes hold. Food in hand, Sidney asks if Caleb is up for a walk then leads them across town to where Caleb's interview will be. From there he shows how to get to the proper subway so Caleb will know the route tomorrow. All this time Manhattan confounds Caleb. The city speaks a hundred languages, excluding him from its conversations time and again. Each building-crammed block seems a distinct town harboring its own population of fellow dreamers, but the guarded stares of everyone he passes hint at loneliness. A Bentley drives by, a car he has only seen in magazines, so that he watches it disappear back into the honking traffic herd as if it is a unicorn. Glamour mixes with suits and working class uniforms, but scattered everywhere poor people beg or sit and stand talking to themselves, feet apart from everyone else but separate and ignored. Near the auction house, a three-story bronze statue of Atlas bearing the world upon his shoulders reinforces for Caleb how far he's come in a day: from a land bound by scripture to a city where titans bow to passersby. A stab of failure pierces him every time he walks by the many homeless without even a word.

The First Thursday in September

New York Times
    *One man was killed last night and another injured in the Williamsburg
section of Brooklyn. Witnesses say that at approximately 10:30 P M the
deceased, Robert Ray T_____, along with two other men forcibly entered
the apartment of Valerie W_____ with the intent of apprehending her under
authority of a warrant issued by the State Supreme Court of Alabama.
Guests staying with Ms. W_____ intervened and a gunfight broke out. This
confrontation seems the latest in a string of increasingly bloody encounters
between agents of anti-abortion states and organizations dedicated to
guaranteeing abortion access through transport for women in those
jurisdictions.*

A track fire near the Lexington Avenue station delays Caleb's subway
train. By the time he reaches his stop, it is already 9 am. The first chill of
autumn pinches his cheeks as he darts through the crowded streets of
Midtown Manhattan. Showing his ID at the employee entrance to the
auction house, he tells himself it will be alright because he has not been late
before but when he joins the other porters on the loading dock, his boss calls
out, "Caleb, Mr. Guyot in HR wants you."

His friend Rolando wags a finger for the trouble Caleb has gotten into.
He wants to return an unfazed grin but the summons lets loose a ruckus in
his stomach. Mr. Guyot hired him. He also lets people go. Caleb tries not
to consider but can't ignore the consequences if he loses this job—his New
York refuge in jeopardy.

The HR assistant Alicia is thumbing through the top drawer of a filing
cabinet. A caramel complexion lends an exotic flair to her blue eyes and
black hair. Caleb stays back, put off by her attractiveness, and her outfit of
matching blue dress slacks and jacket. Growing up, he didn't interact with
many female professionals and even with the prerequisite Southern charm,
their assured airs put him off. Polished detachment makes the Manhattan

THE PROPHET OF CENTRAL PARK

counterparts even more disconcerting. His diffidence awakes Annaliese who wonders: If I had dressed up more, might I still be around?

"Excuse me. Mr. Guyot sent for me."

From the inner office the manager calls, "Yes, I did." Alicia points him on with a smile.

"Sir, I was only late because my train got held up in the tunnel."

Behind his mahogany desk, Mr. Guyot shakes his head with a kindly disposed authority that stills Caleb's butterflies. The eight months since their last meeting have not changed the man. His thinning hair remains expertly trimmed. Another tailored suit works to hide his slight paunch. The hazel eyes, holding between them the long anchor of his nose, study Caleb for a long pause. Just as on that January interview.

"You are the most unusual hire I have ever made, Mr. Ellison. I still tell people about the application you sent in. Via snail mail."

It was one of several. Caleb also reached out to the prominent companies in Chicago, Philadelphia and Boston. He didn't bother with smaller operations, reasoning that they would take on whoever was ready at hand.

"You know what they ask me when I do?"

"'Why **did** you hire me?'"

Mr. Guyot nods at the astute guess.

Caleb remembers how the applications seemed stupid even as he wrote them, explaining as they did that if the personnel department reached out to his boss and father, the man would give a damning reference to prevent the cosmopolitan life he objected to for his son. Instead, Caleb provided contact info for people he trusted to keep his confidence, a twelfth grade teacher and two consignors he had worked with closely, then he spent the following weeks trying to gather the courage to pack his truck for Columbus and a dishwasher's job. When his cell rang with a 212 number, Caleb ignored it as a nuisance call. The chime of a voicemail was a mild surprise, but when he heard Mr. Guyot identify himself, Caleb checked to be sure no one else could hear.

"You've made me look a genius. I took a risk giving you a job. Others were not convinced."

"I'm grateful for the chance, sir."

P C Burhenne

Mr Guyot taps what Caleb takes to be his file. "And everybody knows that. Your supervisor sure does. He's sorry to lose you. At least for the next few weeks." The manager is ready with an "ate the canary" smile as Caleb peers back. "You're going to be floor support for the upcoming Asia Week. Now these sales are a major part of our calendar. Buyers fly over from China, Japan, Korea, as well as Europe. The world will be watching. What I'm saying is, I'm once again putting my faith in you."

Mr. Guyot raises his eyebrows for a pledge that Caleb will act accordingly. Put on the spot, he almost quotes Jeremiah—to trust is like a tree planted by a stream that bears fruit even in a drought—but stops himself. Apart from the sin of comparing faith in himself to faith in the Almighty, he knows it would sound ludicrous.

"You will always get my best, sir."

"Do well and the promotion will be permanent. And you will get a raise."

Caleb can't help but grin. The extra money would be a relief.

"You'll start on Monday, but check in with Ms. Yuan now. She's in Gallery Five. And, aah, be sure you're not late."

Mr. Guyot returns to the paperwork on his desk but Caleb lingers. "What do you tell those people?" and when the manager looks up again, Caleb goes on, "When they ask why you hired me."

"I tell them I called you out of curiosity, but when you were willing to make the trip for an interview with no guarantees, I knew I was going to give you the job. Don't come across that type of determination often."

Dazed by the good news Caleb heads to the second floor. The supervisor Ms. Yuan is directing the arrangement of pale green plates and scene-decorated vases in a vertical case at the showroom's far end. He recognizes the middle-aged Asian woman from the hallways where she always seems too busy for a greeting. Tall and slender, she has wide dark eyes set high on her face, a flat but delicate nose, and a thin-lipped mouth currently pressed into an inquisitor's frown. The bun tied at the back of her head pulls her hair into a sleek black satin skull cap. She puts up a finger at his approach. When the handler behind the display finishes adjusting its layout per her commands, Ms. Yuan finally turns. "Can you tell me anything about these?"

THE PROPHET OF CENTRAL PARK

He tenses at the unexpected exam. "Well, the three green plates have a celadon finish. The smaller plain one on the end could be Song Dynasty but I don't know for sure. The two vases both have a rouleau form and are either famille rose or famille verte, but again I don't know enough to pick one from the other. I surely can't say if they're real. Except that you're selling them."

A tick troubles Ms. Yuan's mouth, almost a smile. "That's more than I hoped for. Where did you learn the terminology?"

"I grew up in an auctioneering family. My father put Maine Antique Digest in my hands as soon as I could read."

"Good for him." In the next moment the supervisor tilts her head to ask. "Your last name is Ellison, right? E-L-L-I-S-O-N?" and when he nods, she says, "Did you have a relative named William? An uncle or maybe a much older cousin?"

"No, ma'am. No Williams in the family tree."

She maintains her quizzical stare. "Where did you move here from?"

"Kentucky. Town on the Ohio River, a ways east of Cincinnati."

The answer perplexes rather than satisfies her. "You look so much like a well-known Asian Arts dealer, William Ellison. And he was from Kentucky." She taps her forehead with an index finger. "What was the name of that town where he was born? It was in the catalogue for his estate. Heraldsville, something like that."

Thinking it can't be so, he nonetheless suggests, "Harrodsville? H-A-R-R-O-D-S?"

"That's it," and for a second she flashes a pleased grin, then seeing his reaction, she asks, "Young man, is something wrong?"

Caleb realizes he is catching flies with his mouth and shakes himself back into the job. "Just weird, ma'am. I, I've been to that place and there isn't much to it, but like I said, no Williams that I know of. So what do you need me to do?"

Still with a hesitant concern to her voice, Mr. Yuan says, "Downstairs has you today and tomorrow, and you have the weekend off. Report to me Monday morning. I've drawn some company dress shirts for you."

He listens to the rest of her instructions, thanks her for the opportunity and when leaving, remembers to take the uniforms set aside on a nearby case. However, the hugely improbable coincidence sticks to him.

Harrodsville is where his father was born. Where his Uncle Sanford is buried. Once out of the gallery, he ducks into a bathroom to think. Meant for affluent clients, the upstairs facilities shine with large marble tiles and the fixtures on the sink pretend to be gold. He stares at the mirror, wondering how a stranger with the name Ellison can come from his father's birthplace, then he hears again that he resembles this dealer. The phone search brings up the man's obituary, complete with a photo. Alfred Sr.'s face is more starved, Uncle Sanford's was more jowly but William has their sleepy grey eyes and the bulbous swell at the end of the nose. He is undoubtedly blood. The tribute outlines a fabulous life but mentions no Kentucky ties and states that no wife or children survived the man. Caleb fights the urge to rip a soap dispenser from the wall, but beside the anger there is sadness too at what was denied. Sanford was a drunken wretch whom Alfred Sr. taught his children to pity. Why hide every hint or mention of this other incredible uncle?

His cell has no more answers. His father will countenance nothing but a promise to return to the fold and his mother will obey her husband. The flat voices of Carolyne and Al Jr. from previous contacts after his escape made clear Caleb is an outsider now, not to be indulged, let alone trusted. There is no one else to ask.

Caleb's one thought is to find his friend. Downstairs the porters are unpacking the panel truck which they loaded yesterday at a Park Avenue address. Rolando is logging in a nineteenth-century Meissen dinner set when Caleb joins them.

"You won't believe what I just found out."

His friend does not look up from his clipboard. "I can't really focus on that now. Let's just work."

"You'll wanna hear this. It's big." and Caleb leans in to whisper. "My father's done me such a wrong turn."

His friend starts back like Caleb jabbed him with a pin. "Oh, you've been wronged. Well then, hell yeah, let me drop everything to hear how you've been wronged."

Caleb stares back and Rolando presses at the space between them with the inventory sheet. "Let's just do this, please."

"Wait. What did I do?"

"Nothing, C. You didn't do nothing wrong. I shouldn't have snapped."

THE PROPHET OF CENTRAL PARK

There is only tension in the back Rolando turns on him. Caleb hurries to put himself in front of his friend again. "C'mon, something's wrong. You're treating me like I stole your girl. Tell me what I did."

The other does respond but with his clay-colored face devoid of warmth, he is the stranger who intimidated Caleb the first days on the job. In fact, Rolando is more menacing. His thick arms bearing their tattoos of roses intertwined among hooded wraiths flex from a pulse of anger, emphasizing that, though they are the same height, Rolando is the stronger. He asks as an accusation, "Did you apply for the floor?" Understanding that their boss revealed the promotion, Caleb is happy he can answer, "No," to put things right between them.

It doesn't.

"Well, I have," Rolando snaps back. "I've been here five years. For the past two, I've been renewing my application, checking on openings upstairs. And they give it to you, someone just months off the bus. Why do you think they picked you over me?" Caleb can't help glancing at his friend's inked sleeves. Rolando says, "Screw you, blanco. I have shirts that'll cover them."

He does walk away, and after all the rest the day has thrown at Caleb so far, the departure of a rare close friend dazes him.

* * *

Social Media Post from Ghostinthemachine06825

To all Godloving people who are alarmed by the angry voices tearing America apart, join with me in celebrating before the Lord all the things that hold us together, and if you plan to do so, please pass along this message to your friends.

In the next moment, Caleb thinks, Screw you too—I didn't do anything wrong. He goes back to work trying for the other's cold manner. Nevertheless the regret persists. Rolando was the first person to make Caleb feel welcome at work. Finding out where he was from, Rolando asked, What's that Derby like? When Caleb said that he'd never been, that most people in Kentucky had nothing to do with horses, Rolando asked, What's the place about? Caleb didn't hesitate: God, family and farming, with a little football mixed in. Rolando's first smile made Caleb understand he had been wrong to fear the dark-skinned, painted stranger. Rolando told him that it wasn't much different here, that his mama was always whacking him with her Bible growing up but the only farming he knew was his uncle's plot at the community garden. Now they are a team within the team. Well, were.

At lunch Rolando goes outside without a word. Typically Caleb would watch his friend eat; he has never had a noon appetite. Not wanting to spend the break staring at the half-emptied truck, he heads out alone.

The sun has run off the earlier cold and office staffs are draining from the surrounding highrises. Across the Rockefeller Center plaza, the Rainbow Rights Railroad people are out again today. Caleb has visited their table before, drawn by their banner hanging off its front that proclaims in red, "WE PROTECT THE RIGHTS THAT THE SUPREME COURT WON'T." He has studied the leaflets describing their transport network and temporary lodgings for women who need help traveling to different states for abortions. More than once the voice of Annaliese has prevailed upon him to donate. Closer by a homeless person sits on a collapsed box, holding another piece of cardboard with the message, "Please help. I'm hungry and alone." Not sure if the person is male or female, Caleb guesses the beggar is a transgender youth, discarded for the fact. The person is certainly younger than Caleb. The lunch crowd crisscrosses the square. One or two stop at the volunteers' stand. None take notice of the beggar. Or of him either.

The phantom uncle comes back to mind to mock his loneliness. The discovery begs to be shared. He most wants to tell Carolyne. Her rejection cut him the deepest but he misses her the most.

Her phone rings so often, he expects the call to go to voicemail but Carolyne answers, annoyed, "Yes?"

"Father had a brother William he never told us about," he blurts out to prevent her cutting him off. "This William came to New York. Became a pretty big-time dealer before he died."

"Are you . . . How do you know?"

Caleb skips the how. "Google him. There are pictures. He looks like father. Like me."

The chattering of computer keys tells him Carolyne is in her family room. Along with this, he hears his niece let loose a joyful burst that is laugh and squeal both. Caleb wonders how big she is now.

THE PROPHET OF CENTRAL PARK

"He does look like dad!" Carolyne says.

In the agreement he hears again the confidante he grew up with. "Can you believe it? All our lives preaching family first and Father's got this huge secret the whole time."

The more recent angry Carolyne returns to mutter, "Like father, like son."

"I explained why I didn't tell you about New York. How long you going to stay mad at me?"

A hiss flies through the line like a short burst from a coffee maker that seems to break loose her response. "How long are you going to keep lying to me?"

"Hey, don't talk to me—" but she cuts him off. "I know why you left. Really know. You got Annaliese pregnant."

"N, no, she told—"

"She told everyone it wasn't you, you told everyone it wasn't you, but did you think you could keep the truth from me? I mean, really? And I waited for you to share it with me. So I could help. Like we always helped each other. But you never gave me the chance."

Caleb holds his breath at being caught out then lowers his voice to ask, "Did you tell him, Father?"

"That's all you have to say?"

"Please, Carolyne."

She nearly shouts back, "Of course I didn't. That's the point. I wouldn't," then with a sigh, she adds, "Anyway I don't talk to dad anymore. He changed after you left. Became militant about faith."

Caleb scowls at the ground. "He's always been that way."

"Not like he is now. Everything must be as the pastor says, or I should say, as dad tells us the pastor says. If you argue, you're straying from God's will and he will not stand it in his presence." With a strain of anguish she adds, "Terry stopped going over to dinner."

Carolyne's husband was a family favorite, a Bible study regular whom their father hired two months after the young man first took Carolyne out. When Terry took him aside to ask for his daughter's hand, Alfred Sr. announced the news in his booming auctioneer's voice to the farthest corner of the sales pavilion. Caleb clapped with his brother.

"That must make work tense," he offers.

"Terry's working down Cincinnati. He sleeps over every other night in the car. We're looking to move closer."

Just as when they were young, the sorrow behind her words flows into him, the pang unmitigated by the intervening miles. "Oh, Sis."

"No, no, you don't get to 'Oh, Sis' me," she snaps like he is a rude dinner guest. "Why didn't you tell me? Trust me to help? Me, Caleb, me!"

"I couldn't, Sis." Caleb struggles to keep his voice from breaking. "Annaliese, after she was gone, she, she wouldn't let me. I had to keep my word."

"What? Caleb, you're not making sense."

"I can't talk about this now. I'm sorry, Carolyne. I never realized I hurt you."

He punches off before she can answer and sees that his roommate Sidney texted him, "Great idea for Saturday." Not intrigued, he pockets the cell. Of course Annaliese in his head chides him: Still can't say what you did.

When he glances about the plaza, several people who are watching look elsewhere. The beggar, though, nods in sympathy for Caleb's obvious troubles. He goes up to the vagrant and gives over a crumpled bill before seeing it is a ten. "It was kind of you not to turn away."

A violent web of rosacea discolors the face and two large cracks make the lips painful to look at. The beggar nods taking the money and the nodding becomes rocking in place.

"Too much turning away. Everybody just wants to turn away. Turn away. Turn away."

* * *

ProPublica

A year's long investigation suggests that the conservative group One Nation Under God is recruiting like-minded students at universities across the country to embed themselves in federal government agencies. Prospective employees were told that these positions offered unique opportunities to promote right wing ideological goals. The young people interviewed for this article said they were contacted after attending an on-campus speech or debate sponsored by the One Nation association.

THE PROPHET OF CENTRAL PARK

_____ *was the organizer of all the events and spoke personally with each of the students afterwards. Mr. _____, a lawyer and lobbyist, has long time ties to The Federalist Society.*

At the revelation of the pain he caused Carolyne, a verse from the Book of James returns: For where you have envy and self-ambition in your hearts, there you find disorder and every evil practice. Along with everything else, Caleb drags the new burden inside to work. Seeing this strain, Rolando opens his mouth to ask but turns away before relenting. The crew trudges through the afternoon. At five ten Caleb is catching his Queensbound N subway train, his stomach aching for dinner and his mind trying to turn off the loop of his father's pronouncements about family first and foremost. An uncharacteristic lull allows commuters to board without using shoulders and harsh words. Caleb sees the African American woman hurrying with her guitar case from the stairs. He disregards the recorded command to "stand clear of the closing doors". Slipping past him, the woman clamps the pole inside with her left arm, that hand steadying the neck of the case sitting upright now off her foot. "Thank you for doing that."

She is a regular on the afternoon train. Caleb first noticed her by seeing a couple notice her. A young man nudged his girl and during the whole trip they mouthed comments to each other which Caleb didn't need to lip read to understand as thrilled. An obvious guess that the woman is a street performer with a following, common enough in Manhattan, and the city has beautiful women wherever he walks. She is different, though, with a self-possession that lets her accept starstruck attention without being affected by it. He has not stood next to her before. Up close that presence disorients, leaving him unsure whether to move closer or further away, so he returns to "Uncle William." Riders at the next stop push him against the woman. When he looks up to apologize, the guitarist is peering back as if to place him. The skin color that seemed nearly black from a distance shows undertones that could have seeped off the saturated red of her lips, the upper of which is now pressed down over the lower. The closely cut ringlets of her hair barely stand apart from the scalp so that her face alone is before him. Her dark eyes search his own for something familiar but not yet named.

"Tough day when doubt outweighs faith."

That she sees so clearly past his injuries to what troubles him makes Caleb turn aside again. They both lurch a step as the train starts. Caleb wants to be angry but instead panics that the gaps where faith once sustained him are so visible. The crowd keeps them close. The soft sighs of her breathing tie Caleb to her. The faintest musk from hours in the sun carries from her skin.

"I'm sorry," she says at his ear. "I shouldn't have butted in. Please forgive me."

The woman shifts away. Caleb knows at the next opportunity she will separate from him. He plays back what she said, hears sympathy in the sentiment.

She is studying the neck of her instrument case.

"How did you know?"

"It's flying all about you."

"What is?"

"The struggle. Despair and hope. Wanting to find a love that's been lost. I know what that struggle looks like." She faces him again. Her eyes glisten and she does not blink, he thinks so they do not loose their tears. "I know what it feels like."

Caleb thinks perhaps the crowd is keeping him upright because his legs feel unequal to the job. The car is traveling upward, pulling into the first Queens station.

"I have to get off here."

The slow shutter of her eyes as she ducks her head tells him she knows he is lying. Before the car stops, however, she nudges him.

"People should have doubts. I can't trust someone who doesn't. Only God has no doubts and I suspect we give Her pause now and then."

Such casual blasphemy that last. Caleb wants to answer it but his tongue is thick and an ocean roars in his head. When the doors open, he breaks away onto the platform, trying not to stagger among the other riders while still making sure to move out of the guitarist's view. When the train pulls away, he falls onto a bench. His side of the station empties and fills back up before the world rights itself. The next train comes a minute later.

* * *

THE PROPHET OF CENTRAL PARK

USA Today

Flooding has devastated low-lying regions and valley communities from Arkansas to Tennessee as a massive storm front stalled over the southeastern US. Reports of 12 inches of rainfall are common while some areas have received upwards of 18 inches. Many of the affected counties are still dealing with damage from an unusually wet summer and depleted local resources are hampering this round of rescue efforts. So far authorities have confirmed 27 deaths directly connected to the storm but warn the number will rise. Thousands have been displaced.

TVs murmur through the walls when Caleb enters his Astoria apartment building. In his kitchen, he starts a meal of Spam slices sauteed with chopped onions and parboiled baby potatoes and carrots. At the table he pauses to give thanks then, as best he can, eats deliberately "to do so for God's glory." The effort is not one of his best.

After putting away the dishes, Caleb checks how well he tidied his room after this morning's woodworking session. All the tools are in their drawer but a few shavings eluded him on the desk top. Caleb glances to his totems on the floor beside the desk. Between ten and twenty inches high, each is too irregular and most are too fragile to stack. The room is small and the array now hinders the folding doors of the closet. Soon he will need to move them . . . somewhere, but he would rather not think about that. The pieces are a comfort. He began, what? Realizing them? Discovering them? Certainly not just making them. He began with the work soon after he arrived in the city and during his darker spells, the growing collection persuades him that the months since have not been misspent. More than that, the totems connect him to his Pop Pop who first put a penknife in Caleb's hand, though his grandfather might not know what to make of these elaborate constructions. The man taught traditional carving, stick and blade.

After changing, he takes up his latest library book. Usually the freedom to read whatever his interests bring to hand, without disapproving stares or outright rebukes, is an engrossing treat. Certainly his father would snatch away his latest choice, A ROOM OF ONE'S OWN, to use as tinder for backyard fires. However the day's revisions to family history keep intruding on Virginia Woolf's arguments. Caleb doesn't hear Sidney arrive until he steps into the doorway. The roommate sees the turmoil in Caleb's face.

"Whew, what happened to you today?"

No simple lead-in comes to mind. "I found out I have an uncle named William Ellison no one ever told me about who lived and died here in New York." Caleb sits up on the bed to tell how he found out. As he describes the fascinating man memorialized in the Times obituary, Sidney pulls up the article on his own phone.

"Holy shit! Your uncle was seriously wealthy. He owned a brownstone off Park Avenue. By the Metropolitan Museum of Art. That's several million right there. And look at this," the roommate says pointing to a line in the text. "He owned Bonhomme Restaurant. My parents went there once for their twentieth wedding anniversary. Reservation months ahead of time and they saved up to pay for it. Your uncle was a big deal." Then Sidney looks over skeptically. "Are you sure this is the right William. It says he was seventy-five when he died in 2019. How old's your father?"

"Sixty-eight next month. Though you wouldn't know to look at him. Clean living. My father met my mother late in life. And I'm the youngest child. Just like him." Caleb sighs. "This whole thing really is a tease. I find out about an amazing uncle in New York City who died before I ever got here."

"Yeah, but he was important. There are people who knew him, friends and colleagues who'll be glad to hear from you. That lady boss may know some of them. You should ask her."

"Hm, maybe," Caleb allows, unconvinced that he should broach personal matters with his new supervisor.

"Well, I don't know why you're so glum, chum. Somebody's been watching over you. I mean, what are the odds of stumbling on the trail of an uncle you didn't even know existed." He turns back to the main room saying, "You should play the lotto."

Caleb follows, not feeling at all lucky. Sidney pulls a microwave dinner from the freezer, removes it from the package. "Odd that bit about him never marrying," he says and when Caleb answers "Why?" the roommate butts his head forward as if nudging Caleb to the obvious. "Come on. Your uncle was a good-looking man. And rich. Why wouldn't he have married?" Caleb understands even as Sidney announces, "He was gay," elongating the last into a two-second reveal.

THE PROPHET OF CENTRAL PARK

Evening has taken hold outside and they have not turned on the lamp, but the room goes bright for Caleb so that the brown wear circles on the Formica table show where countless elbows have worn away the veneer and the faint line of the sheetrock tape lifting from the wall behind the TV points to a new spiderweb at the ceiling. Caleb sees his father at the Cincinnati bus depot trying to stop his wicked flight. "I can't believe it. My parents think I came here to be gay," and when a suppressed snort catches in Sidney's throat, he says, "Why is that funny?"

The roommate turns from starting the microwave. It hums behind his head as he holds out his hands. "I'm sorry. Really. I didn't mean anything. It's just, I did wonder when you first moved in."

The cold tingling rushes over Caleb that hasn't taken hold of him for years. The moment to decide: cut back in kind if the innuendo is friendly, strike back if not, but answer one way or another. The darkness falling over his face pushes Sidney back a foot.

"Hey, you're fastidious. And sometimes your mannerisms can become a little . . . theatrical. Look, I know you're not. I've caught you staring at a tight skirt when you think no one's watching. And it wouldn't matter to me anyway. I guess it was a much bigger deal back in Kentucky."

Caleb exhales, allows, "In my church being gay is as heinous a sin as having an abortion. An abomination of God's will." Without meaning to, he assumes a harsh gravity to pronounce this.

His roommate frowns. "I didn't think you believed that anymore."

"I don't. I . . . but it's the voice I heard my whole childhood. It's always right there."

Sidney seems glad to look away when the microwave beeps. "Anyway, didn't you date in high school? So they knew you're straight at least?"

Annaliese is in his ear at once: No, you skipped all that foreplay. He looks to his roommate seating himself now, then to the meatloaf TV dinner to escape the inner voice. "Actually, well, I didn't."

"That might have been an inadvertent red flag." Sidney stirs the tray's side of mashed potatoes and in a neutral voice says, "Why didn't you, Caleb? Seems the normal thing—Hey, it's none of my business."

"Oh my goodness, I'm not gay. I just didn't want any attachments." Caleb takes a deep breath and Sidney stays silent. "I knew in my teens I wanted out of Maynardsville. A girlfriend would have been one more string holding me back." He lets out a humorless chuckle. "Lord, you wouldn't believe how many daughters from church my mother pushed at me."

"You must have been lonely."

Caleb sits too and they discuss the highlights of his millionaire uncle: travels throughout Southeast Asia in pursuit of the most exquisite bronzes, his specialty; positions on the boards of several influential institutions, including his neighbor, the Met. Caleb takes heart that someone with his same background lived such a fulfilled Manhattan life. After an hour he retires to his room. Sidney knows better than to ask if he wants to watch a show.

However, Annaliese keeps him from turning many pages of his book. Memories of her as a child, tomboy fast in all the church picnic games. With short dusty brown hair and long slender pointy nose, those pale green eyes square in front of him. "Why you so weird about not playing with anybody?" Little Anna Tompkins. Until she discovered herself in her full name. A song in three syllables, she called it and from then on she would not acknowledge the shortened version. Scandalizing her parents. The very way Annaliese described it to him years later. They chided her for not respecting elders. They punished her when she ignored adults who used the abbreviation, by withholding desserts and doubling her chores, but she was defending something more precious than treats or free time. Once her father slapped her. She related blinking back tears to tell him, "You hit Annaliese." Eventually everyone came to understand that she would always only be that jaunty tri-note tune. Caleb's father watched the Tompkins's struggles for a couple weeks before declaring that the little girl was becoming too worldly. Akin to branding the child a devil worshipper. Caleb stayed clear of her as he knew to stay clear of all outside temptations. Stayed clear through grade school. Through high school. If only he had persevered.

That night Annaliese comes to him, gamboling across the freshly mown church yard in her graduation cap and gown, singing, "Dolly, Dolly, don't you cry. Give me a hug and say goodbye," a gleeful dark sprite barely making contact with that emerald carpet. He wears no such costume, just jeans and a t-shirt. Taking her hand, Caleb draws her toward the neighboring cornfield. When they hurry between two rows, all around him the stalks sough in disapproval. The broad leaves reaching across their way begin to cut his face and arms. When he looks back, Annaliese's gown is rent and bloodied but she keeps up her song, though now more as a plea than celebration.

P C Burhenne

Friday

CNN

The parents of Desirae T_____ have asked the Justice Department to take over the investigation into the disappearance of their daughter, citing a willful lack of activity by state and local agencies. Ms. T_____ was last seen two weeks ago at a gas station one hour outside the South Carolina capital of Columbia. She had traveled there as a transporter for the Rainbow Rights Railroad, an organization that offers, among other services, passage for women seeking abortions to states where the practice is legal.

Caleb wakes to the sense that he missed an appointment and has to slow his panting from panic. The upheaval from yesterday rushes back. Sleep brought no clarity. A pale blue fills the sky. The buildings out his window block the view eastward but he knows behind them the day is rising at the horizon. When he heads to the shower, of course Sidney, scrubbed and polished, is sipping a coffee at the table. The few down hours that refresh the roommate amaze Caleb.

"Oh, good, you're up. The quest for William sidetracked me last night. Did you get my text about the weekend?" When Caleb gives a groggy nod, he goes on, "Tomorrow why don't you and I try to sell your work in Central Park? I'll bring some boxes home. We'll throw down a blanket. I'll be your hawker. You give me fifteen percent of the take."

"You want a commission?"

His roommate's eyes go wide. "What, you want me to help you schlep everything over there for nothing? And who else is gonna draw people in. Are you gonna speak up? I don't think so. You know I will," and Sidney holds his hands out with fingers pointing back, as much to say, That's who I am. "Seriously, though, let's do it. Pay me if I help you sell something but let me help you get your work out there. People should see it."

The idea of people judging his pieces is as troubling as that of parting with them. "Maybe."

His roommate takes a last drink of coffee and heads out the door. "I'm bringing those boxes home."

THE PROPHET OF CENTRAL PARK

After the wash and breakfast, Caleb takes his worries to the work station. Tarp in place and tools on the desktop, he retrieves his latest project from the floor and starts by sitting still before it. When he doesn't listen to the piece, the results have been bland blocks that end up in a dumpster. When he does, the totems bring despair or electricity, either way leaving him cleansed in their wake. Caleb knows only this humble path to receive guidance.

The work-in-progress started as a foot length of 2x4. He beveled one of the narrow faces so that it tapers to a center line but he left slender examples of the original profile at the three and nine inch points. These seemed like chocks to hold the wedge upright. Until the sculpture whispered, intimated that he should stand it tall. He dadoed four new stabilizers shaped like fins into the new base. The past week he hand-sawed wide plies, trimmed them into ovals, and removed the proper cutouts from the middles. They looked like yokes until he slid them about the totem's torso, tightly tucked beneath the used-to-be-feet. At the end of yesterday's session, they showed themselves as correct but not yet complete. In the quiet now, Caleb sees what's missing.

Luckily the thin strips sliced from a crate rib are surplus from an earlier assemblage. Caleb sets up his steam system: electric teapot sending vapor through a hose to a four-feet portion of PVC pipe. Once the wood is pliable, he massages "bends" into them thumbpress by thumbpress and when they encircle the plies, he secures everything with glue and pegs from matchsticks. Finally the totem reveals what it wished to be, a thing embraced, by adult arms above and a child's below. The sculpture sends a blush of being safe through Caleb that carries him through cleanup. Remembering yesterday's lunch break, he prepares a sandwich from the leftover Spam, and still the stream of well-being flows through him. Later riding on the train, he considers that his morning sessions are the closest he comes to acts of faith. That thought inspires hope, then melancholy.

At the auction house Rolando still ignores him, now with forced apathy that seems a matter of principle rather than simmering anger. Sidney's scheme for tomorrow comes to mind to depress Caleb. Rolando is the only porter to whom he would tell the plan. The many times he wore latex gloves because of weeping cuts from the utility knife, his friend alone among the crew wanted to see what was worth the sore hands. As they begin crating bottles of vintage wine and whiskey sold last week, Caleb rues this squandered chance to show him. The morning drags.

At the break, he is glad to see the pitiable figure in the same spot. Yesterday's exchange registered the fact that he has stopped seeing the city's street people. When he first arrived, Sidney's promise repulsed him that the "homeless situation" overwhelmed all newcomers, but Caleb would get used to it. Yet he changed from an almsgiver, dividing what he could spare for as many hands as possible, to just another pedestrian blind to the suffering he passed. Someone who has forgotten, "Whoever is generous to the poor lends to the Lord."

"I got you this," Caleb says, offering the sandwich he made for the beggar. The young person—who somehow seems more a "he" today: stronger-seeming jawline? Broader-seeming shoulders?—sits as before with the same placard. He(?) takes the wrapped food without looking up. Whether from shame, fear or caution, Caleb cannot tell. "I hope you don't mind pork. Well, pork products."

The added wish does draw the beggar's gaze, but the smile that comes suggests a girl's pleasure at being noticed. In a flash Caleb sees not the derelict in a once-blue sweatshirt and jeans fading to the same sooty color but the teenager who might have been if blessed with kinder days. A young person waiting on friends for an afternoon lark in the city. A typical adolescent, anxious to be an adult.

"Too much turning away. That's you. Too much turning away." the beggar says, taking the food.

"Yeah, that's me. Too much turning away."

A voice rises from the square, strained with anger, its accent redolent of the crooked country roads and harrowed fields Caleb left behind. "You're meddling where you got no right to!"

The Rainbow Rights Railroad people claim their same place also. The challenger is before their table. He sports a crew-cut and a farmer's tan below his short sleeves. The friend backing him up has a similar outfit and blazing sunburn. The loungers nearby freeze at the shout then either move away or pull out their phones to record the spectacle. One volunteer holds open his hands to try to calm the agitator while his shorter partner has his own phone out to call for help.

THE PROPHET OF CENTRAL PARK

In his ear Annaliese demands: You didn't stand up for me then—Stand up to them now!

As Caleb starts forward, the plaza shines in high definition for him: the quick steps of a quartet of pigeons hying out of his way; the tense postures of a group of professionals at the event unfolding before them; the trembling that possesses the volunteer as he tries to defuse the hostility. And ahead of Caleb, the circular impressions of snuff tins pushing against the back pants pockets of two men approaching the show. So out of place. Since he moved, he has encountered only a handful of Skoal users, mostly in Queens. Both men have their heads on swivels and their hands balled into fists. Brothers in the same plain clothes to the pair harassing the RRR workers. They go around the gathering to the far end of the table, as their spokesman shouts, "You goddamned murderers helped kill my unborn son!"

Caleb's breathing feels barely strong enough to fill his chest, but his limbs and scalp feel on fire as he shoulders through the gathering to step between the angry man and the stand, so sudden and close that the agitator falls back, bumping his friend back too.

"And you're a woman-hater. Any 'bitch' who speaks her mind."

Shock widens the agitator's brown eyes but the man's second narrows his gaze to take in the new threat. Caleb quickly remarks the bent line of the backup's nose, a fighter's nose, before the spokesman thrusts his face forward again.

"You'd be smart to get your faggot ass out of my way."

Force of habit almost has him hit the man but Annaliese orders him: Think!

"Tennessee, right?" Caleb says. "That drawl a yours? Carolinas maybe. Or farther west." He clucks from the side of his mouth. "You boys drove a long way to tell us up here," and Caleb draws circles above his head with both index fingers to indicate the crowd now shuffling closer, "that we have no right to help people who are asking for it." He raises his voice then. "And everybody listen. These Alabama bully boys are just the distraction." He points left then without looking away from the two in front of him. The spokesman is confused but the fighter is raking his lower lip with his upper teeth, ready for blood. "Those two over there are the ones who are going to trash the display. If you let them." Sounds of argument and jostling start up from that end of the table but Caleb keeps his eyes forward. The spokesman glances that way then back with a growing flush at the quickly unravelling situation.

"This place can have all the queers and transvestite freaks like you they want, but you are sure as hell gonna leave our women alone."

A deep breath and think: Annaliese orders him.

As calmly as he can, Caleb says, "You're kidding yourself if you think Jesus would stand with you. He would be back at your towns trying to ease the pain that you've inflicted there."

"Why you evil sonofabitch!"

"'Evil?' I've seen evil. It holds you down to die telling you it's for your own good."

Caleb smells the beggar before he/she speaks. The spokesman turns to the rank odor too.

"You should go. You shouldn't be here. This is not, this is not, here, now, this is not right."

The rest plays out in seconds, each one clear to Caleb. The beggar is scratching at the air beside both temples to free the thought there. The spokesman says, "Shut up, you stinking piece of shit," as he makes to push the transient away. Caleb knocks the man's arm aside, knocking him aside. His second steps forward to finally throw the punch that he has been itching to unleash. Caleb cannot avoid it, can only turn his head some. The blow lands on his left cheek and makes the bright day flicker. He knows enough to grab the second. His right hand finds the fighter's throat, his left a shoulder, and pulling the fighter forward, Caleb brings his forehead down onto the bent nose. A crunch tells that it has broken again. But before any of them can continue, a painted arm reaches around from behind to half lift, half drag Caleb from what is fast becoming a melee.

* * *

The Brookings Institution

 The deterioration of our country's infrastructure continues to inhibit the nation's poorest from lifting themselves out of poverty, in ways both obvious and subtle. Failing transportation systems hinder productivity and job growth while breakdowns in sewage and water delivery systems force onerous work-arounds and costly health complications upon the segment of our society least equipped to withstand them.

Shouts fill the square. Caleb hears them now and not the rushing torrent that seemed like silence a moment before. Rolando turns him away from the crowd, releasing him with a push that sends Caleb trotting further from danger.

"Holy shit, C, what are you thinking? Those southern boys carry guns."

Behind his friend the gathering has grown. As Caleb watches, the spokesman and fighter break into view as if the roiling throng has spit them out and they run toward Sixth Avenue. A band of red cascades over the fighter's mouth and chin to his chest. Caleb looks down to find the man's blood spattered over his own shirt. Rolando keeps him moving away from the scene.

"Oh, Rolando, I'm in trouble," and Caleb realizes, "I'm going to lose my job."

"Yeah, buddy, you're seriously screwed."

His friend directs him away from the employee entrance and across Forty-Ninth Street. Bypassers gawp at Caleb's bloodied front.

"Turn your shirt inside out, C, and go home. I'll tell them you got sick all of a sudden." Rolando holds Caleb by the shoulders saying this. Caleb nods to the plan then stops when he understands the deceit. "No, no, no, C. Whatever's in that head of yours, do what I say."

Caleb slips out of his friend's grasp to lift the red-speckled garment over his head and reverse it, saying as he does, "The job shouldn't pay for what I did. If the boss asks why, I'll tell him what happened." In answer to his friend's open-mouthed disbelief, Caleb adds, "I'm not going to lie."

Rolando looks skyward muttering "Oh, Dios dulce y amorosa."

When they return across Forty-Ninth, two policemen are questioning the volunteers at the RRR table. When they hurry into work again, Rolando announces to everyone, "We need to get this guy a bib. He spilled soda all over himself." The rest laugh and Caleb smiles shrugging to his friend at the cover story. Within an hour, however, a reddish blue mouse rises from Caleb's forehead like an incipient horn and swelling starts to remove the features on the left side of his face. Rolando conjures up ever more ridiculous reasons for why the bidders spent so much money on the wine they are crating. This buyer will use it to consecrate the wafer at his daughter's first Communion, an event that one thousand of her closest friends will attend in rebuilt Notre Dame Cathedral. That buyer chose that particular burgundy for its consistency which, when properly distributed in eight crystal glasses and activated by the tap of a spoon, provides the most solemn notes possible for a performance of the *Godfather*'s theme song. The other workers, even the supervisor, encourage these inventions to ignore Caleb's changing state.

At five Rolando hurries him out saying, "Get home and get some ice on that."

Caleb tears up. "Thanks for everything today," and right then he decides about Sidney's plan. "Listen, my roommate and I are doing a kind of pop-up art show in the Park tomorrow. If you want to see my sculptures, you can come. You know, unless you're doing something else."

His friend smiles at once, bobbing his head as if the offer is the opening to a favorite jam. "Nah, that's perfect. I got my boy. He loves the Park. Where you gonna be?"

Caleb doesn't know. "I'll have to text you."

"Well, here's hoping for clear skies. Now go. Get some ice on those boo-boos."

The kind words send Caleb's spirits soaring but a grin is now a painful act. Approaching pedestrians do a double-take then quickly turn away so he knows his face is moving toward hideous. Even in the crowded train, commuters give him space. On the stairs of his building, he is glad for the brief spell alone in the apartment.

Of course Sidney picks today to be home early. Alerted by footsteps, he is standing behind the table, arms out to present the four boxes there promised from work, when Caleb enters. At once, his self-satisfied glee turns to horror. "What the hell happened to you?"

By now Caleb's jaw hurts at the slightest movement and a headache beats time to his pulse. "Need ice first. And aspirin. Get me some, please."

While Sidney retrieves the tablets, Caleb bags all the ice in the refrigerator. His roommate takes the tray to refill and Caleb swallows the pills and takes a place at the table. When he puts the cold to the bruises, the discomfort quickly turns to balm and he moans. Moving the boxes, Sidney sits across from him.

THE PROPHET OF CENTRAL PARK

"So what buzzsaw did you tangle with?" With as few words as possible, Caleb tells the story. His roommate begins to squint at what he hears, mouth falling further and further open. "What the hell were you thinking?"

Caleb can only shrug. He notices then how fresh-faced his roommate appears. Though twenty-five, Sidney has a boyish pink-tinged appearance and a pronounced chin that makes for a recess between itself and the mouth above. Caleb realizes his roommate is freshly shaved and is wearing a silk button down shirt and pressed tan chino pants. As Sidney starts from his chair, saying, "It's like the Kansas-Missouri Border Wars, what's going on," Caleb can think of only one reason he would take the trouble after work. On a Friday.

"Have I met this one?"

Sidney stops and purses his lips, a rascal happy to be caught. "No. She's a new sales rep who's been coming in the office."

"Well, you've got me all squared away. Don't be late on my account."

"I do have to head out." His roommate points to the boxes. "You're probably not going to be up for that, are you?"

Rolando's eager acceptance of the invite springs to mind. Caleb doesn't want to risk tearing off the patch to their friendship. "Actually I'd still like to. If I don't feel terrible in the morning. You won't mind being seen with a gargoyle?"

"Are you kidding. It's the perfect sales scheme." With his toothiest grin, Sidney throws both arms forward as if presenting Caleb. "The grotesque draws the customers in, the genius of your thingamajigs sell them. We'll clean up."

"'Thingamajigs'?" Caleb starts to laugh then winces at the immediate ache.

"Hey, save those grimaces for tomorrow." Sidney snaps his fingers and points. "Gotta go, Joe."

In the silence, Caleb's empty stomach rumbles but he continues treating the bruises, wrapping a small towel about the bag so he can stand it against his skin longer. Only when the cloth is saturated from the dripping plastic does he stop. He places the icepack in the freezer to firm up again and makes a meal of grilled cheese and tomato soup, dunking the former into the latter. Otherwise chewing is a mild form of agony.

P C Burhenne

At eight he is again icing his cheek and forehead when Rolando texts him. "How u feeling?"

Messaging is not a thing they do. Caleb goes misty-eyed again at the effort from his friend.

"Alright. Hurts some. Don't look 2 good."

"Didn't look good before."

Rolando's expression after the HR meeting flashes to mind. Caleb wants to say he's sorry about the job, begins to type the words but changes it to, "Understand why u were upset."

"What u gonna do."

Angry at himself Caleb sends, "Text u in the morning." For a while he determines to find Mr. Guyot Monday morning to turn down the promotion, advocate for his co-worker instead, but he worries that doing so will make him seem unreliable while guaranteeing nothing. The resolve crumbles. Caleb feels himself a coward when he remembers Rolando dragging him out of harm's way.

By nine the ice is gone and the new cubes have not hardened. He takes two more aspirin and goes to his bed. Staring at the ceiling, he sees the eyes of the fighter from lunchtime, grey and pitiless, searching for an opening to inflict pain. A predator's eyes. A soldier's. What would Christ do before such hatred? "Love your enemies, do good to those that hate you, bless those who curse you, pray for those who are abusive to you," would that be the response? Or would he "put on the full armor of God so that when the day of evil comes, you may be able to stand your ground?" Caleb certainly stood his ground today, but was he the righteous or the evil one?

"Your Book confuses me, God. 'Yes' on one page, 'no' on the next. Seems it can prove anything. Your followers, the ones I've seen, well, I can't be one of them. So what am I supposed to be?" Muffled music from the bar a block away tells of people celebrating the weekend. His cheek tingles in a way that is almost pain. "Wish you were a little more clear with your directions, God, but I guess that's not going to happen."

The end of Sidney's date draws Caleb briefly awake. The sales rep giggles and moans and the bed springs squeak. When he first moved in, such activities next door left Caleb confused between scandal and titillation. Tonight he rolls onto his safe right side and into sleep again.

THE PROPHET OF CENTRAL PARK

Saturday

People Magazine

Merle W_____ admits he has an unlikely new friend, the irreverent comic Tommy M_____ whose snarky takes on right wing causes typically infuriate blue collar folk like the Oxford, Mississippi carpenter. In fact a news story on a recent show by the performer moved Mr. W_____ to post a colorful, and in spots, profane opinion of Mr. M_____'s work. "I probably wouldn't have been so blunt to his face," the man confessed. Imagine his surprise when Mr. M_____ sought him out over the phone. After the initial shock of introductions, Tommy asked the carpenter to discuss his objections more fully. "What he wrote was pretty nasty," the jokester said. "But I have a thick skin. And something about his tone struck me as funny." They found, if not common ground, then a mutual respect. "I'm still not in his camp," Mr. W_____ said. "But he had a position I didn't see before." The carpenter revealed that his sudden defense of the comedian has cost him some friendships but the contact between the two endures. Tommy says he hopes to meet up with Mr. W_____ when the comic has a nearby performance in three months.

His inner clock wakes Caleb at the normal hour but his body feels too weak to rise so the day outside is sunny when he gets out of bed. His jaw is stiff but relatively pain-free. The dresser mirror shows that purple swaths streaked with blue now cover the two areas of swelling. They resemble the tribal decorations of a South Pacific islander. Caleb starts to doubt the Central Park trip. Sidney returns from outside as Caleb comes from his room dressed. Putting down a deli bag, he stares at Caleb. "Wow! I mean, Wow!"

"I know. I look crazy. I can't go out like this."

"Are you kidding? This, you, that," and Sidney points to the aftermath of yesterday's altercation. "It's better than we could have hoped for." When Caleb wavers, the roommate indicates his purchase. "I've treated you to your favorite. If you turn your back on this . . . ," and he holds his hands up to the heavens. " . . . this god-given opportunity, well, you're going to have to go get your own."

Caleb sighs, hungry and even then remembering his promise to Rolando. "Yes. Okay. We go."

"Outstanding." Sidney tosses Caleb's toasted cinnamon raisin bagel with cream cheese. "For the record, I would have given you that either way but you made the right choice."

Caleb doesn't bring up the "why" of his roommate's good mood as the latter brews coffee. Sidney's boxes are deep enough to contain most of the totems with their cardboard caps in place. However, several ambitious efforts reach above so these go in their own carrier. When all are packed, the relatively empty room brings the sense of displacement that he felt entering it eight months ago, and Caleb thinks how he will be glad to put everything back at the end of the day.

The boxes are bulky but not heavy. They each take two. Sidney carries a blanket with his. Caleb carries the open container atop his second closed one. Outside the air raises gooseflesh in the shade and people stare at Caleb's discolored face. Sidney inclines his head toward Caleb. "Just nod 'hello'. They'll stop looking." Indeed a smile and greeting from Caleb does end the curiosity, both on the street and the subway. They are sitting in the commuters' cocoon of silence when the guitarist gets on the car a couple stops later.

Seeing him, she smiles, briefly, then opens her mouth aghast. The reaction nearly stings him to disembark, but his boxed work and roommate hold him. As she approaches, she lowers her head as if disappointed at embarrassing him. "I won't ask what happened. Are you all right?"

Caleb struggles to answer with his constricted throat. "It's not near as bad as it looks."

"I should hope not."

The woman has on closefitting jeans and a snug off-white t-shirt, both of which show her shape more than previous outfits have. Her body seems as perfect as her mouth and eyes. Feeling himself aroused, Caleb wishes he had a container on his lap, but it is too late to move the top one clamped between his legs.

"Hey, buddy, are you going to introduce me?"

THE PROPHET OF CENTRAL PARK

Sidney shuttles his straining gaze from the woman and back. Caleb wants to say, Really?--After your night with the sales rep. Next he realizes the guitarist is a stranger. "I'm sorry, ma'am, I never asked your name."

"Tawana Johnson."

"I'm Caleb Ellison."

Calluses on her fingertips press like pennies into the back of his hand but a charge from her grip travels up his arm.

"You'll have to pardon my roommate's manners. I'm Sidney."

Tawana extends her hand to him also. When he hesitates letting go, she laughs, a deep-chested rumble, and pulls free. "Ain't gonna happen, playa."

"What?" he says, wide-eyed with innocence, and repeats, "What?" at Caleb's groan.

Tawana's expression flutters then like Venetian blinds being adjusted and she reaches toward the assemblages. Caleb is both excited and alarmed that she has noticed them and he flexes the fingers on his thighs. Seeing this, she freezes and asks, "May I?" and when Caleb nods, she tells him, "You pick one, please." He removes his latest work and she says, "Please you hold it." Then without a word she leans her case to Sidney so she can pass that hand about the piece. Caleb cannot say what she gleans thus but, except for the motion, she is still and breathless. A faint "ah" as she finally takes in air marks the end of the examination. She reclaims the guitar as he returns the piece.

"You made that?" and when he says, Yes, she declares, "What a special, sacred object."

Years in church prod Caleb to be scandalized, but identifying his creations as totems is not far off and he will not renounce their transcendence. "Thank you."

"Yes, they are," Sidney interjects himself back in the conversation. "We're headed to Central Park to try our luck selling them. I'm his megaphone," and Sidney puts an arm around Caleb. "Can you imagine my boy here calling out for people to gather round."

Caleb straightens away from the hug, sensing that Sidney is slyly belittling the competition. She ignores the ploy, focuses on Caleb.

"I'm going to the Park too. Mind if I come with you. I'd really like to see the rest," and paying no attention to Sidney assuring that she can, she asks Caleb, "Do you mind?"

Caleb manages to meet the woman's gaze. "Of course I don't, ma'am."

"Please," she says. "Tawana."

Never-say-die Sidney asks, "So, Tawana, you're a singer?"

The woman chuckles at the perseverance. "I interact with people when something I write moves them."

"So you're a performance artist."

"Some say so," then she holds up a finger. "Please, I need to save the voice."

Sidney laughs at the shutdown but respects it and they three ride in silence until Tawana leans her head to her left to say to Caleb, "Have you done this before? Those two are watching like they know you."

There are indeed two young women sitting nearby—late teens probably and blond—keeping sidelong tabs on him. Caught staring, the one turns away all giggles but the other slides forward on her seat to give him two thumbs up. Caleb lifts a wavering hand back then looks to Tawana in confusion.

"Uh, never laid eyes on them, and that, whatever that is, is a mystery to me."

At his side Sidney asks, "Are you wearing some new pheromone-based cologne? I mean, what the hell is going on?"

Tawana laughs again, this time a delighted peal.

Leaving the Fifty-Ninth Street station, she goes before them as interference to the Park's southeast corner, where a paved boulevard leads into the grounds. A hundred or so feet along, she stops.

"This might be a good spot. Catch people fresh." Caleb and Sidney nod at the reasoning. Tawana gestures to the unbroken line of benches that bound the walkway on both sides. "You could set up in front of these. Easier for people to see you, but a passing cop is more likely to take notice. It might be safer to spread out on the grass."

They follow her advice. As Sidney opens the blanket, the guitarist holds up her phone to indicate she has to make a call. Caleb remembers to text his friend. Rolando responses immediately that he and his son are by the reservoir and will be there in the time it takes to walk with ice cream cones, LOL. Tawana rejoins them a few seconds later to help set up, but where Sidney is an efficient stock boy, emptying his box with care but without hesitation, she inspects each article from her container. Her questions unnerve Caleb. Holding up one totem that suggests two stylized hands losing their grip upon each other, she asks softly, "How long since you moved?" and when he tells her, she grimaces. "You must have been so lonely." Hearing this, seeing Caleb's mute agreement, Sidney takes the piece to hold up as he calls out, "Original sculpture entitled '*Homesick*'. You can feel the longing for things familiar. Just one of many." The unpacking continues accordingly. After Tawana queries Caleb about an item, Sidney announces it to all within earshot. At first Caleb believes the woman is deducing his story through intuitive guesswork but as her asks grow more and more informed, he suspects a wilder possibility: he has been transcribing his history into these three-dimensional pictographs and Tawana is the first person to understand them.

When she comes upon the ovoid statue with a jagged rent down its convex front, he goes cold at what she might glimpse. Indeed she winces at its touch.

"What was her name?"

"Annaliese."

Sidney leans in to take possession but Tawana holds the figure away, all the while watching Caleb. "Do you really want to sell this?"

His roommate boxed the piece. Caleb nearly mustered an objection then but didn't want to give the reason why. He told himself he would withdraw the sculpture if and when someone showed interest. "I'll never sell that," he says before swallowing a sob. With solemn care she returns *Annaliese* to the container and Sidney turns away.

Alone and in groups people begin climbing over the barrier for a closer look. Most of the shoppers congregate about the guitarist so that Caleb suspects they are fans waiting for her performance. Still a young couple, dark-skinned and with Caribbean accents, inquire what *Homesick*'s price is.

Sidney takes Caleb aside. "You're not going to get what your labor's worth. You're a no-name. So what are you willing to settle for?" Faced with the reality of letting go, Caleb finds himself speechless. "How about a hundred?"

"No way!"

"One twenty-five?"

"One fifty. And even that much makes me sick to my stomach."

"That much, you might not have to worry about getting sick, but okay, I'll try."

Sidney goes back to the couple and Caleb removes the last totem from his box. Tawana catches his eye. "Not easy saying goodbye to your children."

"It's not 'goodbye' yet."

"I think it is."

When he swings about, the boyfriend or husband is handing over the money while his girl searches the sculpture asking, "Can he sign it for us?" All grins as he gives Caleb the proceeds, Sidney repeats, "Can you sign it?"

Caleb holds out his hands to the buyers in apology. "I would if I had something to write with."

"Did you two put any thought into this?" the guitarist asks in exasperation and takes a felt tip marker from her case. As Caleb writes his name on the base, a spark pushes back against the pang of loss—the fact that someone thinks enough to pay for his work. Tawana tells him to keep the marker.

A few minutes later Rolando shows up toting his son on his shoulders. The boy's face is rounder than the father's but the resemblance is clear in the shape of the dark eyes and finely-drawn winglike lips. "Not bad, C. Already got a crowd," Rolando says, lifting his son over the benches.

"What flavor ice cream did you get, Reynaud?" Caleb asks Rolando's boy, kneeling so he's at the other's level.

"Strawberry."

"What?" Tawana says behind him. "There's another strawberry fan here." The question startles Reynaud so that he looks up to his dad. Rolando smiles to reassure the boy. The woman kneels beside Caleb. "I thought I was the only one."

Reynaud's grin shows the gaps where baby teeth have made way for their erupting replacements. "It's the best."

She laughs and Caleb stands to introduce everyone. Rolando shakes hands then turns back to the figures. "These are amazing, Caleb. I knew how you talked about them, they were special but, well, they're really special."

Flush at the praise, Caleb can only manage, "Thanks." His roommate saves him having to say more with another piece to sign. A glaze of wonder has settled over Sidney's exultant expression. He whispers, "I may up the price."

When Caleb turns back, Rolando is watching Tawana with a quizzical pout, his balled right hand with index finger up suspended at chest height. On the grass she directs Reynaud to carefully remove from the last container a sculpture bristling a spiral staircase of dowels. As Caleb is about to say, Reynaud's fine doing that, Rolando's eyes go wide as does his mouth. He leads Caleb by the arm a few steps apart.

"How the hell do you know the Prophet?"

"Who?" Caleb says looking back. The woman continues to attend to the boy but she glances toward them and a wistful twitch to her lips slows the smile she gives Caleb.

"That's what people call her. Online. Caleb, she is a big deal."

"What, as a singer?" Caleb remembers how she explained herself. "Or a performance video artist?"

"Eh, no. Her followers take the videos, I think. And they call her the Prophet. As far as I know, she just calls herself Tawana."

"But she's a musician, right?"

"No. I mean, yeah, she sings." Rolando chuckles at his struggles. "Look, she is her own distinct thing. She sings, yes, but she performs her own songs and they're like sermons."

"Sermons!" Caleb barks back louder.

Rolando laughs at the confusion. "Look, you'll find out for yourself. Find out if you love her or hate her."

"What does that mean?"

"It means people are either believers or they think, well, that she's the Devil's or something."

* * *

Pittsburgh Gazette, Letter to the Editor

I've been duped.

My farm has been in my family for three generations. That whole time, the well water was fine. Then a fracking drill started operating on the land next to mine. Within a month my tap was spitting out a brown, stinky liquid. Same for all the neighbors. We had it tested. The lab said the water was unfit to drink. The fracking company say it's not their problem. When I contacted my state rep, he said they're not breaking any laws. He said the company made sure there were no laws to break. Now I've been a "hands-off, government" type my whole life and I still worry about big government but experience taught me too late to fear big business. What do you think is going to happen if I try to get mine back in court. The company will bury me in motions until I'm broke. I see now all those talking heads screaming about the "deep state" weren't looking out for me. They're looking out for the fracking companies and all the other companies that know that my only hope of opposing them is through government. Through "We the people."

"You know, I've never actually seen her perform in person," Rolando goes on. "But how do you know her?"

Caleb is still processing the story and Rolando is intent on an answer so they both start at Tawana's voice beside them saying, "We rode the same subway home to Queens."

She has Reynaud by the hand and clutches her guitar case in the other. The boy snickers at the way they jumped. "We scared you, huh, Dad?"

"You got me, little man," and Rolando pulls his child against his leg.

"Thank you for letting me meet your son. He's quite the observant helper. And thank you for letting me rifle through your . . . very soulful work," she finishes with a languid relish then with a wink meant for both men, she says, "But now it's time for me to go do my 'own distinct thang'."

Rolando blushes and from the tingling in his cheeks, Caleb guesses he is too. She walks a hundred feet farther into the grass and takes out her instrument. All around, satellite groups of people—some sitting on the benches or standing as islands in the walkway, others sunbathing on the lawn—migrate to Tawana so that by the time she tunes her instrument, a crowd waits for her to begin. Still a trio remains about the blanket, along with Sidney who motions to these browsers as he asks, "Am I the only one working today?"

"You're right. I'm not pulling my weight," and to Rolando, "Can you hang out for a while?"

"We came for you." Rolando hikes a thumb to where the guitarist seems in silent prayer with her audience. "And I want to see this." Tawana's welcome to the gathering carries with surprising clarity. "To start out, I'm gonna do someone else's music. I don't know what Rodriguez intended to say, but to me this is about heeding the call to be more, no matter if that means being alone. The song is 'Crucify Your Heart'."

A middle-aged couple approaches Caleb. When the husband asks, "What chisels do you use in your carving, eh?" Caleb places them as visitors from the upper Midwest, Minnesota maybe, or Wisconsin. Tawana launches into the tune so that it is a solemn indictment of her listeners for the stands they fear to take and the habits they hide behind to not do so.

"I don't use chisels."

"Any shaping planes?"

The pressed innocence behind these words tells Caleb that the questioner already knows the answer. "I don't use planes either," Caleb says assuming the smile he learned at his father's auction for the sometimes problematic public.

A satisfied surprise bunches the tourist's florid cheeks. "You should check into some shaping tools. They might let you make a cleaner line."

Behind him the wife lets her gaze float away from a scene that she has witnessed before and she moves past Rolando to stand closer to Tawana's performance. His friend smirks at the trial confronting Caleb.

"You're right, sir," he tells his critic. "I could really have used a v-chisel," and he selects a piece formed like a shield leaning against a narrow incline, its surface scored with an irregular tic-tac-toe grid of grooves. "Especially on something like this."

"Oh, you know about v-chisels," the man says apologetically.

"Yeah, I know them. I just got no place to stow them. You probably figured out, space is at a premium around here. My workshop is my room and my room is a shoebox."

The tourist is happy to laugh. "I do, young man. Our hotel ain't much bigger."

Behind Caleb, Tawana pauses for a deep breath then says, "You're the first to hear this next one."

"You grow up around woodworking?" the Midwesterner asks.

"Sort of. My mom's father, you give him a branch and a penknife, he'd carve you a scepter."

Tawana's singing rolls across the lawn then to sweep Caleb away, to one night on a back country lane a good twenty miles from Maynardsville where the crickets in the field fiddled a tumultuous two-note round and the dark begrudged the truck's headlights only short, narrow tunnels to drive toward. Alfred Jr. and he knew they were lost when the macadam gave way to gravel and they turned into the grass lot of the lighted hall to go back. Plastic taped over the rear window of one car and rust and dents on others. A sign long in need of touch-up, "Gethsemane Baptist Chapel." Friday night service. Before Al Jr. could shift into reverse, a Negro spiritual erupted from the meeting house—a plaintive, hopeful, desperate cry into the dark. His brother shut off the engine so they could listen to the invisible female soloist celebrate and lament, both with unshakable belief. The same faith of the dispossessed imbues Tawana's voice now with its reverent growl and ecstatic heights, and like with his brother, Caleb feels himself rising to share its burden.

The tourist alerts him to the lyrics.

"She can't say that!" he exclaims even as his wife hurries back saying, "George, do you hear what that woman is singing?" Their outburst reaches the audience. Some shush the two. Others come about to stand with arms crossed over their chests as barriers to any disruption. Tawana continues.

"God sent his son/to save everyone/but did the Ghost ask about Mary. Still just a virgin/told to submit/whether or not she was ready."

The sacrilege leaves Caleb shaking and when he looks, Sidney is staring over as if Caleb will explain. The tourist tromps past Rolando with his son and towards the performance, beating the air with his fist and crying out, "You can't say that about her, young lady!" The wife trails behind, mumbling what must be agreement as she nods her head like a woodpecker at a diseased tree. Much of the crowd tries to shout him down and those closest are drawing up ranks to keep the threat from Tawana but some call out encouragement so that Caleb realizes that people have come not only to enjoy the guitarist but also to confront her. In the next moment, he wonders with a thrill of terror if the tourist is armed, if anybody in the increasingly agitated group has a weapon.

Tawana's order cuts through the uproar. "Let him speak. Let him through. You, please, come up here if you have a problem with my song."

Through the shifting crowd, Caleb watches the guitarist beckon the man forward. When the people part, the tourist hesitates to come on stage, so to speak, but does. His wife puts a hand out to stop him but stays behind. As

THE PROPHET OF CENTRAL PARK

Caleb walks closer to hear, Rolando whispers to him, "Told you she was one of a kind." Tawana closes up her instrument for safety then faces the man. He is several inches taller but the guitarist, the preacher, the prophet, false prophet, the charlatan—Caleb can no longer venture a name—she commands the space. Without bluster or hostility. People all about have their phones up.

"What have I said that infuriates you?"

"Are you making fun of me?" he snaps back.

"No," she answers quickly. "I am not and will not do that. I want us to understand each other so, please, what have I said that you find so terrible?"

"Okay, okay, I have a problem with you saying that . . ." and he fortifies himself to utter the words. ". . . that God raped Mary."

"You didn't let me finish the song. If you had, you would know I'm saying the Bible story gives Mary no choice in the matter."

"How dare you!" The man's face is beet red by now. "It doesn't say that."

Tawana makes a show of taking a deep breath as a sign for him to do the same. Caleb is amazed when he does.

"Luke, 1:26-38," she counters. "'The Angel Gabriel was sent from God to a town of Galilea called Nazareth, to a virgin betrothed to a man named Joseph, of the house of David and the virgin's name was Mary.' You know it, right?"

"Of course, I do," he says impatiently. "The angel tells Mary of the great honor God has bestowed on her."

Tawana gestures for him to continue reciting the verses, but when his scowl and fidgeting show that he cannot, she does. "'And coming to her, he said, "Hail, full of grace! The Lord is with you." But she was troubled at what was said and pondered what sort of greeting this might be. Then the angel said to her, "Do not be afraid, Mary, for you have found favor with God. Behold, you will conceive in your womb and bear a son, and you shall name him Jesus--"'"

"I know the damned passage!" then as if regretting the curse, he repeats, "I know the passage."

"Okay, so you know what Gabriel tells her, after she says, 'How can this be, since I have no relations with a man?'" and when the tourist starts to become irritated again, she hurries on, "You're accusing me of slandering the Lord and I'm justifying my statement as what's in the scripture. So the text is important. Prove me wrong with the text."

Coming to her husband's aid, the wife calls out in a trembling voice, "'The Holy Spirit will come upon you'."

"Yes! Yes! Thank you," Tawana says, though she cannot place the woman in the crowd. "'And the power of the Most High will overshadow you. Therefore the child to be born will be called holy, the son of God.' That's the text, right?" she puts to the man. "I've not misquoted anything?"

Her recall impresses Caleb even as the man allows, "That sounds about right."

Tawana nods and in a tone that is calm and kindly, she says, "So where in this passage does Gabriel ask Mary what she wants, let alone ask for her consent to an act to be done to her body?"

This starts an irregular chorus from the audience of "yes"s, "ah-huh"s, and "that's right"s. Beyond opening his mouth, the man has no reply, until one of his supporters shouts out, "'Behold I am the handmaid of the Lord'." Then he grows excited. "Mary says that at the end and, and 'May it be done to me according to your word.' So it's in the Gospel. She does accept God's will for her."

The guitarist nods again which prompts the tourist to smile from equal parts gloating and relief.

"Interesting word you used just now, 'accept'," Tawana says. "But you acknowledge that nowhere does Gabriel ask Mary's permission?"

"Mary consented! You just agreed."

Instantly angry again, the tourist leans forward, fists clenching and letting go. Tawana closes her eyes to a long count of one, her profile one of tranquil repose, and Caleb is again stunned to see the man relax.

"Since you cannot say it, I will. The angel tells Mary what will happen to her, he does not ask."

"But you just agreed--"

"I agreed that she accepted what would be done. I can't know if she consented and neither can you."

The man looks skyward in a theatrical plea for patience. "What kind of new age nonsense is that? It's right there in the scripture."

"Yes, it is. Somehow, though, we are looking at two very different events. Please, tell me what you see."

THE PROPHET OF CENTRAL PARK

The tourist sighs as if she is a child to be placated, then he answers, "An angel, a beautific presence, comes to tell Mary God has chosen her because she is special among women. Mary is frightened at first but she realizes what a tremendous blessing has been given to her, to bear the Son of God."

"Yes, that's pretty much the story that Luke wanted you to read."

"Then what are you babbling on about, woman?"

"Exactly. I'm a woman and a woman would have written a very different Gospel. Same details, very different story."

"There's only one--"

"I didn't interrupt you," and she demands of him, "Please give me the same courtesy."

The tourist glares back but stays quiet.

"A woman writing this would realize at this time in history that Mary is a girl, a teenager who is a virgin, so unworldly, and she is suddenly confronted by a supernatural emissary. Even Luke admits she is 'greatly troubled'. I would be terrified, especially if that supernatural being told me, **told me** that God was going to enter my body by some unknown agency to make me pregnant. Yes, the scripture has her accepting this fate. But is she in any position to say no? Would it have mattered if she had begged Gabriel, 'Please, don't do this to me.'? Did she really have a choice."

"So you do?" the tourist accuses her, unable to contain his indignation. "You do believe God assaulted Mary."

"No, I could never worship a God who would do such a thing. And I don't believe you could either."

"Then why do you insist upon twisting the Gospel into such an ugly thing?"

"I'm reading what's on the page. Nothing more. You infer consent because you have to or else it's a terrible story. But I am reading only what's written."

The tourist puts a hand to his forehead. "So what's the point of all your smartass lawyering?"

At that moment, Tawana strikes Caleb as a paradox, a dark motionless idol and yet a vibrant force of life. "Just this. That Mary and Joseph conceived Jesus the same way all parents do. That the church, because of its neurotic obsession, created a myth to render Jesus free of any taint of sex.

And that in doing so the church made Mary the first woman to whom they denied autonomy over her own body."

The tourist rears back then turns away, whether in disgust or at a loss for words, Caleb cannot tell. As the man returns to his wife, Annaliese tries to shout her approval, but Caleb pushes her down in confusion at how the guitarist's arguments eat like acid at his long held image of God and man. Taking up his salesman's post, he asks Rolando, "Are all her sessions like that?"

His friend shrugs. "Sort of. But today, this was some next level stuff."

* * *

Wired

Over the past few years a growing number of municipalities have instituted or are in the process of establishing community-owned broadband. More and more privately owned providers are taking notice. The industry has tripled spending on PR campaigns aimed at discrediting the viability of these public endeavors and are lobbying state capitals for laws meant to diminish their feasibility. Proponents are fighting back with data from towns that already offer resident-owner systems, pointing to user savings of 25% to 50% for a higher level of reliability. They also cite the ability of improved internet service to attract new business and jobs. While surveys vary in ranking quality of service in the US with the rest of the industrialized world, most agree the cost is substantially higher here.

Sidney sells another sculpture before Rolando and his son wander off. Caleb gives Reynaud ten dollars for his help. By way of goodbye Rolando pantomimes tickling his cheek without touching the skin. "Keep icing your face when you get home. You're starting to puff up again." As they leave Reynaud asks to be put back on his dad's shoulders, then waves goodbye to the guitarist with a frantic flailing arm. Tawana stops what she is saying to call out how happy she is that she met him, and much of her audience comes about to answer his farewell too. The boy blushes and asks to be put down again.

Though Caleb tries not to hear, portions of what the woman preaches and sings reach him. As does talk with and among the listeners. Sometimes anger swells into shouting matches but Tawana steps in to restore, well, respectful discourse. The boisterous atmosphere recalls the revivals that his parents brought Caleb and his siblings to but its openness troubles his sense of worship.

Sidney raises the price to one seventy-five and when two more buyers agree, raises it again to two hundred. People keep hopping the barrier with the decided grins of kids sneaking into the circus tent. Increasingly they request Sidney take selfies of them beside Caleb. The more timid comport themselves on the benches so that their camera phones capture him over their shoulders. Handing over the proceeds from a sixth sale, Sidney says, "I told you that face was gold," then in mock seriousness he asks, "You want me to give you another poke, freshen it up." When a stunning thirty-something woman decked in black spandex tights ignores Sidney's chatting to put her arm about Caleb for another photo, he warns her self-consciously, "Aren't you afraid I'll crack the lens?" The sunlight catches in her red hair like sparkles. "Nonsense. Those are battle scars. Wear them proudly," and pressing herself to him, she puts her lips to the bruised flesh for the picture she takes with her outstretched arm.

"Okay. You're punking me now," Sidney demands when the woman saunters away. "You know her, right. I mean, what the hell is going on today?"

At noon the roommate takes a break to buy lunch. As usual Caleb isn't hungry but hands over a twenty for Sidney's meal, asks for a water. While his roommate is gone, an older man joins a trio of browsers and makes a slow circuit of the sales floor that sees the other three replaced by new shoppers. He is an African American gentleman, over six feet tall so that he kneels off one leg when he inspects a specific assemblage closely. He has a broad squarish face and his wavy hair brushed back from his forehead is a white furrowed field with only a few black strands interspersed. Given his interest Caleb becomes hopeful, even as he is anxious for Sidney's return so he won't need to deal with any haggling. When the gentleman finishes his review, he holds his hand out. The callused hardness of his palm and fingers reminds Caleb of the grip of a mason he knew back home. "William. William Davey Randolph," he says in a rippling baritone. "There really is something of the sacred about your work."

At the phrase Caleb looks behind him. The crowd hides Tawana but her soulful hymn celebrating the oneness of mankind rises from it. When he looks back, the gentleman nods. "She called me. Said I should come take a look."

"Why? I mean thanks for what you just said but . . . ."

"Why did she call me?" the man finishes for Caleb. "I'm a sculptor. Tawana's all about bringing people together. Have you studied anywhere?"

"Like art school? No."

"Why wood?" the sculptor asks as he genuflects to handle another figure.

"What I have to work with."

The piece makes the man smile, but Caleb is too timid to ask why. The sculptor stands. "Do you have a name for what you do?"

"Totems."

Caleb watches for the reaction this elicits, knowing it will direct the course of any relationship between them. The sculptor mulls over the term with a murmur rumbling up from his chest. "That seems right." He begins another circuit back the way he came as if to see each piece from the other side. "You work small."

"I work in my bedroom so I have no choice. Why?"

William does not look. "Every decision we make opens one door but closes others. It's good to know what I'm shutting myself off from. Have you sold anything?"

"Six," and he keeps himself from adding, for now, to not sound boastful. The book of James plays in his head: As it is, you boast in your arrogance— All such boasting is evil.

At the number the sculptor does look over to Caleb. "That means you're connecting with people. Not an easy thing, selling off a blanket."

Sidney returns then with his bagged lunch and two waters. Pointing to the sculptor Caleb says, "This is William Davey Randolph, a friend of Tawana's. This is Sidney, my roommate and front man."

The two wave their hellos, then the man again bends down to reach into a box. "This is 'Anna Lisa'," he states rather than asks as he lifts the ruptured swell aloft.

"Annaliese," Caleb snaps back.

THE PROPHET OF CENTRAL PARK

"Sorry." William breathes in labored "ah"s as he considers the statue, his dark eyes unblinking, like a supplicant in the presence of a relic. "How much?"

The question startles Caleb. If Tawana told her friend the title, Caleb would have thought she told him the rest. "Not for sale."

"Don't even want to throw out a ridiculous price?"

"No."

With a sigh the man returns the piece to the container and moves left two steps to a blunt presence into which Caleb scored a rude mouth and crooked nose and onto which he fashioned an aureole of irregular bristles. "Then how much for this one?"

"Two hundred," Sidney says but Caleb corrects him, "One hundred. Friend of Tawana discount."

As Sidney shakes his head, the man withdraws the money. "Your front man is much better at this."

Sidney turns a hard stare upon Caleb, as much to say, See, even this stranger gets it, then he asks the man, "Do you want it signed?"

William Davey Randolph withholds the payment for a moment. "You live in Queens, on the N line," this to Caleb. "Come to my studio to sign it." He hands over the bills with his card and gathers his purchase. "I'm keeping you from your public."

A pair of young men are hovering close by with their phones at the ready. Caleb steps next to the sculptor to whisper, "This whole selfie thing is weird. My roommate's pimping me like some kind of, I dunno, disfigured mad potter of Biloxi."

The sculptor smiles for the first time, a slow-spreading event that exposes teeth as white as his hair. "George Ohr sold a helluva lot of bowls."

Before Caleb can ask how the man knows the mad potter, he waggles the sculpture as goodbye and steps over the benches, his long legs making him much more graceful at it than Sidney.

The roommate moves a totem soon after his return, so that he has to put down his sandwich for the transaction, and another two over the next hour. The requests for selfies increase so that during a lull even Sidney says, "This is crazy. I'm a salesman par excellence but nobody is this good."

An odd messenger reveals the reason. The petite young woman sports a shaved left side of the head while from the right a full straight mantle of hair dyed blue cascades over that shoulder. The 'do accentuates her several nose piercings and trash chic outfit of grey gym shorts paired with three layers of ripped t-shirts coordinated to keep her covered. The squeal of her voice rings out of character, better suited to an animated duck in a children's cartoon, so that Caleb nearly doesn't catch the import when the nouveau punkster says, "You really showed those bully boys."

He does though.

"Wait, what did you just say, Miss?"

Happy to be questioned, she ignores Sidney handing back her phone. "How you stopped them trashing the Triple R stand. It was the most 'stamp' thing I've seen forever."

"Seen where?"

"Online. The video's everywhere. I think they're showing it on TV," and she does take her phone. "Here, I'll show you."

"No, no. Thank you really but no."

Caleb puts his hands up to stop her. Aggrieved by the put-off, she pouts in rejoining the foot traffic beyond the barrier. She seems the only parkgoer not looking his way. Paranoia, he knows but suddenly the sun seems to be shining solely to put them on display. Sidney has abandoned his barker responsibilities to search on his own phone.

"Oh, buddy, she was not lying. You've gone viral."

Caleb doesn't want to watch but like a possum in a car's headlights he can't look away when Sidney holds up the footage. The person recording was to Caleb's right so that he and the provocateurs are in profile. When Caleb points to the silent partners at the stand's far end, the amateur cinematographer raises the phone and captures the one Skoal-user hunching forward with arms lowered and hands turned outward, about to flip the table. Captures the people about him knocking down those arms. Caleb cringes at how pretentious his pronouncement on Jesus sounds, his take on evil. When the fighter launches his blow, Caleb flinches away. "Please turn that off," and when his roommate does, he asks, "Where did you get that from?"

"Slate.com. They call it, 'Southern Samaritan Stops Alabama Bully Boys'."

Before Caleb can cringe even more, a voice startles them both. "That was incredible."

THE PROPHET OF CENTRAL PARK

He is a tank of a man with dark hair. A wrestler's body, upper weight class and about Caleb's age. The woman beside him adds, "You didn't just stand by. You . . . you answered the call."

Several spectators in a semi circle nod their eager agreement. One joins in, "Absolutely." Caleb realizes they have been watching him watch himself, waiting for a reaction like some late night fan show, "Talking the Southern Samaritan." Even more so now, Caleb feels exposed. "Heat of the moment thing. Not me at all. One minute, folks." Caleb pulls Sidney behind their layout to whisper, "We have to get out of here pronto."

Unfeigned shock from his roommate. "Are you kidding? We could sell out by dinnertime. You can't buy the kind of publicity you're getting right now. Why not?" This last in response to Caleb's emphatic headshakes, No.

Caleb tells him. "People've been snapchatting, tweeting, telling the world I'm here." Sidney grows animated at this but Caleb hurries on. "Not everybody who's seen that video is happy with me. Some of them boys show up, we could be in the middle of a riot like the one you just saw. How good are you at taking a punch?"

This last challenge drops Sidney's jaw so that his face is like the comic decoration painted around the opening of a ball-toss game, then he snaps around to the customers, clapping his hands.

"Okay, everybody, if you want something, buy it now 'cause we're closing up."

* * *

BBC WorldWide

American ATF officials are reporting a significant uptick in firearm purchases by members of LGBT and other left leaning associations. Flak vests and other riot gear are also being acquired as these communities form their own militias. This phenomenon of the political left robustly exercising their Second Amendment rights seems a response to highly publicized instances of armed groups with ultraconservative bents showing up at events organized in support of transgender, abortion and other rights championed by liberals.

P C Burhenne

They sell two more statues before the rest of the totems are boxed. As Caleb pens his name to the second, he realizes that all morning he has been signing away his anonymity. As they hurry onto the walkway, he looks back but Tawana's audience screens her. On the train he faces a door with Sidney positioned back to back to him as a buffer to other commuters. In Queens Caleb gets his roommate to move with him to another car in case somebody is following them. Nobody does. By the time they reach the apartment, Caleb's head hurts.

He leaves the boxes in his room, empties his pockets onto the table, then bags ice. The cold makes him wince and shiver as it seeps into his cheek and he closes his eyes in his chair. "So how much?" When there is no reply, he looks over expecting to find his roommate counting the now ordered mounds of bills.

Instead Sidney stares at his phone. "This is way bigger than we thought. You have a crazy amount of views." With a wistful smile he adds, "It has your name."

After sorting and running the tally twice, Sidney reveals the day's take as, "Nineteen hundred and twenty-five dollars," surprise bordering on awe in the announcement.

"You take three hundred. Your commission."

"Are you sure? Given your," and the roommate bobbles his head, "celebrity, you probably didn't need me to sell anything."

"I wouldn't have tried if not for you," Caleb says.

"And you'd still be the unknown Samaritan."

"The way this has blown up, people would have tracked me down anyway."

He shakes the bunch of bills so that his roommate accepts them. Sidney springs for dinner, Thai, to celebrate Caleb's first successful show. They use UberEats rather than go out. The food is outstanding, but Caleb can't help feeling that he is the diner on the Titanic who knows the ship will soon hit an iceberg. After cleaning up he goes to his room with another compress. The boxes wait to be unpacked but he lies on his side on the bed so the cold pack balances on his cheek. Like that he again takes up Virginia Woolf.

The first call comes an hour later.

"You fucking homo!" the man shouts. "You're gonna get more than a dick in your ass if you don't mind your own business."

THE PROPHET OF CENTRAL PARK

Caleb gasps in the quiet afterwards.

The next caller says simply, "I'm gonna kill you. I know where you live and I'm gonna kill you." The third, "Get right with the Lord, young man, or you're gonna burn in hell."

Sidney comes in then, saying, "What's with all the--" but freezes. Caleb is on the bed, back to the wall and knees clutched to his chest. He looks up from the phone on the mattress beside him. "It's started."

"Turn it off," and Sidney comes to do so himself. As he snatches up the cell, however, it rings again. He asks, "Who's Carolyne?"

Caleb takes back the phone, saying, "My sister." Sidney leaves. Without preamble, Carolyne says, "You're in trouble, Caleb," a statement of sympathy.

"I know, Sis," then he grasps the full extent of her words. "Oh, God, people there are watching the video? Mom and Dad?"

"Everybody's seen it. The church elders called a special meeting. Mom says she doesn't know how she can go out anymore."

A woman of causes, his mother meets multiple people every day, people seeking help, seeking advice, those touching base. He grimaces at what he has taken from her. "Does she hate me?"

"She's mourning you."

Caleb summons every bit of will to not burst into tears. "Dad?"

"Dad came here today to tell us, not only are we not to talk to you ever again, we're never to mention your name again. Terry told him, we don't speak with you now," and she quickly explains, "He doesn't know I called. But Terry told him that if you reached out, he wouldn't stop it. He wouldn't do that to me. Dad went wrath of God on him, us. How dare we entertain the blasphemer."

The line goes silent but Caleb knows there is more. "What is it, Carolyne?"

"I told him about William Ellison. He made me so mad, he didn't even care how you were so I told him you knew. I've never seen him like that, shocked and guilty. Then he was someone else. Scary. I thought he was going to hit me. Terry stepped between us, told Dad if he wouldn't respect our house, he isn't welcome in it. Everything's coming apart."

"Because of me."

Another pause. Then, "How bad is it? Your face, I mean?"

"It hurt yesterday. Not so much today."

With nothing to offer that will repair the destruction he's caused, he almost tells her, Goodbye, but she coaxes him, "Why didn't you say about Annaliese?"

"She made me promise to be quiet." Caleb can picture again the furious stare and adamant line of Annaliese's mouth as she extracted the oath from him. "It was the one time, a mistake. We actually laughed afterwards. She was never going to keep the baby. She had plans to leave. And she knew her parents, my parents, everybody would have pressured us to marry if they knew I was the father."

"But why didn't you let me help?"

"All that happened was so ugly, I just hated everybody. I lost myself for a while in the hate."

A beep from another call breaks in.

"Do you need to get that?"

"Not a chance," he says without thinking then he figures he may as well explain. "I've started getting some pretty nasty calls. A lot of people would have been happy if those hicks had succeeded."

"Have you called the police?" The chord of concern and indignation in the question echoes from their childhood.

"I was just about to turn off my cell. It's been a long day. I'm exhausted."

"There's something else," she says to keep him. Caleb steadies himself for another blow but her voice carries the first note of music he's heard from her in ages. "I saw you in the park today. Another video. Your pieces I could make out, they set my heart alight. And they would have done Pop Pop's too. I know he would have said something like 'Thank God I put a penknife in that boy's hand.'"

The praise leaves him mute for a moment but she waits for an answer. "They're all down to him. I just wish I could tell him that."

"He knows, Caleb."

Speaking to the person he once trusted with every pulse and part of himself, he has to ask, "What would you have done, Sis? Yesterday with those shitkickers?" then he lets go the real question that has tormented him for months. "Am I wrong? Have I been deceived?"

THE PROPHET OF CENTRAL PARK

When she doesn't answer right away, he believes she is weighing the kindest language for her condemnation. Instead she whispers, "I don't know," then "Little Stephanie's out of bed. I gotta go."

Caleb powers off his cell and goes back to Virginia Woolf but a pack of imagined threats hound him. When he looks outside, there are street lamps and the bright windows of other apartments but the neighborhood otherwise cloaks itself in shadows. Where he imagines unnamed malice watching him. Though he turns off his own light, the fear stays and he can think of no antidote.

"God, I'm not . . . an agitator, an activist. I'm just . . . I couldn't stand by. I'm somebody that couldn't stand by. Does that make me so bad? Why is this happening? Please tell me. And please, please help me make it through."

In the living room Sidney watches TV till late. The canned voices help Caleb make believe he is not alone. He distracts himself to sleep, repeating over and over that last simple prayer.

Sunday

The Hill

Progressive members of the Democratic caucus in Congress yesterday unveiled a plan for a federal use tax to replace federal income tax, this in response to repeated calls from the Freedom Caucus for a federal sales tax. The Left's proposal differs from the conservative one in that it would apply to all purchases, from chewing gum and home sales to one corporation's buyout of another and each and every stock and bond transfer. Proponents claim the use tax would be more egalitarian because it would reflect citizen and corporate participation in the economy that government functions maintain. Republicans immediately labeled it "another ridiculous scheme unfairly targeting businesses" that would hurt working men and women by stifling wage and job growth. Experts project that such a revenue-generating device would substantially lower the tax burden of lower, middle and even some upper class segments of American society.

In the morning the swelling is down and the bright colors are fading. Caleb decides to replace the plies of wood he used on sculptures during the week. The focus to maintain an even cut delivers peace for those hours. When he turns on his phone, twenty-seven messages are waiting. Not recognizing any of the numbers, he deletes them and powers off the phone again. At ten he cleans up and goes out to the kitchen. A wide brim cap and sunglasses rest on the table.

"I dug those out for you."

Sidney is at the sink washing dishes with his back to Caleb.

"Just what I need. Thank you."

The roommate takes his cell from his pocket then so that Caleb realizes he has it on vibrate. When Sidney puts it away after a glance, Caleb makes himself ask, "It's happening to you too?"

"Started early this morning."

"Oh Lord, Sidney, I'm sorry I got you into this."

THE PROPHET OF CENTRAL PARK

His roommate continues to face away. "I'm not in the best mood right now, Caleb, so maybe just give me some space."

Caleb has not heard this sour tone from his friend before. For a moment he expects Sidney to swing around with a wide "gotcha" grin but the roommate keeps staring down at the sink. Caleb takes the hat and glasses and goes.

He orders an egg and cheese sandwich at the nearby deli. William Davey Randolph's card comes out with the money. He switches on his phone, trashes the new batch of messages then calls. "This is Caleb Ellison. From the Park. You invited me to come down to your studio?"

"Yes, I did."

"Can I come today? Now?" and thinking that sounded presumptuous, he adds, "I mean in an hour. I was going to walk."

"That should work fine. Call me when you get here. Take the elevator to the third floor."

The appointment is a relief. Even with Sidney, Sundays have been empty spaces where Caleb used to gather with family. The Ellisons observed the Sabbath together, first with prayer in pews then with boisterous appetites beneath the homestead's seven oaks. Alfred Sr. was an enlightened man: the women cooked, the men cleaned up. On his way now beneath the elevated tracks, he hears rebuke in the lingering notes of the steeple bells about Astoria calling their members to eleven o'clock mass.

The floppy hat and glasses help him feel unseen. He arrives feeling only slightly tired from the walk. William Davey Randolph's building is a five-story, red-brick industrial affair from the turn of the last century. The many banks of large metal windows opening upward and outward suggest high ceilings meant to house machinery. The sculptor buzzes Caleb in at once but the freight elevator labors to take him up with a determined hum.

The lift opens onto basically the entire third floor. Some rooms cluster about the elevator shaft but otherwise the only partitions among the support columns are movable screens and makeshift curtains hanging from the ten-foot ceiling. Caleb sees a squat stage off near the left wall. The sculptor waits to greet him wearing a leather apron over jeans and a t-shirt.

"Going incognito today, huh?" he says instead of a welcome, then confirming that he has seen the video and guessed the aftermath, he asks, "How bad is it?" When Caleb's open mouth cannot express the anxiety that has seeped through him since last evening, the sculptor adds, "A lot of people are cheering what you did."

"They're not calling me, Mr. Randolph."

"It's Davey." He motions Caleb to follow him right. "Seems like that's always the way. Only scared people who want to silence you go to the trouble. But I have friends in the movement. You're a hero to them. This is me."

They step through two sheets of heavy cloudy plastic into Davey's work station. A block of marble sits on a rough table hammered together from two-by-fours and a plywood top. The sculptor has only removed one front edge from the stone, has not approached the profiles sketched onto the two sides forming that corner. These suggest that a hawk waits to be freed. Drawings beside it support this. Welding tanks and a torch rest on a dolly against a column. Near it Caleb's piece sits on a stand, along with a felt tip. Caleb smiles for the first time that day, then hurries to put away that pride. "You don't take Sunday off?"

"I work while the work is flowing. I stop when it stops. So how did you come to be, what would you call yourself, a poet in wood?"

"Lord, I'm nothing so grand as that." He looks again to his totem, remembering how it guided him to its final form. "If anything, I'm a spokesman for the piece." Turning back to the sculptor, he says, "Maybe that's even too fancy pants."

"Have you always worked with wood?"

"My grandpop got me started. He whittled since he came back from the war. Korea. Said the carving kept his mind from slipping back to that terrible place. He joked that if they had PTSD back then, he'd have never picked up a knife." Caleb runs his fingertips over the stone. "Funny thing, marble. Unyielding as it is, I always feel if I squeeze hard enough, it will crumble in my hand."

Davey reaches out to the block too. "You have a sculptor's hands at least."

Out of habit Caleb retreats from the subject of his Pop Pop. "Other good thing about wood, I can scavenge it off the street. Ready supply of material."

"As long as you work small."

The sculptor dangles each word before he releases it. Caleb hears criticism in the drawl. "Like I said, catch as catch can."

Davey smiles, holding up his hands at the displeasure Caleb can't quite keep from his voice. "Whoa. Wasn't trying to give offense."

"Sorry. Didn't mean to be prickly," but Caleb still does feel the pointy edges. "Why did you mention how small my work is again?"

"Yes," the sculptor allows so that the final "s" sizzles for a second. "Look, I understand working with what you got: a cramped apartment, no money. And I also understand not wanting to mess with your process because it's the crucible that helped you make that," and Davey wags a finger toward Caleb's sculpture.

Caleb knows it is coming, doesn't feel like waiting. "But," he says for the man. Yet again he speaks the word with more force then he intends.

Aside from licking the corner of his mouth, the sculptor is motionless as he takes in Caleb. Then, "'But' nothing. Good job."

He moves away and Caleb knows the man is closing a door behind him. In under five minutes Caleb has brought his only ever meeting with an actual artist to an end. Anger at his own thin skin makes him blurt out before he thinks, "Where there is strife, there is pride but wisdom is found in those who take advice."

The man comes around with a wariness, but he does say, "I agree. Proverbs rarely lead me amiss."

Caleb grips his head with both palms at the show he is putting on. "Lord, you must think I'm well short of a dozen." The sculptor raises his eyebrows to tell Caleb he is not wrong. Caleb no longer feels comfortable calling the man Davey. "Mr. Randolph, please understand, since I came to New York, I'm closer to these totems than anything. I guess I have trouble hearing I might be doing them wrong."

Again the judicial pokerface from the sculptor. Until with mild irritation, he clarifies, "I never said wrong. I suggested other directions are available to you."

"Please, sir, explain what you were going to explain." Caleb waves back to himself, "I'm listening. I wanna know."

The sculptor clucks to himself then he points to the table. "Look at those drawings." Caleb sees they are studies from all five visible sides of the desired figure. The sculptor asks, "Do you think that's where I started?"

When Caleb shrugs, the sculptor crooks a finger for Caleb to follow him. The opaque curtains form a square about the space. William Davey pushes through a part at the rear into a much more cluttered area that has three tables covered with tools, sketch pads and, of course, more of his pieces. Caleb recognizes a cluster of these as iterations of the object underway out front. The sculptor puts his hand over the simplest of these, two plywood hawk shapes bearing opposed vertical cut-out channels that allow them to slide together perpendicular to each other like a raptor-themed mobile. "I started with an idea, a static idea, then I played with it." He moves his hand over a smaller clay bird bearing the imprints of his thumbs and palette knife and says, "I looked for ways to introduce tension to the pose," and as his hand travels the timeline of his efforts, he adds, "to introduce drama that, if I'm successful, ultimately suggests a story."

William Davey sweeps open the partition then so that Caleb knows to go out front. He expects the sculptor to point out the rewards of the process on the outlines of the hawk scrawled on the marble block. Instead William Davey puts on his safety glasses from the table and Caleb knows he has in no way repaired the damage he caused.

"You have an intuitive sense of form," the sculptor says in a tone that he might use for any stranger. "I've only wanted to encourage you to explore your subjects more, whether that means working bigger or smaller. In the future, of course. When you have more space."

Caleb hears the dismissal. "Thank you for taking the time."

Before he is through the plastic, though, the sculptor exclaims, "Oh damned! Tawana wants to say 'hello'. If you have a moment." The man snaps the last, clearly annoyed at having to offer the invitation.

"Tawana lives here?"

"She stays here sometimes. Has a room upstairs." He waggles his chisel off to his side. "Easier to take the stairs. Corridor to the windows. Right to the back corner. She's next to them, one floor up." Then as a parting aside, "You should ask her how to deal with the crazies. She's been doing it for years."

* * *

Graffiti painted on a bridge over I-90 in Chicago

THE PROPHET OF CENTRAL PARK

"Why do you hate me?"

Along the improvised hall other figures move behind the translucent partitions. An iPhone croons softly from somewhere. At the wall a kitchen area takes up the corner to the front left. As Caleb goes right to the back and up the stairwell, he wonders at how Tawana has popped up the past few days. Though he planned this visit an hour ago, the coincidence is strange.

She is there when he pushes open the door. Her outfit of grey sweat pants and grey pullover hoodie emblazoned with "Queens" in red catches Caleb offguard. He hasn't considered that she could be relaxing in cozy clothes. However, the casual attire does not dampen the strength of her presence, which again scrambles his thoughts so that he wavers between holding out his hand and raising it. She settles the matter, showing her cell to say, "Davey texted me." Caleb sees that the dark nuanced complexion of her skin is the same, though the red of her mouth is not so striking; apart from lipstick, she doesn't wear make-up.

Catching himself staring, he looks down. "He said you wanted a word."

She gestures to a nearby open door. "Yes. Thank you for coming up. Though I must say, your visit seems a bit short."

"Ah, yeah, I kinda messed it up."

The austerity of her room strikes him. Aside from a bed—already made —a desk and two mission oak style chairs, there is a floor lamp and a framed print of a geometric stone grillwork, Caleb guesses from a mosque. Her guitar case leans into a corner beside a backpack. He is surprised to see a Bible open on the desk. Following her in, he leaves the door open, not just for propriety's sake. Given her charismatic effect, he doesn't trust being alone with her. He takes the seat beside the exit.

"I'm sorry to hear that," she says as she sits too. "He was very impressed with your work. Which is a big compliment."

"Don't mind me asking, what is this place? Some kind of commune?"

Tawana chuckles. "Not as far as I can tell. It's an artists' loft. Cheap enough for all of them together to afford, along with the rooms up here. Apart from Davey, there's two other sculptors, I think. A bunch of painters. There's a playwright. Some of her troupe live here too. She does interesting stuff. Not always my flava." Tawana leans closer, her mouth hinting at a conspirator's grin. "She gets a little preachy for my tastes."

"You're not part of this, though? Mr. Randolph, ah, Davey said you stay here just sometimes."

"I let this room a couple nights a week, but, yeah, I sleep around," then embarrassed by what she just said, she looks aside. "I mean, I rotate where I stay. Friends help me out."

Davey's "crazies" remark returns to Caleb. "Oh my God, you have to worry that much about stalkers?"

The woman sits up on her seat and in that way, reclaims—he's not sure what to call it—her tranquil self.

"I've learned to be careful."

Given his present predicament, the unrefuted prospect of danger alarms Caleb as much for himself as for her. "Have people actually physically assaulted you?"

She remains self-possessed, says simply, "It's good to be cautious." then she allows with a soft sigh, "I didn't do you any favors yesterday. I didn't know about your . . . intervention at the RRR table when I joined up with you. Or the videos. If I had, I'd have given you the chance to tell me to get the hell away. Followers posted recordings of me at your pop-up market. Which I'm afraid puts some of my baggage in your cart."

Tawana's song that incited the Midwestern tourist returns to Caleb. "Your views on Mary make it online?"

"Oh, yeah." A tremor infects the woman's voice and for the first time she seems vulnerable. Caleb looks away as if he has happened upon her changing. She continues, though. "I prayed for God to take that song back for the longest time. But once they're given, they're my responsibility. That one, though, I knew it would ring louder than the rest." Subdued and in her sweats, she could be a teenage girl despondent because of a coach's criticism after a team practice.

"What do you mean, 'when your songs are given'?"

She studies him to decide if she will share more. "These—you call them songs, I call them verses, psalms—they come to me after I've prayed for guidance, for peace. Because they start with a doubt that, that," and she presses a hand to her chest, "upsets my very soul so that I can't be free of the question. I have to be delivered from it." She takes a bracing breath. "Writing down one of those 'songs' can leave me, it can wipe me out. But you aren't buying this, huh?"

THE PROPHET OF CENTRAL PARK

Caleb understands that he is wearing his skepticism and he shakes his head as if it is water to be dislodged. He still feels it, though, at the idea that Tawana is receiving divine visions. "I've just never met a real live mystic before."

Without rancor at the irony in his reply, she asks, "What's the biggest problem for you? That I'm a woman claiming to be touched by God? That I'm a black woman claiming it? Or that I practice my ministry with a guitar in the Park."

The challenge to him is a gentle one but a challenge nonetheless so that once again during this visit, he works to control his tone. "If I'm telling the truth, I don't know that I believe your messages come from God."

She nods. "Oh, yes, am I being deceived, that keeps me up many nights clinging to my Bible." She places her still-open Good Book onto her lap. Caleb can see even upside down that it is the self-same passage. "Gabriel with Mary, this story has always—if I was being polite, I'd say it vexed me but it has been the biggest pain in my ass. The girl as a vessel, filled upon command. It's not the only part I can't reconcile to the Spirit that comes when I am scared and alone." She closes the Bible to hold it up. "Places in here make God biased, vindictive, full of bloodlust. And always 'He', always male." She sets the book back on her desk.

Similar qualms plague Caleb but he cannot bring himself to fall in line with her.

"So," she goes on. "My belief has evolved. I take the Scriptures to be divinely inspired but the work of man nonetheless which means they're flawed like everything we humans touch. Still I find comfort in much that is written." She straightens then. "As for the reason I wanted to talk. You said something in the video that I—what's wrong?"

Caleb has closed his eyes at the quote he suspects she is interested in. "The thing about evil." When he opens them and she nods, he says, "I don't want to discuss what that's about."

"Neither do I really, not the story behind it anyway," and at his cynic's frown, she holds up her hands. The pink of her palms is striking against the black of her arms. "For a long time I've been struggling with the idea of evil. What is it? How do we identify it? In the video you both call the other evil. Basically, right?"

When he considers the exchange, he knows she is right.

"For him it's clear," she says. "He has God's word, from his preacher presumably. Anything that contradicts it is wicked. But for someone like me—and you, I'm guessing, since you got between him and his mission from on high—it's a crucial matter. I no longer have the infallible word of God in my back pocket so how do I know Her will for us. How do I know what is evil? How did you?"

Caleb needs a second to realize this last is not rhetorical. "I know. I just . . . the thing I saw, it was so ugly, every part of me knew it was wrong."

Tawana's nose snuffles at the breath she takes in, holds, and yet again her pitying regard makes him worry that she had read his awful history with Annaliese in a thousand small tells he cannot control. "Apart from the difference between 'wrong' and 'evil', I don't accept the 'I know it when I see it' test. The man you stopped at Rockefeller Center sees evil in the RRR movement just like you see it in what he stands for. Every war ever fought, certainly any war over religion, both sides saw the Devil in their enemy's midst. Evil can't be that subjective or else God is a cruel puppetmaster pitting us against each other through revelations. Do you see what I mean?"

Caleb does and doesn't care. The violence against Annaliese was an unholy sin, and he denounces it as such. "What I saw, they didn't care about her, if she lived or died, as long as she did as she was told. She didn't matter. They only cared that they be right."

"Now that's a deeper look at evil," she says, giving each part a moment alone before speaking the next, but he does not see the look that accompanies her hesitation. His hands tremble on his legs, will not stop though he wants them to. Annaliese reminds him, You were part of it too— You could have stopped it and you didn't.

"Oh, please," he begs. "I wanted to. I, I tried to get to you."

Caleb senses Tawana brush past him, but Annaliese continues in her most ruthless voice: I needed you to save me—You were my only hope.

"I tried. Oh, Annaliese, I tried. They wouldn't let me help. Your parents, they wouldn't . . . they wouldn't . . . ."

His face is wet suddenly then his hands too from the drips off his chin, and though he tries he cannot stop crying. Can't stop gulping air as his accuser continues: You let them kill me, because you're a coward.

"I am a coward. Yes, yes I am."

THE PROPHET OF CENTRAL PARK

A hand covers his forehead. The cool, dry flesh thrills and confuses him. Tawana is in her seat (again?) leaning toward him with her arm outstretched and her eyes closed. "God, please help Caleb," she prays low so only they two can hear. "Now. He needs You so very much. Help him bear this pain. Help him let it go."

A charge passes down from his scalp through to his limbs that brings in its wake the repose of the saved, as if the tingling has flushed the guilt from his body. The abrupt delivery dumbfounds Caleb so that he can only stare with his untroubled vision at his now still hands. For several seconds remaining beneath Tawana's touch, a contact he is loath to end. When he does straighten, she leans back too, her gaze full of concern.

"What did you just do?"

Tawana relaxes at the question. "I asked what you could not."

He looks about to be sure he is in the same room and pats his chest to be sure he is the same person and of course he is. Yet he knows he is different from the broken soul of a moment before. "You did something. I'm . . . ." He has no name for the change. "You did something."

Her head shake is a single slow back and forth and she smiles as if he is a child to be gently corrected. "I didn't. I saw," and she shrugs and says, "that you were ready to share your burden. You did it. I simply asked for you." He shakes his head this time at the simple explanation, inadequate to the renewal he feels within. Her face does not waver. "Really, Caleb, I didn't do anything but speak the words that were caught inside of you." Before he can argue, she goes on. "Tell me something about your Annaliese. Tell me how you best like to remember her."

His chance meeting with her two years ago August crowds into his mind, as if heeding Tawana's summons. The last of daylight was relinquishing the sky with a fiery western farewell, but the town still radiated heat off every surface. It poured in when he stopped at a sign or light but changed to a chill tongue licking his sweaty neck and arm when he drove so he kept his pickup window down and the a/c off. The red neon sign with its two-letter message in white shone over the roadside stand like an oasis in the sticky Kentucky night.

"I guess when I found her working at the Dairy Queen. I knew her before then. We were in the same class. Went to the same church, though she had quit coming for a while by the time I, ah, stumbled across her there."

The line hugged the building in almost a complete circle. Taking a place at its end, he was surprised to see Annaliese on the other side of the glass darting about the other harried workers.

"I thought she was long gone. Growing up we were never in the same group but everyone knew she wasn't gonna stay. She was never meant for Maynardsville."

Though dressed like the other employees in red shirt and light tan slacks, she seemed an outlier as she always seemed to him, even before they became close. A visitor to their small town who tolerated its simple ways but was not seduced by them. Before he had always rated her a pretentious snob but that evening he found himself happy that she hadn't yet left.

"I didn't really go to the Dairy Queen before that, not something my family did, but I had started spending more time on my own."

Because the rift with his father had grown wider over time, an unspoken disagreement that isolated him. The rest of the family didn't dare side against Alfred Sr.

"That was one of her two jobs. She still hadn't saved up enough to move. You know, I hadn't been particularly nice to her growing up. Not that I was rude but if we ever had reason to talk, I made it clear I had no time for her. She could have been the same way to me, but she acted like she was glad to see me."

Tawana nods but otherwise is still and Caleb remembers how as he crept forward in the line, he hoped that Annaliese would take his order. When she did, she greeted him with a double take then made a show of looking past him as she said, Where's the rest of Bible study? But she told him afterward that he looked so forlorn, she decided to play nice and so said that being by himself showed off his best side.

"I saw her that night for the first time, for how strong she was. Annaliese was comfortable being different. She wasn't a churchie like I'd always been, and my family and her family both were, but she wasn't a stoner or someone who slept around. She just stood apart without making it a big deal. I was starting to be different too and I found out real fast how lonely that was in Maynardsville. Annaliese gave me hope."

"So I'm guessing you went back."

THE PROPHET OF CENTRAL PARK

"I did start eating more ice cream."

Tawana tisks, says, "You're one of those lucky people with a high metabolism," then panning to his feet and back, she adds, "You're pretty slender."

"I've dropped weight since I moved here but, yeah, I've always been skinny."

Annaliese wasn't working the second time he stopped. Caleb stayed in line, not yet willing to admit his real reason for being there. Nevertheless the Dairy Queen was a welcomed destination. Before his drives had been aimless efforts to escape the homestead after dinner. By then the ostracizing silence and pointed stares of his parents were a campaign to cow him back into the fold of the faithful. Before Annaliese, moving out never seemed an option. The Ellison children stayed under their father's roof until marriage.

"The next time I saw her there, she called me out in this actress sort of way of hers. She planted a hand on her hip and stood sideways with her head back and asked, 'Twice in one week. Have you gone sweet on me, Caleb.' People laughed, I think, but I didn't know what to do."

Because the truth was, he didn't yet understand what she meant to him. Her looks fooled him for a while. Her tomboy's body had developed in the most distracting way and her face had filled out making her features with the pointy nose as striking as they were pretty, especially her green eyes which could scatter Caleb's thoughts if he got caught too long in their stare. Annaliese loved doing that to him.

Tawana is kind enough not to agree when he says, "I've never been much good talking to girls. If it had stayed down to me, we'd have kept catching up through the order window. She finally suggested we meet after her shift. She took me to this coffee house I never knew existed in the basement floor of a building downtown. Turns out waiting tables there was her second job."

Annaliese called it, the cafe. The nightstand lamps with low-wattage bulbs cast the tables in tepid pools of light interspersed among shadows. The coffee station was in the far corner. The hiss from the espresso machine startled Caleb the first time he heard someone warming milk for a cappuccino. Annaliese rolled her eyes when he asked, What's that?

"I remember worrying about someone seeing me, like it was a drug den."

Tawana does chuckle. "Wow, you **were** sheltered. Sounds like nothing more than a neat little place."

"Hey, sometimes people smoked dope around back," then Caleb smiles too. "Okay, I was a bit . . . yeah. But 'Alfie's Place'--that was its name—it was a shock to me. The closest thing to an underground scene in Maynardsville."

Right off Annaliese warned him to not embarrass her with talk of the football team and when he overheard snippets from neighboring conversations, they were about shows in Cincinnati, jobs in Columbus and shops in Lexington and Louisville.

"Anyway that's where we would meet up. It became a regular thing. Annaliese knew everybody in the place. Pretty soon they all knew me."

Back then the others seemed like cutting-edge hipsters to him. A roomful of fedoras and berets with the odd cowboy hat thrown in for irony's sake. Tweed jackets coupled with plaid shorts. Various colored tights worn beneath short skirts or silk blouses over leather slacks. His jeans and work boots were an exception. Along with Annaliese, who didn't own any shabby chic attire.

"She really was the right person at the right time for me. Someone I could talk to. You probably got that my family is ultra religious."

Tawana says simply, "Yes." As in the Park yesterday, there is something monumental to her patient attention. Caleb's mind flashes to bronze figures of Buddha. A similar deep-anchored quiet shows in her face.

"Her family was the same and she had got clear somehow. She still lived with her parents, to save money, but she had quit the church by then. Matters of faith didn't eat her up like they did me, but she understood what I was going through. And I knew she wouldn't share anything I told her."

After he left Kentucky, Caleb realized that those regulars he considered fashionistas were really timid folk relying on vintage clothing to bolster dreams they would never make real. Annaliese didn't need a wardrobe to convince her she was leaving. A room in Cincy was waiting for her the following spring by which time she figured to have nearly ten thousand dollars saved.

"If not for her, I'd still be back there, unhappy but too afraid to change. I might even have fallen back in line with the family. Started mumbling things in church that I didn't believe like some kind of zombie. She opened the door out for me."

Tawana winces in sympathy. "Losing someone like her, who was a big bright sun in your world, must have been terrible, but you can't ignore that pain. You have to feel it or the pain just rots inside you. Feeling it's the only way to be free of it. You don't have to carry it alone, though. People will help if you share your burden with them. You don't have to do it with me but remember, you don't have to do it alone."

Looking about, Caleb sees that the door is closed. The woman has isolated him. As if snapping out of a trance, he realizes that for the past several minutes he has spilled memories which for months he kept on purpose to himself. Treasured memories not to be fawned over or misinterpreted or clucked at.

Starting from the chair, he reopens the door. 'It's probably not proper we be shut up alone."

A smile freezes Tawana's face for a second then she bursts out laughing. "Oh my God. No, no, no, honey, you are way too young for me."

Caleb can't decide whether to sit back down or leave and so remains at the door and without thinking says, "How old are you?"

Tawana screws up her face. "Don't you know any better than to ask a sista that?" but as he stammers out, "I'm, I'm so sorry," her big smile blooms again. "Just messing with you, Caleb. I don't care. I'm thirty-four."

"Really? That old? I thought you were my age."

She shakes her head but still with a smile. "Almost the right thing to say," then she stands too. "I can see you have to leave, but can I ask, are you working tomorrow?" When he nods and answers, "Yes," she points to his face. "Are they going to be alright with you looking like that?"

Cold cascades through Caleb as he grasps the answer. He opens and closes his mouth but says nothing. Tawana winces in sympathy. "I'll take that as a 'no'. I can help you with this at least. Will you let me?"

Afraid now, he bobs his head without asking what she will do. Tawana steps past him and goes down the hall away from the stairs. He follows to an apartment on the other side of the floor where she knocks. "Hope she's in."

P C Burhenne

"She" turns out to be a short older woman in a red and blue striped billowing dress. White streaks her black, frizzy hair and her thin-lipped smile shows nicotine stains on her teeth. The stink of cigarettes wafts from the apartment.

"You're with us today. How wonderful," she greets Tawana, her voice raspy from her habit, then she notices Caleb. "Oh, my, you've got a stray."

"Someone in need of your expertise, Wilma. Can you do it?"

Wilma cocks her head in mock affront. "Mon cherie, of course I can."

"Wilma is the very talented playwright I told you about. She is also a wiz with makeup." Tawana holds his eyes with her own so that Caleb knows not to repeat her earlier critique of the woman's work.

The playwright takes hold of his chin to turn the bruised side toward her. The nails threaten to draw blood so he does not resist. "Okay. Follow me."

She leads them past a sofa to a corner of the living space where a three foot by three foot mirror rises from the back of a vanity, the surface of which bristles with a broad sampling of cosmetic supplies. The playwright pushes Caleb into the chair there, even as she tells him, "Now pay attention so you can do this yourself if you need to." Tawana leans against the wall to watch. Wilma's breath smells like an ashtray, one of which he spots among the makeup on the vanity top, but she does not light up while she works and she needs a remarkably short time to make both cheeks match and his forehead appear unmarked. Afterwards she writes down what he needs to duplicate her efforts.

"Thank you so much, ma'am," Caleb says as he pockets the list. "You saved me a lot of grief."

"Dear boy, you can thank me by coming to my next production. I wrote what you need on the back of a flyer." She pinches his unharmed cheek. "Say hello when you come."

Tawana comes forward to hug the woman. "Wilma, you're a lifesaver on short notice," and when the playwright lingers over the word, "Well," Tawana assures her, "Of course I'll be at your show."

"Splendid." Stepping back, Wilma points to the door. "Now get out. I have work to do."

With that they are in the hall, then at the elevator. Tawana faces the door as she presses the call button but says, "It's a shame about you and

Davey. If there's a way to set things right, you might want to try. He's very generous when he wants to be."

The elevator opens before Caleb can answer. Tawana waves goodbye as the door shuts him in. Feeling manipulated, he sends the car to the ground floor, but once there he remains inside, twisting his hat in his hands as the words of Job play in his head: How many wrongs and sins have I committed?--Show me my offense and my sin. "Sometimes I wish I didn't know the Bible so well," he says but he knows he will better serve himself repairing the damage than walking away from it.

Back on three, "chink"s from chisel on stone greet Caleb. When he approaches the sculptor's work space, the man must recognize his silhouette through the drapes because the noise stops. "What did you forget?"

Caleb steps through the partition seam. Davey watches him, tools still in hand, but goggles up on his forehead. "I just wanted to apologize. You didn't have to have me over. I should have been more respectful."

The sculptor closes his eyes to sigh. "She sent you back."

"'Nudged' be a better word for it."

The man's regard is not quite a glower but several seconds of it has Caleb thinking he should leave. Then Davey points his chisel at him, the sculptor's lips puckered as if he has a particularly sour lemondrop on his tongue.

"I can read two things in you, Caleb, as clearly as newspaper headlines. One, you got something, talent, a gift. You speak through wood." The praise sets Caleb's mouth twitching but before he can smile, Davey says, "And two, like most white people, you don't wanna hear any directions from a black man. I'm not gonna waste my time fighting you to take my advice."

In a maneuver of surprising digital strength, Davey replaces the eyewear with both forefingers and thumbs while the pinkies grip his tools. Caleb's face prickles at his dismissal framed in that return to work. Realizing how his expression must look, inflamed red running into the pale color of the made-up splotches, he leaves. On the ride down, as he pulls on the hat, dons the sunglasses, humiliation gives way to anger. "Screw him. I disagree with the man and he calls me a racist. I mean . . . screw him."

* * *

P C Burhenne

Reuters

This past week the Arizona legislature narrowly passed the controversial Social Contract Voting Requirements Act along party lines. The law would allow poll workers to turn away any prospective voter who has not adhered to basic standards of hygiene. Participation by the homeless greatly increased in the last state election and advocates, whose efforts helped make this group's enfranchisement a reality, claim the statute is intended as another obstacle to their clients making their voices heard. The governor has vowed to veto the bill.

The openness of the empty street makes Caleb feel as if he has broken free of a maze. When he considers the last hour, he wonders if he escaped instead. First the wannabe mentor insults him when he doesn't swallow wholesale the man's suggestions. Then Tawana coaxes loose the secret of Annaliese—the beginning anyway. This by a woman who claims those, well, blasphemous songs come to her after intense prayer. The woman is talking about visions from God. The warning from the Gospel of John returns to Caleb: Beloved, do not believe every spirit, but test the spirits to see whether they are from God, for many false prophets have gone out into the world.

But how? How does he judge anyone else when he is no longer sure what he believes? In that way he is like Tawana. She admits she is struggling to understand what makes people's actions right or wrong.

In sudden understanding, Caleb blows out a disgusted "ah" then at his naivete. Of course she claimed the same doubts. Just a few days ago on the subway she sensed his crisis of faith, so she makes herself out to be the same questioning pilgrim. She's targeting him because he's vulnerable. Though her building is now out of sight, he glances back, and in his mind the strange honeycomb layout of the workfloor and the anonymous sleeping quarters above now resemble an urban compound.

"It's a cult!"

As Caleb walks away faster, the test becomes clear. Could someone like Tawana be the mouthpiece of the Lord? A woman who riles up people in Central Park with her guitar. Savior as internet sensation. Caleb cringes at his gullibility. He even realizes that in her own backhanded way, she also

THE PROPHET OF CENTRAL PARK

called him a racist if he didn't acknowledge the mantle that she has pulled about herself.

He stops at a pharmacy on the way back. When he opens the folded sheet from the playwright, the inside of the leaflet shows the dates for Wilma Kupinski's "Debbie's Dirty Panties: A Tale of Female Empowerment." He nearly bins the flier but, aside from needing the list on it, the promise which the woman extracted stops him. The items take some hunting; he has never searched for cosmetics before. His indignation at the so-called mystic and the not-to-be-contradicted master sculptor is still a tart lozenge in his tongue as he heads to the check-out. The customer waiting there to pay makes it instantly dissolve.

The black man has a holstered gun at his waist. Even in New York the occasional gun advocate carries in public but Caleb senses a menace to this man and freezes several feet away. The armed shopper is older—late thirties, maybe forty—and wears an emerald green windbreaker that covers just the butt of his weapon. The roll of flesh circling the back of his neck makes his shaved head seem pressed into his broad squat body. When he turns his bulk to glance around the store, Caleb almost walks away into the nearest aisle and when the man guesses something of this disturbance, Caleb looks down. After a few seconds he raises his eyes again but the man has waited him out, seemingly to challenge Caleb to his face, but instead he mashes his lips into a frown of disgust and shuffles forward for his turn at the counter. Caleb worries for the cashier, worries for the store and wonders if he should have his phone ready to dial 911, but the black-haired woman at the register scans and bags the man's purchases with haste, her gaze on her hands the whole time. The man leaves, his posture rigid in dismissal of the lot of them.

Caleb pays a moment later and is on the street with the makeup. He scans the way home, prepared to loiter if he sees the other customer ahead, but there is no sign of the man's smooth dark scalp. Nevertheless the brief encounter stays with Caleb. He knows he prejudged the man but he doesn't understand why the incident aggravates him like a pebble in his shoe. Something in his thoughts wants to answer the jabbing hurt, but he can't quite catch it for the next few blocks. Can't as he considers jumping on the subway then doesn't. Can't until finally Black Joe reaches out to seize him.

P C Burhenne

After the Supreme Court rulings, a number of his neighbors who never felt the need before began bearing arms out and about. Crime in Maynardsville was almost entirely misdemeanors. The new militiamen, or militiapersons—their number included women—did so to assert the right in the face of liberals doomsaying that the country would be less safe because of the struck-down regulations. Alfred Sr. started bringing his Smith and Wesson on inspection calls and onto the auctioneer's podium. His father offered to gift Caleb his own, more than once. He declined each time with a respectful "thank you" that left his father pursing his lips so that Caleb expected him to quote Luke, "and he who has no sword sell his cloak and buy one." All those 2nd Amendment supporters were God-fearing and white —except for one that was quickly dealt with.

Everyone knew him as Black Joe the mechanic. "African-American" was not a widely used term in Maynardsville. Caleb hadn't cared enough to learn Joe's surname until afterwards. Joe was good with farm equipment and would carry his tools into a field. He didn't say much but when he spoke, his opinions carried a tone implying long consideration. Some didn't care for that. When he began exercising his expanded Constitutional prerogatives, more were upset. People said as much congregating after services. Even in the cold. Then Joe stopped.

The chief of police went to their church. Caleb's mother said he was a good linebacker in high school. Caleb couldn't see the athlete in the belt-straining, middle-aged man. The chief was friends with his father as was every important person in the community. Caleb overheard the lawman bragging on why Joe's change of heart.

"Every time he came into town wearing that piece, I pulled him over. Asked to see his carry permit every time so he'd get the message. Wrote him warnings at first—failure to stop, yield—then I cited him for a broken taillight somehow slipped his attention." The man said this with a chuckle before breathing out in disbelief. "Stubborn black bastard just wouldn't take the hint. So last time I told him, department didn't have the resources if a group of concerned citizens showed up at his place in white robes and hoods." The chief slapped his father on the shoulder. "That done it."

Caleb knew his father was no activist but believed him a righteous follower of Christ so he waited for the outrage at this man for proudly owning such an injustice and outside the church no less. Expected his father at least to rebuke the chief with silence.   Even now the same aching disappointment in his gut as then, the pain he imagines a tumor inflicts. His father nodded, said, "Seems to have." That moment was a wedge between them.

His father felt it.

Just the three of them in the TownCar after service. Carolyne was with Terry by then. His older brother married too. Waiting until he caught Caleb's eye in the rearview mirror, his father told him, "There's an order to how people should live. It keeps us at peace, everybody happy. You see that, don't you?" His mother hadn't heard the earlier exchange. In the front seat, she looked aside to see what the matter was. Caleb stared back, suddenly tingling at what he was about to say.

"No."

His mother drew breath as if the word had cut her, then she swiveled about to demand, "Tell your father you're sorry." Her frown, a rare occurrence up to that point, deepened the lines about her mouth and forehead so that her face, which usually hid her true age, showed all her then fifty-one years. In the mirror his father's grey eyes had taken on a flinty cast.

"Do you want me to lie?" Caleb asked and not rhetorically. "Both of you, is that what you want?" His parents glanced to each other but neither spoke. Caleb shuddered at the effort to utter the next seven words, "I don't believe as you do, Father."

The Lincoln's engine grew loud then. So too the keen of its tires on the macadam. His mother lowered her window, as if she hoped to replace the air which had gone from the car. His father did not object. At home she hurried into the house. His father said to him over the rooftop, "Caleb," a command to stop but within that a note seeming to seek a truce.

Caleb turned, not knowing what to expect. Alfred Sr.'s stern bark and unblinking gaze had always been enough to chasten him. But Caleb had never defied him thus and his father had never appeared so distracted. Where before he would have been stone still in correcting his son, that day a slight palsy agitated his head, imbuing a frantic air to the gaunt features.

"Listen to me now. This is important," and when Caleb nodded, he said, "God's will is not always clear to us."

Caleb heard a crack then like thunder overhead, though the sky was the flawless blue crystal carapace of a freezing winter's day. He shook his head as if the report had jolted him from sleep. Which it did perhaps, rousing him from an adolescent daydream. Suddenly to his woke eyes, the family property staked in place by seven giant oaks and the pond to the side of the homestead and the blue grain silo in the neighboring farm, which all had been familiar before the service, seemed suspect because the lodestar he had abided his whole life had showed itself to be a will o'wisp.

"How can you say that? You've been reading us His will before every meal. 'Do unto others'," then Caleb's voice pitched upward. "Unless he's a black man."

He waited then, still hoping his father would repair the shattered space between them but Alfred Sr. fidgeted a moment, touching fingertips to his mouth, before regaining his usual adamant pose. "'Honor thy father and mother', that is His will."

Caleb could not hide his sense of betrayal and shockingly his father turned away first, unable to withstand what stared back at him.

Two days after the chief's boast, Caleb crossed paths with Joe in town, though he did not place the mechanic at first. This man had none of Joe's presence. Rather he hurried with head down, hands in pockets and shoulders hunched as if wary of what was in front of him but anxious to leave what was behind. Caleb was two steps beyond when he connected the harried figure to the person he had been.

"Mr. . . . Mr. Joe?"

The mechanic stopped but hesitated turning. A hard frown made his lips thin and, when he lifted them, his eyes squinted with a distrust that held embarrassment and resentment both, an expression that Caleb had never seen from the man before but seemed familiar. Joe waited. Caleb could think of only one thing to say.

"I'm sorry."

Seeing that Caleb knew of his humiliation, Joe grimaced, forced to relive it. Shame froze Caleb, not just for the pain his pity caused but for the manner in which his fellow churchgoers had so reduced the mechanic. Looking about he experienced the same displacement that he had with his father at home. The red-brick three story buildings on both sides of the street, along with the similar surrounding blocks, were the cradle for his childhood, the playing field of his teenage years, but the patina from his memories fell away, leaving him in the midst of a mean, unjust place. Caleb remembered where he had encountered the sour glance that Joe gave him. Only a handful of blacks lived in the area. From time to time one of these had turned the same indicting face upon him. He had thought it strange and rude without ever wondering where their anger came from.

Caleb has since identified those two moments as the catalyst that made him the person who he claims to be, but as he approaches the apartment, he knows that a white customer in line earlier with a gun would not have frightened him nearly as much.

* * *

The Atlantic Magazine editorial

The Political Correctness movement has been a terrible failure. I know that this statement will unleash a tidal wave of angry, and in some cases, threatening letters, but a dispassionate discussion of our country's public forum is necessary if we have any chance of reclaiming a semblance of civil discourse. First off I want to make clear: I applaud the aim of PC culture. Racist namecalling and other forms of trope labels add nothing to an argument beyond the attempt to belittle one group while appealing to another holding similar prejudices, but the indiscriminate shout of "bigot" at someone whose view I find ignorant does nothing to dissuade my opponent of those opinions. It simply pushes both sides to seek out like-minded allies and ultimately shuts down dialogue. And in the case of those people condemned as intolerant, the practice renders them susceptible to demagogues happy to announce that they are justified in their convictions. Hasn't our recent history shown this to be true? Today a stark question confronts us. Do we believe that people's opinions can change? If the answer is no, the future is bleak. If yes, the way forward will include the maddening process of engagement along with the equally uncomfortable exercise of scrutinizing our own tenets.

Burdened with the shame of discovering he is still his father's son, Caleb is happy the apartment is empty. At once his Pop Pop's voice encourages him: Let your hands rein in your craziness, and Caleb sits at his work station, remembering the visit when he received the advice.

It was back when his mother still took him and the others to see her parents. Caleb must have been seven or eight. The grandparents lived below a slope bristling with oak and ash trees though back then it was a mountain soaring up before him, the summit obscured by a dense, dangerous forest, and to his eyes their house was a fantastic construction of peaked blocks stepping up the incline. Inside was a warren of rooms, each separated from the next by two or three steps. A perfect place for hide-and-seek or make-believe in a castle or a strange metropolis. No TV. Pop Pop said that life was too short for such a stupid distraction. At that time the decision persuaded Alfred Sr. that Pop Pop's was a suitable environment for his children.

That day Pop Pop was at the back of the yard, whittling with a penknife, a larger carving knife beside him on the bench. He flicked the latter like a spear into the ground to make room for his grandson. Caleb had seen the canes and other figures that his grandfather made but this was the first time he had questions; How did Pop Pop know what to carve? How'd he know what branch to pick? How'd he keep from cutting himself? At the last his grandfather pointed out the scars on both his hands which must have frightened Caleb because the man held up a finger for Caleb to wait while he decided what balm to administer to the fear. The three lines in his forehead deepened and his grey eyes peered at the horizon. Caleb's mother said that when she was young, Pop Pop had been easily irritated so that her own mother was always reasoning with him to try and relax, but Caleb couldn't remember his grandfather snapping at anyone.

"We do the things that mean the most to us despite the cuts they cause," Pop Pop said at last.

"Why does carving mean so much to you?"

"Because it keeps my head on straight."

"How does it do that?"

"Well, have you ever had something on your mind that you can't stop thinking about?"

"Yes, sir," Caleb said but he didn't admit that he often worried about Jesus watching to catch him at bad acts.

THE PROPHET OF CENTRAL PARK

"Well, so do I. My old noggin can just turn me in circles if I let it. But I've discovered, if I keep my hands busy with this penknife, I'm carving and nothing else. In some parts of the world, they call such a thing mindfulness. Would you like to try?"

Pop Pop had offered to teach Alfred Jr. but he had no interest which was why the older brother was inside with Carolyne sampling their grandmother's baking.

"I would, sir."

"Then let's get you something to start on."

His grandfather went with him up into the trees so Caleb was not afraid. They found a stick big enough to be shaped but small enough that he could hold it. Pop Pop showed him how to place his hands then suggested that the crooked branch looked like a copperhead. When it was time to go, his grandfather promised to keep his work-in-progress safe. Trips to Pop Pop became Caleb's favorite thing, a treat withheld when he sinned too gravely, a reward for extra chores done or progress at school, especially Sunday Bible study.

Then Alfred Sr. removed his blessing. He had preached "family" for too long to demand they stop going. Instead he greeted announcements of a visit with the opinion that Derek (Alfred Sr. never used Pop Pop) was not a man of God in a stern and disappointed voice until his wife stopped offering to drive there and his children, Caleb included, stopped asking. As best as Caleb could gather afterwards, Pop Pop committed the sin of not believing that their house of worship provided the only path to Heaven.

The edge of the chisel is dull. Caleb draws its beveled face over the whetstone until it threatens to bite the light tap of his thumb. The shallow notches he has made in the wood resemble scales and in a flash he sees ahead an articulated snake. Perhaps a copperhead. The model would be his most complicated ever, requiring many parts and even more demanding cuts. Requiring many days. Caleb tells himself, if they all remind him of Pop Pop, the time will be well spent.

He remembers the sense of loss when the visits stopped. Only ten, he felt it for a week as a bug with vomiting and a fever that brought dreams of his grandparents calling from within a cave's black interior. His mother nursed him without her usual upbeat encouragement that he would soon be better. Caleb needed years to understand that she was suffering too.

Eventually after he recovered, Pop Pop became Caleb's first act of rebellion from his father's sacred authority.

His fingers still knew the telephone number when Caleb summoned the nerve to defy his father's wishes. Though the homestead was empty, he hunched into the hallway phone to not speak too loudly. His grandmother squealed when she heard his voice then immediately asked what was wrong. Nothing, he told her, He just wanted to talk to her and Pop Pop. For a moment she sounded short of breath then she called her husband. They three spent fifteen minutes catching up on any mildly interesting event since they last spoke without once broaching the reason for the blackout. After that Caleb called once a week. Before he had only carved at Pop Pop's, but buying a penknife with his allowance, he began whittling at home, a pointing stick with a finger at its end. Pop Pop and he kept each other updated on their projects. When she could be alone with him, Carolyne joined in the call. Neither told their older brother. It was a twins' secret.

Alfred Sr. stopped to stare for what seemed a full minute the first time he came upon his son at the new hobby. Caleb felt as if his father had caught him looking at a brochure for ladies' underwear but managed to say, "What do you think, Dad?" as he held up the turtle he was working on. When his father asked, "Why are you doing that?" he answered, "I like carving. It keeps my thoughts from straying where they shouldn't." Caleb was ready to admit where he had learned. He wouldn't lie. However, his father wandered away without another word. The first time Caleb slipped badly with the blade, he pressed down the urge to cry so as not to give his parents a reason to take away the knife and stopped the bleeding with his handkerchief.

His father found out, probably from the phone records. One afternoon at the auction hall, he took the broom Caleb was pushing, saying rather than asking, "You've been talking to your grandfather."

Caleb's heart became a bird trying to escape the cage of his chest. "Yes, sir."

"You know how I feel."

Moment by moment, Caleb forced himself to return his father's gaze, guessing that if he looked down, he would lose what he had struggled to hold on to. "Yes, sir."

"Then why do you call him?"

THE PROPHET OF CENTRAL PARK

"He's family, sir. He's my elder."

"You have other aunts and uncles, cousins. Why Grandpa Derek?"

Caleb can see now that beside his twin, Pop Pop was the one person he felt close to. Even at that age Caleb felt apart from the non-believers at school but not quite in step with the members of the congregation. Shutting up the taunts of the other kids left him that much more isolated. His ten-year-old self tried to express this loneliness when he answered, "Because it's easy for me to talk to him."

His father's first response failed before reaching his open mouth. Caleb waited, still watching, prickling with the fear that his father would decree, No more contact. Going against his parent's wishes was one thing. Back then he would not disobey a direct command.

"I only want what's best for you, Caleb. Both for your body and soul. If I find you straying in any way from God's word, you will not be allowed to speak with your Grandfather Derek again. Do you understand?"

Caleb cannot remember feeling more loved by his father, a bond that held for years afterward, beyond Pop Pop's death from cancer, tethering him to a home that seemed both his right and responsibility. It was a bittersweet juxtaposition to their episode over Black Joe.

The first segment shows Caleb that the snake project will involve more waste than usual. Donning the hat and sunglasses, he goes out for a wood scavenging run that sees him return as the sun is setting. After depositing the construction site discards next to the desk, he starts dinner—franks, beans and rice—the most complete meal left in his cupboard. He puts on water to boil then makes a grocery list for after work tomorrow. The food is nearly ready when footsteps grow louder in the stairwell. The plodding pace doesn't sound like Sidney's usual haste but a moment later the roommate enters with a plastic grocery bag. Finding Caleb there Sidney removes a paper plate covered in aluminum foil. "Mom made this up for you. Roast. With broccoli stalks and scalloped potatoes."

Sidney studies the delivery he has placed on the table.

"Your mother's a saint." With a spatula, Caleb transfers the sauteed dogs from the pan to the rest of his meal. "Wish I'd known before I made this but it won't go to waste."

P C Burhenne

Sidney nods as if a breeze is moving his head. He is still looking down. Seated now, Caleb doesn't want to ask but knows he will find out soon enough. "What's wrong?"

"I made a mistake." The roommate lifts his eyes finally. His fleshy face, usually alive with mirth, is settled into a morose frown. "I told my parents what's going on. My dad tried to call me this morning. When I went over, he wanted to know why I had my phone off."

"Okay?"

"They want me to move back home." Caleb puts down his spoon, hunger scattered by the idea of him alone in this apartment with no more stories of crazy customers, no one to make him laugh. At his expression Sidney hastens to add, "I didn't say I would. I just . . . all these hateful messages, it's . . . I'm having a hard time."

Caleb realizes that his roommate is seeking his okay and though he wants to accuse Sidney of abandoning him, he can't. "You don't deserve this, Sid. Because I stuck my nose in. I should have just minded my own business."

"No!" his roommate snaps back. "Stepping in like you did, I'm proud of you for that, man. I wish I . . . ." then Sidney shuts his eyes and clamps his mouth so the lips disappear.

Caleb sighs, shaking slightly at what he guesses is next. "Do what's right for you, Sid."

The roommate takes the plate to the refrigerator and goes to his room, mumbling, "I've got work to do for tomorrow." Caleb forces himself to eat then stows the remainder beside what now seems like Mrs. Weiss's guilty conscience gift.

"A Room of Her Own" lies finished on the floor beside the bed, needing to be returned to the library. He starts "The Satanic Verses" but his mind wanders to the flight from Kentucky that brought him to this Queens apartment.

After confirming the interview with Mr. Guyot, he knew he would not be coming back. New York, though, was a frightening prospect of criminals and other more subtle corrupters of the soul. With no contacts to help him find a place, he did a computer search for "emergency lodging in NYC". The phone volunteer at "North Star Safe House" nearly hung up when he admitted he was not gay or transgender and certainly not a reproductive

THE PROPHET OF CENTRAL PARK

rights refugee, but he begged her to listen and when he explained, she relented. An hour later Sidney called. In Caleb's mind the voice conjured a big-bellied man, balding with suspenders over a pinstriped shirt like a clerk or ticket taker. Caleb laid out his plan to Sidney, such as it was, and swore to the potential flatmate that if the auction house position fell through, he would wash dishes or get a job parking cars. "Good luck with that, buddy. Some of those valets make good money," Sidney told him, then, "I'll prorate this month's rent. How soon you getting here." Later when Caleb was somewhat settled into the apartment, he asked Sidney why was he so kind to a stranger. The new friend revealed that a grandfather had been a freedom rider during the 60's and had now come to believe that the South had never conceded its battle against Civil Rights but was in fact expanding it. Helping Caleb was Sidney's attempt to live up to the family tradition.

Accepting that the book is a waste of time, Caleb sets it on top of Virginia Woolf. Sidney has been a constant of Caleb's NYC life. A future without the roommate frightens him.

"God, why are you taking everything away? Again. Am I so wrong that you have to punish me like this?"

The ceiling is an abstract of dark charcoal with a diagonal of yellow streaked over it from the street lamp. The traffic from Ditmars Boulevard is a distant undulating chorus. Neither answers the question.

P C Burhenne

Monday

Politico

Staff members announced that the junior Senator from Missouri will introduce a measure today denouncing the "unprovoked attack upon peaceful protesters" that occurred Friday in New York City. Videos of the incident posted to social media have inflamed passions on both sides of abortion and LGBTQ debates.

In the morning after his shower Caleb is able to replicate the playwright Wilma's efforts. He gives silent thanks as he reviews the result in the mirror. Sidney is waiting for the bathroom when Caleb comes out holding the cosmetics. "That's right," his roommate (for the time being) says, chuckling. "I knew something was different with your face last night. Good thinking."

"Better late than never."

The hours at his desk result in one more serpent segment but also a better process. He decides this model will be shorter as a learning exercise for a next larger, longer sculpture. The face paint goes in a paper bag in case he needs a touch up at work. The number of messages on his phone convince Caleb to keep the shades and the hat, even though the day is overcast. A fine mist is falling when he emerges on Fifth Avenue. Caleb wishes he had brought an umbrella.

The vagrant sees him from the square, waves a sad hello from his or her cardboard mat. The guard at the employee entrance stops Caleb. "They want you in HR."

"Do you know why?"

The guard shrugs. "Just told me to send you straight there."

A warm sting of nerves makes him want to go to the bathroom but he does as he is told. When Alicia motions him into her boss's office without a word, Caleb know he has lost the floor position. Mr. Guyot stays seated when he enters. "Close the door." Doing so Caleb realizes he still has on the shades and hat. As he removes both, the manager smacks his lips. "I'm not surprised you need those."

THE PROPHET OF CENTRAL PARK

At that Caleb knows he is losing more than the promotion.

"This house cannot be associated with what happened Friday. Many of our clients are not fans of the RRR."

The manager's frown is solemn and regret slows the blink of his eyes. Caleb can do nothing but relax. "Mr. Guyot, I just want to thank you for taking such a big chance on me. I'm, I'm sorry I let you down."

A spurt of anger sets the man's head to trembling. "Oh, Caleb, why couldn't you just keep out of it?"

"I been asking myself the . . . ." but before he can finish, Annaliese orders him in outrage: Stop that—You as much as anyone know why. He collects himself to tell the manager, "They had no right, those men. What they do ruins people's lives and they don't care about that at all."

The force of this stuns Mr. Guyot for a moment then with a sigh he says, "Effective immediately I am terminating your employment, Mr. Ellison. I've been able to persuade the company to give you one month's severance." He points to a document on Caleb's side of his desk. "You'll have to sign that non-disclosure form to receive it and you can't talk about why you were let go."

Caleb stares at the typed sheet waiting for his signature, his acquiescence, then pushes it away. "Thank you for going to all that trouble on my account but I don't take handouts."

For the first time, Mr. Guyot appears agitated, pushing the NDF back toward him. "Young man, don't be stup--, I mean, don't let pride make you do something you'll regret. You're going to need that money."

"I don't take charity." The manager stares, expecting Caleb to snap to his senses. In answer Caleb goes on, "Please tell Ms. Yuan I'm sorry if I put her in a tough spot."

There is a knock at the door and a security guard enters. My. Guyot takes one last look at the blank form then raises a hard stare as if he wants to staple the sheet to Caleb's chest. "Actually she asked to see you before you go," then to the guard, "Take him up after he clears out his locker."

A thought jumps to mind. "You should let Rolando take my place on the floor. He taught me more than anybody here and he's loyal to this company, sir."

Mr. Guyot has returned to his paperwork. "Some people are not qualified to be out front."

"Give him a long-sleeved shirt and he's more qualified than anyone."

Caleb leaves with the chaperone without waiting for the manager's reaction. In the basement Rolando sucks in his breath to keep from crying as Caleb is led out. Caleb makes himself grin with a shrug to hearten his friend but his eyes well up too.

The Asian Arts director is in a far gallery. The floor staff stop what they are doing as he walks under guard to her. He struggles to be calm in the face of their stares but suspects this only gives him the air of a condemned man. More than anything now, he wants clear of the place.

"I'm sorry to leave you in a lurch, ma'am," Caleb greets Ms. Yuan.

"I'm sorry too," A brief smile flickers across her face. "But I'm glad you did what you did." She glances back to the two female assistants behind her. "A great many people are."

"You wanted to see me."

"Yes," and she reclaims her professional attitude. "I reached out to the executor of your uncle's estate, Mr. Haruto Yamaguchi—What's this now?"

The director is peering past him and the guard. Caleb turns to find Mr. Guyot approaching with two men dressed in dark suits and slacks. The older walks splayfooted under his round belly in a hurry-up gait to keep abreast of his taller, younger and more fit partner. Both men appear Hispanic. Latinx? Mr. Guyot no longer seems like a disgruntled supervisor. As soon as Caleb faces them, the manager looks down and he turns back several feet before the others reach Caleb, not wanting anything to do with the pair's business beyond delivering them.

"Caleb Ellison?" the older man says in a surprising baritone.

"Yes?"

"I'm Detective Torres. This is Detective Jonas. New York City police. We'd like you to come with us. We need to ask you some questions about what happened Friday."

Caleb stares from one to the other, unable to make sense of this summons by law enforcement. "But why? I got hit in the face. I almost passed out."

The taller detective's attention appears to flicker. His partner Torres says, "Are you going to come with us voluntarily?"

Ms. Yuan steps forward to say, "Gentlemen, are you arresting Caleb?"

THE PROPHET OF CENTRAL PARK

The woman's voice of authority flusters the detective to the point that he takes a step back before he can stop himself. Caleb would smirk at the apparent dance move if he wasn't panicking.

"We've been instructed to arrest him if he doesn't comply."

"What charge?"

The detective breathes through his nose in annoyance. "Inciting."

"What precinct are you taking him to?"

"Mid-Town Precinct North."

Ms. Yuan puts her hand to Caleb's shoulder. Though her fingers seem like the delicate ribs of a folding fan, their grip is firm. Up close her eyes show creases arching upward from their corners, quotation marks enclosing her concerned stare. "It will be alright, Caleb. Go with them." With that she hurries away. Impatient now, Det. Torres takes hold of Caleb's arm. Again people watch him leave but now their attention comes with whispered talk of "police" and "arrest". Caleb realizes his mouth is open, the unreality of the last ten minutes leaving him numb. The detectives take him toward the front entrance, but when they come in view of the door, Det. Jonas exclaims, "What the fuck!"

"Keep it together, Jonesy," the older man growls at him.

Outside the glass partitions, several teams of reporters and cameramen call to each other, energized at the trio's appearance. The police crowd closer to Caleb, each one putting an arm around his back and with their other, they push open a gauntlet through the media. Microphones are thrust at Caleb, but their questions shouted simultaneously are the babble of disturbed geese. Caleb is happy when they shut him into the rear seat of their sedan then he slumps back at how ridiculous that thought is.

In the front Det. Jonas turns to his partner who is starting the car. "How the hell did they know we were picking him up, huh, Jav?"

One of the reporters runs with her equipment man. For a second Caleb thinks they are seeking a vantage point to film him being taken away then Caleb spots their news van parked up 49th Street.

"We have a job to do, Jonesy. Let's just get him back to the house."

When Caleb glances behind, the rest of the media are sprinting toward their own vehicles to follow him too.

"Tell me that wasn't bullshit," the younger detective says back. "Tell me somebody didn't leak that we'd be here."

P C Burhenne

Detective Torres has a bald spot atop his head. Hunched forward, he seems to address the steering wheel. "Way above our pay grade."

Caleb is tired of suddenly being invisible. "All I did was get hit in the face."

The older detective glances at him. "Then you got nothing to worry about."

As they merge into traffic, Detective Jonas radios in their return. When the dispatcher responds that officers are ready to help them into the building, the younger man spits out, "Son of a bitch!"

"Why more police!" Caleb almost shouts in disbelief. "I'm coming peacefully."

Detective Jonas stares at his partner as he says, "They're not for you."

Caleb guesses then what is waiting for him. "This is crazy." He rocks on the seat at the insane drama he finds himself in. "I'm just a guy who got punched. That's all I am."

The three fall silent and Caleb stares out the window at the other New Yorkers traipsing through their work days as he was doing less than half an hour ago. Then Detective Jonas swivels about. "That **was** a helluva shot you took, Ellison. You must have an iron chin."

"Cheek," and Caleb taps the spot, wincing at the contact and says, "He hit me in the cheek."

When they turn onto the precinct's side street, CNN and Fox News vans are stationed in front of the building sprouting broadcast antennae high above their roofs. Among the cluster of reporters at the foot of the steps, Caleb recognizes two from the national news. Four policemen push back the crowd to form a lane to the door. Caleb knows that his family, everyone in Maynardsville, will see this. The passage springs to mind as he steps out himself: My God, my God, why have you abandoned me?--Why so far from my call for help, from my cries of anguish. Reporters from the parade tailing the detectives rush up to join the others as the police usher him inside. Caleb realizes everyone is calling his name so he will turn to the cameras for a better shot. He keeps his eyes forward and his face as blank as possible and yet again is glad when the doors of law and order close behind him. Like the staff in the gallery, the officers in the lobby stare. A desk fronts this entranceway and the man stationed behind it calls out, "Hold up, you two. Torres, a word please."

THE PROPHET OF CENTRAL PARK

The desk officer is tall with a handsome, lined, square-jawed face. Caleb spots the sergeant's chevrons on his uniform as he leans forward to speak into the detective's ear. Detective Torres starts at what he hears and both glance back at Caleb so he wishes he could run away. Seeing this too, the younger detective starts muttering, "Ah, bullshit, bullshit, bullshit." Torres holds one finger up to the sergeant then comes back. This time he takes hold not just of Caleb but of his partner as well to move them closer to the wall.

"We can't question him yet. An ADA is going to conduct the interview," and before Jonas can express the outrage widening his eyes, the older detective whispers to Caleb, "Listen to me, kid. When we get in that room, you ask for your lawyer and don't you say a word until he shows up. I mean, not a fucking word."

The partner seems as surprised by this order as Caleb but again before he can respond, Detective Torres motions to an officer waiting by the sergeant's desk. The younger detective finally finds his voice. "Aren't we taking him up?"

"No, he's gotta wait in the holding cells. Again, ADA says so."

Clenching his teeth, Detective Jonas pokes at Caleb's chest saying, "Do what my partner told you," then he swings away to hurry upstairs. Detective Torres follows and the officer takes him to the desk sergeant who bags his belongings.

"Sorry, kid. Been a busy morning," the man's voice is full of scratches as if his throat is dry. Genuine regret shows in his frown. "Gonna have to share a cell."

The officer takes him through a side door into a small room occupied by two pens. The one further away is empty so Caleb doesn't understand when his handler locks him in the first. The other prisoner is a wide man wearing a dirty brown sweatshirt over a t-shirt and baggy denim jeans. He sports a crew-cut and his skin is a shade of cinnamon. The bench is long enough for two but the way the man leans his elbows onto his open legs in possessing it makes Caleb move to the adjacent wall so that looking forward he can keep the man at the edge of his sight. For a few moments the man continues peering down at the large boats that are his trainers, then he lifts his head the barest amount necessary to look at his new cellmate. The hairs on the back of Caleb's neck stand up as he recognizes a predator's eyes taking stock of him. The man's smile does nothing to change the opinion. More than anything, Caleb wants to look away but he knows only prey would act that way so he wills himself to return the gaze without a blink.

"Why don't you sit by me, boy?"

"Thank ya, I'm fine."

"Now that's no way to start a friendship."

Caleb can think of no good response so works to keep his face blank. The man cocks his head forward like a giant snapping turtle. His smile grows more nasty.

"Are you wearing makeup? You are! You're a professional, aren't you, Cupcake?"

Caleb can hear the beat of his heart in his skull sounding an alarm that he has to fight.

"You're gonna have a hard time downtown, Cupcake," the man goes on. "You're gonna need a friend."

In answer, Caleb raises his hands to be ready and turns himself more perpendicular to the threat.

"Why you little puff!" When the man starts up, Caleb sees that he has a hundred pounds on him and ears that stick out like sails but this in a flash. With uncanny nimbleness the man is in front of Caleb, a hand around his throat, the hateful smile now baring yellow teeth, and Caleb thinks of the ears. Grabs them with both hands, pulls down with all the strength he can muster, tries to rip them off. The man's head goes up and his mouth opens to a scream that catches in his throat before growing into a bellow. The grip loosens but does not let go and with the other hand the man tries to free that ear, but Caleb holds on too and pulls and pulls hoping, hoping the flesh will tear free. Suddenly the man lunges his head forward and clamps down with his teeth on Caleb's injured cheek. The throttling turns Caleb's own scream into a retching noise and the man's yell becomes a growl as he continues biting down and Caleb yanks all the harder, knowing he dare not let go.

The end of the baton hits Caleb's chin as a policeman pushes the club between them. Caleb glimpses the officer behind his attacker through tears. When the other lets go, Caleb falls forward gasping for air and receives a kick in the chest as the man is dragged away. Two sets of hands hold him up. He gulps for air, his throat not fully open and his lungs stunned by the last blow. The pair of policemen half lead, half carry him from the cell, from the room and to the front lobby.

The sergeant who now is out from behind the desk grimaces at the spectacle Caleb makes. He mutters, "What a fucking disaster," then orders his officers, "Get him upstairs and for God's sake, get him some ice." Finding his feet at the steps, Caleb shakes himself free of his helpers while telling them, "Thank you. I can walk now." The aftermath of the savaging feels like picks jabbing the side of his face. His chest aches with each step. When he glances down, the several officers below are silent spectators to his progress. Wondering how he became this battered prisoner in such short order, he begins to sob.

When Caleb enters the second floor, Detective Jonas starts from his desk then, his expression frozen in rude disbelief, settles back. Coming out of a kitchen, his partner gestures with the cup of coffee he carries to a door past them. "Oh Jesus, Lou, put him in two."

The interview room is everything Caleb expects from the few police procedurals he has seen. Four metal chairs surround a metal table that he finds bolted to the floor when he leans against it. There are no windows and a large framed mirror that he guesses is see through from the far side. The escort leaves him without a word. His reflection shows teeth marks as a broken red outline of a football on his once again engorged cheek, and tears are washing away the mascara there in tracks so that irregular purple stripes run through this. The speed of the swelling frightens him but when he gapes at the change, sudden agony from his jaw makes him gasp. Disgusted by the sound of his own snivelling, he takes several determined breaths and wipes at the wetness, carefully about the new injuries. The palm of his left hand comes away pasted with makeup.

The two detectives enter with grim frowns. The younger man hands Caleb a bag of ice and a small tube of what turns out to be antibiotic ointment. As the pair sit, Caleb applies a dollop of this salve without actually touching his fingertip to the wound. Detective Torres is watching him. "The ADA will be here soon," this through a sneer as if the title is curdled milk on his tongue. "Do you remember what I told you?"

Caleb trembles as the policeman's rage becomes his own. "I . . . want . . . a lawyer."

Detective Torres nods and both men turn away. The precinct outside murmurs, types, and occasionally trills with a phone call. Caleb closes his eyes against the growing pain that the ice only blunts. The melted water starts to trickle down his arm so he places the bag on the table and lowers his head slowly as if his cheek might shatter if pressed too firmly down.

The ADA enters a few minutes later. Caleb sits up to find a man in his forties with short cropped brown hair, of average height, wearing a blue suit that seems well fitted over his pudgy frame. The man's eyes widen at the damage to Caleb's face but the prosecutor purses his lips to suppress any further reaction so Caleb knows that the people downstairs told him what happened. The anger returns.

Detective Jonas gets up to make a place for the ADA and stands in the far corner.

"Mr. Ellison, my name is Assistant District Attorney Jacob Kunis. I imagine you have been read your rights."

Caleb puts the ice pack to his cheek again, all the time glaring at the man. Instead Detective Torres says, "He's not under arrest. He came voluntarily."

ADA Kunis puts his briefcase on the table. "Well, I think it prudent to go ahead and read him his rights."

Through a look of boredom the older detective says, "No need. He's invoked."

The seat beneath the ADA seems suddenly to heat up; squirming on it he nearly addresses Caleb. Instead he licks his lips to tell Torres. "Well, Mr. Ellison would be wise to reconsider that decision. If we can come to a plea agreement in this room, I can guarantee the gentleman a suspended sentence but if he forces me to take him to trial, he is looking at significant jail time."

By the end of this speech ADA Kunis is again staring at Caleb. The threat of going to prison, after what he just endured, nearly crumbles Caleb's resolve but Detective Torres ducks his head almost imperceptibly as a prompt. The fact of a policeman urging him to not deal convinces Caleb. "I want a lawyer."

Puzzlement seeps into the prosecutor's frown. "Did you say 'a lawyer'?"

Behind Mr. Kunis a blue uniformed arm pushes open the door for a tall slender man of fifty carrying his own briefcase. He has a thin nose, dirty

THE PROPHET OF CENTRAL PARK

brown hair that has withstood balding and a naturally pouting lower lip. He begins to say, "I believe my client just asked--" before he freezes at his first look at Caleb. Shock opens his mouth but a meaner sentiment closes it. "What in God's green earth happened to him?"

ADA Kunis is up from the table searching the wall behind the new arrival for an explanation. From his seat, Detective Torres says for him, "Mr. Ellison was attacked in the holding cell," this in the same weary tone as before.

"Why would you keep him there?"

The older detective holds up the back of his hand to study. Still in the corner, his partner answers, "Orders."

ADA Kunis grows angry as he realizes he has no allies in this room, but Caleb feels like he is missing a script as he tries to understand how rescue has come in the form of this unfamiliar attorney. The Psalm verse echoes in his head, "The Lord also will be a refuge for the oppressed, a refuge in times of trouble. And those who know Your name will put their trust in You, for You, Lord, have not forsaken those who seek you." Caleb knows, however, that he has moved far from God these past several months and he pants at the thought that God has stayed close to him.

"Mr. Ellison has to answer for his actions, Mr. Strauss," the ADA finally says. Caleb is encouraged that the, or rather, his attorney is prominent enough for the prosecutor to know his name.

"Why are you even talking to him, Jacob? I called the precinct to say I was representing Mr. Ellison."

"I didn't get the message. It's a busy day for the house from what I hear. Mistakes happen."

Detective Torres rolls his eyes. The ADA doesn't see but Caleb's attorney does and he mashes his lips. Caleb too sees the prosecutor's deceit and he grips the table to keep himself in his seat. "You bastard, that's why you tried to rush me into a deal. And the cell. There was an empty cell. You told them to put me in with that monster."

The outburst makes pain flare in his batted jaw and his cheek. The prosecutor's face could be sunburnt, it has gone that red, but Caleb ignores the man to again rest his injury upon the ice bag.

"I have no control over what prisoner might be in a cell."

Mr. Strauss's voice becomes a sharp-edged weapon. "Is Mr. Ellison being charged? If so, I need to go alert the media to get an 'after picture' at arraignment."

Caleb holds still to not miss the answer.

"Goddammit, Cliff," the ADA exclaims, "Let's not make this circus any bigger than it has to be."

Mr. Strauss replies, "You called the circus, I'm just taking advantage of it. If I have to." Before the ADA can respond, Mr. Strauss goes on, "Have you even apprehended the man who viciously assaulted my client?"

"Your client assaulted his friend."

"My client prevented the attacker's partner from striking another bystander and was struck first. The world has seen the video, Jacob, as will a jury. So, how close are you to arresting Mr. Ellison's assailant? I suspect he lives south of here. Have you identified him? Filed an order to the proper jurisdiction for extradition?"

"We are investigating the matter. That's why we need to interview your client."

Mr. Strauss smacks his lips before saying, "Given the many improprieties that have transpired this morning, my client will not be answering any questions. Will you, Mr. Ellison?"

"No," Caleb answers without lifting his head.

"Is he under arrest?"

Caleb hears the fabric rustle of Detective Torres resettling in his seat, then the ADA's curt response, "No, your client will not be charged at this time." Caleb lets go his breath.

"I think we both can agree that Mr. Ellison should leave the building through the back."

There is no audible response beyond footsteps departing. Mr. Strauss's voice takes on a sad softness. "Jacob, I hope what comes of this is worth doing a favor for your friends at Justice."

A sound like a raspberry is the ADA's answer. Caleb struggles with the pendulum of his emotions as relief gives way to a powerless indignation, followed by a deep well of sorrow at the hatred lurking in man's soul.

"Caleb," and again Mr. Strauss says, "Caleb."

THE PROPHET OF CENTRAL PARK

Caleb whispers, "Thank you, God. Now please help me go forward," and sits up. The mirror shows that the wet bag has dissolved most of the remaining makeup so that his cheek now resembles a hunk of chum.

The attorney holds up his cell phone. "I need to make a call before we leave. Detectives, do you mind? A moment only."

Both officers nod. As the attorney steps outside, the older detective leans close. "Keep the cold on it, kid. And you better see a doctor."

A weariness takes hold as he waits. The attorney's voice recalls him from a place that is not quite sleep but far from the room about them.

* * *

Washington Post

Pragmatic-minded legislators from both parties in the House and Senate have been meeting informally for the past two weeks to discuss reforms to keep Social Security and Medicare solvent. It is unclear if caucus leaders have sanctioned the meetings and the most conservative and liberal members of the Republican and Democratic parties are not participating. Discussions across the aisle among the centrist policymakers found common ground in the idea that rigid ideology is preventing any solution to preserve the safety net programs. Unidentified spokespersons say that while progress has been slow, all parties agree that any effective law will include a higher income cutoff for taxation and a higher age threshold to access benefits.

"Thank you, detectives. Do you want to show us out?"

The ice bag is a sopping mess so Caleb leaves it. At the front desk the sergeant hands over Caleb's things without a word. Mr. Strauss has him don the hat and glasses before they go out to the street behind the precinct. A town car waits there, thankfully without cameras or microphones. When the driver opens the door for Caleb, he stares at Caleb's chest, pretending not to see the savaged flesh. The attorney's cell rings before Caleb can ask any questions so he waits, arms trembling, amazed at the sudden change to his surroundings: metal chairs to leather seats, cement block walls to tinted windows. Mr. Strauss interrupts his conversation to ask, "Do you have a doctor?"

"No. Not here. No."

"I have someone who will see you now. You need that treated right away and I want the damage documented."

"I can't afford . . . I'll go to the drugstore, get some hydrogen peroxide. Bandage it myself."

The attorney takes a kind but firm tone. "You're not risking an infection in your face. The doctor's visit is taken care of, along with my fee. I'll explain in a minute."

The infection threat sends a shudder through Caleb so that he nods okay. The attorney gives his driver an address on upper Park Avenue, which makes Caleb grateful indeed that he will not be responsible for the bill, though now he is confused by the anonymous benefactor. Mr. Strauss puts away the phone. "First off, son, how are you?"

Caleb almost cries again as he answers, "I'm not feeling a hundred percent but I'm sure glad you showed up." Then he holds up his hands. "How, though? How did you come there?"

"Mr. Haruto Yamaguchi hired me to represent you. He instructed me to remind you of a Ms. Yuan's promise that things would turn out all right."

At the supervisor's mention Caleb almost smiles but his cheek refuses. A thought occurs to him. "Why would he do that though, this Mr. Yamaguchi? He knew my uncle but I never did, know my uncle, that is."

The hint of drama raises the attorney's eyebrows but he says only, "Mr. Yamaguchi should explain that. He asked if you would see him after the doctor. We'll drop you off there, of course."

Caleb leans his head back to relax but the ache from the bite feels like a trapped rodent gnawing through the skin. "Are they really going to arrest me, Mr. Strauss?"

After a pause, "I don't know. Anyone else in the same circumstances— video proof he was attacked, his only provocation preventing the attack of someone else—I would say categorically no, but the viral nature of your recording has propelled the episode into the political realm."

Caleb remembers the attorney's solemn warning to the ADA. "You think the government is involved?"

"There are attorneys general from the South and Midwest agitating that you violated the free speech rights of those thugs. Ridiculous really, but we are living through more and more ridiculous times."

"But the Justice Department?"

THE PROPHET OF CENTRAL PARK

Mr. Strauss sighs. "I'm hearing whispers that Washington will do anything to keep the firestorm from heating up any more than it already has. Seems their solution was to frighten you into pleading to some minor charge to placate the abortion states."

Caleb stutters slightly to say, "S, So I could really go to jail?"

"There are no guarantees at trial. Taking a plea would be much simpler. I would see to it that you received no jail time but you would have a conviction on your record and you would be admitting that what you did was a crime. The prosecution might even demand that you elocute to that in open court. However, if they do indict you, it would be one of the worst abuses of prosecutorial authority that I have ever witnessed and I don't believe any jury in this city would convict, especially with me as your advocate because I am very good and I would be righteously pissed off." At that moment Caleb imagines the attorney to be a reincarnated Templar Knight inflamed by the new Crusade.

Annaliese suddenly pipes up in Caleb's head: So did you commit a crime? "I believe in what I did and I would do it again."

The attorney's smile seems to hold recognition so that Caleb feels he too has been knighted.

By the time they reach the physician's office, Caleb is rocking in pain. The driver lets them off at the door of a first floor suite in a brick highrise in the 80's. Mr. Strauss's call ahead results in the receptionist waving them through the waiting room. Doctor Sapori is a man of dark brown complexion with a big button of a nose and a large stomach pushing forward his white frock. He gives Caleb a shot to numb the area then cleans and dresses the wound without comment so that Caleb knows that the attorney advised the professional of what happened. Mr. Strauss takes photographs throughout. Gradually the mauled area fades behind a numb shell. The doctor gives Caleb six Percocet tables before they leave.

Mr. Yamaguchi's brownstone is ten minutes away. The attorney stays in the town car.

"You're not coming in," Caleb asks, suddenly anxious to lose the man.

"I do get paid by the hour. Go up. He knows you're coming." Indeed an Asian man opens the door at the top of the stoop. "Be sure to thank him."

Caleb's savior is six feet tall like Caleb himself, but the broad chest and thick thighs of an aging tradesman fill out Mr. Yamaguchi's dress shirt and jeans. Creases scoring his forehead and drooping skin beneath his dark eyes make Caleb guess the man's age at late sixties or early seventies. His mouth quivers when in a lilting voice with precise enunciation he says, "Oh, my poor boy, what have you endured?"

Caleb can only think to answer, "I figured Mr. Strauss told you."

"He did, but his call did not prepare me for this carnage."

"I cannot thank you enough for sending him, Mr. Yamaguchi," Caleb says, holding out his hand, and he considers a moment how to describe the impact of the attorney's arrival. "He was a bright light in a dark, dark place."

Mr. Yamaguchi's grip is firm but careful. "That is the most rewarding 'thank you' I have ever received. Please come in."

Though new to Caleb, the brownstone's interior is similar to others that he has entered for work, delivering or picking up. Through doorways he recognizes articles of Chinese furniture and porcelains, as he would expect, but also continental works of art. The reality hits that he will no longer have daily contact with such beautiful objects and Caleb catches his breath at yet another loss. Mr. Yamaguchi leads him to the kitchen in the rear of the house. A bowl of soup waits on the table there.

"It's minestrone. I thought you might be hungry. Don't feel you have to eat if you're not."

At the food's aroma, Caleb's stomach growls for him to take up the spoon. "No, I appreciate it,"

The soup is delicious and though the one side of his mouth now feels stiff, Caleb ladles in three or four swallows before he thinks to ask, "Sir--"

"Haruto."

"Yeah, Haruto. Why are you helping me?"

The man has his chair away from the table so he can cross his legs and clasp his hands upon the upper knee. "Because I know that's what Will would have wanted."

Caleb's face rejects his attempt at a confused frown. "But he never met me. My family, my father erased him. I just found out I had another uncle." Caleb is surprised that it's only been four days since Ms. Yuan revealed the long hidden relative. He goes on, "He wouldn't even know me."

"Your uncle knew who you were. And your brother and sister. Will tried to keep up on all of his family in Kentucky."

THE PROPHET OF CENTRAL PARK

"But how?"

"In your case Will kept in contact with your grandfather Derek while he was alive."

"Pop Pop never said a word," and with a sense of betrayal, Caleb goes on, "How could he keep that from me?"

Mr. Yamaguchi holds out a hand to stop that thought. Caleb notices how he tucks the thumb into the palm. "Your grandfather couldn't risk doing that. Will told me. If your . . . Pop Pop?" and when Caleb nods that that is right, the man continues, "If your Pop Pop did mention Will and your father found out, he would have ended all contact. Isn't that so?"

Caleb gives out a grudging, "Yes." He hears the pouting there but he feels that on all sides throughout his childhood people deceived him.

"It's a shame Will didn't live to meet you," Mr. Yamaguchi allows with a sigh. "As long as I knew him, he, well, he didn't actually regret leaving. The life he fled suffocated Will, and he wasn't given a choice anyway. But he mourned the family denied him. Having you near would have been priceless. Especially since he missed your father most of all."

"Wait. My dad and your Will were close?"

"Saying goodbye to his Alfie—your father was just seven at the time—Will said it was the worst thing he'd ever done. Your father cried and wrapped himself about Will's leg and when Will, well, peeled your father off, Alfie punched and kicked the floor. Any mention of Kentucky dredged up that last image of his brother, confused and inconsolable. My dear Will would go stone-faced."

Bitterness vibrates in Haruto's voice but his term of affection for Caleb's uncle brings home that being partners, as Caleb guesses they were, meant being lovers. He is surprised that he now struggles to look Haruto in the eye as he did so naturally before. "What happened that he had to leave?"

"He was caught with another man. *En flagrante*, as they say."

Haruto taps a curled finger against his pursed lips. Caleb understands that the man is deciding how much of his beloved's painful past to reveal. To forestall details, Caleb says, "I get it. The poor man."

"Do you?" his host answers with an edge that makes Caleb wonder what line he stepped over, then Haruto asks a softer version, "Are you, are you gay?"

"No," Caleb snaps so that Haruto frowns and Caleb fears he has insulted the man again. "I'm sorry. It's just people, other kids have been asking me that for years. Not in a kind way. Because I don't act or gesture like other guys do. But I'm sorry how I jumped back at you."

A smile lifts the corners of Haruto's mouth then disappears as he wets his lips. "You know, even in this city, when I was growing up, there were only so many places in which I was safe to be a homosexual. Your uncle's hometown provided only the most sordid opportunities. I'm sure you can imagine what they were. Will would have left on his own eventually but the deepest cut was how his father used your father to justify driving him out."

Caleb senses a door opening that has always been barred and he doesn't speak in case the wrong word slams it shut again.

"Will's father swore he would see Will dead before allowing him to corrupt his younger brother. As if Will would have recruited your father. Will thought the world of his Alfie but he believed the threat." Haruto's words are growing more indignant. He reverses his crossed legs to reclaim his composure. "Then to rub salt in the wound, his father blamed Will when Alfred began using drugs."

"Wait, what?"

"Your father had a serious . . . oh," and the older man holds his fanned fingers across his mouth. "Perhaps that part isn't mine to tell."

"My whole life everybody has been hiding the family, my family history. Protecting me from it." The anger recalls a faint but ominous pang from his cheek. He tamps down his upset. "That hasn't stopped it from affecting me. Please, Haruto."

The old man tucks his chin to his chest, his hand again obscuring his mouth but he decides before Caleb has to press him. "Your father had troubles in his twenties. Your uncle tried to help. I know Will paid for two stints in rehab. That's all I'm comfortable sharing about that. But I will tell you, what finally got your father straight was religion. Will was ecstatic for Alfred, but your father's new beliefs left no room for a homosexual brother." Once more Haruto clasps his upper knee with both hands to indicate that he has told all he would. "Did the doctor say if you could put ice on that?"

"He did say it was all right," Caleb allows as he raises his hand to the wound, then he exclaims, "Oh my God!" at the extent of the new swelling.

THE PROPHET OF CENTRAL PARK

Haruto locates a plastic bag. The refrigerator with an ice dispenser in the door is a Sub-Zero. Haruto wraps the cold compress in a hand cloth. It is an odd flower against Caleb's bandaged skin, a tingling circle about a void. Haruto takes his seat again. "May I ask you a personal question?" Given the man's generosity, Caleb feels compelled to nod. "How did you come to be here? In New York? Suddenly a symbol of the fight against the repression of women? Against intolerance?"

"You like to get the easy ones out of the way up front, don't you?"

Haruto chuckles. "That was a broad ask, wasn't it? Let me try this. You seem to have changed a great deal from the young churchgoer Will would tell me about. I haven't kept up his periodical, huh, reviews I guess you'd call them. What prompted your transformation? If you did indeed change. You see, everything I know about you is secondhand. Well, third hand really."

"Eight years ago, right, when Uncle William died?"

Haruto's answer is a flutter of the head yes. Caleb has no words to acknowledge the pain there so he acknowledges instead, "I **am** a different person. That boy believed. Deeply. Everything he was told. That we alone, our church community, and churches like ours, were living God's will for man."

"And now?"

Caleb stares at the table between them, holding the ice to his wound like a telephone to his ear. "I have holes. I know what I don't believe, not what I do."

"What changed?"

Haruto asks this in his own soft voice, as if he fears, as Caleb did before, that the wrong sentiment will end the conversation. In Caleb's head, Annaliese dares, Go ahead—Tell the man what happened. Without thinking Caleb answers her aloud, "It started long before you."

"What started?"

Concern mingles with confusion in the old man's frown. Embarrassed, Caleb considers pretending that he didn't say this last but he doesn't want to lie. He taps his temple on the uninjured side. "Sorry. Talking back to the voices in my head," and to move the talk on, he says, "I guess what happened is, I started to ask questions."

"That's a bad thing?"

P C Burhenne

Caleb remembers the ninth grade when the guidance counselor called him to the office. Worried as always that he had sinned, he was surprised when the man questioned why he wasn't taking an advanced science class for the next year. Mr. Phelps told him, You're more than capable of getting into a good college if you start taking the right classes now. UK, University of Louisville. Even Vanderbilt is not out of the question.

"In my house it was. Especially if I didn't just accept the answers. You know, I wanted to go to college but that wasn't done in my family."

"Why ever would your parents object to that?"

On the bus ride home after the meeting with Mr. Phelps, Caleb stared at the horizon, and where that morning he had seen a boundary, there now was the promise of "beyond". A prospect that both frightened and exhilarated but filled him in a way that he hadn't felt before. At the homestead, he hurried to share the counselor's encouragement. Dark disapproval suddenly turned his father into Moses ready to hurl the Ten Commandments to the ground, almost freezing the news in Caleb's mouth, but the newborn thing within insisted he finish.

"Because education teaches a person to question that which we must accept on faith. My father's words why he wouldn't allow me to go to college."

"'Wouldn't allow'!" and Haruto quivers in anger. "You're an adult. You can continue your education if you choose to."

His father made clear that not only would he not help in any way, but defiance on the matter would mean Caleb was no longer part of the family, a terrifying threat. "I was fourteen." Caleb realizes how dry his mouth is. "Could I bother you for a drink of water?

As Haruto starts up, Caleb remembers how after his father's ultimatum, the distant hills refused to hem him in like before. The school library, that before had been a quiet spot to finish an assignment, became a site of rebellion as he began seeking out forbidden knowledge. For the next three years as his classmates discussed their plans after graduation, his resentment grew and though he did not have the courage to be on his own, more and more he stared after the far away clouds, wondering at the lives unfolding beneath them. The old man places a Perrier bottle before Caleb with a glass already containing half its contents.

"Tap would have been fine."

THE PROPHET OF CENTRAL PARK

"Drink." His host sits again as Caleb makes himself not swallow in gulps. Haruto says, "So being denied college was a turning point."

"Yeah. For me and my family." Caleb presses the cold against his cheek again. "My parents started fixing me up with girls from the church. I really think they hoped I'd get one pregnant so I'd have to marry. I went along with it for a while, but not really. I was afraid to leave but I didn't feel a part of the community anymore either."

Haruto lifts his head to let out an "ah" then "Whispers that you were gay started because you didn't show interest."

"More than whispers."

"You said you went along for a while. When did you stop?"

"When Covid came."

In his library sanctuary, Caleb followed the virus's progress like the weeks' long approach of a hostile army. The stream of warnings from medical experts, each more dire than the last, started him washing his hands at every opportunity but Alfred, Sr.'s response to the reports filled him with dread.

"Like most members of our church—in the beginning anyway—my father believed the virus was nothing more than a bad case of the flu. The doctors were worrying people for no good reason and mandates, well, it was every citizen's duty to resist those government intrusions into our lives. When I started wearing a mask, I became the tax collector Levi in my own family."

"Who?" Haruto asks at the reference.

"I was a traitor," Caleb explains, and he recalls his father's angry intake of air the first time Caleb pulled a mask on to leave the homestead. He quickly told how he only wanted to help keep everybody safe. His father answered that Jesus would protect Caleb if only Caleb let Him. "My sister knew it was the right thing, but she just couldn't. She's my twin. As people started getting sick, I was so scared for her. For all of my family. And I was scared of them. It was a horrible time. Almost as bad as now."

"Haruto leans forward. "Did you lose anyone?"

"Close to me? Thank God, no."

When the shutdown came, their church refused to suspend in-person services. Alfred Sr. was the most vocal church elder demanding they heed God's commandment, not man's Godless law. He ordered Caleb to sit apart

P C Burhenne

if he persisted in broadcasting his lack of faith, thinking the punishment would force his son to submit but Caleb was glad to be alone at the back of the hall. Caleb tells Haruto, "But twenty-two people died in our congregation. I'm not sure how many more spent weeks in the hospital." As longtime members disappeared from the pews, others joined Caleb in the further reaches, many wearing the light blue mouth guards. For Alfred Sr's part, he would not look behind, refusing to bear witness to the frailties on display even among the Lord's chosen, and he insisted that the prayers of true believers such as himself delivered those who passed through the ordeal, not soap and fabric swatches.

"I remember those stories." Shame turns the old man's head aside. "At the time I took satisfaction in reading them. The superstitious getting their comeuppance. I never considered what it must have been like in those communities, like yours."

Caleb sets aside the ice for another swallow of water and more soup, and he remembers how his father became in full the Alfred Sr. that Caleb fled. After the crisis some survivors left a church that demanded they attend dangerous services. Alfred Sr. condemned them as the deceived and celebrated the remaining congregation as God's true warriors. The community withdrew even more from the town around it.

"What was it like?" Caleb says returning the compress to his face. "The pandemic was a fire, Haruto. It burned away all but the most . . . hardcore followers."

"Well, that sounds ominous. Is that what made you leave?"

Caleb does lie then that "Yes, it was," even as Annaliese challenges him: You coward—Tell how it took my life to get you to finally break free. He closes his eyes and cannot seem to open them.

Haruto's voice pitches higher. "Are you all right?"

With an effort he looks at his host again. "I just need a moment to gather myself."

"That's not it," and Haruto comes around the table. "You've hit the wall, young man." With a hand gently lifting at Caleb's arm, he suggests Caleb rise too and leads him to a guest room at the end of the hall. "You need to rest. Trust me, please. You're exhausted."

Caleb does not wish to be vulnerable in the gay man's house. However, the weight of his day so far bears down upon him. He remembers stretching out on the bed only.

* * *

Vice.com

Rumors are circulating that Attorneys General from several blue states are planning a meeting next month to discuss a united response to US Supreme Court decisions that they take issue with, both on matters of law and the safety and well being of their constituents. What their possible answers might be are unclear. Republican governors of deep red states blast the endeavor as hypocritical in the face of their decades long endurance of court decisions with which they categorically disagreed. However, this development along with the continued call for a national divorce from more radical members of the GOP are raising the specter of a coming constitutional fracture.

The pulsing ache wakes Caleb. He sits up draped in a thin striped coverlet and with a sensation that the sun is beating down on his already burnt cheek. The pain pills are in his pockets. His shoes wait paired beside the bed. He replaces the loafers, mortified that his host removed them. His hat and shades are on the side table. When he goes into the hall, Haruto's voice carries from the front of the brownstone. His alone. On the phone. Caleb returns to the kitchen. The table is cleared. Caleb cups his hand beneath the faucet for water to wash down the Percocet.

"It's hurting again?" The old man stands in the doorway. He flinches when Caleb turns, says, "You'll need to change that dressing. The blood is seeping through."

When Caleb checks his reflection in the glass of a cabinet door, the bandage bears a red print of teeth marks. For a second his attacker has again latched onto his cheek, the hatred in the man's eyes inches from his own, the grip throttling his neck. Caleb takes a shaky breath to steady himself. The sun has moved during his nap. He guesses it is late afternoon. "I have to get going, Haruto."

"You don't have to if you don't feel ready. Maybe you should sit down," and the old man hurries on so that Caleb suspects he's betrayed unease at the invitation. "William would want me to do everything possible to help."

"You've done more than I could ever have prayed for."

A smile wavers through the worry on the old man's face and he shakes the hand Caleb offers then holds on a moment longer. "Before you go, I have some things to give you. Elliot, Mr. Strauss, he said I should get . . . ." then the host holds up a finger as he leaves for the front room again. He returns with a cell phone and a paperback book. "Mr. Strauss thought a pay-as-you-go would be the easiest way to communicate. He said you might be having trouble with, ah, nasty calls on your regular line."

Caleb stares at this perfect gift. "I should have thought of this. How'd he know."

"Elliot is the most insightful human being I have ever met. And one of the most empathetic." Haruto points to the device. "I've already programmed his direct line in. Hit 'memory', then '1'. He already has this number. He said he'd call with any developments." Haruto clears his throat. "Hit 2 to reach me. Please, Caleb, if you don't mind, stay in touch. Connecting with you is like having part of William back. I want to know that you're all right." Then before Caleb can mumble agreement, Haruto goes on, "Oh, yes. 3 is for Yuan Lin, your supervisor. She asked that you call her too. I told her what's happened today. She is beyond concerned."

"Yes sir, I will. I owe her my thanks at the very least. If not for her . . . ." Caleb shrugs then he nods to the book. "And that?"

Haruto passes it over and Caleb recognizes William on the glossy cover, sitting at the front room window of this very brownstone. "Your uncle wrote this. It's a long essay really, about his early years in New York. His start in the business. I thought you might want to learn more about him. In his own words."

Caleb stares at the man in the photograph looking over from his desk, a whiskey glass in hand, family and stranger both. If he is a true Ellison, he'll tell only the truth he wants known but even half of William's story is more than Caleb knows now. "I would. Thank you. And I'll keep it safe."

"Yes," and Haruto reaches a hand to brush fingertips over the image of his partner. "Please do." They go out to the stoop. When Caleb lingers a moment to put on his two articles of camouflage, the old man says, "By the way, I think your art is exceptional."

Caleb almost asks how the host knows about the totems, then the videos come to mind. "I keep forgetting, just about everybody in the world knows my business anymore."

"Yes, but this is one instance where celebrity can help you, Caleb," Haruto says sharply enough for Caleb to look back again. "If I were you, I wouldn't sell any more pieces until I explored dealer representation. You'll get a lot more for your work in a Lexington Avenue showroom than on a blanket in the Park."

The idea aggravates Caleb, as much for being right as for the effort needed to make it happen. "When I can catch my breath, I'll check it out."

"Yes. Of course," and Haruto opens his mouth to another thought but thinking better of it, waves instead.

The cool air makes Caleb wish he had a jacket. He heads down Fifth Avenue, feeling miles, not yards, distant from the parkgoers enjoying the afternoon beyond the stone wall on his right. No one seems to recognize him but most stare at the bloating with its bloodied cover that disguises him. The bandage is a red and white flag waving at the bottom edge of his vision. Caleb keeps eyes on the sidewalk and so does not see Tawana until she cries out, "Oh, sweet Lord, what's happened to you?"

They are at the southeast entrance to the Park. The damage wreaked upon Caleb transfixes the guitarist. Then she hurries up to him.

"Are you okay?"

Not sure, he shrugs.

"What happened?" then quickly she adds, "Never mind. Not here."

Without asking she takes his hand as if he is a lost child and leads them into the subway. The Queens bound side of the station is deserted so he knows they just missed a train. Tawana draws them to the far end of the platform before facing him again. "How badly does it hurt?"

The ache is still keeping time with his heartbeat. "I just took another painkiller. It'll kick in in a minute."

The woman puts a hand to her mouth, then says, "How did this . . . ?"

Caleb thinks that narrating the story will distance him from it but as he recounts the day, the reality of being jobless takes hold again, as does the trauma of the attack, and the threat of prosecution becomes all too real.

Commuters file in as he speaks. They look away as he starts weeping. Another train creeps to a stop beside them. He asks, "Why is this happening to me?" and Tawana pulls him to her, away from the exchange of passengers, and holds him in a swaying embrace. The remnants of perfume linger upon her neck. The suggestion of lilac almost masks the urine smell rising off the floor. "I'd wish I'd never gotten involved," he mumbles to her shoulder.

"You've paid a high price, but do you really wish that?" she whispers to his ear.

Tawana still grips her guitar case. Its weight slides off him as he steps back. "Why wouldn't I?"

She shows him a kind but subdued smile. "Because you know what those men wanted to do. Of all the people in that square, maybe you alone could have stopped them." The telltale frayed circle of a snuff tin on the one agitator's back pocket leaps to mind for Caleb as she goes on. "How would you feel today if you had not acted? Yes, these terrible, terrible things would have passed you by but would you be guilty knowing you were moved to do something and didn't?"

Caleb stares through rather than at the woman now. The words of Matthew rise to his lips. "'Enter by the narrow gate. For the gate is wide and the way is easy that leads to destruction and those who enter by it are many.'"

"'But the gate is narrow and the way is hard that leads to life, and those who find it are few'," she finishes for him. "We can't know God's will for us. We can only hope to stay open to it. But from what you told me, God has not abandoned you. A woman you barely know contacts the partner of an uncle you never met so that a lawyer can arrive when you need him most," and again she assures him, "God has not abandoned you."

Caleb tries to smile again but fears it looks like a grimace instead. The hug has aggravated his cheek so that tiny claws seem to be digging at it and a knot in his chest denies him full breaths. Seeing this, Tawana offers her open palm to him. Caleb shies away.

"I just want to help you, Caleb."

"How?"

Instead of an answer, she asks, "Do you believe me?"

THE PROPHET OF CENTRAL PARK

He looks from her patient gaze to the hand between them and straightens. With the barest contact Tawana cups the injury. Her touch is cool. She closes her eyes and her lips move about unspoken words. Caleb hears riders collecting again behind him and with a sidelong glance he sees that the crowd across the tracks is watching their drama. Then, as a downtown train blocks this audience, a pinprick of heat, or perhaps of intense cold, starts in his cheek. It grows between them like a stream and though he cannot say its direction, the current binds them so that he can only tremble at what is not pain exactly but an uncomfortable activity alive on the side of his face. This until Tawana withdraws her hand as if his skin scalded hers.

"What did you do?"

"Nothing," she says.

The guitarist flexes her fingers. Caleb brushes the backs of his own against the dressing. The wound is calm now. He realizes that tightness no longer constrains his breathing.

"You did something. I can feel it. Could feel it."

At the tent revivals from his youth, the laying on of hands was always the high point. As a teenager he needed all his self-control to not roll his eyes when the arthritics leapt from their wheel chairs. The preacher was always happy to accept the worshipers' praise. Now Caleb discovers a genuine healer who wants no credit whatsoever. A train pulls up beside them as she decides to answer his stare. "You've forgotten to ask for help when you need it, Caleb. All I did was ask for you."

They ride in silence. He is anxious at the profound event that he knows just happened but she is at ease in the jostling car, so much so that, when she remains still at her usual stop, he thinks she is caught in a daydream.

"Isn't this you?" he asks, tugging at her sleeve.

"Not today. I'm going to make sure you get home okay." As he readies himself to object, she shakes her head. "You may feel better but you don't look good at all. Like an albino," then with a smile. "Going incognito."

Caleb touches the sunglasses self-consciously but accepts her verdict. Again they do not speak, even as they disembark at Ditmars Boulevard and head down to the street. Caleb is surprised to see Sidney beside the bottom of the metal staircase. His roommate goes open-mouthed at his state.

"What . . . now!" Sidney exclaims as they reach him, and making a leap —because of Tawana's presence?—the roommate asks, "Did you get mugged in the Park?"

"No. In jail."

"What?"

Tawana balances the guitar case in front of her to put a hand to the shoulder of each of them. "You should probably talk about this back at your apartment."

"No! No, no, no." Instead of explaining right away, Sidney goes around beneath the steps, gesturing for them to follow. "News crews are all over our building." Wanting only to be safe inside, Caleb feels himself on the verge of crying again as Sidney goes on, "Not just the local channels, either. Fox News has a crew there. And Reuters. For you, I'm sure, but why?"

Caleb wonders what to do even as the guitarist asks, "You don't have anywhere else to go, do you?"

He looks down, says, "I'm thinking."

"Take that as a no." She steps away, pulling out her phone.

As she makes her call, Caleb tells his roommate, "I know I keep saying it, but I'm so sorry, Sidney. What are you gonna do, go to your parents?"

"No, I'm gonna wait them out. They'll get tired of standing around."

"They get paid to stand around," and Caleb ducks his head to catch his roommate's eyes. "Why wouldn't you go home?"

"I go home now, I'm afraid my mom won't let me leave." Sidney purses his lips as if the next words are bitter. "She and Dad are pressing me pretty hard to, you know . . ."

"Get as far away from me as possible," Caleb finishes for him, and despite his predicament, he smiles as best he can. "They're not wrong, Sid. Next to me is a dangerous place to be anymore."

"Shouldn't matter, though." His roommate's elastic features settle into a solemn regard. "I want the courage to do what you did. The least I can do is stand by you." Flustered by the praise, grateful for the support, Caleb is at a loss to respond. "And don't try to smile," his roommate says to fill the silence. "It makes you look like a gargoyle. More like a gargoyle. And what happened? Somebody bite your face?"

"Yes, somebody bit his face," Tawana answers for Caleb as she steps back. "I just spoke to Davey. He said you can hide out at the lofts."

THE PROPHET OF CENTRAL PARK

The sculptor's parting assessment makes Caleb fidget. "Really? He said it was all right?"

"Davey don't pull punches about what he thinks but he's got the biggest heart of anybody I know," Tawana tells him, betraying that she knows what passed between the two yesterday. A smirk suggests she is enjoying Caleb's upset even as she dispels it. "He wants to help."

Still unsure of his reception, Caleb asks, "Can Sid come too?"

Sidney's face lights up. "It would be a huge help. I'm just standing out here waiting for all those turds to go away."

When the guitarist studies him, Sidney hangs his head, assuming a child's quivering pout. "If you behave yourself, you can come. No strutting around like you're sex on a stick." She heads back up to the platform.

Sidney winks to Caleb. "You hear that. Tawana thinks I'm sexy."

Caleb cringes, hurries to step between them on the stairs. Without looking back, the guitarist answers, "Not what I said at all. And don't be staring at my butt, you two."

The order has the opposite effect; where before Caleb had been respectful, he now has trouble looking away from her wonderful shape flexing at the climb.

* * *

Politico

Demographers and climatologists both are warning that the tension between artificial state borders and natural barriers to human existence will only increase over the coming decades. As changing weather patterns continue to raise mean temperatures along with the levels of the planet's oceans, coastal regions and those in the tropics will become less able to support the dense populations that currently reside there. Migration away from the equator and the world's shorelines in general will only increase. Scientists are imploring politicians everywhere to start preparing now for this seismic shift in where people will safely be able to live.

Like yesterday the elevator opens to the waiting sculptor, though this time on the fourth floor. Forewarned by Tawana, he holds a bag of ice. The present everybody gives Caleb now, he thinks ruefully, but he accepts it with thanks. Davey shows no reaction to the injury beyond staring at it a moment. Instead he looks to Sidney.

"I see you brought the smart-aleck roommate."

Before Tawana can respond, Sidney says through a happy smile, "You remembered me."

A grin flickers at the corners of the sculptor's mouth. "So much for a quiet evening." With that he leads the way along the hall.

"Wilma still in rehearsal?" Tawana says as she follows.

"Yeah, but they'll be finishing soon."

"Why do you need Wilma," Caleb asks.

"We don't need her," Tawana says back. "We need her to be occupied. You're supposed to be hiding out."

"And that woman can't keep a secret in an empty room," Davey finishes for her.

Unlike Tawana's monastic cell, the sculptor's apartment is decent-sized, by New York standards. It has a main living space with a kitchenette on one side. Facing this are three doors. Davey opens the third to show Caleb where he will be sleeping, indicates the second as the bathroom, and tells Sidney that he gets the couch. The two large windows glimpse the furthest of the Queensboro Bridge bastions rising beyond the buildings across the street. Several pieces of sculpture—Caleb presumes Davey's work—anchor the room. The largest is a giant's arm rising from the floor to raise aloft a short handled sledgehammer. A painting of a woman, distorted as if she is leaning toward an irregular lens through which viewers see her, grabs Caleb's attention. The depiction is nothing he would seek out, yet it fascinates him so much that Davey's voice at his shoulder makes him start.

"That's by a friend, Natashya. Amazing talent. She's clawing her way to something great." Caleb can't pretend he knows how the artwork makes him feel. Davey must see this because the sculptor makes his mouth a pensive, oh, then says, "Something new's opened your eyes. Who'd have thunk it."

Caleb hears the slap in the remark but hears too a note of surprise and he needs the place to stay. He turns back to the painting.

"You have a first aid kit, don't you?" Tawana asks the sculptor.

The kit does not contain a big enough gauze bandage. Commenting that maybe it's a good thing he came after all, Davey sends Sidney to the nearest drugstore with the sculptor's cell number in case the roommate gets lost. When Davey's phone rings, he rolls his eyes in answering. Next thing he says, "Good idea," and asks the room, "Pizza, everyone?" When Tawana raises her hand, he preempts her with, "Yes, I'll tell him no meat." The guitarist cleans the wound with daubs of hydrogen peroxide on cotton balls. Caleb hears the faint buzz of the disinfectant but feels only the barest tap of talons against his cheeks.

Before Sidney returns, Tawana says to Caleb, "Can I see your new phone?"

As he hands it over, Davey turns with a questioning frown. When she starts working the punch pad, the sculptor says, "Wait, Tawana, are you sure?" Caleb looks on, uncertain what both are about but more uncertain of his standing to ask.

"I am," the guitarist tells her friend, then finished with the task, she hands back the device. As Davey walks to the windows, she says to Caleb, "I've programmed myself in under 'T'." She draws a line between them with her finger for him to look her in the eye. "I've dealt for years with the harassment you've experienced for a few days. I only give my number to people I trust. If you give it to anyone else—your roommate, anyone—I'll get a new phone, and I won't trust you again."

She stares at Caleb until he realizes that she is waiting for an answer. "I understand."

Sitting back, she grimaces in apology for saying, "I wish your roommate would return already with the bandage. Your face is really gruesome."

Still across the room, Davey asks, "How was the Park today?"

"Volatile. More people are coming to argue."

Caleb pockets the new phone, decides to sort through and trash the messages left on his old one.

"Troublemakers," Davey says.

Tawana swivels toward her friend. "You know I don't like that label. That's why I'm out there. To engage with people who disagree. Maybe learn from them."

"But?"

Like before, if Caleb doesn't know the number, he deletes without listening.

The woman sighs and says, "It's becoming so much bigger. Not just the . . . argumentative ones. The people wanting to hear too. Keeping them apart, trying to get them to talk to one another, it's getting harder and harder. I moved twice today to stay in front of the police. I don't know, Davey. It's like . . . ."

After a moment, Davey prompts her, "It's like what?"

A name rather than a number in the list grips Caleb like an invisible hand squeezing his chest.

"Every day is building towards, I don't know what. An event. A catastrophe. A great reveal."

Caleb finally lifts the cell to his ear just as there is a knock on the door and Sidney calls from the hall, "Hey, open up. This box is hot."

Davey lets him in, asking, "How'd you get up here?"

"One of your neighbors came in with me. I said your name and Allah Kazam," then at a higher pitch, Sidney says, "Holy shit, buddy, what's wrong?"

For Caleb, there is no wound anymore, no legal difficulties or money problems. All three people face him now, alarmed by his attempt to repeat his father's message and when he accepts that his mouth will not speak, he plays it on speaker for them.

"I have failed you, son. Our leaders have made me see that. I allowed you to settle in a city that denies the glorious kingdom of God which so much of this great country has embraced. You're coming home. Put in order whatever affairs you need to put in order. Say your goodbyes. I'll be there soon to collect you."

Sidney still balances the pizza with one hand, holds the bag from the drugstore with the other. "Wow! That's the voice of crazy!" As Davey nods, the roommate hurries to say, "But who gives a shit? He can't make you go with him."

Tawana's eyes widen. "You're really worried. Why?"

Caleb finds his voice again, says, "Sid, put that down. We may as well eat," then to Tawana who has not stopped watching him, "Okay, I'll tell you why that scares me."

The sculptor pulls out plates, Sidney deposits a slice onto each, and Caleb describes his exodus from Kentucky. How in the months before he left, he withdrew from the life of the Ellison homestead which prompted sermons from Alfred Sr. on filial piety and the deceit of Satan meant to lure the unguarded to ruin. How he emptied his bank account to have his savings ready in cash and finally arranged a job interview and a place with Sidney, even as Alfred Sr. tried to keep ever closer tabs on him. How Alfred Sr. pursued his bus for sixty miles like God's own bounty hunter to bring Caleb back. When Caleb finishes, fear pinches Sidney's unblinking gaze and Tawana reaches for Caleb's hand.

Davey breaks the quiet by telling Tawana, "This is a little more involved than you let on, girl."

She turns to the sculptor, kind but unfaltering. "Yes, it is. Does that make them less worthy of our help?"

Davey makes a sound falling between "M-hmm," and a groan.

Caleb manages to finish the slice on his plate but no more. Evening has fallen outside. Despite the earlier nap, he struggles to not lay his head on the table. Sidney wants to know how he got bitten but even the roommate realizes that is too much for Caleb. After applying a new dressing, Tawana goes to her room and Caleb does the same. Though he takes along his uncle's book, he is too tired even to look at its photos. Before lying down, however, he remembers that he owes Ms. Yuan a call.

"Is this Caleb?" the woman answers and when he says, yes, her anxiety comes over the line. "Are you alright?"

He knows she has spoken with Mr. Yamaguchi so she knows about his assault. "I am, Ms. Yuan. Though I am sort of in hiding."

"I wondered if the newspeople would be at your home. They were outside the gallery all afternoon."

"Mr. Guyot must have loved that," Caleb says with a laugh, then he hurries on. "Thank you so much for reaching out to Mr. Yamaguchi. You can't know what a big deal that turned out to be."

"Yes, well, a simple act. As to Mr. Guyot, I'd say you don't owe him anything."

Caleb glances down at the company logo on his shirt. "Oh, darn, I do owe him some uniforms. I wonder if the reporters will be back there again tomorrow."

"You could give them to me and I could hand them in." This a surprisingly hesitant suggestion. Before he can ask how, she goes on more decisively. "Bring them around twelve thirty. I'll treat you to lunch."

"It's Asia Week. Won't you be too busy?"

"I still eat lunch over Asia Week. So, see you tomorrow?"

"Yes. Thank you, ma'am."

"Stay a block or two away to be safe and call me when you arrive."

The supervisor clicks off, leaving Caleb to gape at Mr. Strauss's phone, wondering if the invite actually happened. Exhaustion doesn't let him wonder for long.

Tuesday

New York One
    The District Attorney's office of New York has reportedly identified the principal actors involved in a Friday disturbance at Rockefeller Center, videos of which have since gone viral. Social media had discovered the name of Caleb Ellison before authorities questioned the Queens resident yesterday but though online sources claim to have found the other two participants, authorities will not confirm the details of the pair, except to say they do not reside in New York state.

    In a dream he trips to the sidewalk hurrying along a city street and one after another the people coming behind step a foot to his face. This coalesces into the revived pain from the injury. He starts up in bed panicked in the nearly pitch black, convinced his father lurks there about to seize him, then he places himself and turns on the lamp. It is four AM. As he goes for the bathroom, Sidney rolls over on the couch and murmurs that a package has not arrived yet. Caleb uses the toilet, downs another pill, then looking at himself in the mirror, realizes he needs a change of clothes if he is going to hand in the auction house shirt. And there are more back at the apartment. Caleb decides that if he is risking a trip to Ditmars, now is the best time. He grabs the hat but leaves the sunglasses.

    To Caleb's ear, the hum of the elevator intrudes on the silent building like a radio suddenly turned up loud. The chill outside shocks and he determines to grab a jacket too if the media have ceased their watch on the apartment. Alfred Sr.'s message keeps playing in his head. Walking to the train he shies away from doorways, the alleys between buildings, half-expecting his father and brother to jump out to drag him back to Maynardsville. On the subway platform, he searches the street below for them but the few figures out at that hour belong to the neighborhood. Knowing this Caleb understands that he truly has become a New Yorker, and he grows angry. What does Alfred Sr. hope to achieve by forcing Caleb from his home? Does his father believe a few prayers will snap him back

P C Burhenne

into his adolescent self? He boards the train prepared to fight off any hands that grab for him.

In Astoria no news vans are obvious but he turns onto a side street before his address to search for any that may be hiding. Junk and the electric bill wait in the mail box. After he changes upstairs, the serpent in progress almost draws him to his work station, but he can't squander the cover of darkness. The shirt he slept in has a blood smear on the chest. He hand washes it, along with the other injury-marred garment from Friday, until the stains seem a faint wrinkle. Separating the wrung-out clothes in a plastic bag, he stuffs it and any other uniforms in a back pack. He grabs the money from the weekend sales and at the last minute selects a new outfit for his roommate. Dressed for the cold, he heads back down.

The woman hurries to him, microphone in hand and cameraman in tow, when he steps outside. Her husky, slightly rushed call of "Mr. Ellison," is straight out of the local broadcasts that he has come upon his roommate watching. Caleb sees that retreating will trap him inside. The extra time could allow more reporters to show up. He considers pretending that he is not Caleb Ellison until she confronts him with, "Is it true you were assaulted while in police custody yesterday?"

Caleb heads to the train, acting as if he has not heard. The reporter paces him on the left side so the camera records the bandage. The woman is smaller than she seems on TV; she has to reach the microphone up to him after she asks, "How did you come to have Elliot Strauss represent you?" Astoria is still asleep for the most part. Caleb sees only one other person ahead, a worker in jeans, jacket and work boots with a scuffed canvas pack. The laborer is Latinx and about Caleb's age. Glancing over his shoulder at the rapid-fire questions thrown at Caleb, he walks faster to not be overtaken. Caleb tells himself that she will not follow onto the elevated station if he maintains upright disinterest going through the turnstile. When his shadows do not follow, however, he sags forward. Still, on the platform, paranoia makes everyone who comes up after him a possible tail, and from this comes a melancholy that even at five in the morning, news hawks pursue him. Anonymity, which he didn't recognize as gift, is no longer available.

The pay-as-you-go phone rings while he is on the train. Knowing the cell's purpose, he answers in a dither but Tawana greets him, "Are you all right?"

"Oh, damn, I should have left a note. Yes, I'm fine. I thought early would be the best time to go back to my apartment."

Even his own ear hears the pouting. Tawana hears it too. "You sure you're fine?"

"I am, I am," then to change the subject he says, "Have you guys eaten yet. I can get something on the way back. Small thank-you to Davey."

Tawana asks then relays their breakfast orders. Through her the sculptor informs Caleb of a bodega near the subway stop. Before punching off, Caleb adds that he has gotten Sidney a change of clothes. His roommate's shouted, "That's my boy," and Davey's, "Don't be waking my neighbors like that," carry from the background.

Caleb is the lone passenger disembarking at the stop. The bodega is newly opened when he arrives. Neither the grill cook nor the cashier care enough to stare at his patched face. At the loft Sidney welcomes him with an excited whispered, "Thank God, you thought of this. These clothes are starting to stink."

As they eat, Caleb finally does tell about the ambush outside the apartment. Sidney says, "That was Jessica Salome. I like her segments," as if the meeting was a treat. Tawana closes her eyes in a quiet show of sympathy. The sculptor stares at his food, scowling like the sausage in his sandwich is off. Caleb says, "Sorry, am I bothering you with my problems?"

"Yeah, kid, you are. You're sitting at the wrong table to be playing the martyr."

Uninformed as it is, the slap of the label stings. He shouts back, "You have no idea what's happened to me."

Tawana speaks before the man can. "I've told them everything you told me."

Caleb hears a warning in the way she levels that at him, feels he is being lectured. "Yeah, well, I had to go through it. Am going through it. You're not, Mr. Randolph."

Contempt stares at him in the sculptor's eyes but Caleb will not look away. Tawana places her hand on the table without touching her friend's. She tells the sculptor, "Calmly," which Caleb hears as a backhanded rebuke to himself so that he considers gathering his book and bundle of company clothes and leaving right then, but Davey exhales and the temper leaves his face.

P C Burhenne

"Yes, you've been wronged," the sculptor says. "What upsets me . . . ." and the man takes another bracing breath. "Unfortunately what you're going through, though unique, isn't special. Not to me. Or Tawana. It's all too familiar." He asks Sidney then, "How many times have you been arrested, or even stopped by police?"

The roommate offers a hesitant, "Well, never."

"And you," the man says to Caleb. "Other than yesterday, how many interactions have you had with the law?"

Caleb glimpses that the questions is going to deprive him of any righteous indignation. "None."

"I've been stopped over ten times in my life. I quit counting after ten. This is me walking down the street. I've been cuffed and put in the back of a police car three times. Once because they didn't like my tone while they rousted me." Davey sees something in Sidney's reaction that he takes as incredulity because he challenges the roommate, "I know because they drove me around for awhile before they found a deserted alley." To Caleb he says, "They didn't bite my face but they did beat the crap out of me then laughed when they dumped me miles from my neighborhood. Nothing happened to them. The word of two white cops against mine. All of that when I've never done a damned thing. Never even littered. 'Cause I know better."

Davey glances from one to the other for a response. Sidney actually shakes his head in a skittish, no. A resolute strain imbues Tawana's composure, the peaceful resolve faced toward the storm. It unsettles Caleb more than Davey's dare to comment.

"Actually, I've been lucky," the man goes on. "I've never been arrested. I've never been incarcerated. I know lots who have been. Some deserved it. But I have one friend in prison right now who I know is innocent."

"Ah, Julius," Tawana says in a husky whisper, then more loudly, "I need to go see him next visitors' day."

"Yeah. Remind me. I'll go with you," Davey says to his friend, then picking up the argument's thread, he tells Caleb and his roommate, "And I 'don't think' he didn't do it. I know he's innocent. But there he sits up in Dannemora." The sculptor wets his lip to slow himself. "Young man, I'm not trying to diminish what's been done to you but you have no monopoly on suffering, injustice. Not in this room." With that Davey looks to the guitarist. When she gives him the barest shrug, he goes on, "Tawana's story is not mine to tell but, believe me, sitting next to her, you look petty and naive complaining about how the world's mistreated you."

Caleb squirms with the sensation that, though invited, he is intruding upon an intimate moment between the two. Sidney takes a nervous bite from his meal as if a similar notion has seized him. Davey gets up for more coffee. With a look about the room Tawana clasps her hands together. "That's more than enough soul searching for this early in the morning. Thank you all for the company," and getting up she says, "I need to prepare for my day."

After the guitarist leaves, Sidney asks to use the shower. Davey says, "Sure," tells Caleb, "you too," as he places last evening's first aid materials on the table. With that the sculptor announces, "I've gotta start work. The door locks behind you," and he too goes from the apartment.

"Damned, Caleb, you really get under his skin."

"What d'you mean?"

"I had a great time bullshitting with him last night. He's funny. Except around you."

"Go take your shower already."

His roommate does and Caleb clears the breakfast table before going back to the guest room. At first he is loath to sit on the bed and considers clearing out right then, but he realizes he has no other good options. The apartment is obviously still not safe. The idea of asking Mr. Yamaguchi for a room, well, Caleb must admit, he is uncomfortable with the prospect of staying with a gay man. A hotel will break him inside a month. Especially now that he has no job. That reality makes Caleb shudder. He settles against the headboard and picks up his uncle's book. A photo of a young William Ellison standing before a Laotian temple occupies Caleb when his roommate calls, "I'm outa here, Dude. Call me about what's going on for later," then with a laugh, "Try not to piss our host off anymore."

The other residents of the loft have started their mornings. A radio deejay mumbles next door about river crossing delays and an upstairs bathroom releases a flume through a waste pipe in the wall behind the bed. Caleb rifles the book for other travelogue snapshots. The ones showing ancient overgrown cultural sites trouble him. He almost puts the book away but the mystery of his newly found uncle pushes aside the qualms.

P C Burhenne

William introduces himself by writing:

I grew up in the family business of antique/chattel arbitrage, or as it is known more colloquially, 'picking', the pursuit of valuable pieces of furniture, artwork and other items for resale. My father taught me that phrase as soon as I was old enough to understand it then made me promise to never use the term outside the house just as he would never admit to knowing such a "ten-dollar word" in public himself. We lived in southern Kentucky where people viewed with suspicion anyone tainted with a cosmopolitan whiff. At the farm auctions and estate sales that were the setting for my youth, my father Tobias Ellison cultivated a persona of a country hayseed, complete with a straw stalk that he chewed as he inspected the merchandise offered. His bib and overalls act duped many a stranger who bid against or sold to his backwoods character but even his colleagues, who knew that he was more savvy than he let on, did not realize to what degree this was true. Though in my later professional life I have met experts with encyclopedic grasps of their field, I have never met anyone with as wide a breadth of knowledge of markets as my father possessed.

Unsurprisingly he achieved his expertise through lifelong study. Where other households tuned into the games of the state's beloved Paul Rupp Wildcats or other popular broadcasts, our television was typically cold during evenings and the radio provided classical music as an aid to thoughtful reading. Our library contained volumes as varied as "Furniture Makers of the Colonial Period" to "A Collector's Guide to Clay Marbles". Knowledge of value came from trade magazines. Articles in these not only revealed prices obtained for highlights in major sales but also discussed the changing buying habits of customers who walked into showrooms. My father's curiosity was never satisfied when it came to his business and he pressed his sons to develop a similar appetite for learning.

The second source of my father's success was regular attendance at antique shows in any of the number of cities within three or four hundred miles of our podunk town. Adherence to this calendar of events allowed him to cultivate a network of high-end dealers to whom he could sell on or "flip" his finds. Typically each contact specialized in a niche market, about which Tobias familiarized himself by perusing the merchant's stall. By the time I began accompanying him, years of handshake deals and telephone promises had cemented most of these relationships, though my father was always on the lookout for a new reliable "outlet". I soon realized that a great many of his purchases were sold before he ever bought them. We traveled to these shows in a panel truck full of merchandise earmarked for specific vendors. Transactions occurred in hotel parking lots the day before venue doors opened.

Keep in mind that Tobias assembled his web of regional associates before the advent of the internet. Though not unique in creating such a professional model, he was nonetheless remarkable for doing so from such a rural base of operations. I grew up in tune to the cycle of harvesting and curing tobacco leaves. Two of our neighbors sharecropped the plots of others. Tobias was certainly an example of a man rising above his circumstances.

My father's "aw shucks" act might lead readers to consider him something of a wolf in sheep's clothing. In truth, as I grew older I became uneasy with the hayseed charade. The marketplace certainly condones this sort of subterfuge, but as I approached adulthood I rejected his life of maintaining a public and very different private persona. The examples from my father's world which appealed to me most were the dealers we visited in Cincinnati, Chicago, St. Louis and Memphis. These men owned their acumen as they owned their stores: with pride and self-possession. Theirs was the life I decided to pursue and if that meant transplanting to the big city, then I resolved to go to the biggest city of all. The greatest city in the world. The Big Apple. New York City . . . ."

Knowing what he does from Haruto, Caleb chuckles at his uncle's dig at Tobias in that last paragraph, then he rereads the section for any missed mention of his father. There is none and in the book full of photos, only one from that time exists, an image of his uncle as a teenager holding a vellum vase identified in the caption as Rookwood, "one of my first big successes". With that William dispensed with his life in Kentucky.

* * *

The Guardian

P C Burhenne

The DOJ warns that larger and larger swaths of rural America are falling outside the control of law enforcement. An Agency memorandum obtained by this organization states that the number of communities with populations of 5000 or less which can no longer depend upon a response to a 911 call is growing at an accelerating rate. Residents living outside these villages can expect even less protection. The perception of police forces under attack has made recruitment more difficult over the last decade but a lack of funds has also hampered hiring efforts as new officers follow the trend of young adults opting for larger towns and cities that offer higher salaries, in addition to greater social amenities. Traditionally made up of a conservative populace that is skeptical of government agents, more and more these isolated homeowners decry "the Wild West" environment that their areas have become. Officials at the DOJ worry that these expanding regions of lawlessness are a perfect haven for illegal enterprises, not to mention domestic terrorist organizations.

At nine, his normal start time at work, Caleb thinks that Rolando might be concerned after his sudden firing.

"C, there you are!" his friend greets his call. A truck speeds by in the background. "Man, are you okay? I been trying to get you."

"I'm sorry. I'm getting so many crank calls, I've been ignoring my phone. Yeah, I'm okay."

"I'm hearing some crazy shit's been going down. The whole loading dock knows you got arrested."

"Actually I didn't," and he abridges the entire interview room episode to, "They just wanted to get my side of things."

His friend continues in a hushed voice. "People are saying you got raped while in custody."

Pincer-points of pressure are once again trying to collapse Caleb's windpipe, the stink of phlegm and pot breath fills his nose, and suddenly he has to work to draw air. "No, that didn't happen. Thank God, that didn't happen, but I did, well, I did get bit."

"Bit! How?"

"I got put in a holding cell, for not that long. Another guy in there . . . I don't know why it happened. I don't know why any of it happened."

"Jesus, Caleb, it's bent what's going on. Guyot came down to the basement yesterday, told us not to talk about you to anybody. When I went out for lunch, newspeople swarmed. 'Do you know Caleb Ellison? Has he always been an activist?' They were stopping people in the square, asking if they saw what happened Friday."

"They were at the police station. They're even at my apartment. I couldn't go home last night."

"Do you have a place, C?" Rolando snaps back. "You ain't on the street, are you?"

"No," and not wanting to lie and not sure Tawana wants her part known, he says, "An unlikely savior found me a place."

"Ow, sounds mysterious." Rolando laughs. "But I'm glad somebody stepped up. And listen, if that place falls through, I'll always hook you up."

"You know, that means the world to me, Rolando. And I might be calling you on that too."

"It's there for you any time," then before Caleb can say goodbye, Rolando asks, "How did you do Saturday? Did you sell any of your totems?"

The reminder of that happy experiment just three days past makes Caleb smile. He endures the cheek and jaw ache. "You're not gonna believe this. I sold eleven pieces."

"Of course I believe it. They're good. You got talent, C. Gotta go. Keep in touch, man."

The book keeps Caleb company for the next few hours but once the story moves to New York, William may as well have been an orphan. He does write extensively of the mentor whom he worked for early on, a "legendary pioneer" in the field of Asian Arts, the dealer Lisa Comey. Snapshots show a tall woman with school teacher good looks but even the static poses convey a gravitational presence. After serving a decade apprenticeship, Caleb's uncle describes striking out on his own. This included frequent buying trips to Southeast Asia. Caleb closes the autobiography to get ready for lunch.

Sleep and the morning trip have loosened his bandage. The bathroom mirror also shows a welt on his jaw, below the white covering. He touches the sore bruise wondering what caused it before he remembers the policeman's baton striking there when the officer dragged the attacker off.

Baring his cheek, Caleb showers, careful to keep the stream away from the chewed area, then he dabs it again with the hydrogen peroxide before redressing the wound. Rolando's voice repeats in his head, "I'm glad somebody stepped up."

The sculptor barely looks over from a mallet strike when he steps through the plastic curtain. Marble shrapnel skitters to Caleb's feet. "I seem able to get under your skin just by the way I say your name, Mr Randolph. Yet you took me in. Me and my . . . slightly obnoxious roommate. Thank you for doing that."

Before he can leave, the sculptor clears his throat. "I like Sidney. He's a good time."

"Most people do."

The sculptor does finally face Caleb. "You, on the other hand, are a challenge to—how does Tawana put it—my capacity to see the potential in others."

Caleb has no answer, shrugs.

"That accent?" Davey says. "You're from the South somewhere."

"Just because I'm from Kentucky doesn't mean I'm a racist."

The sculptor shrugs this time in a way that dismisses the statement. "It means you were bathed every day in a racist wash. I don't know how much you absorbed but you absorbed some."

Caleb quits trying to be nice. "Who's prejudiced now?"

Davey actually points the hammer at Caleb with a wide smile so that the his white teeth light up his dark face. "We all are, son. That's our inheritance from America. Of course the prejudice of blacks rarely causes harm to you white folk. But that's not what makes you a challenge."

Caleb is not sure he wants to know but asks, "What does?"

"Your attempt to rid yourself of those hand-me-downs."

"Cheese and crackers, man, I'd have thought you'd call that a good thing."

"Cheese and what!" Davey says back, amused at Caleb's brush with an expletive. In the next moment his grin snaps into a thoughtful frown. "It's not a good thing. It's a wonderful thing. It's also a dangerous one. You're trying to shed those commands from family and friends that shaped you. You're no longer a caterpillar. But there's no guarantee you'll turn into a butterfly. Those remarks of yours that get under my skin, they're your past looking for new handholds. Not everyone who seeks in the wilderness for a better self finds it. I've known a lot of hateful, angry older souls who danced in the mud of Woodstock. Tawana sees a deep pool of love within you. I worry what you might become if she's wrong."

Davey seems to glimpse an image suspended between them that sets his head to bobbing and he repeats, "Deep pool, deep pool, deep pool within us." Setting aside the hammer and chisel, he starts about the work table to grab a nub of charcoal and a sheet of paper. Drawing renders the man oblivious, but the uncertainty that he voiced syncs with Caleb's own doubt about what will fill the void left by the beliefs he has disavowed. Watching the sculptor's total immersion in this moment of creation, Caleb is jealous, wishing he was at his own station.

"What happened to your friend Julius?" and when Davey straightens, Caleb says, "How could he end up in prison like you said? Innocent." The sculptor continues to stare at his rudimentary sketch. Caleb can't see it well enough to distinguish the intent. He doesn't want to move closer. "I'm sorry. Not my place to ask."

"A liquor store got robbed in Julius's neighborhood," Davey starts without preamble. "A place Julius used to go into but stopped after he had an argument with the owner. Well, the thief wore a ski mask but the owner identified Julius. Said he could tell by the voice and body language. Which was total bullshit because Julius was with me all that evening."

"Then why is he in jail?"

Davey cocks his head at Caleb. "Because of our companions. We had a double date that night. Never left my apartment the whole evening. This woman Anne came into town every few months, she would call me when she did. She had a friend came along this time. Asked me if I knew of a nice guy who could join us. Julius was the nicest guy I knew. When the police came asking me to confirm his alibi, I gave them Anne's number. I only knew the other woman's first name. Well, when they contacted her, not only did Anne not acknowledge the date, she told them I threatened her trying to get her to back up the story. Turns out Anne would do anything to keep her family finding out she consorted with a black man."

Caleb finds himself angry and ashamed at the same time. All he can think to say is, "Did, did that get you in trouble?"

The sculptor's laugh was an angry report through a twisted sneer.

P C Burhenne

"They said if I didn't retract my statement, they would prosecute me for witness tampering and four or five other fucking things. I said, Do it—I looked forward to testifying for Julius." The sculptor runs his gaze back and forth about the partitioned space. "Never got the chance, though."

Anguish delivers a tremor among these words. Caleb waits for the rest until he understands there will be no more unless he asks. "Why not?"

"Julius took a plea. His lawyer, the guy was alright. He tried. Julius wasn't just some black thug to him, trying to get over. But he told Julius straight. Anne muddied up the alibi. Even without her taking the stand, my account was uncorroborated. The testimony of a close friend. A black friend. Trial was a crap shoot."

"There's no way to find the other woman?"

"Anne wasn't about to tell. And the woman didn't say much about herself, she mostly asked about him and me. Mostly him. Julius is an entertainer, he was happy to carry the conversation. About all we could remember about her was that she was a secretary." Davey turns away to continue. "We were both pretty much focused on the night to come."

The sculptor puts on the safety glasses, takes up his tools. The first "chink" from the chisel is Caleb's dismissal.

* * *

Vice.com

A mental health advocate angered policymakers with a comparison between the US's response to mental health issues and that of Nazi Germany. During his testimony before the Senate Committee on Health, Education, Labor and Pensions, Doctor Edward Lansbury criticized the "anemic efforts" of this country to aid its citizens currently dealing with serious psychological afflictions. When various senators pushed back that a system is in place, the advocate countered that, for far too many sufferers, the system's final solution is a life of homelessness, then he commented that at least the Nazis had the decency to euthanize its mentally ill rather than condemning them to the depredations of street predators, adding that America's attitude to its most vulnerable is not that of a compassionate society. Among the ten wealthiest nations, residents of the United States are the least likely to have access to psychiatric or psychological counseling.

THE PROPHET OF CENTRAL PARK

Again with the floppy hat and shades, Caleb catches his train. He holds the bag of uniforms between his shoes and opens the book on his lap. During the ride, his uncle describes, among contacts made and extraordinary objects discovered, the deterioration of his relationship with Lisa Comey. By this time she had moved to Japan where she would spend her final years. Early on, buying trips to the Far East included a stopover in Tokyo, but the visits became increasingly contentious until she stopped welcoming him altogether. William called her withdrawal from their friendship one of the most heart wrenching losses of his life but he claimed ignorance of why she did so.

When Caleb calls, Ms. Yuan directs him to meet her on Lexington Avenue. He feels hidden within the parade of pedestrians so keeps moving up and down the block until the supervisor arrives. Forewarned she falters for a second only on seeing him. She does say, "I hoped it wouldn't look as bad as Haruto said."

Mrs. Yuan leads him to a nearby upscale bistro. Caleb is glad he opted for dress pants, not jeans. The hostess guides them to a table in the rear as the supervisor requests. Caleb hands over the uniforms, puts the book beside his place setting.

"Firing you has backfired a bit. A lot of the customers keep asking staff to point you out. Especially the Chinese."

Caleb shakes his head, in a disjointed sort of way because of the ache. "How do they even know?"

A waitress fills their water glasses and leaves menus.

"After yesterday, your name got tagged with the auction house," the supervisor says. "It found its way onto one of their threads. They see you as standing for order. They don't understand why you've been fired."

Ms. Yuan flickers a smile, expecting a pleased response. Caleb cannot dredge one up. "I liked working for the auction house. I was really excited to be part of Asia Week." A blind falls over the mischief lurking in her face and Caleb fears he has failed to speak the proper appreciation for her news. "How is the first day going," and he asks about the reception so far for the highlights pictured in the street windows. She discusses them as if he is an expert and he asks questions because she is one.

P C Burhenne

When the waitress leaves with their orders, Ms. Yuan changes subjects abruptly. "If you want, Caleb, I can help to find you another job. Or I should say 'we', other supervisors and I. That's why I invited you to lunch today, that and to see that you're alright, of course."

With the offer, Psalm 146 springs to mind: He gives justice to the oppressed and food to the hungry, but Caleb struggles to say, "I, I would . . . that would be a big help, the biggest help. I wasn't sure . . . Oh, Lord, ma'am, I can't begin to thank you. For everything."

The supervisor glances to the tables about them and Caleb sees that his stumbling outburst has caught their attention. He mouths, Sorry, to Ms. Yuan. A suspicion of a smile again dances over her lips.

"We'll look into that for you then. I see you're reading your uncle's mini memoir."

"Yes. From Mr. Yamaguchi."

"Learn anything interesting?"

The newly found relative is a happy discovery in the midst of this terrifying set of days. Caleb does not want to sully the surprise but a notion gnaws at him. "You didn't know my uncle but you know his reputation, right?" Ms. Yuan assumes her professional distance in nodding. Caleb presses on. "There are pictures. He seems to be in, I don't know, maybe not the jungle, but in overgrown sites. He's digging up artifacts in those photos, isn't he?" When the woman still does not answer, he forces himself to say, "My uncle was a grave robber, wasn't he?"

At that Ms. Yuan drags the crook of her finger three times down the short bridge of her nose. Then, "Yes. Undoubtedly yes." At what he knew would be the answer, he looks down. William's expression in the cover art now seems like a thief's smirk as he enjoys his ill-gotten gains. The supervisor goes on. "By the same standard, Indiana Jones was one too. In their era, however, both were admired as adventurers." When Caleb looks to her again, she raises her hand. "I'm not justifying what either did. It was clearly looting of historical sites. I'm only suggesting that, given the mindset of the West at the time, it was much harder for your uncle to recognize his excursions into the wilds for what they were."

The waitress arrives with the lunches, fettuccine for her and jaw-friendly minestrone for him. After a few bites, the supervisor points her fork at the book, saying, "I remember when word got out that your uncle was working on that. It was highly anticipated in our little world. And everyone, the editors who importuned him to do it, everybody in the business who read it, we were all mightily disappointed."

As he knows he's meant to, Caleb presses her with, "Why?"

"He makes no mention of the event that he is most famous for. Your uncle made maybe the best buy since the Dutch bought Manhattan. And it was the source of his fortune. Not those trips over to Southeast Asia."

"What did he buy?"

Ms. Yuan takes another bite of her pasta. "The estate of Christian Tollier. He was an influential collector. Before my time but a name one sees on provenance statements. And not just for Asian works either. He came from European bankers. French originally. Or Belgian. Very wealthy family. Which made what happened all the more curious."

Caleb eats as she does then says, "Yes, ma'am, I'm still listening."

She nods in appreciation at his oblique prompt. "Christian died young, in his early forties, and he died with outstanding debts that the executor could not satisfy with the estate's liquid assets. So, per the terms of Christian's will, the lawyer conducted two sales. One of Christian's home— as I remember, a lovely brownstone off the east side of Central Park—and one of his 'chattel'. All the furniture and items from his collection in the brownstone or in storage or elsewhere."

"Excuse me, Mr. Yuan. Is it so unusual for a rich person to die owing people money?"

The supervisor waves this off, swiveling her upright left hand as if she is hastily unscrewing an invisible light bulb. "That wasn't the curious part. Christian wrote the will not long before he died because it explained how he wanted his obligations handled, and most of those were contractual pledges to charities which he made not long before he drafted the will."

"Okay, that is more weird. Why not make those gifts part of his will, right?"

"Right, indeed, but that still is not the most curious part." A teasing light animates Ms. Yuan's eyes and in that second Caleb glimpses how much this stern professional enjoys conducting the ebb and flow of the story. "What is most intriguing is that the Tolliers could have easily claimed the estate. Christian was divorced and had no children so the family could have come forward with the shortfall and the estate would have passed to them instead of the proceeds. Supposedly Christian was estranged from them, especially from his brother, and they had no use for his passion for all things Asian."

"I'm sensing a big comeuppance," Caleb offers.

Her robust chuckle, more loading dock than gallery floor, startles him and flusters the supervisor herself so that she retreats from it behind a hasty forkful of her lunch.

"The lawyer liquidated the estate as directed," Ms. Yuan goes on as before. "He knew enough to properly advertise the chattel sale. All the right Asian dealers participated. The preview was at the brownstone. Interested parties left written bids at the lawyer's office and he contacted all the runners-up with an opportunity to counter the high bid. Your uncle's. No one did. I've heard the others who took part thought his number was insane at the time. Seven million, I think they said. Maybe eight. An astronomical price for back then."

When she pauses, Caleb sees in her patient regard a dare that he guess the big twist, but all he can say is, "Well, it's no country auction, I'll grant you, but it's nothing extraordinary either, except the part where William has that much money. Okay, Ms. Yuan, please tell me what makes this the stuff of legends."

"The sale was for all of Christian Tollier's property excluding real estate. Everyone else was bidding on the objects in the townhouse. Only your uncle knew that the townhouse held only a fraction of the man's collection, that the vast majority was out on loan to museums around the country."

The supervisor sits back to enjoy his reaction and Caleb rewards her with a view of his tonsils until he regains enough composure to demand, "How in God's name did only he have that information?"

"Because he brokered all the agreements," and Ms. Yuan leans forward again. "People knew that Christian bought from William. They didn't know that William was Christian's exclusive advisor and that Christian bought most of his collection anonymously through your uncle. Over 95% of those items never made their way into the man's home so the other buyers didn't know they existed."

"How much did my uncle make?"

THE PROPHET OF CENTRAL PARK

"No one can be sure but at a guess I'd say . . ." and the supervisor touches a knuckle to her lips before arriving at "three to four hundred million dollars."

Caleb whistles too loudly then hunches toward the supervisor who wears a gratified smirk. "The Tollier family must have been upset when they found out."

"I doubt they ever did." Ms. Yuan takes a sip of her iced tea. "As I said, they were not interested in Asian antiquities so they wouldn't hear the gossip and that's the only place to find this out, from an insider. And the trade didn't begin to grasp the scope of what had happened until years later. Your uncle needed that much time to retrieve all the items that had been lent out."

"Why?"

The supervisor bobbles her head. "Of course, that wouldn't make sense to you." She points her fork at him. "Little known fact about museums: they're happy to receive rare items but not so much to return them. If a benefactor dies, they certainly don't contact the estate about the valuables on loan to them. They keep quiet and hope the items fall through the cracks. I imagine your uncle had to go to every institution with a death certificate, a letter from Christian's executor and the original loan agreement then follow up while the museum director dragged his or her feet. I say 'imagine' because people didn't start putting this together until these pieces started hitting the market with Christian Tollier/William Ellison provenance and exhibition history at such and such museum."

The waitress is at their side again to refresh the drinks. At the young woman's awkward manner, Ms. Yuan cranes about. When Caleb does too, a few of the diners have their phones trained on him, others are openly watching, and among the people crammed outside the front windows are two shouldering cameras. The cafe has turned into a fishbowl. The restaurant manager, a forty-something beanpole of a man wrapped in a grey two-piece suit, is shifting from foot to foot by the door as if the world is shifting beneath him.

"You better bring the check," Ms. Yuan tells the waitress and when she leaves, the supervisor tells him in the same "take charge" voice, "The bathrooms are through that doorway on the right." She nods to the back of the room. "To the left is an exit out to the building's lobby. At the rear is a

P C Burhenne

stairwell. Go down two flights and there is a passage to one of the platforms at Grand Central Station. Just follow the signs."

"How do you know that?" he asks, startled by the sudden way out.

"A friend works upstairs." Her smile is a shy offering. "Given what you're going through, I thought it might come in handy."

"Thank you," and struggling to express all she has done, he can only say again, "Just thank you."

She flicks her four dangling fingers in a shooing motion.

* * *

Post from CincySue123

Dear Ghostinthemachine06825, what a wonderful prayer. No requirements except a willingness to come together.

Post from LetsgoMets31

Absolutely, Ghostinthemachine06825. Something to hold us together, not tear us apart. I'm all in.

Post from Southernboy

Ghostinthemachine06825 is right. Everyone, pass this along and have everyone you reach pass it along too. And lets pick a day, a day of national healing.

The way down is where Ms. Yuan said it would be, descending to a well-lit but drab yellow corridor that ends with a set of hollowed stone treads. These rise to a walkway clinging to a brick wall beside one of several train tracks winding through the mass transit catacomb. Giant steel columns, earth red with rust and set at twenty-yard intervals, separate the sets of rails as they reach up to support the ceiling and the skyscraper above. Unfiltered by shades, the bulbs here give off a more jarring light but the overall darkness dwarfs them into illuminated points hanging over the tunnels so that the underground complex seems like a menacing industrial night with low hanging stars liable to blink off at any moment. The bright piers of the terminal far to his right show the way back to the city but Caleb entertains the notion of exploring the shadows to his left for a hiding place. Reporters would never think to chase him here. A week should see the news cycle turn upon some other poor soul. Remembering his father, Caleb knows the man will never find him in the bowels of the terminal. He could buy a flashlight, a store of batteries. Pop up when he got hungry. He could stand the filth and isolation if it meant he emerged a nobody again.

His Uncle William's example shames him off this fancy. Like Caleb, the young man fled a difficult family situation. He arrived friendless in big scary NYC, like Caleb. However, far from running from the obstacles that the city surely threw up, he extracted a legendary fortune. Well, legendary among a small circle.

The walkway becomes a platform, one currently not in use. In the great hall, he hurries as if with purpose through the swirl of commuters; speed is his disguise as much as his roommate's props. Outside he goes north. Large mountains of clouds and the highrises closer by combine to make the sun's warm touch a wonderful surprise when it finds him. At the entrance to his N train, he decides not to head back yet. After the morning's discussions with Davey, Caleb isn't even sure if his place in Queens is secure. As he heads into Central Park, he almost calls Tawana to find where she has set up before thinking that the interruption might be rude to someone . . . at work? Is that what she calls her efforts? Caleb is sure it's not, even as he has no idea how to locate her. The Park seems to grow larger with each step. After several minutes of wandering, he realizes who may be able to help.

Caleb texts his friend before he understands that he is bothering Rolando at work instead. "Had to come into the city. Thought I'd see Tawana preach again. How do people find her?"

After a moment, "People post when they see her. #WHERESTAWANA." Then, "Want me to check for you?"

"If it doesn't get you in trouble."

After an interval of blank static screen, Rolando types back, "She just finished by ball fields. Don't know where she's headed. Gotta go."

Caleb switches to the burner phone. As he pulls up the guitarist's number, Annaliese challenges him too: You do know, she has no use for you that way.

"Yes, I'm not stupid," he snaps back.

Tawana picks up right then. "Who's stupid?"

"Sorry, sorry, talking to myself. Not you. You're not stupid."

"Are you alright, Caleb?" Both concern and exasperation pull at her question.

"I'm fine. I had an appointment here. I mean, I thought I'd come listen to you." Caleb doesn't want to admit to tracking her, says, "Are you still . . . performing."

"Just wrapped up. Where are you?"

"By the zoo."

She says she'll meet him at Strawberry Fields. On the walk to the west side of the Park, Annaliese derides him for visiting all the sights that she planned to see before he helped to kill her. Making the ascent to what he realizes is a terrace within the Park, he murmurs, "Please forgive me," a mantra to appease her voice. She answers: At least you won't hurt Tawana —She's too smart.

The guitarist has not yet arrived. In tribute to his absent friend, he walks a slow circuit about the Imagine mosaic, sidestepping the several bouquets left on its perimeter. Afterwards he sits on a bench. The craftsman in him tries to tease forth the method used to create the intricate yet precise sunburst pattern. Tawana suddenly asking, "Have you been waiting long?" starts Caleb from the reverie.

"Didn't mean to sneak up on you," she says with a bashful smile.

Caleb stands. "You didn't," then when she raises her eyebrows, he adds, "I mean you did but it wasn't your fault. I was engrossed. Never mind. Are you taking a break?"

"Stopped early." Glancing away she continues toward the street so that he could almost believe he has caught her in a lie. "Put-off" is not a posture he has encountered from her. When he catches up, a shush from the case keeping time to her steps reaches him.

"Is that castanets?"

"That? That's just change people dropped in there. I haven't counted it yet. That's where I'm going." She leads them past the backlog of vehicles stopped and impatient at the light at Central Park West. "How was your meeting?"

"It was kinda great really," and his summary sees them head toward the Hudson River then turn up West End Avenue. He is explaining the museum angle of the Tollier story when Tawana groans. "What did I say?"

"It's not you," and Tawana ducks her head forward with the face of someone experiencing a muscle cramp.

THE PROPHET OF CENTRAL PARK

Across the side street they have reached, a woman is coming down the steps of a yellow brick church. She's a brunette in her thirties wearing what Caleb guesses are designer sweater and slacks. The crisp clips of her dress shoes announce a business person with no time to waste.

"Thank goodness, I picked the right soup kitchen. You disappeared from the performance so abruptly."

"I've told you, Ms. Kapoor, they are not performances," Tawana says, more exercised than he has seen her before.

"Yes, right, the communion with your followers," Ms. Kapoor says, discarding her mistake with a wave of the hand while at the same time overriding Tawana's objection. "Some of them may still be waiting. I hope you didn't disappear because of me."

"Of course not. Had I seen you, I would have told you 'no' right then so you didn't waste your time chasing me."

Ms. Kapoor nods at that kindness. "I should have realized you couldn't pick me out from among that crowd. More than a thousand people. Your communions keep growing." Then, "Have we met? You seem very familiar."

This last catches Caleb staring. He glances from the woman to Tawana's annoyed frown to his feet and back again. "No, we've never met." but he doesn't get a chance to introduce himself.

"Nothing's changed, Ms. Kapoor," Tawana announces. "I'm not interested in monetizing my mission."

"Well, monetize it more." The woman smiles at the guitar case where coins rustle with each adjustment Tawana makes to it. Her pale blue eyes shine with calculated mirth. Until she again swivels to Caleb, perplexed furrows disturbing her otherwise lovely dusty brown skin. "Are you sure, because I'm certain I've seen you before?"

Her slow groping towards recognition of him alarms Caleb. He tells her. "No, ma'am. And I would remember you." To Tawana he says, "I'll wait over there," and he walks past Ms. Kapoor to the steps she just vacated, hoping his abrupt leave doesn't make her more curious. The conversation carries to him.

"As you pointed out, I have a haul needs counting so I'm going too," Tawana says.

Ms. Kapoor actually puts a hand to Tawana's shoulder. "Please, I didn't mean it like that."

The guitarist stares down at the soft restraint until Ms. Kapoor removes it then answers in a kind tone that Caleb did not expect. The professional woman either, judging by the way she cants her head to understand this strange gambit, or perhaps to appreciate this rarity in her world, a sympathetic refusal. "I know you didn't but as I said, I've not changed my mind."

Tawana starts toward Caleb. Ms. Kapoor keeps at her side.

"One moment please. This time I'm not here to enroll you." and when the guitarist relents, the woman hurries to say, "I'm here on behalf of another client. A TV evangelist. Don't ask me who. I can't mention his name. Not at this stage anyway, but I guarantee you know him. He wants to do a show with you. A national broadcast of a communion, if you will, led by the both of you."

Tawana has taken on the wide eyes of a lamped deer. "Why would he want that?"

Anticipating an excited response, the woman continues with more urgency. "He's seen you on social media. He sees what everyone sees, the spirit within you. He wants to do a sort of ecumenical crusade, he called it. I looked that up. It--"

"I know what it means. I don't know if he means it."

"Then talk to him. Share your doubts. He wants to speak with you."

Tawana presses her lips together and shuts her eyes for a moment in coming to a decision. "I won't waste this man's time either."

Ms. Kapoor darts to put herself in the guitarist's path so that her back is to Caleb. "Don't throw away this opportunity. According to this man, there is a movement growing on social media for a day of coming together, of communion like you do. That's what's inspired him to reach out to you. Think of all the people your message will reach."

"Thank you for delivering the offer but it's not for me."

Tawana moves around the woman towards Caleb. Ms. Kapoor turns after her, frustration contorting her face. "So what are you gonna do. Keep running away when the crowds grow too big? I saw what happened today. You've started a movement. Like I knew you would. And now it's gotten

THE PROPHET OF CENTRAL PARK

too big for street corners and patches of grass by the bridle path. Okay, you walk away from this broadcast special. Where **do** you go from here?"

Tawana pushes the buzzer beside the church door pretending she hasn't heard, but almost imperceptible false starts betray her anxiousness to get away. Caleb gives the woman below a nod goodbye, not in apology but in answer to the awkward parting.

Right then Ms. Kapoor opens her mouth wide even as she smiles and Caleb also wants the people inside to hurry. "You're the Prozac man!"

"The what?" he can't help himself asking.

"The Prozac man. You're Caleb Ellison. I didn't recognize you with that bandage and the glasses," then the woman covers the gasp she lets out with both hands. "Are you two together? Say you are. The synergy of your brands opens up all kinds of possibilities." The grey-haired woman who opens the door is startled by the exchange she has stepped into and hesitates before moving aside. As the two of them go in, Ms. Kapoor calls after, "Tawana, Tawana, please, we should talk."

After shutting out the street, their attendant reaches to Tawana with motherly concern. She is a plump woman in her seventies at a guess, wearing baggy blue pants with an elastic waistband and a button-up knitted red vest over a beige blouse. "Is that a problem for you, dear?"

"No, Florence. Just an over-enthusiastic fan," then she gestures aside. "This is my friend Caleb."

Florence leads the way down a hall. As they follow he says aside to the guitarist, "Do you know what that 'Prozac man' thing was about?"

"I'll tell you in a minute."

The older woman stops at a stainless steel table in a kitchen that could have been removed from Caleb's old church. A large mound of potatoes waits there beside a cutting board littered with brown peels and a bowl holding the ones Florence has skinned. She says, "Stew today."

"I'll do this out there," Tawana says, lifting the case so it again shushes her.

Caleb follows Tawana through a swinging door to an empty dining area with a serving counter along one wall. She opens the carrier on the nearest table. When she takes away her instrument, bills stick to its back and a quarter lets go to fall to the Formica top then onto the black and white checkerboard of the linoleum floor. The rest of her contributions paper the bottom of the case. "I shouldn't leave the change in there but I don't get the chance to separate it out anymore." She delivers this fact as a sad reality, while she wipes the notes off her guitar. After clearing the rest of the money from the case, she returns her guitar to its safety.

When she sits to sort the contributions, he asks, "Can I help," and takes the seat she points to. "So why am I Prozac man?"

Tawana twists her mouth into a pucker pulled rightward to suppress a grin but its humor glistens in her eyes. "You've become a meme." Caleb closes his eyes, preparing himself for this next blow. "After your video went viral, somebody doctored it to have you saying basically the opposite of what you did say and captioned it 'Caleb Ellison is Pro-What?' Then social media gremlins ran with that, tailoring your image to all kinds of 'Pro' captions. Like 'Pro Wrestler', your head pasted onto the body of a WWF person. Finally someone titled that moment of you looking like you're spitting a curse out 'Pro Zac' and that's taken on a life of its own. People are posting it to say that something is so crazy, they need to calm themselves."

"Great."

He finishes dividing his half of the money and pushes the piles across to Tawana, then he starts with the change. A question that he isn't sure about asking has him glance up at the woman three or four times before she finally tells him, "You want to know about Geeta Kapoor."

"Well, is everything okay? You seemed flustered when she mentioned how you left the Park."

Tawana goes back to counting so Caleb does too. After a moment, though, she sighs. "You probably guessed, Geeta is an agent/manager type. She's wanted to manage me for some time. Which . . . isn't me. But Geeta's right. I am afraid of what the gatherings are becoming. I've always fashioned what I do as forums. People disagreeing. Questioning me. And I always felt that a spirit held us together even when we argued. But lately that spirit seems stretched to the point of ripping. Every day now, when I get up, I'm afraid of what's going to happen."

Her vulnerability catches Caleb off guard. Brings back evenings spent with Annaliese watching the Milky Way from his truck hood or waiting on the river bank for the next "ploink" in the dark of a catfish breaking the water's surface. Past hours together made those heart-to-hearts possible. With Tawana he is unsure what is too familiar, too cold.

"What is it you do?" he ventures. "I mean, what do you think it is? I'm guessing you don't consider yourself a performer."

"I share what's been shared with me."

Tawana says this without a pause or qualm. It galls Caleb, another so-called 'man of god', or person, knowing His will. "You mean your song lyrics?"

His snarky edge brings the woman's attention back upon him. After a moment her mouth twitches with what might be humor. "Do you know much about the Koran?"

"Not taught where I grew up."

She does smile then with a benevolence untouched by pique so that he feels guilty for his tone. "Silly me. Muhammad received the verses of the Koran after intense meditation on issues that troubled him. One of his most important early converts said that the beauty of the language convinced him they were Heaven sent. God revealed his truths as poetry."

Still Caleb cannot stop himself. "Your songs come from Heaven?"

"They come when I am most upset. After I've prayed and prayed then have quieted myself to listen. The ones that have real meaning hold together when I sit alone with them afterwards. The real ones are an anguish and a joy." Then the dark mood takes her over again. "Of course, Muhammad was forced to flee Mecca not long after his visions started."

She returns to her count of the bills. For a moment Caleb continues with the coins. Then, "You could stop for a while."

Tawana closes her eyes, to wince at that option rather than consider it. "Believe me, I've tried. I'm meant to be on this path. Whether as God's messenger or Her fool. I don't know which, but if I turn away, all I have to look forward to is the dread of being lost. God chooses our purpose. It may feel like a burden at times but that purpose is the only thing that makes us whole."

* * *

Popular Mechanics

P C Burhenne

A recently developed grout and advances in AI technology are reinvigorating hopes to harness the oceans as a source of clean renewable energy. The temperature difference between warmer surface and cooler deep waters, the disparity in salinity between fresh and salt water along with the constant movement of marine currents all contain huge amounts of inherent energy. If tapped this storehouse could produce up to 80,000 terawatt hours of electricity, according to the International Energy Agency. However, the high impact and otherwise destructive environment found on and beneath the seas have so far hindered efforts to unlock this natural battery. The qualities of the new grout render it much more impervious to corrosive decay while delivering remarkable compressive strength, and programs that utilize artificial intelligence are allowing sea-stationed devices to better conform to the turbulence of open water.

Tawana doesn't announce the final total but Caleb guesses there is over four hundred dollars on the table. She gives most to Florence who, after counting the donation again herself, hands back a receipt. Jotting the transaction in a small notebook, the guitarist tells Caleb, "For my taxes." Tawana then helps prep the soup kitchen's evening meal. He joins in. Apropos of nothing she passes on that Davey said Caleb and his smartass friend could stay over another night if need be. "He's really taken to your roommate. I wouldn't be surprised if they become the best of friends."

"Of course they will. Everybody loves Sidney," and without looking up he says, "Don't you?"

The woman's chuckle slows to a growl. "Hard not to see all the trouble that comes with your roommate. Not bad trouble, mind you, but nothing I'm looking for."

When the stew is simmering and the bread is baking, Caleb checks his old phone to find that his sister has left three messages for him to call in a fraught voice. His face betrays his fear because Florence asks, "What's happened, dear?" and Tawana hurries over.

"I don't know. My sister didn't say, but something's wrong," then he says, "I'm going go outside for this."

The kitchen manager goes with him to unlock the door. "Ring the bell when you're done."

THE PROPHET OF CENTRAL PARK

The side street is empty but when he goes around the corner, a queue of homeless waits along the church for the meal inside. When his call goes through, his sister snaps, "Oh, thank God, Caleb. Where have you been? I heard you were arrested. I heard you were attacked."

"I've been turning off my phone because I'm getting a lot of crank calls. No, I wasn't arrested."

"But you were attacked. Don't say you weren't. I know."

She leans on the last words to make clear that their twins' radar revealed this. "Okay," he says, and checking that he is clear of other pedestrians, he relays all the encounters of the past day and a half, both awful and incredible. At first when he finishes, she can only say, "Really?" Not as disbelief but in breathless wonder.

"It sounds like a Grimm's fairy tale, I know, but yes."

There is a pause then, "This uncle we never knew about, was he actually all that people say he was?"

"Yes, I think so."

A bitter tremor enters Carolyne's voice. "We should have been able to meet him."

Caleb think so too but says instead, "Anyway, it looks like I'm gonna be okay so you don't need to worry."

Fright once again rushes his sister's words. "That's not just why I called. I'm worried because of what's happening here."

"You mean Dad's message that he's coming to take me back home." He assumes a dismissive confidence. "We're past the point where Dad gets to tell me where I can and can't live."

"It's more than just Dad. Mom called me yesterday. At her wit's end. She said her and Dad are getting pressure to make you renounce what you said on that video."

"Pressure from who?"

"She wouldn't say but, Caleb, she was scared for you. And that woman? Tanaeya?"

"Tawana. What about her?"

"She really has everybody crazy. Dad. The people talking to him. That you're with her."

"With her!" Caleb realizes the people in line for a meal, anxious to watch someone else make a scene, are staring at his loud reaction. He lowers his voice and hunches toward the phone to further muffle it. "I'm not with her. She just helped me when I needed it. And how do they know about Tawana. I just met her a few days ago."

"I don't know. There are videos online. Was she there when you sold your work in the Park?"

Caleb exhales like he is blowing out candles on a birthday cake. "Yes. Yes, she was."

"Well, you and her in the same place have people really upset. I don't know who, but people want Dad to stop that." Carolyne becomes the little girl who turned frantic when she lost sight of Caleb. "What are you going to do?"

Caleb has no idea. "Buy some mace, I guess. Maybe I should buy a gun. It's what Dad always wanted."

"I'm serious."

"Just got this information, Carolyne, so haven't quite figured it out yet," then he takes a breath, and another, and regrets his tone. "But I will. Now that I know. Thank you for telling me." He makes himself a curious brother. "So how is Terry settling into the job?"

"Are you seriously changing the subject?" Carolyne laughs then but only for a second and the effort turns to sobs, through which she begs him, "Please be careful. You're in so much trouble, Caleb."

The cell goes quiet. He looks from it to the homeless shuffling in line. Many are still watching his discomfort, entertainment to discuss over dinner. The prospect of answering, or evading, questions inside propels him across the avenue. The ground slopes downward. At the bottom of the block, the rowhouses cease and green space opens up across a street which a sign identifies as Riverside Drive. A highway bounds the narrow swath of grass a hundred yards away. The undulating whoosh of traffic is the soundtrack for the neighborhood residents lounging or walking their pets there. He sits at an empty bench to watch a brindle-colored dog fetching a tennis ball back to a man about Caleb's age dressed in black and white waiter's garb. Soon, though, Caleb is again considering the tunnels in Grand Central as the best place to ride out this tempest that will not move on from him.

The pay-as-you-go phone pulls him back.

"Has something happened?" Tawana says instead of hello.

THE PROPHET OF CENTRAL PARK

Caleb opens his mouth, falters then says, "I'm not sure. My sister told me something that, I don't know what it means. I need to be alone."

"Okay," then she asks, "What do you want me to do with your book?"

At that Caleb reaches for the hat that is not on his head, the glasses that are back at the cafeteria. "Oh, damn, my disguise!"

"Yeah, and your disguise." Caleb isn't sure now if the pet owner is glancing at him sidelong, trying to place Caleb's face, or waiting for the right moment to take a photo. "I can walk these over to you if you want. If you're still nearby. I can drop them off and leave."

"That would be . . . . I'd appreciate that, Tawana."

He describes where his is sitting and a few minutes later the guitarist crosses the drive to deliver the left-behind things. As he dons his camouflage again, he tries to laugh at his forgetfulness but the result sounds more like a weak cough.

"You know, the biggest part of this park is on the other side of the highway." She points the neck of the guitar case northward. "There's a through way to it up there. You want me to show you?"

Caleb really doesn't want to be alone. As he follows, he wonders about sharing what his sister told. He doesn't want Tawana thinking she is just one more problem to him but a suspicion won't let go that Carolyne's report holds menace for the guitarist also. The highway is a series of rumbles overhead as they pass beneath it. They emerge onto a stone terrace that looks out over the Hudson River which seems ridiculously wide at this up-close spot. A marina hugs the length of shore below them. Stairs lead down to a walkway which, when Tawana veers to the left, takes them to an open field. A trio has spread themselves across this to pass a Frisbee among themselves.

"That looks like fun," she says. "Let's join in? Maybe they're our new best friends."

Soon enough Caleb's book and Tawana's instrument have joined the backpacks of the three players beneath a bench and he is trying to recover his old disc-throwing form. Their new friends are students at Columbia University. They do laugh at his efforts but their technique corrections and several reps enable him to not make them run too much. The play transforms Tawana into a gleeful child, squealing as she chases down errant pitches and dancing herself in a circle, hands slapping the air above, when her own tosses glide to a slow motion touch down onto their targets. By the time the group breaks up, Caleb's cheek again aches and Tawana's winded breath punctuates her goodbyes. If the three recognize either of them, the collegians keep it to themselves.

On the walk back to a subway, Caleb calls to let his roommate know they still have a place to lay low.

"Davey already told me," Sidney says to the news.

"You two got chummy fast."

"Don't worry. You'll always be my number one guy. Gotta go. The boss is looking at me funny."

Tawana's laughter rumbles as he puts away the phone so he knows she overheard.

Finally on the ride back to Queens, he tells what Carolyne told him. At first Tawana only runs a forefinger back and forth through the groove of her lips. He worries that she will be upset that he has brought his family's insanity to her door when she has her own craziness to negotiate. Instead she turns inquisitive eyes upon him as if he can explain their situation. "I've spent the past several years asking God to reveal Her will for me. I have to believe that is what is happening. Her purpose promoted through our meeting. I pray I have the strength to do my part."

* * *

Journal of the American Water Resources Association

Latest surveys suggest that certain parts of the Great Plains will deplete their water resources from the Ogallala Aquifer more quickly than expected, in some cases, in as soon as 20 to 25 years hence. The affected states rely upon the aquifer for crop irrigation and, in response to the looming disaster, farmers throughout the region have been instituting various conservation schemes. However, a sustained drought and a sharp increase in days with temperatures 96 degrees and over have hampered these efforts while at the same time population growth has increased demand. Experts believe a new industry-wide approach to food production is necessary to stave off a dramatic decrease in production from this large swath of land often labeled "the breadbasket of America."

THE PROPHET OF CENTRAL PARK

The cloud cover obscures the sun when their subway train emerges from beneath the East River and the day is chillier because of it. At the loft an exiting resident recognizes Tawana so they don't have to bother Davey. On the third floor the interplay of several music sources and the movement of people behind the layers of translucent partitions suggest a bazaar of suspect merchandise. Until Wilma claps her hands to complain, "No, no, no! I want more outrage. More disgust. This is an insult to you as a woman."

The sculptor looks up startled then reaches for his phone when they push into his space. "What time is it?"

Caleb goes to the great bird that Davey is freeing. A jagged excess layer still only suggests its body but Davey has made much progress fashioning the head of the alert raptor.

"Sorry we're interrupting work hours. We came back early," Tawana says.

"Wow, you've gotten so far since this morning," Caleb tells him.

The sculptor looks from one to the other of his distractions. "The marble's been cooperating. Doesn't always. So you two pass the day together?"

The hawk makes Caleb miss his own sculpting tools. He inches about the table.

"We met up in the afternoon," Tawana says. "He finished his lunch appointment and I was done in the Park."

"Early exit again." Davey implies a question in the statement.

"Biggest crowd yet. Very uneasy spirit. Police were getting ready to shut me down." She shakes off that unsettling thought as she waggles her guitar case. "I'm gonna put this upstairs then buy fixings for dinner."

Davey rears back. "Staying over two nights in a row?"

"I inflicted these two upon you. Least I can do is help entertain them."

She leaves with a nimble use of the case neck to part the drapes. Caleb thinks about following but hesitates to presume on what might be her alone-time. Which leaves him with nowhere certain to go. He takes two start and stop steps toward the resettling partition. "I should let you get back to your project."

"No," the sculptor says in a near growl. "This feels like quits. Help me clean up."

Caleb doesn't like the barked order but takes the broom Davey pushes at him and starts sweeping the perimeter while the other wipes stone chips from the table. All the while the sculptor's mouth practices an argument playing in his head so that when he speaks aloud, Caleb does not immediately realize that the man is addressing him.

"Tawana doesn't do strays. Her call to come see your work was a shock, but thinking that means there's something special between you two would be a mistake."

Davey stares over, his rigidly stern face meant to deter disagreement. Which puts up Caleb's hackles.

"That's not what's going on but if I thought it was, I'd discuss it with her, not you."

Davey's abrupt guffaw almost makes Caleb drop the broom. "That would be an embarrassing conversation. Kid, I'm not telling you this for her sake. I'm telling you for yours."

That raises a question. "Why has she helped me so much. She's your friend. Why?"

Uncertainty runs off Davey's grin. "I don't know. Tawana helps people but she doesn't let them into her life like she has you. I'll tell you this though. The reason comes from her mission self, not her private self. When it comes to the girl she keeps safe inside, well, you're never gonna see that girl, and if you did, you'd never understand her."

"Because I'm white?"

"Yeah," Davey puts down the whisk broom and takes the large one from Caleb. "What do you even know about Tawana?"

"I know that her songs come to her as visions while she meditates."

"She told you that?" The sculptor stops a moment wide-eyed that Tawana trusted Caleb enough to share the fact. Then, "Of course, that's from her mission side. Did she tell you anything about her life before she took up her calling?"

Instead of admitting that she hasn't, he says, "So, again, why are you warning me off?"

Davey keeps sweeping. "Hey, do what you want. I just thought you've had more than your share of heartache these past few days and I see how you look at her."

THE PROPHET OF CENTRAL PARK

Annaliese mocks him then: Go ahead—Tell the man he's wrong—You're only kidding yourself. Caleb has no rebuttal for either so he watches the sculptor gather the marble chips onto a dust pan and dump them into a pail under the hawk's perch. When they go up to the apartment, Caleb's cheek hurts enough that he asks for ice. He has the dressing off and is pressing the bag against his face when Tawana returns.

"Oh, let me see how it looks today," she says setting aside the groceries on the counter.

"It's fine. Keep doing what you're doing."

Ignoring this, she puts her hand over his to lift the ice from the wound. A flush cascades down from his scalp and he knows he must be glowing crimson. Annaliese suggests in her meanest way possible: You know she's having a hard time—She's a perfect candidate to have her life ruined by you. Davey empties the grocery bag without a glance their way.

"It's good. It's starting to heal." She presses his hand with the ice back in place. "The color's better today. When you're ready, I'll help you put on another bandage."

Before he can summon a polite reason why she needn't bother, Davey says, "Making your meatloaf. What do you want me to do?"

When Caleb says he wants to help, both tell him to keep the cold on the bite. A few minutes later, the sculptor buzzes Sidney up. The roommate enters with his own brown bag from which he pulls first a carton of chocolate peanut butter ice cream then, in case either of his hosts has a nut allergy, another of vanilla. Holding both over his head, he parades around the table singing, "We're havin' a party." Davey wipes away a playful smirk before calling Sidney a menace to peace and quiet. "Are you mad because I didn't bring syrup?" then plunging a hand back in the bag, he announces, "Because I did!" In an aside he asks Caleb. "How was your day, Prozac Man."

Caleb gives him a bland frown back. "Yes, yes, I know."

Tawana laughs at Sidney's disappointment but Davey squints at the lot of them. "What the hell are you talking about?"

With that the roommate begs Caleb. "Oh, please, please, let me explain." When Caleb waves him on, Sidney describes the online storm track that delivered the meme, then pulls one up on his phone to show them. Caleb looks away.

"Wow," and in the first show of sympathy that Caleb has heard from the man, Davey says, "This shit show just won't let up for you, kid."

"You know, if you managed it right, this notoriety could launch your brand," Sidney says.

"Yeah, so I've been told."

"By who?"

Sidney cocks his head asking this. Realizing this is not his story to tell, Caleb glances to Tawana. Of course the others do the same so that Caleb wishes he hadn't. The guitarist sighs and to Davey says, "Geeta Kapoor tracked me down again today," and before Sidney can ask, she tells him, "Geeta is a talent scout."

"Same old spiel?" Davey asks.

"Actually this time she came on behalf of someone else." As she mixes her meal's ingredients, she describes the meeting and its proposal with a dispassion meant to dismiss it.

"Did she tell you which evangelist?" Davey says.

"Didn't ask."

Looking to each of them, Sidney announces, "It has to be Noel Osterhaus, doesn't it?"

At once the cavernous modern cathedral backdrop for the preacher's broadcasts comes to Caleb's mind along with the welcome of the man's wide smile which seems to promise God's favor in the Gospel which the preacher spreads.

"Why?" both Tawana and Davey ask.

"They just announced his event. Next month on the Great Lawn in Central Park. There's supposedly this movement online for a universal day of prayer. This is his answer to it. Here, let me pull it up."

Davey steps forward to better see as Sidney navigates the web, but the guitarist looks to Caleb. He sees in her unblinking dark eyes and tightly poised lips an appeal. To be rescued? To be guided? He cannot decipher its meaning but sets aside the ice to stand between them and her.

Sidney looks up. "Who's Billy Graham?"

"He was a preacher. TV personality. Before your time but huge," and Davey takes the phone to read from its screen, "In confirming the event, the highly influential Christian personality expressed his hope that the nationally televised service would be a first step in healing the divisions that afflict our country. 'The message of Jesus is intended for both the poor and the wealthy, the mighty and the weak. I offer this celebration of His Word as balm for our distressed nation.' Officials believe the crowd for this day could exceed fifty thousand, many of whom will travel from other states. Such estimates recall the crusades of Billy Graham from the last century." Handing back the cell, Davey says, "Kid's right. It's gotta be him."

Sidney holds up the phone. "Holy shit, you're gonna be part of this?"

"I'm not." Tawana turns her attention back to the meal. "I told the woman no."

"But isn't this a chance to reach millions?" When Caleb stares hard at Sidney to quiet him, the roommate goes, "What? Am I wrong?"

"Are you sure?" the sculptor says softly to her. "It's an opportunity."

"Is it?" she counters without looking up from the ground beef she is kneading. "I don't know what his real purpose is. It's his stage. He'll control everything."

"It's your message, the message entrusted to you." This still a quiet suggestion.

Her hands cease their task though she keeps watching them. "What if he makes a fool of me?"

The tenderness with which Davey encourages her, the fear she confesses to him, they make Caleb feel like he is intruding on that part of Tawana's life which the sculptor just warned he could never comprehend. Nevertheless a response rises within him, lifted by the presumptuous notion that it will comfort her.

"Jesus was an itinerant preacher. He didn't start in the capital. He traveled the countryside talking with anyone who would listen and the rumor of him grew." Davey's eyes are locked on Caleb now and though Tawana keeps her chin down, she peeks aside at him, though Caleb cannot tell if either resents or appreciates what he is saying. Sidney encourages him with a slight bob of the head. "Moses was an oppressor of God's people until He called the man to lead the Jews to freedom."

"That didn't end well for Moses, though, did it?" the guitarist finally says. "Didn't end well for either of them."

"Well, you haven't broken anything of His yet." When Tawana doesn't smile, he hurries on. "I don't know what God wants of you. Only you can come to that but, well, if you want to know, maybe you should ask Him."

P C Burhenne

Tawana goes back to her dish. Davey points for Caleb to sit back down. Sidney stretches his mouth into a "yikes" expression and joins him. As Caleb re-applies the ice, Annaliese berates him: What a hypocrite—You, the apostate, tell her to pray for God's will. Once her dish is in the oven, however, Tawana retrieves the bandage, tape and salve from the bathroom, comes to Caleb's side.

"No, no, you don't have to. I'll do it."

The guitarist pushes him back into the seat when Caleb tries to escape. Sidney teases him to "Do as you're told, roomie," as Tawana takes the ice bag away to the sink. Returning with a paper towel, she has him swivel about more towards her. Covering a hand with the sheet, she cups his injury to dry the area.

"I know you only want to help."

Her touch sends a charge down to his groin that each brush of her hip and thigh against his arm only exacerbates. Sure his arousal is showing, Caleb dare not look at his roommate so he stares straight ahead and distracts himself by focusing on how far he has traveled, not just in the past few days but from his jumping off point in Maynardsville. He has crossed a vast wilderness to an exotic locale that would baffle the folk back in Kentucky.

It would scandalize them.

"Did I hurt you?" Tawana asks pulling back her fingertip with the antiseptic ointment.

"No. I just, a thought surprised me."

He nods for her to continue and imagines his mother's shock at how easily he surrenders to the home of these colored people. Hears an appalled Alfred Sr. demand, "You let these blacks (a label spit at Caleb) tell you what to do?" The community he left behind would condemn him for the taboo he is breaking. They would wink and smile if he screwed Tawana, the men anyway, but not for embracing her. Not long ago he would have agreed, with the notion of keeping separate anyway. Yet just now he had to remind himself of those barriers. Tawana has become a perplexing and magnetic figure, rather than a black street hustler of God. Davey is now an irascible but deep-down generous sculptor rather than an angry menacing black artist. Of course they haven't changed at all.

THE PROPHET OF CENTRAL PARK

Tawana is tamping down the adhesive with a pianist's touch. Kindliness tics at her mouth and once again Caleb fancies that she somehow glimpses the epiphany just visited upon him.

* * *

US News Today

A recent poll revealed a surprising level of dissonance among Americans. Asked if they would support a candidate for office who held their political positions but had a history of profiting from human trafficking, 86% responded, no. In the same survey, 79% voiced support for George Washington if he ran for President today.

Though tangier than his mother's, the meat loaf is every bit as good. Caleb tastes a cumin accent and perhaps a note of lime. When he asks about the seasonings, Tawana shakes her head. "Family recipe. You should have offered to help." Davey puts his fork down, he laughs so hard, a chain of guffaws that Caleb thinks must hurt the man's throat. After the meal, Caleb and Sidney clean up, even giving the floor a quick sweep. Davey has a record player, plays what turns out to be classical music. Sidney snaps his fingers, "Tchaikovsky!" and the sculptor snaps his back. "There's hope for you yet, Mr. Hipster." The guitarist makes a pot of tea then asks if Davey has any prospects for a show. The sculptor is describing a disastrous opening in Newport, Rhode Island where a drunken guest stumbled into one of his pieces when Sidney checks his vibrating phone.

"Gotta take this."

The roommate steps away and Davey resumes narrating how the abstract tentacled sunburst broke into several pieces on the concrete floor. Until Sidney's rising voice overrides the sculptor's.

"No, Dad, that doesn't mean I have to come home!"

The roommate has his back to them, is pressing a palm into his forehead. "No, Dad, it doesn't mean it's time . . . No, Dad, I'm not doing that . . . Look, thank you for calling me about this. I'm gonna go and see for myself." Sidney pockets the cell as if that is the only way to truly silence it. When he finally does step around, he looks at Caleb. "You're on TV. One of the right wing talking heads is breaking news about you." An

P C Burhenne

uncharacteristic detachment constrains the roommate so that Caleb can almost believe it an inquisitor's stare. "Something about you and a girl you got pregnant?"

He tells the sculptor, "Turn on the TV."

Davey stands still. "Are you sure?"

"I need to hear this."

The sculptor stops the music. When the television mounted above the turntable comes on, he brings up the proper channel. Caleb's senior year photo is superimposed above the commentator in the upper right corner. A legend at the bottom of the screen reads, "Abortion rights extremist deserted mother of his unborn child." Pointing at the defaming text, he tells the room, "How can they put that up. That's not true." But at once Annaliese argues: Then what do you call what you did to me when I begged you for help? Caleb starts gulping fish-out-of-water style.

The commentator states, "As I have said, we cannot definitively confirm that Caleb Ellison was the father of Annaliese Tompkins' unborn child but the community widely believes this to be the case."

"What? What?" Caleb swings about to the three of them. Sidney who no longer appears detached as he sidles away. Davey who watches through narrowed eyes and with a cat's tenseness and Tawana who has her arms up like guardrails to calm and contain him. "'The community' was too busy calling me a queer behind my back to think I had gotten a girl in trouble."

"For her part," the commentator continues, a tremor beginning to affect his words. "Annaliese would not reveal the identity of this man. Members of her family have told us they think she was frightened of this person. Did this ultimate deadbeat dad threaten her? Did Caleb Ellison threaten her?"

"That's just made up!" Caleb answers. "That's not what happened at all."

The apartment has fallen away and all he sees is the TV sneak's indignant scowl flexing and pursing. "Certainly when the expectant mother's condition became dire, Caleb Ellison was nowhere to be found. When this young woman was in the hospital, on her death bed, struggling with her final gasping breath to deliver their child, this," and with a sneer the man says, "I'm forced to say 'nameless individual' could not be bothered to support her during the tragic conclusion--"

THE PROPHET OF CENTRAL PARK

The screen goes blank and Tawana steps in front of it to take his face in her hands. "Caleb," she intones like a lullaby's opening.

"That bastard, that f . . . bastard. He twisted everything. Made me a monster and her family the victims. They're the ones. They're the ones what killed her."

A flute glides into the apartment, sailing above them, calling the rest of Tchaikovsky's composition to follow. Tawana still cradles his chin and jaw. "Caleb, please, don't stay with that man. Be here with us." Her dark eyes hold him. Her touch begins to drive off the distress that possesses him. "Be here with people who care about you."

"That's not what happened at all," he pleads for her to believe. "It was terrible but not like that."

"I know." She releases him to first touch her heart, then his. "I know you," then even as Annaliese tells him meanly, She's wrong, isn't she?, Tawana speaks more forcibly, as if trying to speak over the voice in his head. "But, Caleb, for your own sanity, you have to let go of this awful thing you've been holding on to. Speak it out loud. I'm not suggesting it has to be me. But find someone. Someone you trust."

His muscles tremble but from the intensity of the previous moment. He is calm again. "I trust you."

Tawana accepts this without a smile. "Should we go somewhere private?"

He pans to the other two in the room. Caught staring at the intimate exchange, Sidney looks away. Davey opens his mouth but the thought will not be spoken so he catches his broad nose with a thumb and forefinger and waits.

"No. They've heard the slander. I want them to hear from me."

Tawana motions for everyone to take their seats. The voice in his head tells Caleb, Finally.

"Annaliese and I grew up going to the same church. From the start she didn't fit in. She didn't want to. I did. For a long time. When I started to have doubts, we kinda found each other. Two outsiders in a small town. Me, I was sleep walking but she had a plan. See, her parents wouldn't help her go to college. They wanted her to get married, have kids. Like mine wanted me to do too. But she was determined to live a life that she chose.

She was saving every penny to move. If she hadn't befriended me, she'd be living her dream right now."

In danger of panting, Caleb stops to steady himself. The tears in his eyes distort the apartment, Tawana as she asks, "Tell them what she was like."

He closes his eyes to find an answer. "She was a song I could remember during my day to help me keep going. To give me hope." He looks to them again. "She showed me there was a way out of Maynardsville."

A soft nudge from the guitarist. "What happened?"

"We started plotting an escape together. To Cincinnati. Pittsburgh. We talked about Cleveland." The way his pulse would speed up when Annaliese found him with more apartment listings comes back to Caleb. They pored over her research sitting in the bed of his pickup at the edge of a farmer's field. Out of earshot of any and all so that no whisper of their scheme could make its way back to either family. "The shared rent made leaving suddenly a lot more possible. We figured, a couple months at most, we'd have a place." As their escape became more and more real, the secret charged their meetings with an almost crackling tension. "But we mistook the excitement of finding each other, you know, of having an ally, we mistook that for attraction." They were by a cornfield, reviewing her latest find, a two-bedroom in the vicinity of Pittsburgh's university row. She gripped his thigh when she came to the locale, then left her hand there as she read on so that he did not hear any more. When she finished, neither of them moved, until she began caressing his leg. Side by side they leaned to each other to kiss but when she started tracing his erection with her finger, he had to pull away, grab her hand. No?, she said without accusing or belittling him. He was afraid to move, he was so close to cumming and managed to tell her so. "We just did it the once but once was enough." She pinched him, she said to pull him back, then asked if it was his first time. He got out a muddled, Uh-huh. Her mouth was a soft, vibrant probing pressure against his own. Her eyes up close full of questions he didn't understand. She said how the corrugated metal was uncomfortable so they walked into the field which should have been the frustrating end of the encounter. Close to harvest, the plants were fully grown with unforgivingly rigid stalks and leaves that scoured the skin like giant dry cats' tongues.

THE PROPHET OF CENTRAL PARK

However the narrow lane they hurried along opened into a few feet of ground where the seed hadn't taken and the weather had leveled the furrowed ground. Annaliese was stepping out of her pants as she entered the bare spot. "We both knew as soon as we were done that sex wasn't the thing between us," Caleb says and cringes recalling how obviously ill-advised their hook-up was. A minute maybe of ungainly haste, a couple unsuccessful jabs until she guided him into her while he grew frantic that it wouldn't be in time. Which was nearly the case. A release that left him winded and hollow and Annaliese silent. He raised himself off her and when the last of his semen dripped onto his leg, he swiped the goo into the dirt as if that would get rid of the shame spreading through him. Annaliese sat up, at once pulled on her panties, saying, well, that was a mistake. He murmured to his knees bent beneath him, Sorry. She kicked him then with the one foot not yet through its pant leg and told him, He didn't do anything wrong. She chuckled in continuing that he didn't do anything right either but it didn't matter because sleeping together wasn't them. Then she knelt too facing Caleb so he had to see her say, But how could they know if they didn't try first? Now they knew, then hopping up she said, Get dressed— They had an apartment to find.

Caleb realizes he has drifted away, that Tawana and the others are waiting for him to return. Night holds outside the window and a chorus of wind instruments from the speakers suggests a merry crowd hiding in the room. Without judgment the guitarist says, "She got pregnant," then leans forward with a tissue to wipe tears away from his dressing.

"Thank you." He takes the tissue. "Yeah, she got pregnant. Everything was fine for a few weeks. We went back to being partners in our great escape. Then Annaliese started ghosting me. I had a bad feeling. The sex happened so out of the bl—well, no. I could feel the . . . whatever building between us. I should have been prepared but I didn't wear a condom so I had a feeling what was keeping her away. Then when she finally did ask to meet, she made it at the same field where we, you know, so I was ready. I was scared stupid and, looking back, pretty darned depressed but I told her I'd do the right thing." Her reaction was a grimace like she had stepped in a cow pie, then she pushed him away, another shock. She had never been angry at him before, mad as heck as she demanded what good would that do either of them. "Turns out, that was the last thing she wanted. She was asking me to go with her to Maryland to get an abortion."

Caleb cannot stop his jaw quivering, and drawing breath raises an ache behind his Adam's apple. "But I didn't, I didn't help her. When she needed me the most, I didn't help her." It haunts him to this day, will do until his final moment, how the fierceness in her dissolved like a finger painting in the rain when he said they shouldn't kill their baby. That he wouldn't. And the more he pressed her to let him help as he wanted to help her, the more she stared at him as a traitor. Until he had broken everything that had grown between them. "I had turned my back on the church, I thought I had, but all those years of 'Thou shalt not's' were still here. I ruined everything, our friendship, her chance to get away. She told me that I no longer had a part in the decision. She'd take care of it herself and she made me promise not to say anything." And in his mind Caleb hears the rest of her renunciation when he argued that he didn't think he could stand by. With a glare that made her a hardnosed woman unknown to him, she swore that if he tried to interfere, not only would she deny he was the father, she would tell people he couldn't be since he didn't sleep with girls. "After that she was quit of me. Didn't answer my calls, looked right through me when I tried to see her. She only ever spoke to me the two other times."

The tissue is mush in his hands so he drops it on the coffee table. His roommate fetches him a paper towel. Caleb struggles not to sob.

"A couple weeks later, though, she did call me to make sure I'd keep my mouth shut. She'd been crying. Her mom found out. Annaliese had written down the date and address for the appointment and her mother came across it. Anyway when she couldn't talk Annaliese out of it any other way, her mother said she'd have Annaliese arrested when she came back. God, that gut-punched me. I'd put myself in the same camp as her. Anyway Annaliese told them—the father was at her too—if she had to carry the thing, she'd never hold it and neither would they. The adoption people would take it and she'd never speak to either of them again. That's when the parents started asking what I wanted, trying to get her to admit I was the father. She told them it was a one-night stand with a visitor gone she didn't know where." Caleb remembers how the bitterness hissing like steam through her rushed explanation made clear he was now another person that she needed to free herself from. She said she didn't care if everyone called her the town slut, she'd be shot of the place in the end, but if the god-fearing people of the church knew he was responsible, they'd be on a mission to see Caleb and her married. Nonstop visits from the reverend, prayer groups, concerned mothers, all to save their souls. Annaliese half demanded, half begged him not to put her through that extra ordeal. He promised, again because of what they had been. "She was right to call me too. An hour later Mr. Tompkins found me at my father's auction house."

"Speeding into the parking lot? Skidding to a stop?" Sidney clarifying disrupts the room like a car backfiring so that they all turn to the roommate. He throws up his hands. "Sorry, sorry. I just mean, how angry was he?"

"Annaliese's father was a deliberate man. Never saw him blow up. He was upset. Got in my face. Tell him honest, was I responsible. And my father came over to see what Mr. Tompkins wanted, so my father started asking too. And I did what Annaliese asked. I lied. The baby wasn't mine. She hadn't told me whose it was. I lied. And every time I did, I felt like Peter denying Jesus."

Bile rises in Caleb's throat. Tawana goes to the sink for a glass of water. As they wait, Davey watches with an interest that seems clinical. Caleb guesses that elements of this scene will appear in the sculptor's future work but Caleb feels too fragile to object. He thanks Tawana for the drink.

"I'm not sure how much Mr. Tompkins believed me. My father was convinced." Caleb doesn't share the childhood terror that gripped him when Alfred Sr. made Caleb clasp the office Bible to his chest and swear he took no part in Annaliese's troubles. In his head Caleb asked God to please understand before he bore the false witness. "A lot of the town didn't believe me. That was a bad time. It had to be horrible for Annaliese. People used to think we were weird but we had each other. Now they were whispering that I was a sleazebag and Annaliese was a whore and we were both alone. I got into a fight over it. Two smart mouths I grew up with talking about her so I could hear." Specifically the bigger one who said through a smirk they should go see if she was still putting out since she couldn't get any more knocked up. Caleb was leaving the convenience store with a candy bar. His taunter didn't see that something snapped in Caleb. He had just read that a punch in the center of the chest could take a person's breath away. Which it did for a moment. The big boy's friend hit back for him. No one tried to stop them. Caleb had no friends and the pair were a-holes. They swung themselves out, stood panting at each other then walked away. When his father saw the aftermath, he sniffed once and told Caleb to clean himself up as if the swollen eye and split lips were justified. "Still things should have turned out okay. I mean Annaliese was a prisoner which was . . . I don't understand how her parents could do that to her but, but they did worse."

Caleb pauses to steady himself and his nose whistles because of the snot running there.

"She called me, frantic. She'd just gone to see the doctor. The embryo hadn't gotten down to the uterus. It had gotten stuck."

"In the fallopian tube," the guitarist says for him. "An ectopic pregnancy."

"Yeah, yeah, that's what it was. And the doctor told her that the fetus wouldn't survive and that it should be removed as soon as possible, it was a matter of life and death. But the doctor said she couldn't do the procedure. Because of the laws that had been passed. Then when Annaliese told her parents, they . . . they refused to help get her to a state that would save her." Caleb hears his rising voice and feels anger cording the muscles in his throat and closes his eyes against Annaliese's plaintive appeals reverberating in his head as if she is shouting them through a megaphone, crying, for Godsake, please help her. Her mother had lost it. Was ranting that Annaliese's "situation" was a test, a chance to redeem her soul after her sin of fornication. His friend repeating, He was her only hope. "So I raced there. I didn't care anymore about the 'Thou shalt not's' that had been drummed into me. All that mattered was rescuing Annaliese. But I couldn't. I'd had a chance to save her but it was gone."

The regret is a vengeful beast in his chest. Caleb bares his teeth against its punishment and lets loose a whine that is so high-pitched, it is nearly silent. He has his fists jammed against his eyes. Tawana pulls these down to his lap. With a patience that draws him back within the caring circle in the room, she tells him, "You should finish. If you can. Let this last horrible part go."

He nods and wipes the wetness from his face but he cannot stanch the tears.

"So I'm at her house and the parents won't let me in. Mostly the mother. And I'm pleading with them, with the father really because he looked shaken. He wanted to be convinced. I said let me take Annaliese. They could say I'd kidnapped her. The police could arrest me when I brought her back but his daughter would be alive. And the mother was hanging on the father's arm now, telling him they were protecting their daughter's life eternal. Then Annaliese came out from her room. I wondered why she hadn't come as soon as she heard my voice." The scene from the porch of the Tompkins' ranch is as clear to Caleb as Davey's apartment. Mr. Tompkins looked every bit the insurance salesman he was as, behind his glasses, he calculated the benefits of Caleb's proposal. Missus was an upset matron in her yellow floral frock, desperately chattering out her church babble. In the next moment they both swung about at their daughter's squeal of pain and past them Caleb saw Annaliese pitched forward, clutching her stomach, her face pinched in agony.

"I was too late. That thing, her tube, it tore while me and her parents were arguing. There was no time to take her any place that would help her. The local hospital said the same thing that her baby doctor said a few hours earlier—they couldn't take the chance of operating. No one would look at me except the nurse who said Annaliese wanted to see me. The parents got mad, said they were the family, but Annaliese had already said not to let them in the room." Then in a wail he says, "Lord, God, I don't want to remember her like that," and he rocks on his seat at the image he doesn't want. Annaliese's bloodless face, her blanched arms jutting out from the gown and the white sheet covering her body stained by the irregular red teardrop below her groin. The air heavy with the iron tang of congealing blood. The nurse warned him Annaliese might not speak sense; they had her on a morphine drip—the extent of their help. When he entered, her head wavered on the pillow, then she let out a soft gasp in abandoning that effort. Her dazed stare left him dumb for several seconds until at last he told her, Please don't go. Her first attempt to answer did not make it past the workings of her lips. When he leaned down, her breath smelled of bitter reflux along with the sour stink of a dry mouth. This time she managed to say that she could feel the tear growing inside her. When he straightened she was gone. Her body suddenly seemed as if it had shrunk.

"I watched her die."

P C Burhenne

Caleb weeps. The three let him be until finally he blows his nose and realizes that the makeshift handkerchief will absorb no more. He discards it in the kitchen and returns with a replacement.

"And as awful as that was, it wasn't the worst part. That happened a few days later when the preacher came to our house. To comfort me. Which meant trying to convince me to pray with him that God forgive Annaliese and we, the ones left behind, find the strength to accept His will. As if people like the preacher, and my parents, and the Tompkins, and me, people like me, as if we didn't have everything to do with her dying. And I said none of that. It was booming in my head and I just sat at our kitchen table staring at him." That was the first time Annaliese pushed her way into his thoughts. He remembers how her voice on that internal PA system seemed appropriate and though she could not taunt him into completely abandoning the deference of his upbringing, because of her he did not parrot the slogans of her murderers. The preacher genuinely wanted to help, grew agitated when Caleb would not accept the solace that faith offered. His mother urged him to join in seeking the Lord's grace in that dark hour and Alfred Sr. told him that only by bowing to God's plan could he find peace. Caleb closed his eyes and with as much conviction as he could muster, asked God to forgive their sins, naming each person in the room, himself included. A proper prayer, but not the one they wanted. The preacher exhorted Caleb to let go of his anger or it would surely keep him apart from the Almighty's chosen people. Caleb said he would try and thanked the man for coming. "I was a coward."

The record has finished. Caleb's windy sobs fill the room. Tawana pulls him to the couch. Within her embrace he feels anguish and remorse that calcified after Annaliese's death break loose. These erupt in spasms that wrack his upper body, but each one leaves behind a cleansed space inside and he surrenders until he is emptied, and he worries that the emotional vomiting might have hurt the guitarist. When he pulls back, Tawana grips him by the shoulders to peer at the aftermath. Hers a healer's face assessing the state of her patient. Sidney gives him a smile that falters but perseveres. After a once-over look that reassures the man, Davey gets up for the turntable.

"There are no easy decisions about abortion," Tawana tells him. "At least there shouldn't be. They are a burden of thorns that everyone involved

THE PROPHET OF CENTRAL PARK

wears afterward. Thing is, God doesn't want us to carry it alone. He will respect our choices to do so but it's not what he wants. I know very little about the Divine, but of that I am sure."

"I think you need a little 'Clair de Lune', young man," Davey says as he starts a new disc.

As the speakers whisper the opening notes from a gently-plied piano, Tawana takes a deep breath that becomes a yawn. "Well, that's me for the night," then, "Caleb, can I have a moment?"

He follows her into the hall.

"Speaking that story aloud couldn't have been easy. I hope you got some relief." He wants to tell her he has but Tawana goes on. "If you really want to be at peace, though, it's only a first step. You're going to have to deal with a lot of issues that you don't even know are affecting you right now. You'll need to talk to a professional."

"Can't you help me?"

"Of course I'll help you." She squeezes his hand. "But I don't know the right questions to ask. You need a trained therapist for that." Caleb wants to withdraw further but she keeps her hold. "I know the idea of baring your soul to a stranger is scary. It was for me too. But it made all the difference to who I am today. Please think about it."

With that she leaves. Inside the apartment Sidney and Davey have moved to the table. The sculptor is shuffling a deck of cards. Caleb can't imagine concentrating on a game.

"We saved you a seat," Davey says without turning around.

"Too tired. I'm gonna call it a night too."

Far from upset, Sidney leans forward. "Just you and me, Mr. Stonemason."

In the guest room, his uncle's book reminds him to call Mr. Yamaguchi. Now that he has finished reading the memoir, he worries he'll lose it like he almost did today. The call is ringing before he considers that maybe Mr Yamaguchi is an earty-to-bed type also.

"Caleb, are you all right?" The greeting comes in a rush.

"I'm fine. I hope this isn't too late."

A surprising tinkling of amused "Te-he-he"s returns to him, then, "I'm not that old, son"

"The reason I called, I read the book you lent me. Really enjoyed it but I need to get it back to you."

"There's no rush on that, but actually I was about to call you." Then in a voice suitable for church, he asks, "Did you see the segment earlier?"

Caleb wants to shout his answer, instead worries the anger and dread in his hushed words make him sound guilty. "That's not what happened. He made up stuff. Ignored so much."

"I thought as much. You need to come over tomorrow, as early as possible, to meet with Mr. Strauss. He can be here in the morning, first thing."

"Why? It has nothing to do with my case."

"That segment is already the "breaking news" on my phone. Your case has become so much more that a courtroom affair. You have to tell your side. I've hired Elliot to represent your interest and he knows how to combat a smear campaign. Can you come?"

Caleb peers about his hideaway. "Yes."

They agree on nine.

Outside the door Sidney announces, "Gin," with a gleeful chortle. Davey exclaims, "Sonofabitch. I'd swear the cards are marked if they weren't mine." Caleb turns out the light and crawls into bed, marveling at how crowded his world has become over the course of a week, with unlikely enemies and allies both. The promise of Isaiah returns to him, "So do not fear, for I am with you! Do not be dismayed, for I am your God. I will strengthen you and help you; I will uphold you with my righteous right hand." Alfred Sr. didn't recite the verse, addressed as it was to the tribes of Israel, but the pledge always brought Caleb hope before. Now given the absurd obstacle course of events through which he has pinballed, Caleb can accept the presence of the Lord sustaining him. But why? He has been a wayward servant these past months. Not observing the Sabbath. In no way seeking God's will. Yet that Purpose seems to have found him. Caleb knows that the outlandish ways in which he has been delivered from harm should give him faith but the gathering storm grows darker and more dangerous each time he stops to look about himself. He goes to sleep, murmuring, "God, please, I am such a weak man."

Wednesday

USA Today

Arkansas's attorney general is reportedly refusing to cooperate with New York's investigation of the Rainbow Rights Railroad incident that occurred last week at Rockefeller Center. According to an official close to the situation who spoke on condition of anonymity, the AG's office in Little Rock rebuffed requests by Manhattan's district attorney's office to question two individuals believed to be involved in the near riot. The source went on to say that the state's head law enforcement officer felt compelled to protect the rights of his constituents against the unfair focus that he believes police are directing upon them.

In the second morning in the new room, the fuzzy sensation in his face has receded. His fingers hovering over the injury confirm that the cheek is regaining its normal shape. When he turns on the light, out of habit he looks for his work station, remembers too late that it waits a few miles away. He washes out of the bathroom sink and in the dark kitchen steps with the exaggerated care of a cartoon burglar but the hiss from the kettle rouses Sidney from the sofa and light appears beneath Davey's door as Caleb pours hot water over the coffee grounds. When Tawana knocks, the sculptor has a cup ready for her. The other three have a breakfast of toast. Soon the guitarist and the roommate are off and in a not so subtle hint, Davey asks, "So where are you going now," as he puts away the cleaned dishes.

"I have to head into the city later but I was hoping I could watch you work for a little bit, or, or does that sound too weird?" The sculptor is peering at him through a squint and scowl that implies it is. He hurries on, "I miss my wood pieces."

Davey tisks, bobs his head in a vague "okay" and flutters his great paddle of hands to hie Caleb out the door.

He sits on a high stool, his back touching the opaque drapes, stifling the questions raised by Davey's efforts to extract the hawk from its stone captivity. Uneasy with the silence, however, the sculptor soon begins a gruff narration of his steps and choices. Caleb moves his perch closer and by the time he leaves, he is handing Davey the proper next tool. Without looking up, the sculptor tells him, "You're welcome to come back tonight if you need to. Your dopey roommate too."

The day is cool like yesterday. The clouds are a thin tufted sheet hanging from the sky. A panel truck with produce painted on its side rumbles up the street. On the sidewalk opposite, a pair of men wearing similar dark blue windbreakers shake hands and go their separate ways. On the subway people staring at their phones remind Caleb that he has made the news feed. For the whole ride he pretends to read his uncle's book on his lap behind his shades and floppy-brimmed hat.

The impatient Manhattan crowds calm him. He walks up Fifth Avenue on the Park side, taking out his old phone to check and delete messages. Among the usual vile threats is a text from Rolando: "Call me." When he texts back, "Now okay?", his phone rings a moment later.

"Thought you should know, some guy stopped me after work yesterday asking for you," his friend tells him. "Said he was a friend of yours. Sounded like he came from your part of 'Friday Night Lights' America too."

The breeze suddenly gets colder and Caleb swivels left and right for who might be after him. "Did this guy look like me? How old was he?"

"Nah, no way he was family, C. He was clean cut like you though. Not sure how old. Maybe thirty?"

"Listen, text me if you see him again, and if you can, get a picture."

For the first time worry rushes his friend. "Jesus, C, are you in trouble? I mean, more trouble?"

"I don't know, man. I don't know. Weird things are swirling around me, Rolando."

His friend's voice drops almost to a whisper. "I heard about them running you down on air last night."

With his free hand, Caleb rubs at his face. "Ah, I can't talk about that right now."

"Hey, C," this spoken with a force to hold Caleb's attention. "I'm with you. Nothing they can say will change that, man."

Caleb manages to get out, "God sent you to me, Rolando. Thanks."

* * *

THE PROPHET OF CENTRAL PARK

BBC America

Management's stranglehold on the American factory floor seems to be slipping, especially in the South where unions have had a particularly hard time organizing over the last several decades. During this last election cycle, a surprising number of Democratic candidates won with platforms championing workers' rights. As legislators they are now proposing bills in multiple states to revoke "Right to work" statutes and otherwise strengthen the ability of employees to bargain collectively. These developments reflect a growing support for unions in both the blue and white collar segments of the work force. Experts cite a growing awareness of the shrinking middle class in the country for the change, along with several well-publicized stories of workplace injuries or illnesses caused by a disregard for employees' safety by corporate ownership.

No one follows him, as far as he can tell. He has composed himself by the time he rings Mr. Yamaguchi's doorbell. Haruto's, he reminds himself. The man has on an apron when he opens the door. He cants his head to the right to study Caleb's face. "You're healing. Good. Come on in."

The interior is familiar on this second walk through and Caleb sees more of it. A painting stands out on the far wall of the parlor. An exceptional Hudson River School landscape boasting a crimson and orange burst of sunset and a mountain lake in the foreground that deftly mirrors the display.

"Is that an SG Robinson in the front room?"

His host shoots back an impressed smile. "You are your uncle's nephew."

The dining room table is set for three but Haruto leads them to the kitchen. "Please keep me company while I finish. Elliot, Mr. Strauss called. He's running ten minutes late." Caleb sits in his seat of two days ago. He puts down the book. Bacon sizzles in a pan on the stove.

"I enjoyed reading this. Thank you."

"William would be pleased. He derived great satisfaction writing it." Haruto cracks an egg and gently empties the yolk and whites into a shallow dish. "Learn anything?"

"A lot of stuff, but mostly that I got cheated out of a really great uncle."

The chef pauses from opening another egg. "Yes, you did," he agrees in a choked-off sort of way.

Fearing he upset Haruto, Caleb hurries on. "Of course, Ms. Yuan told me the most incredible thing. We had lunch together yesterday. About his legendary purchase of the Christian Tollier estate. I could barely credit it, the lick was so, well, mythic."

"'Lick'?" Haruto says, pausing his deposit of the eggs into the hot water.

"Oh. 'Hit a lick'. People don't say that around here. Means to make a really big score, a really good buy."

"Ah." The chef hesitates to go on after that single remark. He starts a timer, depresses English muffins waiting in the toaster, turns off the burner under the bacon. The indecision lasts until he pours a cup of ingredients into a blender, then he contorts his lips into a bud that blossoms into a smile. "Yes, that is a notorious story in an insular world and hardly any of it is true. William was pleased the fiction held but since you seem to care about the facts of his life, I'm sure he would want you to have the truth. One moment."

The hum of the machine takes over, leaving Caleb open-mouthed. Haruto is deliberate in introducing melted butter into the agitating sauce. Thirty odd seconds that seem forever.

"That entire sale was a piece of theater orchestrated by William and Christian. Even the attorney who served as executor didn't know he was playing a part."

"Wait, are you saying that that whole sale wasn't really a legal proceeding?"

"Oh, no. It was a legal court-sanctioned auction. That was the point. It was binding on the heirs. You see, Christian was the love of William's life, and visa-versa, as William told it." Haruto has poured the Hollandaise into a gravy boat. This he transfers to the oven. "Don't want the sauce to congeal."

"But I thought you and my uncle were . . . ."

"I loved William and we were committed to each other but I always knew there would only be the one great passion for him." The toaster expels the muffin halves. Haruto examines, approves and places these on plates. With a fork he covers each with a portion of bacon. "They met through William's shop. Tollier was new to the field of Asian arts. His family was more traditional in their collecting tastes. They were more traditional in every way. And William had only recently struck out on his own after working, well, what had been a decade-long apprenticeship under his mentor." The chef removes a perforated ladle from a drawer, checks the timer. "Almost."

"His mentor, that was that woman Lisa Comey? She seemed fascinating."

"By all accounts." Haruto taps his chest with the slotted spoon. "I never met her. She had moved to the Far East by the time I became involved in the business but people have told me she was a very striking woman. Very imposing."

"They had a falling out, my uncle and her? He doesn't give a reason in the book though."

Haruto grimaces. "I know he regretted their fractured relationship but he never spoke of why." The timer dings and he scoops the poached eggs onto paper towels laid upon the granite counter. "Anyway, William and Christian became lovers but neither was 'out'. It was the eighties. Very few men admitted they were gay. But as much as the closet allowed, they were together," the chef says as he blots the tops of the entrees with another towel.

"Christian got sick," Caleb says for him.

"Yes. A very aggressive form of bone cancer. Again, the eighties. The diagnosis was a death sentence. William was devastated. He put his life on hold to spend that last year with his soulmate. Which at first Christian very much didn't want William to do. He worried it would cripple William financially. Pardon me," and Haruto concentrates on transferring the eggs onto the English muffins without rupturing them. Removing the gravy boat, he coats the dishes with the sauce, garnishes each with a sprig of parsley and shuts the plates themselves back in the stove. "Hope Elliot isn't too late."

Caleb prompts Haruto with, "So Christian is worried for my uncle."

"Oh yes," and the host takes a seat across from Caleb. "Christian knew any bequest he made would end up being a problem for William. As I said, the Tollier family was, and probably is still, very traditional, which translates to very conservative. They couldn't stop Christian being with his gay lover but they would certainly challenge any gift made to such a person in

Christian's will, even a small one in recognition of the care William provided in Christian's last days. So Christian conceived of his grand plan to have his possessions go to the person he loved and at the same time get his own back from the people who never accepted him. Over that last year they moved the vast majority of Christian's collection, and certainly its most important examples, to museums around the country, on loans governed by agreements that Christian had drawn up himself. Also he pledged sizable gifts to various charities that would be obligations against the estate. Some of the causes surely upset the family—Gay Men's Defense and Support Funds, AIDS research, shelters for battered women, PETA—but that was a bonus. William said he was a good man who wanted to help.

"Anyway the net result of William's prearranged and apparently exorbitant bid was just enough funds to satisfy those obligations with only a few odd dollars left over for the heirs. Because the family had no interest in Asian artifacts, they never questioned the value of what had been sold. They simply wrote their relative off as a wastrel and a homo. So said William. And in order not to draw attention to what he actually purchased, William retrieved the loans from the museums over the course of several years. Of course, that didn't work out as well. People in the trade put two and two together when so many spectacular pieces with their names in the histories kept hitting the market. Still they never guessed the whole truth." Haruto rubs his hands together. "I'm so glad I finally got to tell that story," then he wags his finger at Caleb, fixes him with a suddenly serious stare. "Not a whisper of this to anyone. Right?"

"No, no. William deserves his secret."

"Right then," and the man jumps up from his chair. "I'm having a coffee. How about you?"

"Yes, please." Caleb pans about Haruto's home, William's home first. As well-appointed a New York townhouse as Caleb has set foot in. "So all of this, and everything you inherited, it came from their . . . time together?"

"Mm, yes and no." Haruto stirs sugar into his drink. "His relationship with Christian established William's fortune, yes, but I did not inherit it. William made sure I'm taken care of as executor of his estate but the money passed into a trust which I oversee." The buzzer sounds from the front hall. "Finally we can eat," and as Haruto leaves to answer this, he says, "Do you mind bringing those plates out?"

THE PROPHET OF CENTRAL PARK

Caleb is transferring breakfast to the dining room when the attorney enters. He also inspects Caleb's bandaged face, commits only to "Better." Once they are seated, they both compliment Haruto on the wonderful breakfast. The attorney dines on small bites that he raises in a slow smooth motion over his tailored suit. The practiced care constrains Caleb's usual attack when the food is as delicious as the eggs Benedict. Afterwards Mr. Strauss says, "So I reviewed the account that aired last night. Now I need your side of the story." Annaliese whispers, Twice in two days, but otherwise does not torment him. When he finishes, Mr. Strauss places a small notebook beside his plate and reaches inside his jacket lapel for a pen. Caleb recognizes it as a Cross.

"You never made any admission that you were responsible for this Annaliese's pregnancy? Please, think carefully."

Guilt makes Caleb hesitate rather than any need to reconsider. "No. I out and out denied it." Then he remembers his twin. "My sister did tell me recently she always knew the truth. And I admitted it to her, recently. But she has never said anything. And never will."

Mr. Strauss says slowly, "Are you sure?"

"Absolutely."

"And as far as you know, Annaliese never named you?"

"Definitely not."

The attorney writes a note with an unhurried hand. Until "Do you know where she made the appointment for an abortion?"

"Somewhere in Maryland."

"Do you know the clinic?"

Again remorse makes him loath to admit, "I wasn't part of the planning."

The attorney enters another line. Before, "Would Annaliese have confided in anybody else?"

Caleb feels his eyes grow moist. "No. She only had me."

"Do you think any of her family would confirm the appointment? The coercion?"

Caleb lets out a hate-laced chuckle. "Certainly not the mother. I don't know about her two brothers. They were out of the house by then." He remembers the fear and indecision that swiveled Mr. Tompkins's head about as Caleb begged for Annaliese's life and Mrs. Tompkins, her soul. "Maybe the father. Probably not but maybe."

Again a pause for recordkeeping. "Do you remember the name of the nurse whom Annaliese told not to let her parents into the hospital room?"

"No. Sorry."

"Describe her," and after entering the details of the woman that Caleb recalls, he says, "Anything else you think might be important?"

Caleb shakes his head, then makes himself ask, "What good is any of this, though? It's all true, but how does it have anything to do with last Friday."

"It's the court of public opinion," Haruto interjects. "You're being tried there too and you need to defend yourself."

"But so what," Caleb says in a controlled manner to make clear he is in no way mocking his benefactor. "So people say nasty things about me. I'll ignore them. You're already spending a small fortune to keep me out of jail, Haruto. You shouldn't have to pay for my PR."

A pained frown takes over Haruto's expression. "What's going on feels more organized than just the gossip mill churning."

"I have to agree with Haruto," Mr. Strauss says with a matter-of-fact conviction that alarms more than the other's concern. "A strange dynamic seems to be driving the prosecutor's interest in your case. Mr. Kunis, the ADA you met, is looking for work in the private sector. Rightfully so, but his misconduct along with the total lack of any evidence of wrongdoing on your part should have the DA running. Yet he hasn't closed the book on the matter. We need to take this smear campaign seriously."

Both men are staring at Caleb to see that he is on board. "Okay."

"Good," the attorney says. "I have a contact at the New York Times who will help with this. You're a huge story. She'll welcome the heads up and she's thorough. Which, from what you've said, can only help us too." Then Mr. Strauss again holds Caleb's gaze. "That is, if you've not held anything back that might put you in a bad light?"

"No."

"Excellent," and he taps the notebook before pocketing it. "I'll get this to her this afternoon. So, is any of that wonderful coffee left in the carafe?"

The meal concludes within the half hour. When Caleb offers to help clean up, Haruto says, "Elliot's taking you downtown so don't keep him waiting. It'll cost me too much." The older man draws Caleb in with surprising strength. Caleb overcomes his unease to return the hug. The attorney's town car waits double parked on the street. As soon as they buckle up, the attorney asks, "Where do you live in Queens?"

"You can drop me at Fifty-Ninth."

"We're driving you home. We need to talk alone." Mr. Strauss employs the same professional detachment as before. "Haruto can get overwrought, and this is not the time."

The alarm sounds again for Caleb as he says, "People are putting me up," and he gives the address.

"The pressure on the DA to proceed is coming from the US Attorney," Mr. Strauss explains. "The feds can't act against you themselves. For the very good reason that you've broken no federal statutes. And because if they do get involved, they would have to go after those two thugs from Arkansas." The man smacks his lips. "You were close when you said 'Alabama'."

"Well, why don't they, especially if they know who those freakin' troublemakers are." Caleb hears the shrillness carrying his words. He collects himself. "Why are they picking on me, sir."

The attorney holds up a hand for a moment as if to ready himself to admit what he would rather not. "The Justice Department is at war with itself. People I know tell me an ultra conservative faction has embedded itself there, and in the FBI too. The types who would have been right at home framing Black Panthers in the sixties. The Attorney General hoped a quick misdemeanor plea from you would keep the episode at Rockefeller Center from igniting tempers in the ranks. He didn't count on you having friends. Now he doesn't know what to do but he, and the US Attorney, keep hoping a guilty plea from you for anything—trespassing, littering—will turn down the heat. That's why we can't ignore the possibility that last night is part of a campaign to turn public opinion against you."

"Turn it against me?" Caleb exclaims and he fishes the old phone out of his pocket. "It's already against me. I can't even look at this anymore, I'm getting a hundred death threats a day."

With a chuckle Mr. Strauss turns more fully toward Caleb. "You really have been keeping your head down. There is a huge groundswell of support for your actions around the country. To millions of people, you are the poster boy for protecting the weak and those in trouble." As fast as it came, the humor drains from Mr. Strauss's face. "That's why these powerful interests are focused on you. Destroy the symbol, destroy what it stands for. And that's why you need to tell me everything. Even if it seems unimportant."

Like a fisherman's hook, this last catches hold in Caleb's thoughts. The attorney sees the idea surface. "What?" and when Caleb grimaces in trying to dismiss it, Mr. Strauss persists, lingering on each word, "Tell me what you're thinking."

"My father left me an odd message."

Caleb replays the recording for the attorney then repeats all he can think of that relates to Alfred Sr., from the drama of his flight from Kentucky to what Rolando told him just that morning and Carolyne's warning yesterday. When Caleb is done, Mr. Strauss peers forward, oblivious to the back of the front seat. "Your father knows where you live?"

"Probably. My mom had the address. But I haven't stayed at the apartment since Monday."

"Good. Don't go back there. For the time being anyway."

Caleb visualizes the next extreme he will carom toward when he outstays his welcome at the grumpy sculptor's. "You think I could crash on this back seat when my friend kicks me off his couch? It's real comfortable." The attempt at gallows humor falls flat to his ear but Caleb can't help continuing. "Or I saw an abandoned tunnel at Grand Central. No one would find me there."

Mr. Strauss stares at him. "Take a deep breath, son. If you haven't noticed, Haruto would never allow you to end up like that."

"I can't keep asking people to take care of me."

"This from the voice of experience, accept the help friends offer." Then the attorney sighs. "And this isn't just about you. You stumbled into the middle of a much bigger fight."

Mr. Strauss looks away. Out the window, the girders of the Queensboro Bridge trip by, transforming the brown roiling East River into a motion picture projected slowly enough that its still images are revealed.

"I'm grateful that you're at my side, sir. I don't think I've told you that but I am."

THE PROPHET OF CENTRAL PARK

The attorney gives out a throaty chuckle. "Caleb, you're the client lawyers hope walks through their door then dread when they sit down. Most every person I've represented this past year committed some illegal act. A few didn't realize what they'd done. Most did. My job's to mitigate the damage. But you, you saw an injustice you couldn't abide. Now it's up to me to make sure you don't get fed to the grist mill. It makes for sleepless nights." Finally he looks over again. "You still have those threatening messages?"

"I erase them but they replenish themselves right quickly."

"Well, don't erase any more. Tomorrow we're going to the DA's office to get this harassment on record. I'll call you later about when." Again the attorney's words hook a notion in Caleb. Again his demeanor betrays its rise. "Let's not go through the same dance. Out with it, young man."

"It doesn't have anything to do with my situation and it's absolutely not something that should concern Haruto."

Mr. Strauss puts his hand forward to indicate the way before them. "We still have time before we reach your . . . home away from home."

"Well, okay, I'd appreciate your opinion. As much as you can give me without charging anyway."

As best as Caleb can remember, he retells the story of Davey's friend Julius. After the first few details Mr. Strauss goes still. Only his eyes are active, shuttling from Caleb to the floor beneath Caleb's feet. They keep up the back and forth for a few seconds after Caleb finishes.

"There must be more to the case than that," Mr. Strauss says, finally fixing his gaze on Caleb as if expecting the withheld piece.

The demand leaves Caleb torn between his two rescuers. He answers, flustered and resentful both, "You think Davey lied?"

"I think . . . I don't have all the facts."

A few minutes later they are approaching the cross street for the warehouse.

"You can drop me at the corner. I'm going right and the street is one way."

The driver double parks near the intersection. Honking, the truck behind them goes around. Caleb steps out but before he can close the door, Mr. Strauss says, "I'll look into this Julius thing."

182

The statement—offer?—leaves Caleb at a loss for a second. The people on the street all walk in a hurry as if anxious to escape the gloomy day. The tradesman in another truck having to go around the town car throws Caleb a dirty look. A loud, two-fingered whistle carries from behind him.

"I didn't mean for you to go to that trouble. I just wanted your opinion."

"My opinion is, I don't have all the facts. It's just a phone call. Call it professional curiosity."

Caleb waves the attorney off. He has only just started toward the warehouse when screeching tires and more horn blasts come from that direction, but the town car is speeding away by the time he hurries back to the corner. Shrugging he again starts for the lofts. As he nears the entrance, a man crosses to his side of the street. He wears pants and a rain slick, both blue, an outfit Caleb knows he has seen recently. Before Caleb can place it, however, a figure exits the back seat of a sedan two spots away with a familiar spryness. The Smith and Wesson on his hip stands out. His father's sudden appearance stuns Caleb. Too late panicks him. "God is calling you back to Him, son," Alfred Sr. pronounces. A hand comes around from behind to clamp a cloth over Caleb's mouth and a wasp stings his butt. He struggles for a second until his arms and legs are no longer his, and he is pushed forward.

Outside of Time

A faint voice reading scripture reaches him through a dark tunnel. He doesn't move but the sound comes closer. A musty stink fills his nose, rouses a vat of nausea to bubbling inside him. The smell brings to mind a cave, dirt floor dank from scat and guano and the moisture dripped off weeping stone walls. A headache makes itself known, couples with the sickness and he feels he will vomit, but his arms and legs won't move when he tries to lean forward. He is sitting but his limbs refuse to do what he wants. The gospel speaker grows louder and a sense takes hold that he should get away, but though he struggles, he cannot move. The pain in his skull presses outward, he fears flesh and bone will not contain it. He retches forward as best he can.

Puke cascades down his front, splats onto his lap. The moist warmth of it soaking into his jeans and shirt, the acidic tang wafting back up makes Caleb gag and throw up again. A bottle is put to his lips.

"Rinse your mouth out."

Caleb does so, spits the vile taste into some catchall held beneath his chin. The headache draws down several notches, but he realizes the terrible thirst he has. "Water. More water please."

"No."

Caleb recognizes his father speaking. He realizes his ankles are tied to the metal legs of a chair, his arms bound together by the wrists behind the backrest he is leaning against. His vision is blurry but more light shines at him than a cave should allow. Hands start wiping away the vomit. The Bible passage is from Matthew, Chapter 3, Jesus healing the crippled man on the Sabbath.

"Why not?" and Caleb gasps, "Please, water."

"Only in distress will this evil spirit leave you."

At once a stranger speaks up with a broken-reed quality to a statement that nonetheless carries authority. "We are not here to conduct an exorcism. We are here to pray over this young man that he may again accept Jesus into his life."

Caleb waits for Alfred Sr. to rebuke whoever dared correct him but his father remains silent. Another voice, a somewhat childish one, certainly not Annaliese's with her sharp tongue, but one Caleb knows he has heard before, cracks a joke in his head. Caleb laughs despite his circumstances, though his parched mouth breaks this into three distinct parts.

His father snaps, 'We are here to save you. What about that do you think is funny.'

"Just surprised how Bible study's changed," Caleb says, repeating what was quipped to him.

His vision clears more. The bright spots are two halogen search lamps trained on him atop tall stands. The heat from a third beats against the back of his neck.

"You've strayed far, Caleb, if you can laugh about this."

The voice of Caleb's juvenile companion tells him three times: Love your father, not his methods, like the refrain of a nursery rhyme. His father's face comes into focus.

"My God, you look tired," Caleb says, working his jaw to try to draw some moisture to his tongue. "You okay?"

Darkened skin hangs in buntings beneath Alfred Sr's eyes, and he seems to be sucking in his normally gaunt cheeks, they have receded so. His mouth quivers with a deep sadness. "How can I be okay when a son of mine has caused so much damage to the Lord's work."

The scratch-prone but commanding voice emerges from the figure that stands behind Alfred Sr. "We're here to lead you back into God's glorious embrace, son."

Caleb squints to correct what he sees but the speaker continues to be someone wearing a white hood with cutouts to see and talk through and a long white cloak that drags along the hardpacked ground. When Caleb looks about, two more people in matching robes are there, one stuffing a grain sack into a trash bag that Caleb guesses is covered in throw-up and another nearby at attention behind the light poles. Neither seems to be reciting Matthew's gospel which has progressed to chapter 4.

"You've brought the Klan back?" Caleb looks to the figure in charge. "For me?"

"We're here to help you repent your sinful ways."

THE PROPHET OF CENTRAL PARK

Caleb's last conscious memory from Queens returns. The soreness of his bottom against the chair reminds him of the injection. "You kidnapped me," he says, trying to become angry but still too woozy to do so.

"You were lost and now you're found."

The enclosing walls are crudely mortared field stones. Overhead handhewn timber joists reveal the underside of a plank floor. At the far end of the room two-by-fours and plywood lengths form irregular sections of shelves. Caleb identifies the source of the Bible reading there—an app on an iPhone sitting up in a charging station.

"Kidnapped me back to Kentucky."

"Caleb, you have a chance to undo all the damage you've done." His father sits in front of Caleb. He leans forward to promise, "I won't fail you again. However long it takes, I'll stay here until you take the Holy Spirit back into your heart."

"Torturing me in a root cellar," and he moans, "Water. Please, water."

"Give him some water, for goodness sake," the hooded supervisor says.

Alfred Sr. shoots a frown back at the man but gestures with an impatient flick of the hand for the garbage disposer to do so. As this captor raises a bottle, the expensive Bulova that his wife bought for his birthday emerges from the long sleeve. Caleb gasps as looks up to his brother's eyes. "You too."

Al Jr. quickly claps his other hand over the wristwatch and Al Sr. pushes the bottle away. "You aren't that thirsty."

A tuneless hum carries from upstairs, muffled by the floor but clear enough for Caleb to know it as a portable generator. An extension cord snakes upward behind the shelves. The headache has not ceased its insistent beat. "Where's your hood?" he asks his father.

"I do not need to hide doing Christ's will."

The other three stiffen but Al Sr. pays them no mind. Caleb can't move his tied hands; the jailers secured them to the backrest. When he tries to rock side to side, the chair is held in place though the floor is earthen. Caleb lets his head fall backward, rolls his eyes about. "Quite the set-up."

Al Sr. takes hold of Caleb's chin so that he must look at his father's earnest face. "For as long as it takes."

The eyes before him shine with unblinking faith. Without mercy. The hours to come in this chamber, the days, unspool in Caleb's imagination—

the agony of his dry mouth, hunger stabbing his belly, the pounding in his skull. His limbs already feel like balloons about to burst. Unceasing unless he relents. Caleb is too dehydrated for tears. "So you'll break me down. Brainwash me."

The simple-minded voice that Caleb knows he's heard before promises him: I will not desert you—I'll stay—I will—This is terrible but I will stay with you. Seems the companion is staying.

His father squeezes Caleb's jaw. "You've **been** brainwashed. I've seen the video." Spittle strikes Caleb's face. He tries to rear back but his father pulls him closer. "You're with that degenerate woman. In that Central Park. I've seen the videos of her too. She dares to deny the Bible. That, that . . . ."

"Go head. Say it." The admission makes Caleb want to cry. "It's who you are."

Alfred Sr. flings loose his grip and leaves his chair. After a moment the supervisor takes his place. Caleb guesses he is a flabby man. He has pudgy eyebrows. "What you said when you thwarted God's soldiers last week has led many people astray but you will lead them back to salvation. Them and many, many more." The man presses a palm against Caleb's forehead. He does not want the contact but the cold flesh is a wonderful shock. Caleb's grateful sigh encourages the supervisor to pray more loudly. "God, help this lost son take up again his role in your divine plan. To eliminate the horror of abortion once and for all so women can no longer reject their sacred duties." Caleb tries to butt himself free of the man's touch but the supervisor seizes the back of Caleb's head so that the hands are a clamp. "To root out acceptance of the obscenities of homosexuality and so-called transgender persons. All so this land can again be pleasing to You." The man finally releases Caleb, tells him, "Your redemption in Christ will wash away all the sins that your fall gave rise to."

The new companion whispers: Don't forget there are green places away from here—There is comfort—Healing. Caleb steadies himself. "He restoreth my soul. He leadeth me."

"Yes! Yes!" The supervisor looks about to be sure the others are listening. "God's Word on your lips. The Spirit has taken you over."

As the man raises his arms in praise, Caleb goes on, "This is the valley of death."

THE PROPHET OF CENTRAL PARK

The man's open paws begin to tremble. Caleb expects a punch but the supervisor starts from the chair like his father had. Alfred Sr. says, "He's not ready."

Alfred Jr. takes the seat. "What happened to your face?"

Caleb has forgotten about the injury. He doesn't even know if the bandage is still in place and tries to check. "Jail."

"You were in jail?"

Caleb nods. "Cellmate bit me," then, "Water. Please, water."

"Get away from him," Alfred Sr. orders his oldest boy and hurrying over, he pulls a hood over Caleb's head. "I told you, he's not ready."

* * *

Matthew progresses to Mark. Caleb needs a bathroom. His jailers release him from the chair but with the hood on and his hands still tied at his back. They lower his pants and underwear, press him into a squat over what he can feel is a plastic bucket. Shame makes him blush, the tingling tells him so, but they can't see his face and the need is urgent. They wipe him afterward, raise his pants and fix him in his seat again. Caleb thinks how he just expelled the remains of Haruto's wonderful breakfast. He is expelling New York. Then someone lifts the hood enough to push a bottle mouth against his own. His brother says, "Drink." and he does until another hand knocks it away. A new voice, the fourth sentry, tells Al Jr. with a snarling quality, "We didn't say give him that." Al Jr. snaps back, "I didn't ask." Hope sluices through Caleb with the swigs but the water soon disappears into his terrible thirst and the dark engulfing him swallows the other.

* * *

The narrator concludes Luke's Gospel. In the pause before John, no one speaks. A cow's lowing penetrates the chamber, a morose call from far away. "Dairy farm," Caleb mutters to himself. His father 's startled reply. "What? No." Against the shadows wrapped about him, Caleb pulls up a snapshot of the church's Saturday service, goes through the pews searching for families with a herd. The third owns a hundred acres. Caleb spies the old barn barely visible at the distant end of the field. Built into a hill that is crowned with a grove of red maples. Plank siding weathered charcoal grey. Where it is exposed, foundation of irregular boulders. "Huh," Caleb lets out. "Mr. MacIntosh's place." Beyond the black, his brother snickers. At once Alfred Sr, snaps, "You're happy about him knowing? And if we don't . . . succeed?" Caleb corrects his father, "Break me. Don't break me." The supervisor takes charge. "This isn't helping. The Lord will come if our faith is strong. Let's pray over him again." Hands press on Caleb's head and shoulders. He shudders. Nevertheless the supervisor calls out to God on the wretched sinner's behalf.

* * *

"Water. Please. Please. Water."

* * *

The lamps blind him when the hood is pulled off. Caleb squeezes his eyes shut, looks away as best he can. A wet terry cloth is pushed into his mouth. Heaven. He sucks in the wetness, contorts his mouth to rotate the fabric when the section goes dry. His vision gets used to the bright.

Flabby man is gone, along with the barking sentry. Before Caleb the new boss sits with a hunched back in his cloak. A few stray white hairs have fallen down into the eye holes of his mask. The new guard behind him is basketball player tall. Al Jr. is still in the room. Caleb takes comfort from his brother's presence then wonders if he should. To the left Alfred Sr. watches with the scrutiny of a livestock agent searching for qualities to merit sparing an animal the slaughterhouse.

"Caleb, your father has explained your upbringing to me." The man is an "aw-shucks" type of preacher, everyone's best friend, happy to lead even the most confused to the correct choice. He is also very skinny. At a nod from their father, Al Jr. pulls out the water rag. Caleb's mouth stays open in mourning. "Your parents raised you right. Immersed you in the Scriptures." The elder makes a creaky glance back toward the shelves where the iPhone relates Peter's summons from Jappa, Acts of the Apostles, Chapter 11. "To which we are reacquainting you." The man scoots forward to touch Caleb's chest. Liver spots show on the back of the hand. "That proper boy, that decent young man resides inside you still, waiting to be called forth. That is why I am certain that here and now, surrounded by people who love you, Caleb, you will recognize the depravity that has taken root within you."

The stew of the vomit congealing down his front with the sweat growing stale on his skin and the aftermath of the poor job cleaning his rear stings Caleb's nose. "I stink," he tells the man. "Don't you smell it?"

This seems to excite the man, as much as a scarecrow can be excited. "We will wash that stench away, and so much more filth with it, once you renounce the depravity within you. Cast it out so you can proclaim God's saving truth."

The companion returns, almost meekly assures Caleb: Nobody talks to the stinky—They don't—They pretend they don't see. At last Caleb places the voice. He lifts his head more to let loose a hoarse, "Ha, ha, ha," then "Why are you here?" The companion's answer: You gave me your sandwich —You saw me.

The scarecrow preacher peers about for help at the non sequitur, gets none. "Son, I've told you, I'm here—we're all here—to draw you back inside the community of His redeemed. But you must renounce your sinful beliefs. You must denounce abortion."

Caleb prefers the companion in his head. "What kind of sandwich was it? The voice replies, Spam—It was Spam.

The patient tone stops. "Are you mocking me, young man?" At his side Alfred Sr. appears hardpressed not to intervene.

Caleb wishes he'd been given more time with the rag. "I don't believe . . . what you do."

"No, no." The scarecrow makes a fist, stretches the digits straight in frustration. "The boy who grew up hearing the Bible every evening before dinner knows that abortion is wrong."

So many words to say and so thirsty. "God breathed into his . . . nostrils the breath of life."

"How dare you quote me Genesis like you're a Bible scholar." Gentle persuasion is out the window. The scarecrow would reach for a rod if one was at hand. Instead he reaches for the front of Caleb's shirt, his fingers scrabbling for a moment before they find purchase. "The Scriptures have illuminated my whole life." Caleb does not allow himself to be pulled. The scarecrow's effort actually draws him forward in his seat. "Jeremiah 1:5.

'Before I formed you in the womb I knew you, before you were born I sanctified you!"

Caleb can imagine the scarecrow's self-satisfied anger under the hood. Tawana's habit of speech comes to mind. "So She's confusing us?"

The scarecrow lets go of him. "'She'? Who's She?"

"God."

The preacher looks aside to Alfred Sr. as if he must bear responsibility for the heretic. In turn Alfred Sr. leaps forward to clutch Caleb's throat as he thrusts his face inches away. "Don't you dare mock us. When we're here to save you," and he screams, "Save you! We're here to save you! Don't you understand?"

Caleb grimaces at the knife tips that the shout plunges into his ears and he gurgles at the throttling and his answer comes out as "Wahe." Then Al Jr. is trying to break their father's grip, calling out in a child's plea, "Dad, Dad, stop, please. You're gonna . . . please." Alfred Sr. throws off his son's hands, yelling, "Don't you dare interfere." Al Jr. steps back, holding up his arms in surrender and Caleb steels himself for the assault to continue but their father steps away also to double forward, palms on knees, and his chest heaves in drawing his wheezing air. Caleb sees the old man his father has become.

The scarecrow preacher has not moved. His pose suggests, if not glee at the violence, then acceptance of it as justified. Caleb would like to massage his throat. He would like to swallow better. "Why 'He'?" he manages to say.

"What's your nonsense now?"

"Why 'He', not 'She'? Think God has genitalia."

A spasm passes through the scarecrow's bent body. Behind him the basketball player is inching forward. The preacher cries out, "Haven't you heard a word your father said? We're here, we all are here to save you."

The companion reminds Caleb: Nobody sees the stinky. Caleb tells the tilting scarecrow, "Never smelled this bad?"

"You've not earned the right to be washed."

Caleb holds the man's eyes through their peepholes. "Last time you smelled this?"

The hood puffs out, exasperation, then, "Son, I bathe daily."

THE PROPHET OF CENTRAL PARK

Caleb shakes his head, still staring into the other's eyes. "Last time, clothed the naked . . . . Fed the poor." The scarecrow erupts, "By God, you smartass, I nourish men's souls," drowning out Caleb's last question, "Bathed the stinky?"

At that the basketball player does approach, but Al Jr. steps in the way, punches the man in the chest with a straight arm. "You're not touching him." As the tall man recovers, Al Jr. raises a length of hickory wood handle. Caleb didn't spot it in the cellar before.

Their father barks out Al Jr.'s name, a reprimand and a warning, and the preacher enjoins him, "Young man, we must not waver." His brother could be crying, or seething, Caleb can't tell through the hood. "He's not touching my brother." For several unobstructed seconds the iPhone recounts Saul's meeting with the false prophet Elymas in Cypress.

"Cover his back up," the preacher says in disgust. He flicks a hand for his will to be done. Alfred Sr. studies Caleb for a brief moment through a pained, cross frown, seeking the son he once knew, then plunges Caleb back into the dark.

* * *

He drops his chin down onto his chest, sleeps.

* * *

A burst of apnea brings him to. The complete blackout makes him whimper, then he remembers. The iPhone is off. There is only the rustle of one of his captors resettling and the fuzzy hum his mind makes of the silence. An owl hoots outside.

He imagines the bird hunting among the stand of maples. A shadow arching through the branches. Not a sound from its wings. Caleb half-expects the final squeal from the owl's prey as the predator strikes.

He barely gives sound to the question, "Are you there?" The companion promises: I won't leave you—I'm here—I won't leave you. Caleb makes himself ask, "Am I going to die in this cellar?" The answer simply: I don't know. Surprise at this. Anger. "How can you not know?" In a calm, sad youngster's tone: I don't know what people are going to do.

Caleb's throat hurts at that but there is no moisture for tears. "You're not who I thought you were." His companion promises: I'm someone who won't leave you.

* * *

A nudge awake and a cupped hand over his mouth. His brother's voice at his ear, barely heard, "It's me," and a denser shape than the surrounding dark when the sack lifts up. Then water. Precious, precious water. "Drink slow," and his brother pulls the bottle away so Caleb will. Until it's empty. The silhouette still before, beseeching. The pleas again a murmur but as dire as any shouted alarm. "Just say what they want you to say and get out of here."

"I can't."

"Why not, for God's sake."

Caleb wonders if Al Jr. truly means that last phrase. "He's here, Al, in this cellar."

"Who is?"

"God. He's here. I'd be lying in His Presence."

His brother wraps an arm about Caleb's head to bring them together, ear to ear. "They're not gonna stop."

"I know."

* * *

The iPhone wakes him, Corinthians I. The stiffness in his neck stabs down though his back when Caleb tries to raise his head. A new day.

* * *

The veil rises and the flabby supervisor has returned, his sentry again stationed a few feet behind. They have a roster, Caleb thinks to himself, to his companion. Alfred Sr. claims his same spot to the right of the interrogator's chair. A track of impressed dirt on the left pant leg and sleeve show that he was one of the guards last night. The lines dividing his face run deeper this morning, the dark pouches threaten to rupture at the bottoms.

THE PROPHET OF CENTRAL PARK

He seems shrunken and his shirt hangs untucked on the one side, a sloppy look Alfred Sr. would not normally tolerate. Caleb does not want to embarrass his father by saying so aloud. Can't spare the saliva anyway. He catches his father's attention, uses his gaze as a pointer until Alfred Sr. notices the loose tail.

"Let's talk about Psalm 139," the supervisor says.

Al Jr. is off to the man's left. Caleb can feel his brother willing him toward obedience. The companion tells him: Everybody's afraid in this room—Try not to be afraid. "Why?"

"So that His teaching can deliver you from your terrible mistakes."

Caleb takes in his inquisitors ranked about the adapted cell and tries not to be afraid. "Don't believe that."

"But it's true, son, and just one small nod of faith will allow that teaching to enter you so the process of redemption can begin."

"Don't believe it's God's teaching."

The companion says: Now he's really afraid—He's so afraid. Caleb watches the supervisor's eyes bug out, hears him suck in like he stubbed something and answer, "He's angry."

"Yes, I'm angry." The supervisor holds up a black leather covered Bible. Caleb didn't notice it before. He notices the wide-banded gold ring on the supervisor's flabby finger. "I'm angry that, after all the benefits of your upbringing, you could so revile this divine document."

"No." Caleb looks to his father whose anger shows as a trembling spirit passing through him and more than anyone else there, Caleb wants Alfred Sr. to understand. "Think it's beautiful. And human." A jolt goes through his father's expression, hardens it as if Caleb could not sling an uglier insult. The supervisor's upraised hand quakes. Caleb braces for the blow from the Bible. "I don't believe what you do," he says.

The supervisor finally lowers the menacing book. "Since you reject the Bible, tell me, young man, what do you believe in."

Caleb wants to tell the man, swear to his father, that he questions the Bible, he doesn't reject it but he doesn't have the strength. "I don't know."

"For the love of God, you poor confused soul, why won't you let us help you?"

* * *

In the hood Caleb asks, "What do I believe? What should I believe?" The simple-minded voice says: Simple things—Believe in simple things. Caleb asks, "What does that mean?" as beyond the shroud, the supervisor says, "Is he muttering?" Footsteps grow louder and the wave from someone's approach brushes Caleb's body. His companion answers: Believe in giving a Spam sandwich to a hungry man who stinks. "Doesn't really stack up to 'In the beginning'." Standing over Caleb his brother reports, "I can't make out what he's saying."

* * *

Again the bedazzling lamps. Caleb whines at their piercing pokes. The flabby supervisor has reclaimed his seat. The bow-backed scarecrow preacher is now behind him while Caleb's father and brother are in their usual places.

"We realize now that you have been deceived by this false prophet in New York. This Tawana Johnson."

The companion tells Caleb at once: They're really afraid of her—She scares them more than most anybody else. Caleb bobbles his head to escape the brightness. "Why? She's just a Park performer."

The flabby supervisor jabs two fingers toward Caleb. "Is this what you're talking about? How do we know he's not faking?" He claps his hands inches before Caleb's nose. "Focus, son."

The companion tells him: Try not to be afraid. Caleb answers, "Okay-dokey."

"We now understand that freeing you from her thrall is the key to your salvation."

The voice asks: Does she scare you?—She did—You wondered if she ran a cult. Caleb slumps his head forward to stare at his bound legs. "She never tied me down."

The scarecrow grows irritated. "You really need to stop dwelling on the . . . cruder examples of our concern for you. We are not the source of your distress. This Tawana Johnson is."

Caleb remembers the horrified shock when the guitarist first saw his injured face, remembers how she lessened his pain. "Never starved me."

He looks from one to the other of the bosses. "Gave me water when I needed."

The scarecrow presses forward. "I imagine she gave you more than that. Did she use her sex to mislead you?"

Caleb recoils from the grubby presence the man projects, of sweaty palms and sneering stares at the first glimpse of flesh. The companion laments with sympathetic regret: Oh, these men, so twisted by what they want—Can only take pleasure in the locked office, pushing someone up against the bookcase. Caleb asks, "Who's the girl against the office bookcase?"

This time the scarecrow recoils, demands, "What did you say?" so that the flabby man looks aside then moves the scarecrow back with the bar of his arm.

"Tawana Johnson is not the saint you think she is." The strength collects inside Caleb to be angry. "Never said 'saint'," but the flabby supervisor goes on as if Caleb hasn't spoken. "She sold her body on the street when she was young. She probably murdered her unborn child."

Steel rises up through Caleb, straightening him on the chair and the change unsettles the supervisor enough that he glances to Caleb's father for guidance, but Alfred Sr. only stares at his son with severe disappointment. Caleb says to the companion, "A waste talking to them."

The voice tells him: Don't stop talking—Silence changes nothing—Talking changes people." The interrogators, all confused now, find their fellows the same.

"Talking hasn't changed a thing," Caleb says.

The voice tells him: You don't know that.

"I'm a die. They're gonna watch."

At that Al Jr. turns to his co-conspirators for their denials but they remain still in facing Caleb as if awaiting inspiration. At last Alfred Sr. steps forward. "Your obstinacy is a sin, Caleb. If you would only allow the least bit of His saving grace in, this would all soon be over."

With an effort, Caleb keeps his back erect and gazes unblinking from one to the other to the third of them, mute, until the hood is back in place.

* * *

P C Burhenne

The spells of light grow more brief. The jailers preach. Caleb stares back without a word. The sack goes back on.

* * *

"My head," Caleb mutters before he catches himself. A vise squeezes his skull.

* * *

The iPhone announces the Letter of Paul to Titus. Caleb wonders what happened to the several Letters that came before.

* * *

Beneath the shroud, beyond it, away from it, Caleb glimpses a weakening of the dark, can almost make out his companion. When he looks too closely, the figure, shape, the silhouette blinks away.

The voice reaches him: You're always fighting—always pushing back.

"Tied to a chair."

Fighting through silence—With what you have—Will you fight till the end?

Too weak, too depleted to sob, he manages only, "Am I gonna die?"

The form wavers. Stands? Moves closer? The gentle admission: I told you, I don't know.

"Right. Constant companion." Caleb feels himself slipping away. Into sleep? Unconsciousness? "Don't you get mad?"

The shape is coming closer, a dark fire growing in size, a wave drawing itself up in the void to cover him. The voice says: I try not to—Little good comes of it, given what's underneath.

* * *

Like the night(s?) before, his brother sneaks him water. "Please don't do this," Alfred Jr. begs Caleb. The fear that squeaks in the brother's whisper almost crumbles Caleb's resolve but he cannot bear false witness.

"I'm not doing it." His brother's voice breaks in saying, "So stubborn," and he needs a pause to finish, "You're just like Dad."

* * *

The Bible recital resumes. Caleb does not bother to identify the place in Scriptures.

* * *

An argument in heated murmurs. Until Al Jr. speaks up, "No, no, that's not what we said." The rough and tumble of a struggle. Then again God's word. Caleb asks the companion, "Know now?" Still the answer: No.

* * *

The construction lamps beat on the top of Caleb's skull. He keeps his chin on his chest to avert his eyes. The scuff-scarred work boots on the ground are his father's.

"Look at me, son." Caleb lifts his head by inches, squints. The powerful halogens backlight Alfred Sr. in the chair. Caleb's blurring vision makes this a halo. He snorts at the idea but it sounds like a choked-off cough. "Son, you must see that the path you're walking leads to death."

Talk to him, the voice urges. Caleb responds with a slow blink.

"God still has a plan for you," Alfred Sr. continues. "Despite all that you've done. He has a part for you in the heavenly crusade that is unfolding even as we speak."

"Amen"s greet this announcement. Caleb recognizes the flabby supervisor's self-important delivery. The meek companion argues on: Tell him what you know of God—You may never get another chance. Caleb grows angry with the cellar.

"And, son, please listen to me, son. If you put your hand to His will now, the benefit will be just that much greater. Don't you see, you are the prodigal son, and his reward for your return would be just as great. And, and so would mine."

Hope and despair tug Alfred Sr. to proclaim one second, wheedle in the next. Caleb's acclimating eyes see how something has fallen away from his father—an aura of certainty, an investment of power—leaving a desiccated and forlorn man. Further back the supervisor with the basketball player and the sentry coalesce from the haze. The scarecrow preacher is not in attendance.

However, Caleb's undeterred silence provokes a hardness when Alfred Sr. goes on, "Of course they're wrong about that mammy charlatan being the start of your fall. Annaliese Tompkins is the one who led you astray." Caleb's sympathy disappears. Alfred Sr. takes heart at the glint which replaces it. "I told you to stay away but you wouldn't listen. Then when she dies, you go and make a martyr of her." His father stands over him, suddenly enraged at Caleb's disobedience that has brought them to this place. For his part Caleb is trembling and the surge of emotion again resurrects his tortured hands, but he would use them nonetheless if they were free. "You stupid boy, you couldn't see her death for what it was. God's cleansing justice. His answer to her sinful act and one that very well may have redeemed her. You were too weak to accept her death, her terrible death as God's merciful will."

"Your will!" Caleb finally spits out. The collapse of the wall he erected brings the other jailers closer. "Their will. Her blood's on all your hands."

Alfred Sr. grabs him by the hair. "Why were you so put out, boy. Some whore dies for her sins. Was the child yours? Tell me! Was that why?"

His father's nose presses against his own, the manic eyes would drill into him if they could. Caleb almost shuts down again but sees another shine in those fierce grey pupils. A wish there. "You want that. Me the father." Caleb's laugh is a dry gasp. "Know I'm not gay. I'm not William."

The punch sends the cellar away

"Don't you say his name! Don't you dare say that awful name!"

Part of Caleb yearns to surrender to the sleep slipping over him. Another part wants to strike back in the one way he can. "He paid for your rehabs. Never stopped missing you." The swirl of colors again solidifies into his father, fist raised to deliver a second blow. The other three make no move to intervene. "Never stopped caring about his Alfie."

"He left me there!" his father screams and Caleb waits for the fist to fall. "Left me with that monst—He left me in hell."

THE PROPHET OF CENTRAL PARK

At Caleb's back comes a bang and the cracking of wood, and Caleb thinks, So that's where the door is. His father darts past him as if the noise marks calamity and the other three start forward with the same frantic jerks to action. A second later Alfred Sr. cries, "What?", his tone startled as much as indignant, and he stumbles back into view, barely able to keep to his feet. Al Jr. comes into the cellar carrying something. Caleb contorts his eyes to make out the handgun then realizes his left eye is swelling shut. He thinks grimly, Why can't people hit the other side for once. Then the bonds behind him fall away and molten lava rushes back into his hands. At his anguished squeal a voice pleads, "Sorry, sorry," at his ear. Relief overwhelms Caleb so that he pants for air to answer, "Sis?"

"How can you do this, Junior? You know how important this is."

"I'm not gonna be Cain."

Al Jr.'s voice wavers, but the bullet he fires at the feet of the two advancing guards is decisive. Caleb winces at the shot, tries to cover his pierced ears but his arms aren't ready to respond. The person freeing his feet lunges flat to the dirt. He looks like Annaliese's father, Mr. Tompkins, but Caleb knows he is not seeing straight. His brother says, "Next time in your knees." and from outside Carolyne's husband hollers, "Are you alright, girl?"

Behind Caleb, his sister hollers back, "Yes," then to his ear again, "Can you stand?" His third rescuer raises himself off the ground to finish cutting the ropes about Caleb's ankles and the man will not stop being Mr. Tompkins. "I dunno," Caleb admits.

The flabby supervisor draws himself up to say, "Young man, think about what--" but Al Jr. turns the gun on the spot where knees would be behind the robe.

"This is finished."

Carolyne hoists Caleb from the chair and the man who is indeed Mr. Tompkins scrabbles up to step beneath Caleb's left arm. Good thing too. Caleb's legs buckle at his body's weight. Al Jr. guards their retreat. Beyond him their father has gone ashen at all three of his children arrayed against him.

"William loved you, Dad, and so do I," Caleb calls out.

Far from melting Alfred Sr., this goodbye looses a dark shadow over his face, the corners of his mouth sunk under contempt. "'Children will fight against their own parents and will have them killed. Everyone will hate you because you follow me. But the one who remains faithful to the Lord will be saved.'"

The promise of Matthew follows them up the stone steps. Caleb's sister and Mr. Tompkins practically carry him from one to the next of these, and onto MacIntosh's field. His brother-in-law's Chevy pick-up waits idling a few yards away, the tailgate down. Terry behind the wheel. The world is suddenly warm after the dank cellar. Across the pasture several of the dairy herd watch his escape as they chew their cuds. His handlers help Caleb scoot into the bed. He peers at the father of the ghost in his head and tries to ask, Why?, but the question doesn't quite pass his lips and the man says only, "Hurry." Over the closed gate Carolyne stares horror-stricken at her first clear view of him, but Al Jr. pushes her toward the cab, ordering, "Come on, we hafta go," then he vaults over the sidewall into the back too. Caleb feels light-headed from the exertion but he stays sitting up as they pull away, looking to catch his brother's attention. Al Jr. clocks the movements of the jailers who have now emerged from the cellar. No one hurries for a car behind the barn but still Al Jr. rigidly refuses to look aside. Caleb understands why.

"You saved me, Al." His brother twitches as if this is more a slap than praise. "I don't leave that room if you're not there."

His brother sniffs and still will not face Caleb. "You really do smell to high heaven."

The companion whispers: Blessed are the stinky and those who help them. Caleb tries to laugh, wants to cry but can only gag.

* * *

Seems Terry drove down a section of fence to enter the pasture. Leaving the same way, he heads west. Carolyne hands back water which Al Jr. relays to Caleb. "Sip it if you can." Caleb tries, fails. By the time he empties the bottle, Terry has looped around on the back roads so they are going east.

"Where's he taking us?" Caleb asks.

The passing wind whistles among them. When Al Jr. shakes his head, Caleb thinks he couldn't hear. Instead Al Jr. leans close. "Not Terry. Mr.

Tompkins's giving directions." He shrugs at the confusion Caleb must be showing.

Dog tiredness takes hold then. Caleb slides down onto his back. The ribbons of clouds above trail after them, unruffled by the overhanging branches that whisk past. The effect could almost be hypnotic but the jostling from the macadam keeps the aches all over his body too fresh for sleep. Soon the gift of freedom feels slippery; fear creeps over him that he will end up back in the root cellar—or in another claustrophobic room, this one untraceable. Mr. Tompkins' presence suddenly seems suspicious. Caleb reaches up to grip his brother's arm. "You're really helping me, right? This isn't some trick to break my spirit?"

Al Jr. reacts with surprise, then gaping regret that shows how desperate is the face Caleb turned to his brother. Al Jr. covers Caleb's hand to give it a squeeze. "No. We're gonna get you away."

Fifteen minutes pass, maybe more. A discussion starts up in the cab, his sister's voice bringing heat to it. Caleb can't hear specifics. Only when the ride starts bucking his battered body, does he push himself back up. The country road is moving away behind the tailgate. Terry has veered them onto a dirt track between a tobacco field and a dense growth of ash trees sprouting out of a bramble of raspberry bushes. He guides them into the latter at a break in the underbrush. Caleb begins to shake when the limbs blot out the sun. "Where's he taking me?"

Again Al Jr. takes his hand. "I dunno but it's all right. I promise."

"Where are we?"

"Somewhere out Tyson way."

The path opens up. They park beside Mr. Tompkins's blue Subaru. Carolyne is out her door before the truck stops rocking. "We're gonna get you to a hospital, Caleb. Don't shake your head at me. You have no idea what you look like."

A bed in a ward in town terrifies Caleb. "I want to get outa here."

Mr. Tompkins is at Carolyne's side. "We'll get you someplace out of state."

"Wanna go home. That's all. Give me a phone. Roommate'll come get me." Terry is out of the cab too. When they four hesitate to answer, Caleb asks, " Why have we stopped?"

The paranoia in his voice brings a single sobbing burst from his sister.

"We need to change cars," Mr. Tompkins says, stepping in. He pauses to calm himself, maybe calm Caleb. "The sheriff and his deputies are not our friends. We can't drive you a long way in the back of the pickup anyway." The man gnaws his knuckle. In the indecision Caleb recognizes the man he almost persuaded to let Annaliese go for help. "There's an FBI headquarters in Cincinnati. We could take you there."

Caleb knows he's about to cry, works to swallow off this impulse. "They'll put me in a hospital there. Wanna go home."

"I don't know." A serious ring inhabits Terry's usual unbothered drawl. "You look to need help."

"I'll get it. Soon as I'm back. Please, a phone."

Carolyne's will to argue collapses. She cries into the opening of her prayerful hands. Caleb wants to reach out to make her see that he will be fine but doesn't have the strength.

"Okay." Mr. Tompkins nods his head in a flutter. "If that's the only place you'll see a doctor, I'll get you to New York." Carolyne and Al Jr. stare at the man in disbelief so he says, "We can't wait for someone to come fetch him. For his sake. And we gotta get him outta here now." Decided on the plan, he takes out his cell. "I have to make a call."

When the man steps away, Carolyne takes out her own phone. "You wanna call your roommate?"

Before he finishes punching in the number, Caleb realizes Sidney probably still has his phone turned off. Of all his new acquaintances, Caleb remembers the sequence of only one by heart. He wonders if she will answer.

"Who is this?" Tawana asks, wary and expectant both.

"It's me. Caleb."

"Where are you? Are you safe?" she demands.

Caleb cannot remember her sounding so animated, angry even. He glances about at the family that have put themselves at risk for him. "Don't think I can tell you. Not now. Been rescued."

"You sound awful. Do the authorities have you?"

Again an urgency he's never known from her. "People I know. One's bringing me back." A voice in the background speaks to Tawana. No carefree calls or other outdoor noises intrude. "Not at the Park?" he asks.

THE PROPHET OF CENTRAL PARK

Tawana first tells whoever is in the wings, "It's him! It's Caleb!" in a rush of astonished relief then to Caleb in an exasperated, wounded tone, "You are so foolish. I'm here with Davey. Sidney's been here too. He finally had to go back to work."

"Sorry he missed two days."

"What?"

This a word of alarm. Caleb doesn't understand. "Tell him sorry for the couple days."

"Caleb, this is the fifth day you've been missing. We started to think--" then the order, "Let me talk to whoever's bringing you back."

Mr. Tompkins has rejoined the group. He looks at the phone like it might explode. "Who's this?"

"A friend. She's worried."

Mr. Tompkins steps away again as he offers a wary, "Yes?" to the line.

"It's been five days?" His siblings both nod. Caleb notices the start of a beard dirtying his brother's jaw and lip, the sunken look of his brother's eyes. He tells Al Jr., "You must be exhausted."

His brother exhales with the sound of a punctured balloon and hopping out of the bed, he walks around to the front of the truck. Sighing, Carolyne pushes more water on Caleb.

Mr. Tompkins stutters into the cell, "We, we tried that with him," making clear it is an attempt to wedge his way into a one-sided conversation. Caleb can't imagine the bossy Tawana on the other end. "We want that too," the man states, anger now putting a bite to his words and quick on that, "He has to leave as soon as I get off this phone." In the next moment, however, the irritation freezes on his face then transforms into a smile so broad, his cheeks strain to contain it. "Lady, he's already there," and next, "That's exactly what I'm saying." A faint but undeniable squeal escapes the cell that Caleb can also barely credit to the composed guitarist he knows. Carolyne and Terry hear it too, look to him for an explanation he does not have. Mr. Tompkins brings the phone back to Caleb. Tawana says —almost sings--"You're safe, Caleb. You can trust that man. He's gonna get you home."

Caleb feels himself relax, didn't realize how suspicious he still was. "Can you let Mr. Yamaguchi know? Mr. Strauss? Sorry. Can't remember the numbers."

"We have them."

"How?"

"After you were . . . afterwards, Elliot sought us out. I'll make sure they know. Now go. The sooner you leave, the sooner you're back."

With that the line goes dead. Caleb returns the cell to his sister. Joyful exuberance gone, Mr. Tompkins orders them, "Time to say your goodbyes." Caleb scoots out of the truck bed. When he thanks his brother-in-law, Terry says, "Maybe you can keep your head down from now on." Carolyne hugs him, whispers, "You really do have a new home now." When Al Jr. holds back, Caleb calls to him, "Remember, if you're not in that cellar, I still am."

When his family is gone, Caleb turns to the Subaru but Mr. Tompkins raises a traffic cop's hand to him then reaches in the car to press its horn once and, after a pause, again. "Signal for your ride to head over. Sheriff knows my car too. Hardest part's getting you out of the area."

A late model Bronco pulls into the grove. A bear of a man gets out, older, wearing overalls atop a flannel shirt and a John Deere cap with grey brown tufts of hair curling out beneath it. His nose could be an ill-shaped plum tomato stuck to his face. Because of Tawana's assurance, the stranger doesn't worry Caleb. "So it is him. Couldn't quite believe you were telling me true."

"Caleb, this is Kip. He'll be taking you on." Mr. Tompkins has a brown grocery bag from his front seat. "Here. I brought you a new outfit."

"Oh, thank goodness," Kip says with closed eyes. To Caleb, "No offense, son. You 're ripe."

Caleb can't manage the change with his still tender hands. As they dress him, the farmer asks, "You sure he's up to the trip? Boy looks like a whole month of bad Friday nights."

"Helps waiting at the other end. We can't chance it here."

Their discussion about him without him galls Caleb. All he can think to say, though, is "Don't wanna go out on the town with you, Kip."

The man brings up from his belly a single stretched-out "hah" at that. "Then we're off."

Mr. Tompkins helps Caleb into the passenger seat. At the door, he says, "Kip's got water for you. A couple bananas."

"Got this too," and the driver pulls a second John Deere cap onto Caleb's head.

THE PROPHET OF CENTRAL PARK

"Now you look like his son," Mr. Tompkins says through a smile.

Caleb stops him closing the door. "I know why you're doing this. She does too."

Mr. Tompkins works his lips together for an answer that fails.

* * *

Kip is a cautious driver. "We ain't breaking any laws but given how everybody's looking for you, be a whole lot simpler if a trooper don't pull us over."

"A lot of people looking?"

Kip lets loose another elongated laugh. "Hell, you're the biggest kidnapping since Patty Hearst. Put your seat belt on, son. You look like a good bump'll pitch you right out the door."

Fifteen minutes later, the driver's phone pings with a text. "Helps to know where we're going," Kip says as he pulls over to punch the address into the phone's navigation app. Back roads snake about to an entrance ramp onto I-64. By then the farmer is recounting stories from his youth on the Great Lakes working in the Merchant Marines. A wooziness pulls at Caleb not unlike what followed the abductors' injection. Was it really five days ago? He remembers asking Kip to turn off the A/C, the man surprised because the Bronco's boiling, then the roadside flashing by blurs into a tunnel and the wind within this becomes the only sound to be heard.

* * *

The jab pulls him back but when he tries to move his arm away, it will not budge. A woman's no-nonsense voice orders, "If you can hear me, Caleb, be still." Something is happening in the crook of his elbow, the left elbow. The woman continues, "Christ, he's severely dehydrated." Caleb starts awake, still in the Bronco. Kip has his right arm pinned to his leg while the woman who appears to be his mother's age attaches a clear plastic tube to the port that she just inserted into Caleb's vein. "I'm giving you an IV saline solution." The woman works on him from inside the open passenger door. She has on a brown knit vest over a white blouse and with her black rim glasses reminds Caleb of his librarian back in Maynardsville. "How long have you been denied water?"

"Five days, I think."

The woman looks up in horror. "You should be dead."

"My brother sneaked me some water when no one was watching."

"Bully for him," then to Kip, "He belongs in a hospital."

"One's waiting in New York."

Disapproval shudders through the caretaker as she takes from the dashboard a clear pouch of liquid to which the IV's other end connects. "Can you walk?" she asks, giving the bag a gentle squeeze. At the surge of fluid into his forearm, Caleb opens that hand and presses himself back in the seat.

Kip and the caretaker transfer him from the Bronco to a green Volvo station wagon. They are in a garage, remarkable for how uncluttered it is; tools hang in ranked rows on one wall, large hooks suspend two bikes off the floor on the opposite. In front of the vehicles, white ceiling-high cabinets hide whatever else the space holds. The closed bay doors hide them from the outside. When they have Caleb in the front passenger seat, the caretaker tapes the pouch to the side of the headrest, then spreads a blanket over him. The farmer leans in afterwards. "Sorry this fell on you, son."

Minutes later Kip is gone and the woman drives them through a grid of residential streets to a divided highway. She pulls a large sippy cup from her satchel. "Broth. Easy to digest. They tell me you haven't eaten either. Go slow or you'll throw it back up."

He sighs at the first taste, cannot imagine any soup tasting better.

"Where are we?"

"West Virginia, headed for I-79 up into Pennsylvania."

Since they left the garage, the woman has barely glanced at Caleb. She intimidates him so he can't even bring himself to thank her. At that moment Caleb remembers Mr. Tompkins's sudden delight in the conversation with Tawana, along with her promise that the man will protect him.

"I'm on the railroad, aren't I," he blurts out. "The Rainbow Rights Railroad."

The woman closes her eyes briefly and sneers. "Christ, I hate that name."

* * *

The IV drip moves Caleb if not back to his normal self then at least away from the ledge where he was tottering over death. Just across the state border the woman stops to remove the port. "You're going to need more of these," she says. "But they should be administered in a more sterile environment than my car."

"You're a doctor, aren't you?"

The woman ignores the question but every few moments she orders him to take a sip, until he realizes the mile markers are her schedule. At the next even number he holds up the bottle before she can speak. The woman actually smiles. The container lasts until they're north of Pittsburgh, leaving him as bloated and lethargic as any Thanksgiving meal.

South of Erie the woman goes east on I-80. By then his left eye is swollen shut and the complaints from muscles all over his body have doused the euphoria from the escape. The caretaker pulls into a truckstop off the next exit then slowly rolls through the array of tractor-trailers until she finds the license plate she is searching for. The driver who climbs down from its cab is a wiry fellow in his forties sporting a hunting vest over a t-shirt and a ZZ-Top mustache and beard. Before she'll let the driver continue on with Caleb, the woman trots into the diner for a bag of ice wrapped in a hand towel. She presses this onto his newest injury before hugging him goodbye.

* * *

"Helluva stretch of days you've had."

The driver's southern drawl surprises Caleb as much as the man knowing about his drama. "Keep forgetting I'm on the evening news."

"Evening news, shit. I turn on the radio now, they'll be talking about you somewhere."

"Please don't," Caleb says when the man points to the console, then he asks, "Do you know how this all started?" The man shrugs, the equivalent of "D'uh," and Caleb remembers that the man is part of the railroad. "Right. Well, before that happened, there weren't ten people cared what I did or said."

P C Burhenne

He leans forward to see himself in the side-view mirror. The fresh bruise is full to bursting like a giant purple tick that won't give up the feast and the healing flesh below wears a faded blue sheen so that the color seems to be leaching down from above. Opposite this, the five days of starvation have started to raise that eye socket and cheek bone in relief. It is a marriage of two faces and neither reminds Caleb of the man he was two weeks ago.

"All I did was stop some thugs come looking for trouble. For that they took my life from me."

Caleb reapplies the ice, thinking ruefully, Cold compress, never leave home without it.

* * *

The driver wakes Caleb as they near the next transfer point. Out the passenger window Manhattan is lit up for the night, dwarfing the industrial parks and waterways of New Jersey even at a distance. On his arrival less than a year ago, this sight frightened Caleb so much that if possible, he would have darted across the many lanes of the Turnpike and stuck his thumb out for a ride away. Now the spectacle is a beacon calling him.

They pull into the Vince Lombardi rest stop. Two young men Caleb's age are waiting in a Yaris. Caleb thanks the truck driver and gets in the back of the cramped vehicle so he can stretch his legs across the seat. After their first effusive questions about his condition, the chauffeurs respect his short answers with silence. When they emerge from the Lincoln Tunnel, Caleb swivels about to take in all of Midtown's swirl and babble. He lowers his window so the growl of the traffic reaches him more clearly and the exhaust stink accented with the bite of burnt salt from a pretzel vendor can fill his nostrils. His escort riding shotgun looks back to say, "Welcome home," and Caleb nods with a laugh that, before he can stop himself, turns into sobbing. Again the couple look forward to allow him privacy as best they can. They avoid Times Square but the neon glow from its marquises shines down Forty-Second Street. They cross to the east side in the Fifties and when they turn up Madison Avenue past the Plaza, he realizes the chauffeurs are taking him to Mr. Yamaguchi's.

"Why not Queens?"

Mr. Shotgun shrugs. "This is the address they gave us."

THE PROPHET OF CENTRAL PARK

Caleb sees the hand of Mr. Strauss in the instructions and feels too tired to argue but feels cheated too. Composing the script for a reunion helped Caleb endure the root cellar. Anticipating it stretched the day's journey out like a toffee highway that threatened to never end. He savors the funk that takes hold, ignores Mr. Shotgun's phone call to let the other end know they are almost there. He consoles himself that he might get a second wind before the night is through and as they turn down Haruto's street, Caleb tells himself he can borrow cab fare.

Sidney and Davey wait on the sidewalk for the Yaris. Tawana stands on the stoop beside Haruto. Mr. Strauss is there too with another man dressed in a suit. When Caleb straightens himself from the backseat, the two men hurry forward to help him and the guitarist covers her mouth with both hands, not trusting what she might blurt out. Caleb feels as if the world has righted itself.

"Hey, everybody, did you miss me?"

* * *

Both men hug him, carefully.

"Goddamn, Caleb, you look awful," Sidney says.

"Smell awful too," Davey says on top of that.

"Believe it or not, this is an improvement," then Caleb turns to the chauffeurs. "Appreciate you fetching me here."

The driver nods but Mr. Shotgun holds up his phone. "Can I get a selfie with you?"

Caleb doesn't want to be photographed looking as he does. Before he can explain why not, the attorney is there. "No photographs. No telling how it could be manipulated if your selfie got out."

Mr. Shotgun almost squeaks saying, "I wouldn't send it to anyone."

For the first time the Yaris driver speaks. "Get in the car now." They drive off trailing the start of an argument: "Are you kidding me with that?", "What's the big deal?"

Then Tawana is before Caleb, embracing him, her lips brushing his ear. "I didn't know if . . . ." He tells her, "Neither did I for awhile," and he yields for as long as she will hold him. Mr. Strauss ends the moment.

"We need to get him inside."

P C Burhenne

The stranger in the welcome party turns out to be a doctor. After examining Caleb, he says, "She was right. He belongs in a hospital." The attorney states how an overnight stay would be better for the record but they all seem resigned to Caleb's refusal and the doctor produces a saline pouch. Soon Caleb is again hooked up to an IV drip, the bag hanging from the coat stand Haruto moves from the hallway. The doctor leaves them, promising to stop by first thing in the morning.

The attorney tells the room then, "I need a few minutes alone with Caleb before all of you start asking him questions." When Haruto leads the others to the kitchen, Mr. Strauss says, "I've already notified the FBI of your return. They've agreed to wait until tomorrow to talk to you but they'll be here first thing. I'll be here too but I don't want any surprises. So what happened?"

Despite all the abuses at his father's hands, Caleb has to force himself to name Alfred Sr. When he comes to his brother's role, Caleb continues with, "Hypothetically, what if" but the attorney stops writing. "No hypotheticals."

"But before I tell you any more, I just want to know--" then the regret that moves Mr. Strauss to wet his lips silences Caleb.

"Your brother turned himself in this afternoon. Your father has disappeared."

"They have to know what Al Jr. did for me." Caleb taps the attorney's pad. "You have to tell them."

The rest of what he remembers takes only a few minutes to tell. Different angles from different interrogators but the same effort to "convince" him. So much of the time was spent under the hood. Caleb understands how he could have lost count of the days. He considers leaving Mr. Tompkins out of the story but realizes that his brother might not do the same. When Caleb finishes, Mr. Strauss draws the same line repeatedly on the bottom of the sheet. Caleb realizes this is the attorney seething.

"What's going to happen to my brother?"

Mr. Strauss looks up from his incensed graffiti. "His actions on your behalf are grounds for leniency but it depends on how much he cooperates. Does he identify the other men in that cellar?" The attorney packs his satchel. "Get some rest. I'll see you tomorrow."

Haruto brings Caleb another helping of soup broth, but with toast on the side this time. Between spoonfuls and sips of water, he tells what happened again, ending with the coda which Mr. Strauss just supplied. When he finishes the meal, Haruto brings Caleb ice again. "You should buy stock." When the drip finishes, the man removes the IV port. "I learned how to do this for your uncle." Caleb summons the nerve finally to ask Davey, "I know it's an imposition but can I crash at your place for a little longer?"

The sculptor smacks his lips. "Yes and no." At that Caleb thinks that he has indeed overstayed his welcome but the man nods with a faint grin to Sidney. "I'll let your roommate explain."

In his chair Sidney joins his hands by interlocking the fingers, classic sign he is about to make a pitch. "Thing is, an apartment is opening up in Davey's loft and I think we ought to take it. It's a little smaller than his place but no smaller than ours. Money's about the same and it's several stops closer to the city."

"What about our lease?"

Sidney separates his hands to clap them. "That's the best part. I don't think our landlord wants us back. The other tenants made quite a stink about all the media camped around the building so I think he'd be happy to let us out of the lease. How great is that?"

Caleb looks back to the sculptor. "And the rest of the loft members are okay with this. What about all the bother that comes with me?"

"Everybody in the loft is hungry for more attention, not less."

The good news overwhelms Caleb. Then, "I guess I better find a job so I can pay the rent."

"You will," Haruto assures him. "But you don't have to solve all your problems tonight. And, Caleb, I hope you know you can stay here for as long as you want to keep a low profile."

Caleb lets go of his smile. "Low profile, what's that? I tried keeping my head down until everything blows over, and it didn't work."

Sidney and Davey look to each other for how to respond, and worry takes hold of Haruto. Tawana gives him a sad and knowing smile.

* * *

Haruto offers to put up all four guests but Davey returns to Queens. The host assigns the bed and bath at the back of the first floor to the convalescent. Before Caleb heads to the room, he takes Tawana aside. "I need to tell you about some things that happened while they held me."

"You will. But not tonight." She holds his hand. "You need rest now."

The luxury of a shower makes him truly relax, first through his shoulders, then in his lower back and throughout his whole body so that he shuts off the water before he collapses in the stall. Afterwards he phones his sister on the landline. She guesses who the New York caller is.

"Caleb, how are you?"

"Better. I'm starting to feel like myself. My one eye's swollen shut."

"Listen, I've got something to tell you about Al Jr."

"I know he turned himself in." Caleb feels unsteady on the side of the bed. "How's his wife? The boys?"

For a moment Carolyne's breath sounds filtered through a fan. "They're in shock. Mom's in pieces. Her one son in jail for holding her other son prisoner. Dad's gone, no one knows where. We have her staying here tonight."

Caleb wants to comfort his mother, but he can't risk finding out that she doesn't want to speak with him. "I'm sorry, Sis, that you got pulled into this."

"Did Dad do that to your eye?"

Caleb considers telling her the why of the punch because of their uncle but says only, "Yes."

"I don't know the way forward, Caleb. I don't know about what you said on that video, but those A-holes you hit, I could never stand with them. And now our father and the people who put him up to this, they've taken crazy to a whole new level. Seems there's no place for me in this argument."

No answer comes to mind except, "Thank you for coming for me, Sis. Thank Terry too for me." Before hanging up, however, he thinks to ask, "How did Mr. Tompkins end up with you?"

"That was all him. He reached out to me as soon as the rumors started."

"What rumors?"

"There were rumors you were around here somewhere as soon as the news broke you'd been snatched. I expected the FBI'd find you. Seen them everyday talking to people. Anyway Mr. Tompkins called me, said if I ever found out where you were, he'd help get you away." Carolyne lowers her voice. "He's a different man since . . . Annaliese. Heard he stopped going to services."

"Heard?"

"We go to a different church now."

Regret and resentment live beneath this statement. Caleb can't tell how much she aims these at him so he says good night.

Caleb goes to sleep with the table lamp on.

Tuesday

AP News

The sudden return of Caleb Ellison five days after his abduction from the New York borough of Queens is raising as many questions as it is answering. Private citizens including family members reportedly rescued the kidnap victim from a farm near Mr. Ellison's hometown, an area in which the FBI deployed numerous resources. Reliable sources within the Bureau are claiming that field officers failed to act upon credible tips that would have led to this location because of directions imposed on the search by Washington. This morning members of both the House and Senate called for those involved to appear before their respective Judiciary Committees to answer questions.

Caleb thrashes awake with his arms to free them from the chair, then he sees he is in a lighted room, Haruto's back room. His breathing returns to normal. The clock shows it is his normal hour to get up. During the night his muscles seized up, especially near his wrists and ankles. The aches make getting out of bed a play in several acts. An outfit of slacks and a light brown pullover shirt, socks and underwear wait folded just inside the door, obviously reached there last night by Haruto. The clothes are big but not so he swims in them. Drawing a glass of water from the bathroom tap is the greatest of freedoms.

He walks with soft feet to the kitchen but his host is already up, as is Sidney who raises a coffee cup from the table when Caleb enters. Scrambled eggs, toast and freshly squeezed orange juice are ready when Tawana comes down.

His two friends leave, the guitarist with the promise, "We'll talk later." Soon after the doctor is at the door. The exam is brief; he is pleased with his patient's improvement and hurries off to not be late for office hours. Caleb understands how extraordinary his patron is who can arrange an appointment before the doctor's normal workday begins.

Mr. Strauss arrives next followed by two agents, a man and woman in their thirties dressed in unremarkable blue suits. They interview him in the front room. For a third time he struggles to name Alfred Sr. and takes pains to credit his brother's crucial role in his survival. In this telling he realizes that by the end of the ordeal he was not lucid enough to retain many details of his shuttle trip back yesterday. The attorney watches this performance with lips that go bloodlessly pale, but the man hears nothing that requires a pause so he can consult with his client. Still it's after ten when the three of them leave, Mr. Strauss last on purpose so that out of the agents' sight he can shake his head at Caleb's selective memory. Considerately the lawyer leaves another pay-as-you-go cell.

His host pushes more orange juice on Caleb.

"Haruto, at the end of my time, you know, my father let slip something, well, from a really dark place." They are at the kitchen table again. The animated spirit flickers out of the old man, leaving him disheartened at what he expects next, but Caleb continues. "He never really talked much about his father. I never met that grandfather. Just seen pictures. Did William ever mention anything . . . bad about their dad."

"Never. He never spoke of their father." Haruto draws a deep breath. "But that same dark guarded place was in him too. If I ever ventured too close to his childhood, William would not discuss it and I learned not to try."

They talk of other, more trivial things. Haruto asks about the guests who left. He knows them from their vigils held for Caleb, so not well. What does Sidney do and is his cockiness his normal manner? What are Davey's sculptures like? Was that fascinating woman a performer that Haruto might have heard of? When Caleb explains the guitarist's purpose as he understands it, the joyous surprise at making a connection relights the pilot within Haruto.

"Tawana Johnson! Yes, of course. She's doing that big thing in the Park in a few weeks."

"What? Are you sure?" Caleb puts down his drink. "Before I . . . left, she had decided not to do that event."

"Here." Haruto does a search on his phone and hands over an announcement of "Salvation in Central Park: A Christian Crusade with Conversations Between Noel Osterhaus and Tawana Johnson." The photo of the man is professionally composed, the preacher beaming before a congregation of thousands. The one of Tawana looks like a tourist's snapshot that catches the guitarist looking up but not quite facing her audience. "This upsets you? Why?"

"Tawana didn't entirely trust Noel Osterhaus's motives," Caleb says, holding back the phone. "I just don't understand the change of heart."

"The city's expecting the biggest event since Simon and Garfunkel," Haruto continues, though with not quite as much enthusiasm. "People will be traveling from across the country to attend."

Caleb taps a fingernail against the glass. "Sounds like a huge opportunity."

Haruto moves the conversation on, asks if Caleb has any plans. When Caleb replies that he better start looking for work, the man suggests Caleb take the time to concentrate on his art. Then Haruto snaps his fingers.

"Remember before when I told you I would talk to a gallery owner friend of mine. I did. Agnes is definitely interested. Even more so now, I would imagine. Given all the news coverage."

The prospect of his totems in a dealer's window lifts Caleb in the chair like helium correcting his posture. Until the last comment. "So she wants to sell mementos of the disaster of my life."

"No." Haruto throws this word forward as a roadblock to that train of thought. "Agnes recognizes the value of celebrity but she doesn't lend her name to work she doesn't believe in. I showed her videos of you in the Park. Your sculptures genuinely interested her."

"She really liked them." Hope seeps back.

"You should talk to her." Haruto grins and could be a delighted boy flashing his large front teeth. "I can call for an appointment, if you want. She's a short walk up Park Avenue."

"Well . . . okay."

* * *

Reuters

Social scientists in the US are warning of a small but growing trend of emigration among young adults. The move typically occurs after the attainment of a graduate or post graduate degree, often in the fields of STEM. Companies from Europe, and to a lesser extent Japan and South Korea, are sending recruiters to American campuses, and their message of more affordable health care, safer work environments and overall higher quality of life seems to be resonating among a segment of young adults who have come of age during the increasingly strident and sometimes violent cultural discord of the past two decades. Experts worry that if current patterns continue, they will cause a significant and costly "brain drain" on American society.

The two quotes play in Caleb's head like dueling banjos: from John, "You will know the truth and the truth will make you free," and Galatians, "So I have become your enemy by telling you the truth." He suspects both will prove true.

He is headed toward Park Avenue and the steady rain sounds like the muffled popping of heated corn on the borrowed umbrella. The cover from this obscures him well enough but he stills checks behind compulsively. The appointment with Agnes Lansky is in fifteen minutes. Caleb pulls out the new phone to make the call he didn't think wise at Haruto's. When it goes to voicemail, he leaves a message, "Rolando, It's me, Caleb. Call me back at this number when you can. And yeah, I have yet another cell." His friend answers within a block.

"Man, are you in one piece? Where are you? The hospital?"

"No need for that." Caleb looks down at Haruto's sneakers "I'm on my feet."

"Damn, C, there's no keeping you out of the crosshairs, is there?"

"That's why I'm calling. I need your help." Caleb explains his plan. When he finishes, Rolando's laugh is a slow starting chuckle that takes off like a car engine turning over in the cold. "You sure you wanna do that after everything that's dropped on you?"

"I've tried laying low. Look what that's got me. No, I'm going to tell the story loud."

"Well, if you're sure, you know I'll help you with the show. When you want to do this?"

"When's your next day off?"

"Day after tomorrow."

"Day after tomorrow it is. Thanks, Rolando."

P C Burhenne

"Hey, C," his friend barks out to hold Caleb on the phone. "Reynaud's gonna be so happy I talked to you. The news really scared him. He prayed for you every night. We all did."

The Lansky Gallery is on the second floor of a townhouse on Seventy Seventh Street, shattering the fantasy of his work on display in a prominent window. The woman who buzzes him up is nearly as tall as Caleb and broader. Blue mascara encircles her eyes, a plum red paints her lips and a trio of barrettes fail to keep her greying dark brunette hair forming a wispy white-streaked headdress over her wide forehead. Her outfit is a chocolate brown ankle length leather skirt and a blouse splattered with multi-colored triangles that make him slightly dizzy when he peers too long at the disarray. Her voice is a deep-welled chime that Caleb guesses she can easily convert to a hammer.

"Oh, you poor boy, what's been done to you?"

Caleb opens his mouth to politely make light of his recent past, says instead, "Yeah."

Agnes has them sit at a desk in the rear of the showroom. "So why do you make these pieces you make?"

He considers talking about his grandfather but guesses she is not interested in the roadmap that brought him to the gallery. "I see them, inside the scraps of wood. They reveal themselves to me. They're lost if I don't free them. And I think I'm a bit lost without them too."

She moves the loose fist she has pressed to her mouth. "Have you always been like this?"

"Yes and no really. I grew up whittling but that part of me changed when I moved to the city. I had big empty spaces and that part of me grew to fill them."

When Agnes asks about his methods, Caleb senses he has progressed to another level. She asks about the scale he has chosen and he explains the limits of his work space, then finds himself recounting Davey's suggestion for moving forward to which she nods in emphatic approval.

"I can't make a final decision from video. I need you to bring me a sampling. Say five or six pieces. Are you up to bringing them tomorrow?"

As he starts back to Fifth Avenue, Caleb gapes at the chance that the gallery owner will sell his totems. Yet another extreme to which he is swinging. The weather is no longer oppressive. If not for his depleted energy, he would skip.

Then he freezes.

A man in a trench coat and black fedora darts towards Caleb in front of an approaching cab, the man's gaze locked on him. He swings around to fight off the ambush creeping from behind, but the next nearest pedestrian is just in view from Park Avenue. The horn blast brings Caleb forward again. The taxi is stopped because the man has stopped in the street too, suddenly unsure if he wants to approach Caleb's agitated dance. The taxi driver yells for him to move and the man retreats to the far side and hurries away without again making eye contact with the poor, unstable soul panicking beneath his umbrella. Caleb can't catch his breath until a flash of insight shouts, you're hyperventilating. He pulls his shirt up over his mouth. A few seconds of the strained air slows his heartbeat but the fright holds on so that he has to lean against the wall of a stoop. His body aches all over again and he doesn't know how he will reach the subway.

He makes the trek praying the whole way, "One more step, Lord. One more step." Thankfully, Sidney left money for him this morning. The further end of the subway platform seems a mile away but is unoccupied. However, when the train pulls in and he enters the last car, people begin taking second and third glances in his direction. At his station in Queens, he calls Davey to be ready to let him in. "There's a crowd," the sculptor warns him. Caleb groans then tells himself, Think. Past the corner, the herd of newspeople congest the pavement at the building's entrance. He drops the dome of the umbrella over his face and comes to the crowd between their vans. "What's going on?" A bored cameraman barely looks up from his phone. "Caleb Ellison's around here somewhere." The seconds bought by the question see him most of the way through the clog before the reporters start pushing their devices at him. On the other side of the door, the sculptor is coming from the stairwell. Caleb turns as he closes the umbrella. "Please, folks, I'm exhausted. Please let me be until . . . I can stand up straight." The media people record this and surprisingly out of the group comes a quiet and kind, "Welcome back." Others call out agreement as Davey lets him in.

"Wow, considerate press, don't see that every day."

Davey leads them back to the stairs, Caleb assumes so they're out of sight of cameras more quickly. However, the climb is a chore. On the third floor the sculptor waits by the elevator. "You wanna go up to the apartment for a nap?"

Caleb shakes his head and lets his hurried breath run down to normal. "I wanna see your hawk."

When they enter the studio area, Caleb sees that Davey has detailed to below the breast and down the back so the raptor appears to be shaking off an icy coat.

"It's amazing."

"Gotta push on. Client's getting antsy," the sculptor says, as if Caleb hadn't paid him a compliment.

Caleb notices a pile of wood scraps by the back partition. "Those are for you," Davey says. "I've had people on the lookout." He then holds open the rear curtain for Caleb to go through. His tools and the start he made on the serpent sit on a worktable with his boxed totems on the shelf underneath. "We borrowed a friend's car yesterday after you called. It was pretty clear you weren't going back to that apartment." He corrects the position of the Japanese saw. "Your roommate grabbed a bunch of your clothes. They're upstairs. He returned your library books too."

The unexpected favors stun and relieve Caleb. His fatigue at the small amount of exercise today had him doubting he could gather the samples that Agnes asked for tomorrow. He runs a hand over the segments he completed for his snake. "I've missed all this," and he says, "This means the world to me."

Davey nods and at first Caleb thinks he is accepting the thanks, but the gesture continues as a prelude to, "Your Mr. Strauss sent someone up to talk to Julius. My boy called me. Almost crying. Everything he could do not to. **That** meant the world to me. What's wrong?"

"I only asked his opinion. I mean, he's looking into your friend's case. That's great. It's just," and with a mounting sense of dread, Caleb allows, "I don't know how I'm gonna pay him."

The sculptor narrows his eyes, obviously annoyed. "Not you. We. How are we gonna pay the man?"

* * *

THE PROPHET OF CENTRAL PARK

AP News

Today the American Booksellers Association launched the "Banned Books Repository Website." The ABA intends the online address to be an alternative for readers, many of them students, denied access to titles by state legislatures across the country. The endeavor represents a remarkable moment of cooperation among writers, agents, publishers, and retailers—industry participants often at odds with each other over the question of rights and royalties. Creators say the site is a necessary response to the rising tide of censorship spreading across America.

Davey gives him the key and in the apartment Caleb crawls into the guest bed. Seemingly a moment later he hears Sidney promising somebody, "God as my witness, that's how he got caught," followed by unfamiliar giggling. The phone shows it is six and the pepper-laced aroma of his roommate's chili sets Caleb's mouth to watering. He goes out to the kitchen where Sidney is at the stove dividing his attention between the meal and a petite blond leaning against the counter. Davey, Tawana and—in a bit of a shock—Haruto take in the chef's performance with expressions ranging from amusement to head shakes. Sidney points his stirrer at Caleb. "And this is the sleepy-head you might have been hearing about. Caleb, this is Leila, a talented performer who lives down the hall."

The young actor's smile becomes rigid when she turns. Caleb guesses that the bruising has blown up again. "Sorry, ah, I'm not at my best after a nap."

"No, no, nonsense," and Leila gives out another giggle but one weaker for being forced. "I better go start my dinner too. Bye, Davey. Bye, Tawana," and to Caleb before she leaves, "I'm glad you're safe . . . Mr. Ellison."

"Is my face really that bad?"

"It's shit," and getting up, the sculptor tells him, "You need to ice that more."

"That outfit isn't helping matters," Sidney says. "You look like a witch doctor's half way done shrinking your head."

Tawana lurches forward with laughter and at the refrigerator, Davey wipes his grin into the palm of his hand. Haruto makes himself be upset. "Young man, I did the best I could with what I had."

"Oh, I understand making the most of what you have," and Sidney holds up his arms. "Look at me. There is no reason why I should be so irresistible to women."

Over the meal Davey explains that the group drew close waiting for news of Caleb. Haruto says that the loft reminds him of the East Village community he found in his twenties. Every time Caleb tries to put down the compress, they yell, "No!" in a chorus. He makes a game of seeing if he can reach the table with the bag before they object. He cannot remember a happier meal.

When the kitchen is clean, Haruto heads out for Manhattan, telling them he doesn't miss the couches he slept on in his twenties. Davey suggests Rachmaninoff but Caleb stares at the guitarist and she understands. "Caleb and I are going to talk in private."

She takes him to her monk's cell, arranges the chairs like the last time so he is facing her.

"You need to know, the people holding me, they talked about you," he tells her. "I don't mean my father. I mean the two who were in charge. They knew things that could only have come from investigating you."

She shrugs. "I'm flattered?" then at his hesitancy, she says, "The things bothered you?"

"I'm worried for you. Especially now that you've agreed to this crusade thing in the Park. It can't be a big coincidence."

"What did they say."

"That you were a prostitute when you were younger. That you had an abortion."

A wan smile bothers the corners of her mouth. "Nothing I haven't heard before. Listen, Caleb, I ended up on the street as a teenager. I was homeless for almost two years."

"How?" Caleb asks before he realizes it's rude to do so.

"My father was killed when I was three. He walked into a bodega robbery. The man didn't even give him a chance to raise his hands. That's what I was told. Arthur was his name. He worked so hard and left us with nothing. I often think that was his dying regret. Do you ever wonder about that, if at the end we finally consider the people around us?"

The sincerity of the question compels Caleb back to his grandpa's bedside. To Annaliese's. Pop Pop's last remark for Caleb's ears was at the hospice. Caleb's mom had cleared the others from the room as her father asked. "Don't forget there's a mountain of good outside that church of yours." This even as the morphine failed to blunt the teeth of the cancer. In contrast the agony ripping her apart trapped Annaliese inside herself. "I think probably the way we live is the way we die," Caleb says. "Most people don't do that enough, get out of their heads to help others. I don't. You believing that of your dad probably means he was one of those special few."

"Thing is, I didn't really know him. He was always working. A day job then night school to become an accountant. My one lasting memory is falling asleep in his lap while he read 'Goodnight Moon' to me. Tracing the orange lines on his shirt before I couldn't keep my eyes open anymore. Whenever I see a black man in the crowd wearing a button-down with those stripes, I think--Arthur's checking on me." Tawana stares down as if describing a photograph from an album on her lap. "My mother was amazing, though. I'm sure she cried but she was always strong in front of me so I'd know we would be alright and it couldn't have been easy. She loved my father awful. She never let another man in her life. She said she'd never get that lucky twice." Caleb dreads what must come next. "Just after my thirteenth birthday she dropped dead. Massive coronary. She gave everything to keep us together. I got sent to live with her sister, and the husband." A child could be speaking this last, Tawana's voice changes so. She straightens and looks up and again sounds like the guitarist when she continues. "After my dad's death, the sister kept telling us we should move in with them. They had a house in East New York. Mom would never agree and she told me she would never allow me to be alone with the husband and that I shouldn't allow myself to be alone with him either. Of course the first week he tried to . . . rape me. Because of my mother's warning, I was ready to fight him off. When I told—I can't call her my aunt—when I told the sister, she said I was an ungrateful liar who'd been poisoned against her husband. I ran away and they wouldn't take me back after the police found me. I was in care and on my own after that, dealing with all that comes of that life." The calm that first attracted Caleb's attention on the subway descends upon Tawana. Her full lips purse and her nostrils quiver with her breathing. "My story is my story. I own it humbly and without shame. I certainly won't deny it."

Caleb wants to take on her peace of mind but fear remains. "Have you met this Noel Osterhaus? Do you trust him?"

"We've spoken via Zoom. I trust," and Tawana pauses to review her judgment. "That he has not hidden anything from me."

"Not exactly shouting that 'yes' out from the rooftops."

Tawana chuckles. "I suppose you're right. Well then this. We both credit each other with seeking the same Presence though we haven't seen Him, or Her, in the same way."

"But--"

Caleb realizes he's being nosy and clamps his mouth shut, shaking his head and waving his hands that he's sorry. In that unsettling way of hers, Tawana finishes the question for him. "Why did I change my mind about taking part?"

"Okay, yes. You were very skeptical before I . . . got taken."

The guitarist ducks her head aside. Caleb can't tell whether she is acknowledging this last phrase or shying from it. Then she faces him again. "I'm a servant of the message entrusted to me. And a student. I forget that part sometimes. If I challenge Noel Osterhaus's claim to know absolutely the Goddess's will, I have to challenge my own." She brushes his uninjured cheek with her fingertips. "Whatever he may be doing, I'm not competing with this man. I'm trying to sharpen, or, or, to move closer to that Will. And perhaps this man and I can open the door for the Divine to enter the gathering. That is surely worth the attempt."

Tawana sits back. Caleb's face tingles where she touched it. With that same insight she asks, "Is that all you wanted to talk about?"

She'll say I'm delusional—Caleb warns himself—She'll say it was the no water. Pushing aside the qualms he asks, "What's it like when you make contact with . . . ." and he points upward.

She smiles. "We know each other well enough for you to tell me what you really want to say."

"Someone . . . something . . . a presence was with me in that cellar. In my head. A companion. That helped me hold on."

THE PROPHET OF CENTRAL PARK

Tawana has leaned forward. "And you want to know if God spoke to you?" He nods and she asks, "What did this companion tell you?"

Caleb recounts everything he can remember, even the remarks that seemed very ungodly, then with a bracing intake of air, he admits, "And I recognized the voice. It was a homeless person who begs where I worked at Rockefeller Center."

The guitarist is more intent than Caleb has ever known her to be, taking in not just what he says but the cast of his eyes and any frown marks and all the rest of his delivery as if every element helps inform her of his experience. She sort of whistles her breath out when he's done. "I can't tell you if that was God with you during your ordeal. I will tell you any contact I've had—that I believe is genuine—hasn't come from up there." She indicates the ceiling as he did. "But from within here and here," and she touches her head and heart.

"What do you mean, 'contact that is genuine'?"

"Seeking to know God has been a hazardous journey for me. At times." She looks up from where her eyes had again settled upon her lap. "I've deluded myself at times into believing what I wanted to believe. I've been misled. When we first met, I told you doubt is essential to faith. It is for mine. Without it, I can find myself chasing will-o-wisps into very dark and lonely places." Tawana makes a wincing sheepish face at her own dire tone. "That might not have helped you much."

"It, it, well, no," and he smiles too.

The guitarist takes his hands in hers. "Answer me this. Without thinking about it. In that room, did you believe that your companion was there to help you?"

"Absolutely."

"Then you were lucky the companion was there."

P C Burhenne

Wednesday: Two Weeks, Three Days Before the Event on the Great Lawn

Houston Chronicle
  Political observers in Texas are closely watching a demographic shift occurring in and about Austin. Determinedly Democratic homeowners are migrating from the overwhelmingly blue 37th district to the 10th and 21st which were redrawn in 2021 by GOP lawmakers to safeguard those seats for their colleagues. However, red majorities shrunk over the latest election cycle and surveys conducted since suggest the trend of atrophy is continuing. Republican officials claim that the relocation of so may politically like-minded people from and to the same districts must be part of an engineered campaign but can cite no law that the movement is breaking. Interviews with recent transplants bring credence to GOP suspicions. The Alvarezes, who closed on their new home in July, told this paper, "Since the courts will do nothing to stop the disenfranchisement of Democrats in this state, and specifically minorities, it's up to us to vote with our pocketbooks."

Caleb wakes early but rested. He is surprised to have slept so soundly. Last evening, despite Tawana's reassurances, foreboding for her stayed with him back in Davey's apartment. When he lay down, however, his body overruled his mind.

Toast is the quietest breakfast. Meal in hand, he slips from the apartment with the sculptor's keys. Two news vans wait outside in the morning dark and rain. Caleb exits the building hunched forward like an old man beneath Haruto's umbrella and makes a show of a creaky shuffle away. No one follows. Yesterday he decided he should appear at the gallery with some type of packing between the totems. The New York Post seems the perfect choice. He repeats the elderly performance to get back inside.

Sidney is in the shower. A replacement fisherman's cap sits on the table, weighed down by another pair of sunglasses. He almost calls out, Thank you, but there is no glow from Davey's room. He replaces the keys and takes the disguise with the newspaper to the third floor.

The switches take some finding. He sticks the crumpled sheets of the Post around six works in a travel box then returns to the serpent in progress. The work calms him but can't totally dispel the worries about Tawana. An hour later the rustle of plastic announces Davey.   The sculptor says, "Damned, you **are** an early riser," as he hands over one of the cups he is holding. "Black with sugar." After Caleb thanks him, Davey asks, "What's eating you, kid? It was in your face all last night and it's there now. What is it?"

Caleb tells about his captors' knowledge of Tawana and the history that the guitarist revealed, finding himself relieved to share their burden. Until he notices Davey become more and more antsy.

"Shit, I never thought," the sculptor says. The cryptic reaction doesn't help, but Davey starts and stops himself explaining three times, holding up a finger repeatedly as he reconsiders. Finally, "We met when Tawana was still on her own. This was over in Flatbush. I'd seen her around, hadn't quite put together she was on the street. Probably didn't want to. I was tied up in my own thing. But then I heard this neighborhood pimp was squeezing her to let him turn her out and I decided that wasn't gonna happen. I mean, that same thing happened regular on that block but Tawana, she still looked at you like you might help her. Like you were good. So I got her away."

"You think that's the prostitution story these guys might want to put out."

Davey puts the cup down. "I think . . . I may not know all that went on. I think I got her clear of that scumbag before he had her turning tricks but I don't know for certain." Then the sculptor flails his right hand as if erasing every word of what he just said from a blackboard. "And Tawana's right. It doesn't matter. She was a child got left behind. Just trying to survive."

About the rest, Caleb can just bring himself to say, "The abortion?"

"Not while I've known her," then the man looks up from the floor. "But . . . ."

"You can't know for sure," Caleb says for him. As Davey nods, frustration at the guitarist boils over in Caleb. "Why would she agree to this whole ecumenical show when she didn't trust the guy from the start?"

Davey raises his finger again to referee what seems another internal debate. Then, "She made a deal. She would participate if he publicly condemned your abduction and called for your release. He kept up his side of the bargain. On every broadcast. On his social media."

Caleb can't meet Davey's eyes because of the trouble he's brought to their friend. "I did this to her."

"Hey, hey, this isn't your fault. It's the people who kidnapped you. Tortured you."

Caleb nods but it is a gesture easily missed, and he still won't face Davey. To change the subject he asks the first question he can think of. "How'd you get her away back then."

"My aunt took her in. I convinced her we could save Tawana. Wilfreda's got a big heart. She raised Tawana, got her back in school. She really did save her."

"So Tawana got a family back, in a way," Caleb says, clutching at this one happy ending.

"She's drawn a family about herself, yeah." Davey scratches his jawline as now he looks away. His voice goes, not cold, neutral. "But Wilfreda doesn't speak with Tawana anymore. She's a religious woman. A Bible religious woman. She can't accept the things Tawana professes." Davey takes up his cup. "I'll leave you to it."

* * *

Houston Chronicle

One private company financed the vast majority of mortgages connected to the voter transference trend occurring in and about Austin. Records show that wealthy Democratic supporters are the primary investors in Equitable Texas One. The entity is making loans on terms far more favorable than market rates. Republican elected officials warn that the enterprise sets a dangerous precedent which the GOP will necessarily duplicate in coming years. Democratic strategists respond that if white conservatives were comfortable living next to lower and/or minority households, gerrymandering would not be the corrosive agent to fair representation that is is today.

Davey remembers a basement door at their rear of the building. Caleb feels embarrassed walking by the sculptor for an interview with a dealer

THE PROPHET OF CENTRAL PARK

earned because of his notoriety. Seeing the discomfort Davey gives him a sardonic smile. "Gotta admit, normally I'd be pissed, you getting tossed this chance. Can't tell you how many times starting out, dealers saw my work, called me to meet, then when they clocked I was black, found reasons why my stuff wouldn't sell. But I can't argue, you paid for this meeting." The back way empties into an overshadowed side alley that he has walked by without really noticing. He takes this to the street one over from the posse of reporters. The rain has stopped but he opens the umbrella for cover.

The new hat and glasses keep him anonymous for most of the train ride, but the discolored half of his face draws looks that eventually place him. Riders are angling their phones for videos as the train pulls into 59$^{th Street}$. On the way to the meeting, his heart constricts again when a burly man is walking toward him. This time another man is not far behind Caleb but the stout pedestrian passes without even a stranger's "Hello" and the tail goes into a brownstone. He is glad for the remaining walk to the gallery so he can compose himself.

Agnes Lansky is talking with customers so her assistant seats him with a water. The longer the wait stretches, the more Caleb sees himself as a country rube again, this time with a cardboard box of wood fiddlings. He nearly leaves but the clients do so first and the owner blocks his exit.

"Let's see then, shall we?"

Before he can comply, she removes a piece and begins to walk about the desk to review it so that he steps back out of her path. During this circuit, she swirls and points her arms like a conductor guiding her orchestra, though the flurry of her gold-laced purple caftan lends an oriental flair to the performance. Each time she transfers a totem to the floor by the wall, he finds it harder to not sigh aloud. After inspecting the last, she claps her hands. As he recovers from the ringing finale, she reunites two of the dismissed sculptures with the one now on the desk top.

"I want these."

The selection looses a tug-of-war inside Caleb. Resentment for those not chosen wins out. "Why not the others."

"They are not finished. They are unfinished," and she takes up each to draw attention to its flaws. Though prepared to argue, he recognizes all of these—rough surfaces, ungraceful lines, awkward joints—as shortcomings of craftsmanship and grows more and more mortified. Which seems to satisfy her. After Caleb puts away the trio coming home with him, Agnes has him sign a gallery agreement. "You're lucky to have Haruto negotiating on your behalf," then she has him sign the three she will be exhibiting. As goodbye, she announces, "People will be seeing your work over the next week," tells him to "Look after yourself" as she closes the door. He walks away, unsure if the meeting was a success.

His benefactor—one of his benefactors, Caleb corrects himself—is at home when Caleb phones. Haruto asks him to stop by to tell all about the interview. At the door, his host chides Caleb for not icing his eye enough then leads him to the kitchen where shortbread cookies wait beside a carafe of fresh coffee. "Maybe I should make you a sandwich. Lord, you need to put on weight. Tuna salad?"

Caleb gives out a broken chain of laughter, still distracted by his gallery experience. "I need you to tell me how it went with Agnes."

Haruto looks back from the refrigerator. The sandwich is happening. "What did she say?"

Caleb goes through the encounter as Haruto puts together his meal. The host snickers at the dramatic inspection, rolls his eyes with a knowing smirk at the dealer's criticism, and the vague "people'll be seeing" comment causes Haruto's lips to pucker as if the remark is a vintage wine. Caleb again feels himself a boy from the backwaters but this time happily so.

"Okay, you're still a little loopy, obviously, so listen to me." Haruto places the food before Caleb. "One, she took your work, an important art dealer took your work, and believe me, Agnes is important. Two, she told you what she expects, so you know now what's good enough to bring her. And three, she's been able to generate advance interest in you over the phone. That's called a successful meeting, young man. Eat."

"Sorry. It's just, that woman's hard to read."

"Agnes is a colorful, charismatic bird of prey. You couldn't have a fiercer champion, but always read the fine print."

Caleb starts at a jolt of terror. "I already signed something. She said you had--"

Haruto speaks over him. "Yes. We discussed the guarantees you should have and Agnes wouldn't renege on what she agreed to because, well . . . she knows better than to do that with me. But, going forward . . . ." The man emphasizes these last two words then stares for Caleb to complete the thought.

"Always read the fine print?"

"Excellent!" and content with his student's progress, he pours himself a coffee. "Now eat."

Caleb does and the tuna salad has a wonderfully unusual flavor though he can't guess the spice responsible. "Thank you, by the way. For negotiating for me. I'd have had no idea what to ask for."

Haruto flashes his toothy grin. "Obviously."

As he chews Caleb looks up at the track lighting and eight inch crown molding of Haruto's designer kitchen. That once was his uncle's. "It's strange being here. I mean being in this position that you helped me reach." Across the table Haruto has gone serious. "I know it's you who's done it. Mr. Strauss, Agnes. But it kind of feels like it's William too. Does that make any sense?" His host nods but says nothing. "I wish I could thank him and I wish I could tell him, 'Sorry', too. My family cut him off for no good reason. My dad. Just because he was different. I wish I could tell him that I know how much my dad cheated us all. William, me, my brother and sister. My dad even cheated himself. Looking back, I don't know that he's ever been happy. Just so much unnecessary pain. And despite all that, my Uncle William and you, Haruto, you saved my bacon. Someone fed me a story like that, I 'd call them a big fat liar."

For a moment, Haruto just stares off, his pupils active as if following text down a page. Then he stands up. "Excuse me, I need to get something." As the man leaves, Caleb wonders if he offended Haruto. The man returns clasping an envelope to his chest.

"Please, please, keep eating," and the man holds the item upright on the table. The unsteady handwriting across its face reads, "To my family."

"When William knew he didn't have much time, he wrote a series of letters. He always felt he expressed himself better with a pen. I got one. And he entrusted me with this. It isn't meant for just any family member who might show up. He told me it was for a relative that he and I would have welcomed into our home, and who would welcome us into his or her home. He left it to me to decide."

Haruto slides the letter to Caleb.

P C Burhenne

* * *

Wired

An internet movement born at the start of September has gained momentum in places of worship throughout the country. Posts to Mastodon called for "believers in a God who loves all people" to come together in a spirit of understanding. The message quickly inspired an online community whose mission was a day committed to prayer for "open hearts" as an answer to the divisions in America. Religious leaders across all faiths have taken up the challenge and the subsequent interfaith dialogues have settled many to dedicate their services on October's first Saturday to the ideal of fellowship beyond walls. A survey of churches, temples and mosques in several cities finds that nearly half the respondents plan to participate in some fashion. The observances coincide with the Salvation in Central Park event in New York City.

Caleb rests his fingers on the letter. "I think I'll read it later, if that's all right?"

"Of course."

He returns Haruto's umbrella and, feeling tired with one more stop, he leaves the box of passes. Haruto arranges the totems on the sills of the front windows. "Agnes is right but they're still quite stirring."

Caleb heads out again. The sunshine glows in the fractures of the cloud cover and when he reaches Fifth Avenue, pedestrians speckle the sidewalks so that he is not so anxious about being followed and/or pursued. At the south end of the Park, weariness almost turns him down the subway stairs, but he perseveres to Rockefeller Center. As he approaches the square, the thumping from his chest reverberates through his body as if it is a clocktower disturbed by the toll of a bell, but the homeless person is not there.

Rainbow Rights Railroad volunteers are manning a stand, however. He introduces himself which turns out to be unnecessary. One of the young men exclaims, "Jesus Christ, I thought that was you," while his cohort shakes Caleb's hand. He hurries to explain whom he needs to speak with. Passersby are stopping around the table, much as they did for the event that launched him to this place. The excitable RRR member contacts a supervisor and, after convincing the person that Caleb is really at his side, hands over the phone. Caleb outlines his plan for the following morning to which the woman on the other end responds, after a pause, "I'll need to ask some other people about this."

"Understood," Caleb says. "But I'm going ahead."

The crowd is surprisingly deep about them. People yell out for selfies. Caleb starts pushing through the assembly, telling them, "Please, I have to go," and Mr. Excitable comes to his aid by making himself a wedge in front of Caleb. When they break clear, the volunteer falls behind as an obstacle to the few who keep up the chase all the way to the Avenue. For the first time Caleb questions tomorrow's plan, but he is committed. The female supervisor is making a decision based upon his pledge and Caleb has no way to cancel except to go back to the square which he can't bring himself to do. Anyway he is determined that this time he will narrate his story.

His shoes are weights on his feet by the time he reaches the subway platform. He ignores the other commuters on the train. In Queens the bodega provides him a cardboard box. He enters the loft though the front. Only a pair of never-say-never photographers remain. They snap image after image of the back of his head, all the while calling for Caleb to turn around, until Davey appears from the elevator. The sculptor greets him with, "You need to lay down, kid," then on the ride up, asks, "What's with the Charmin box."

"Arts and crafts project. Do you have any black markers?"

In the loft Davey rustles two up from his desk, hands them over with a key. "For the front door, so you don't have to bother me when you want to come in. I already gave Sidney his."

Caleb flops onto the couch but before kicking off his shoes, he thinks he should confirm that Rolando is still up for tomorrow. As soon as the text goes through, however, he stretches out. Sleep has him before his friend replies.

* * *

Wall Street Journal

A roster of influential jurists yesterday announced the creation of the Establishment Clause Society before the steps of the US Supreme Court. Per their prepared statement, the founders intend the organization as a bulwark against the Christian Nationalist movement and its advocacy of "Christian Shariah" principles informing American government. The group's membership list, released in conjunction with the press conference, contains the names of prominent law professors at Harvard, Yale, Stanford and Vanderbilt along with a number of federal judges and well-known attorneys. The society's mandate is to provide a comprehensive rebuttal to this doctrine of the "new conservative right" wherever it appears—whether in a courtroom, classroom or legislative chamber.

A pinch at his forehead wakes Caleb to the fact that he has slept on his bruised eye. He retrieves ice for a compress then checks his phone for the time. Rolando's message string is there: "Gave you my word/But U still think it's a good idea?/After what went down with your friend?/Call me."

Caleb does at once. "What happened to Tawana?"

"You don't know?" Traffic peppered with a fading Salsa tune is Rolando's background track. "I's hoping you could tell me more."

"First I'm hearing anything." Caleb hears the frantic in his voice, doesn't care. "What **do** you know?"

"Your girl was live in the Park and some armed dudes stormed her spot. Friends from the South, what I hear. And she did that thing we saw her do, called them up to have their say. Some of her supporters weren't so 'turn the other cheek' and a couple had guns too. There was a face-off. Video's up of it already. That Tawana is cold-blooded. Stood in the middle like OK Corral shit. She got them talking to each other. Then the police showed up."

"Is she all right, though?"

"Easy, C. Haven't heard obit talk," Rolando hurries to calm Caleb's fear, then the man breathes to calm himself. "But you sure about tomorrow?"

The quick crowd he drew a few hours ago gives Caleb pause. Then he pictures the two agitators that he confronted in the same square—God's warriors, his kidnappers called them, men sent to silence "the Devil's lie" with their fists. Caleb clenches his own hand. "I won't hold you to coming, Rolando. Spend the day with Arnaud."

THE PROPHET OF CENTRAL PARK

"You going through with it, though. Don't have to answer. I hear you are."

"I won't let these people hide what they did."

His friend sighs. "Can we do it quick? In and out?"

For a second Caleb loses his words at such a friend. Then, "In and out, that's what I want. Get the recording and get out."

"Okay. Ten o'clock, like we said."

When Caleb seeks out the sculptor, Davey knows nothing about the Park commotion. He pulls out his phone. "I heard some shit, girl. Tell me." Then, "Can you talk?" Finally, "Call me when you can." Pocketing the cell he stares through Caleb and the furrows of his face could be the product of his own tools, a basalt mask of concern.

"She alright?" Caleb asks finally.

"Huh," Davey says first, coming back to his work space. "She's fine. A lot of nothing, she said, but she couldn't really talk. She's still with the police." Davey throws up a hand that Caleb takes as, Don't ask me. It's almost six. They head back to the apartment. Sidney comes in as they are preparing a dinner. His grave face betrays that he has also heard, just as their mute looks reveal that same to him.

"Any word from her?"

"She's fine," and Davey points the spatula at Sidney. "How the hell do you know?"

"Story's blown up. NY1 has had the video on their feed for an hour. It jumped national while I was coming home."

Davey puts out four place settings. They eat without small talk, each glancing in turn at the empty plate. Tawana calls as Sidney and the sculptor are divvying up the last of the meal. Davey puts her on speaker.

"You can all relax. People made more of the day than they should have."

Caleb wants to snap back but Davey does first. "Guns make it a big deal."

"Guns are a fact of life. I go on despite them or I stop and stopping's not an option."

Tawana could be a math teacher illustrating a theorem but Davey bows his head with a scowl and Sidney holds his breath then lets it out with no answer except a helpless stare at the phone. Knowing the equation better than the other two, Caleb makes sure not to catch their eyes. "When will you be back?"

"It's late. I'm gonna stay over in the city tonight. Congratulations, by the way. I hear your meeting with this Agnes lady went well."

"How—you're at Haruto's."

"He told me I always have a bed if I need one. Seemed a good day to take him up on the offer."

Davey keeps his attention on the phone. "What did the cops want with you?"

"A statement. Pro forma."

"They kept you a long time to take a statement?"

"What can I say. Theirs is not a well-oiled machine." A melancholy note enters her voice. "I'm exhausted, guys, but I miss you. Even Sidney. I'll see you tomorrow."

Her absence hollows out the evening. They fall back on TV. The episode in the Park mesmerizes them. The throng of people on the hillside next to the Metropolitan Museum is poised to flee the five brothers-in-arms shouting for Tawana to shut her blasphemous mouth. Then a loose cadre of defenders steps forward with their own holstered pistols. Some spectators do peel away. Others inch closer, outraged faces shouting angry orders, so that the mass compresses toward a pressure point of violence. The whole time Tawana still, her head tilted upward, left hand frozen at a chord on the guitar neck and eyes almost closed so that Caleb knows she's praying. The dark magnetic center of them all. Then she pushes the instrument to her back by its strap and her voice rises above the enraged chatter, loud but not a shout. The exodus stops. Everyone listens. "We've all come to speak of God. To know God. And She is here with us now. Can't you feel that Presence." Tawana reaches out a hand to the closest in both of the two groups faced off about her. The brother-in-arms starts at her touch of his shoulder and looks aside, almost alarmed at what he feels there. Her defender opens his mouth as if he is coming out of a stupor.

The video ends.

They three look at each other, dumbfounded for a moment, until Caleb blurts out, "Jesus Christ."

Sidney turns to him, shocked. "What did you say?"

The question doesn't register. "That was a riot ready to explode. How could anybody do what she did?"

"I've never heard you curse."

Sidney waits, an invitation for Caleb to confirm that he has actually broken the Third Commandment and Caleb realizes his outcry was much more serious than his roommate can imagine.

* * *

Wired

The US maternity mortality rate has not only continued to rise but has seen its rate of increase accelerate also. The World Health Organization defines a maternal mortality as the death of a woman while pregnant or within 42 days of termination of pregnancy from a cause related to or aggravated by the pregnancy or its management, other than by accident or incidental causes. While the Covid pandemic was blamed for the jump in deaths from 2020 to 2022, experts cite the shortage in obstetricians for the worsening problem today. Surveys show that many prospective doctors refuse to enter the specialty because of restrictions that the ongoing debate over abortion has imposed on its practice. The reality for expectant mothers is more dire in states that have enacted strict anti-abortion laws. In the last three years the US has fallen 5 places on the WHO's ranking of countries by this metric, from 55th to 60th, far behind all other wealthy nations and lagging even Moldova and its own impoverished territory of Puerto Rico.

Caleb says goodnight. In the guest room he works on making tomorrow's sign from the cardboard box and felt tip markers. The murmurs of Davey and Sidney talking carry through the wall, then a symphony starts playing. Again and again his mind returns to the video. The arrested brawl and firefight always seem, well, miraculous.

The front room goes quiet before he puts aside the sign to finish when he wakes. As he strips for bed, his uncle's letter comes to hand from his pants' pockets. Happy for a distraction, he leans against the headboard and opens the envelope.

Dear relative,

P C Burhenne

If my beloved Haruto chose to give you this correspondence "from beyond the grave", so to speak, then I deeply regret that we did not meet while I was alive. Part of my reason for writing this is to apologize. Age has convinced me that I bear much fault for that lost opportunity. I also want to explain the circumstances that gave rise to my mistakes and to indulge with you, who I am confident are a sympathetic audience, in a few rueful "what ifs".

My father was a brutal man. To think of him even today when I am decades removed from his belt and fists still makes me tremble. My childhood spanned the years after the Second World War. Domestic violence did not exist in Eisenhower's America. Victims hid their injuries from a shame they had no reason to bear. My poor wonderful mother tried her best to shield us by standing in the path of her husband's anger but despair at last moved her to escape by the only route available. For a while after her suicide I struggled to protect my precious younger brother Alfie in the same way as she had done for us but the same hopelessness overcame me. However, I had an avenue of flight not open to mother.

Gossip being the most difficult currency to retain, you've probably already heard why I left Kentucky, but if not . . . . I was discovered in the midst of a gay sexual encounter at a spot notorious for those types of rendezvous. Over the years I've come to deeply regret that episode but not because of my homosexuality, acceptance of which has allowed me a happy and fulfilling life. Rather, because of the cowardice that brought me to that stall. Hindsight has shown me that I engaged in that risky behavior with the intention of being caught, thus forcing myself to do what I so desperately wanted, flee my tormentor. Of course the public report of my "act of abomination" in a God-fearing Baptist town forced me to abandon my Alfie to an awful fate, but I fully expected to reunite with my brother when he was old enough to follow. I did not foresee that the sordid nature of my departure, coupled with the trauma that he suffered as a result, would forever sour our relationship. Alfie, if you can hear, please forgive me. I was just a boy myself. I am so sorry for what I left you to endure.

Dear relative, you certainly know by now that I have achieved quite remarkable wealth. In fact the years after I left home are the stuff of fairy tales. How the son of a backwoods peddler can claim all of these acts as his own beggars even my comprehension. I have undertaken every adventure that I imagined. I have visited every site of wonder that I happened to learn about. My hands have been blessed to hold some of the most exquisite objects that mankind is capable of producing. And I have given back to those whose journey has not been as fortunate as my own. I have satisfied every purpose that I identified as mine. Except one. It may surprise you that I hold myself a failure because of that exception.

Here is the time for those blue "what ifs". My youth haunts me. Not so much its history as my unwillingness to return to my hometown and family unapologetically proud of who I am. As much as anybody, I possessed the means to do so. My return could have changed people's perceptions. Not everyone's, of course. But some. Even one would have been enough. That's how transformation starts. The people who call me evil know this. It's the reason they work so hard to censor any narrative from those they condemn. My silence abetted them.

I should have tried harder to reconnect with Alfie. It's his life obviously. He had the right to speak to me or no. But I should have kept myself available. I gave up too easily. I miss him still.

So, my point? I guess it is this.

If a growing tolerance in our family has led you to my doorstep, know that I am pleased, if not a little sad that I could not enjoy the benefits in my lifetime. But if like me you came here as a runaway, learn from my mistakes. We never completely escape our childhoods. No matter how painful yours was, find a way to make peace with that first home. Confront it, forgive it, never deny it, this all for the sake of the homes waiting to find you in the future.

And again I am sorry that we never met in person.

Yours truly, William.

P.S. Haruto is a good man. He knows my heart. You can trust him.

Caleb lets go the sheets so they fall onto his lap and stares without seeing the wall and its door.

"Oh, Dad."

P C Burhenne

Thursday: Two Weeks, Two Days Before the Event on the Great Lawn

Al Jazeera
Tennessee lawmakers this week will consider a proposal to lower the minimum age to marry with parental consent to 15 years in cases where the girl is pregnant. This mirrors ongoing debates in the legislatures of several other states in the US. Supporters defend the move as an appropriate response to the rise in teenage pregnancy. Detractors call it a cynical attempt to force young women into marriage after removing their right to an abortion. Children's advocates warn such bills will undo the progress gained over decades to stop the practice of forced child brides.

The sign takes an hour to finish in the morning. The question cards another thirty minutes. Caleb puts off breakfast to not disturb Sidney. On the third floor he ignores the work-in-progress to review his totems through the prism of Agnes's criticism. Several pass this test while the more rigorous scrutiny pinpoints flaws in the rest.

Hat and shades in place, he leaves by the back door, the sign folded in half until he is ready for it to draw attention. A glaze of clouds weakens the sunlight. He is glad he chose a longsleeve shirt. Paying for a bodega sandwich reminds him again that no money is coming in while little by little he is bleeding his savings. On the platform he texts Rolando. On the train he sits at the end of his car, face lolling into the wall, and does not look up until he reaches Times Square. His friend paces near the newsstand by the 42nd Street exit. Because of Sidney's cloaking items provided, Rolando doesn't place Caleb until he is a few feet away then his friend grimaces at the state of Caleb's face and thinned out frame. He forgot Rolando hasn't seen any of the damage that the past ten days visited upon him.

"Christ, C, you really have taken a beatdown."

"Oh, I'm getting better."

None of the usual humor shows in Rolando's face. "You sure you don't want to do this in a more private place?"

THE PROPHET OF CENTRAL PARK

"I want the people who did this to me to know, from now on, I'm not hiding."

Rolando holds him with a stare. "Just remember what you said. Fast, fast, fast."

Caleb nods and leads the way above to Times Square proper. Near the Father Duffy monument before the TKTS red tiered incline, two RRR members stand at a small fold-up metal table. Coming closer, Caleb recognizes Mr. Excitable from yesterday beside an unfamiliar woman. When he introduces himself, her voice reveals her as the supervisor on the phone. She winces at the distorted side of his face but says only, "I don't know how long we'll be allowed to set up here so you should get on with it."

Caleb distributes the cards with the questions to the three of them, confirming the sequence as he does. A scattering of loungers occupy seats about the incline. A few tourists take advantage of the top row to snap treetop photos of the crossroads of the world, and the people and traffic flowing through it. He positions himself close to but not alongside the table and when Rolando has him framed in the cellphone screen so the incline is the backdrop, Caleb removes the glasses and hat, holds open the sign so the viewers can read, "I'm Caleb Ellison. Ask your questions."

Rolando recites his line from memory as he starts recording. "What happened after you were abducted off the street?"

"They injected me with something so I was out for the whole drive back to Kentucky. I came to tied to a chair in a cold cellar beneath a barn. While I was held there, my captors tried to brainwash me into renouncing the things I said on the "Prozac man" video."

His answer stops the flow of passersby for a rough hundred feet about the four of them.

"What do you mean, they tried to brainwash you?" Mr. Excitable asks on cue.

"My captors did not feed me or give me anything to drink the whole time they kept me. They did not free me from the chair. If my brother hadn't gone against their wishes and given me water when the others were asleep, I would have probably died."

Those who stopped are now coming closer as if answering a call to prayer and from what Caleb can see the movement is drawing the curiosity of others further out. The supervisor glances nervously at the growing numbers as she asks, "You said you brother was there. Did your family kidnap you?"

"Parts of my family were involved. I know my father was there but everyone else wore hoods and robes. And, yes, you heard me correctly. They wore hoods and robes. I recognized my brother by his wristwatch. There were four others. I don't know who they were."

Ranks of spectators encircle them by now. Rolando rolls his shoulders to push back against the press of them as he asks, "So how did you get away?"

"My brother changed his mind when he saw that the others might let me die. He got word to friends of his willing to help and they rescued me by force from that cellar. Then other people got me back to my home. Wonderful people like these two here." Caleb points to the volunteers and Rolando pans to the table stand with the RRR notice taped to its front. "These strangers helped me like they help so many other desperate individuals around the country."

A female voice from the crowd demands, "Did you get that girl Anna-something pregnant? Are you the reason she died?"

Rolando stares over the phone with an intensity that Caleb knows to mean, Fast, fast, fast, and the two volunteers are steadying their table from the bumps of the audience. The half-circle around them is growing. Caleb senses the time to leave is now, but the accusatory question rankles. He can't break his word to Annaliese, he tells himself that's why he can't admit being the father, but he also can't let the charge go.

"Annaliese didn't want anyone to know who got her pregnant. To the end. Ask somebody else about that, not me. She died, though, because the doctors who could have saved her weren't allowed to."

The mass is becoming an animal with many mouths, some calling to him, others arguing among themselves. Cell phones rise above it like antennae, all trained on him. The supervisor is struggling with Mr. Excitable to fold up the table in the crammed space left to them. Rolando is motioning with his eyes for Caleb to go and Caleb very nearly does.

Then someone hollers out, "How do we know you didn't fake the whole damned thing? You disappear off the street and, poof, five days later you show up again. Everyone looked and looked and couldn't find a trace of you. How do we know it wasn't just a hoax?"

THE PROPHET OF CENTRAL PARK

Caleb believes the anger must be making him swell, it fills him so. Rolando closes his eyes for a moment at the change he sees in Caleb's face, but he keeps recording. The two RRR members are forcing their way behind Caleb and away.

"My brother turned himself in. He's in custody, probably going to jail for what he did. My father's on the run. The doctor who examined me diagnosed severe dehydration after I escaped. He reported this to the FBI. What do you need? Me dead on the ground so you can kick the body to be sure?"

Another spectator jumps in, "You fucking people, anything you don't like, anything that shows you up, it's fake news. You're ruining the country." In response a man shouts, "Abortion is murder. 'You belong to your father, the devil, and you want to carry out your father's desire. He was a murderer from the beginning'."

Caleb recognizes the quote from John 8 and wants to yell back, but Rolando grabs Caleb by the arm, pulls him through a narrow path in front of the Father Duffy memorial. When they reach the street, he flags the first cab that approaches, and still gripping Caleb, drags them in the back seat. "Downtown," he tells the driver who is looking out at the commotion. Caleb glances that way too, long enough to see the animal they created shed most of itself as the casual observers flee the heated arguments breaking out among the more committed. As the driver accelerates into traffic, he asks, "What's going on there?"

"Some idiot street performer," Rolando tells the man, but he stares at Caleb. "In and out, huh?" At the disdain in his friend's face, Proverbs 26:12 plays in Caleb's head: Do you see a person wise in their own eyes? There is more hope for a fool than for them.

* * *

Forbes

The circumstances surrounding an article's acceptance by then subsequent withdrawal from The Journal of Political Economics has ignited a debate over the independence of scholarly research at America's elite universities. The essay in question, "The Cannibalizing Effect of Concentrated Wealth on the Social Fabric of the US", is a collaboration

P C Burhenne

between Professor _____ *of Harvard's Economics Department and Professor* _____ *in its Department of Government. Sources familiar with the timeline say that after the Journal agreed to publish, benefactors to the institution became aware of the essay, in particular a venture capitalist whose hedge fund participates in the practices scrutinized in the paper. After threats from this and other alumni to cease financial support to the school, administration officials pressured the co-authors with penalizing obstacles to their careers which made it impossible for them to move forward with the publication. While neither of the authors has commented publicly, lawyers retained by them informed reporters that their remedy will be sought in court. A growing number of scholars from schools across the country are contributing to a fund to offset the pair's legal fees.*

"I'm sorry," Caleb says. "I messed that up."

Rolando leans forward to the perforated glass partition. "Drop us at 34th."

"This has been a big waste of time because of me," Caleb goes on. "I can't post that back there. It all went crazy."

"Exactly. That's why you have to go ahead." Rolando pauses for Caleb to see what that means. When Caleb stares back, Rolando shudders with frustration. "Everyone watching with a camera is going to post because it blew up. Some probably already have. You may as well post your video so the beginning you want out is out."

The logic is undeniable. Caleb has to swallow a sob at the fiasco he has made of his "stand," then he has to ask meekly, "Will you still put it online for me?"

A chuckle breaks apart Rolando's stern frown. "Yeah, I will. I swear, you're worse than my dad."

As his friend begins fiddling with his phone, Caleb notices that the meter is approaching his limit. "I only have a ten, driver. Drop us here."

As he takes the payment, the driver peers at Caleb. He has the dark brown skin and straight black hair of India, Pakistan. Bangladesh, maybe. "You are the one who was taken," and before Caleb even nods, he says, "You're not dead. Allah has a reason."

Caleb replaces his disguise and Rolando finishes uploading the video, then they enter the 34th Street station and, after backtracking, part ways beneath Times Square. In Queens the pack of reporters at the apartment building is one team larger today. He answers all of their shouted questions with, "Have a good day." On the third floor, Davey looks up from his sculpture which now seems poised to take flight from its rocky perch. Caleb cannot come up with the words to match what he feels so he smiles, which gives way to laughter. Davey accepts the praise by resting chin on chest for a moment. Then:

"Busy morning?"

"Wasted morning."

"Well, then," and Davey rolls his eyes toward the station behind the plastic.

Little by little work's well-being displaces the embarrassed twinges that Caleb brought back from Manhattan. He removes an awkward attempt at a budding leaf from a totem, this to dramatic declarations from Wilma's play rehearsal. He is shaping a more graceful replacement when his phone rings. The hard-earned composure vanishes when he recognizes Mr. Strauss's number.

"Am I in trouble?"

The attorney's measured cadence conveys the strain of his upset. "You need to consult me before you make a public statement."

"I didn't say anything that wasn't true," Caleb offers with diffidence.

"More importantly, you didn't say anything you haven't already sworn to in your affidavit, but the FBI is not happy."

The cauldron bubbling to life in his stomach allows Caleb to only parrot back, "The FBI?"

"Any pronouncement on the record that contradicts in the slightest way the account you've given to the authorities will be used by the defense to discredit you at trial. What you did is dangerous." The foolishness Caleb felt with Rolando rushes back but the attorney continues before Caleb can apologize. "There's something else you should keep in mind. One of your biggest assets so far has been the perception by those sympathetic to you that you're just a bystander who got caught up in the great national debate. This video makes you look like an intentional actor. Some might say an instigator."

Again, anger. "I told what happened to me."

"In the most public place in the city. Then left behind a near riot. Thankfully the police did not make any arrests. Otherwise I would be picking you up for another interview with them."

"Why is it, anybody can spread lies about me but I can't speak up in my own defense?"

"I'm speaking up for you, young man. Didn't you see the arti--" Mr. Strauss eats his exasperation with a sharp breath. "Of course, you didn't. The article we spoke about was printed. The girl's father backed you up, exonerated you. You have to trust me on this; your story **is** getting out." Then exasperation blows through the line. "I really have to stop taking referrals from Haruto."

"What's that mean?"

"Sorry. Attorney-client confidentiality there. Caleb, no more surprise public talks, please."

For the rest of the afternoon he fashions an improved leaf that restores his mood. The floor is deserted when he reassembles the totem and stands back to appreciate the more balanced rendition of budding life. Davey has already gone up. The exquisite bird of prey threatens to leap at Caleb as he passes through.

The others have beaten him to the apartment, Haruto included. The old man is at the stove in an apron preparing the cuts of salmon he brought for dinner. Its dill and butter infused aroma fills the room.

Haruto waves without quite looking over. "I don't need to ask if you're hungry, given the trouble you've been making today."

"So Mr. Strauss called you."

At the table with Davey and Tawana, Sidney lets out a shot of laughter. "Don't think he needed anyone to tell him."

"Oh, no! People aren't bothering you, Haruto, are they?"

The man does turn to scowl at Caleb in withering disbelief. "Not me. Why would you do that to yourself?"

Still chuckling, Sidney says, "I'd hate to see how you handle wasps' nests back in Kentucky."

Davey snorts at that but Caleb palms the top of his forehead as if to keep it from exploding. "What are y'all talking about?"

"You wanted your say," the sculptor tells him. "People heard you, on both sides."

THE PROPHET OF CENTRAL PARK

Sidney says, "You're really not getting how much you're the story right now."

Tawana uses her eyes to indicate that Caleb take the empty seat next to her. "C'mon now, everybody. I suspect Mr. Strauss spanked Caleb plenty already." Then to Caleb, "Anyway, sometimes you just have to speak up."

Her mention of the attorney brings back the man's "client" reference, but Caleb doesn't have to conjure a clever way to broach the subject.

"Of course **you** would say that!" Haruto snaps with a ferocity that surprises them all. "Sorry, sorry." the man says keeping his back to them. "But this Crusade event is just too dangerous. The crazies at your everyday events are becoming bad enough. Elliot's not sure he can keep the city from forcing you to get permits from now on. He's not sure that he should. This event two weeks from now is going to attract lunatics from all over the country."

Davey's face goes flinty with concern. "What's he talking about?"

Tawana rests both her hands flat on the table. "The city is not convinced anymore that the Crusade is a good idea. For security reasons. They're certainly not happy about my normal gatherings. Which truth be told have grown larger, and more unruly."

Remembering Davey's explanation of why she agreed, Caleb jumps in. "Then cancel. You didn't really want to do it in the first place so cancel."

The sculptor has his head down, already knowing his friend's answer. "No," she says, the word gentle and unyielding.

"But why not?" Sidney places a hand next to hers, which surprises Caleb. "This Osterhaus character can't argue if the city is having second thoughts."

"Noel's having his own doubts," Tawana says. "I had to convince him earlier to not pull out."

Haruto exclaims "What!" and grips the corners of the stove.

"These messages I receive, they're not just my purpose, they're my responsibility," the guitarist answers him. "I won't allow people to stop me from sharing them. Though this big stage thing . . . it's not how I'm comfortable delivering those messages." They are all taken aback by the confession. Tawana has her head tilted down but glances upward at them in a sheepish manner. "You all know how I interact with people. It's a conversation. Socratic. But this thing in the Park, it's more preaching."

The other three press her to drop out. Tawana's answer is a sigh. In Caleb's head, a verse from Corinthians plays: And God is able to make all grace abound to you, so that in all things at all times, having all that you need, you will abound in every good work.

"You could ask for help," Caleb says.

The suggestion cuts through the arguments. She asks, "What do you mean?" as they look to him.

"Well, you may not be able to do what you normally do but you can get better at what you have to do." Davey, Sidney and Haruto are watching him now and Tawana shrugs for Caleb to go on. "You said yourself, it's a stage thing. All preachers are performers." Caleb indicates about them. "You're surrounded by performers. And a director. I bet they would love to help you. Talk to Osterhaus about the outline of topics you'll discuss and start working on your dialogue for them—your material—while Wilma and her troupe critique you. As to the debate part, I grew up hearing everything this man is going to say to you. I may not still believe but I do know the teachings well enough to defend them." He shrugs back at her. "You don't have to do this by yourself."

Davey rolls his lips inward on themselves before saying, "I'll be damned." Tawana whispers, "No, no, I don't," before looking away.

"Yes, this is all nice and tidy," Haruto says to them all. He moves about the table so he can speak to Tawana. "But are you going to at least hold off these daily sermons which seem to be getting out of hand? If not for yourself, then for the people who follow you."

Tawana grimaces at the point. "I have thought about that. I don't want to be menaced into silence but I don't want others harmed because of me."

The possible concession appeases the older man and he starts back to the sizzle from the pan, but Sidney snaps his fingers. "You don't have to, Tawana," and he pauses, delighted with his idea. "The crowds are in Central Park, and maybe the rowdy disrupters are targeting you there. But there are a lot of other parks." He holds out his hands in a showman's reveal. "Take your show on the road, so to speak."

Davey reaches over to clap Sidney on the back. "Now that's a helluva thought. Huh, Tawana?"

Haruto sighs this time, disappointed. "I forgot how hard it is to care about dreamers."

THE PROPHET OF CENTRAL PARK

Davey gets up from the table and opens a cabinet by the record player. "Why don't we toast the way forward?" He pulls out a bottle of wine. "Nothing special but it's a decent Cabernet."

Sidney stands, saying, "Where are the glasses?"

Caleb takes just a splash in his. Tawana helps Haruto shuttle the plates from the counter. Asparagus stalks stretch out beside the fish. The sight and smell of these remind Caleb that he skipped lunch. After the meal is in place, Tawana remains standing behind her seat.

"If you don't mind, I'd like to speak to what we have here. I don't just mean the food. It's strange this sudden community we find ourselves in, huh?" She addresses this last to Davey who answers with a rumble in his throat and a single duck of his head. "I have many people in my life who help me, but until you three, I only had Davey as a close friend. It's been an amazing, terrifying and pretty unbelievable two weeks but for all the angina it caused each of us, it also drew us together." The guitarist holds her arms out to include each of them in her benediction. "God, thank you for helping us find each other, for making us a family, and please help us see Your Will going forth."

P C Burhenne

Saturday: Two Weeks Before the Event on the Great Lawn

News One

    City officials have revised upward their estimates of how many people will attend the Crusade for Understanding in Central Park which coincides with the national movement of a similar name. Hotel reservations far outstrip numbers for the same time last year and continue to grow. Midtown establishments are reporting no vacancies, as is more and more the case with those in the outer boroughs and nearby New Jersey. A police spokesperson predicts that the prayer event will exceed in scope the 1981 Simon and Garfunkel concert and could well rival the 1997 "Garthstock" show which saw over one million spectators take over the Great Lawn.

    "Agnes asked me to pass along a message," Haruto says over the cell. "She said you should remember Sinead O'Connor."

    Caleb knows it is bad news if the dealer won't tell him directly but the reference means nothing. "Who's Sinead O'Connor?"

    "Heaven help me, I'm surrounded by children. Sinead famously ripped up a photo of Pope John Paul II on Saturday Night Live."

    Despite himself Caleb laughs. "Why would she ever do that?"

    Haruto doesn't chuckle back. "She was protesting the Catholic Church's decades long abuse of children. She was on the side of the angels and that act basically ended her career."

    Caleb stares at the totem he is "correcting," wonders if he need bother. "So Agnes is sending a warning."

    "She's a businesswoman."

    "And a real champion." Caleb smacks his lips. "I've got to get back to work."

Saturday: 1 Week Before the Event on the Great Lawn

Internal FBI Memorandum

Chatter on far-right websites suggests a planned presence at the New York City Crusade by groups opposed to the event. Specifically emails attributed to Christ's Army for America, an organization that sits at the nexus of Christian Nationalism and White Supremacy, speaks of a response "to the mongrel false prophet" being in place. As yet the nature of the response is unknown but liaisons should notify state and local authorities that the threat level has been raised to yellow, Significant Risk of Attack.

Haruto's gaze is busy guiding his feet to stoop treads. The deliberate descent belies Caleb's image of his friend as merely on the threshold of old age. He does not call out until Haruto reaches the sidewalk. Spotting the box Caleb carries, Haruto can muster only, "Ah." Then, "It's only temporary."

"Agnes said as much. 'Just hitting the pause button.' Of course, understood is that I have to sanitize my image." Caleb looks to the sculpture he just picked up. "She did give me a check, though, for the two she sold before I turned from celebrity to agitator."

"That's not . . . . Her customers are more staid than most. I can find you another gallery this afternoon that would be ecstatic to represent you."

"Just one not as important," then Caleb says, "Anyway I thought I'd pick up those ones I left but you're on an errand. I'll swing by another time."

Haruto shoos this away. "I'm going to the Park. If you're not in a hurry, please come along. I'll even throw in a hot pretzel."

Caleb is happy to extend the break from serious matters. He stows the box inside Haruto's door and they set off. The pavement is not the obstacle that his stoop is; Haruto sets a brisk pace. "This seems the right time to say, I want to keep those pieces you dropped off." The old man looks aside to tap Caleb's arm. "I want to buy them."

"That's not necessary. You've done so much for me already--"

"This isn't a gift," Haruto cuts him off. "I've come to cherish the sight of them when I return home."

Despite what the man says, Caleb recognizes charity. "Then they're yours. But you can't pay me for them."

The man is shaking his head before Caleb is through. "I won't accept such an expensive gift and you don't understand that you'll be giving me a bargain. I'll pay you what Agnes paid you which saves me her commission. Either that or you snatch those incredible pieces from someone who loves them."

"Well, if I have to, I will. But maybe for the time being you could just hold on to them for me."

Sad defeat settles over Haruto's expression. "You're as stubborn as William."

At the pretzel stand the old man has the vendor apply mustard without asking permission and after one bite Caleb is grateful. As they walk with the snacks, Caleb tells how Ms. Yuan has found some job opportunities for him. Haruto is plaintive in urging Caleb to not give up on his totems. He assures Haruto that he has not but, in the next breath, explains that art has not proven to be a reliable source for the rent. "Anyway I can't start up anything new until the Crusade's over. It's like a mountain in my way."

They have reached the Great Lawn. Across the field workers assemble the stage for the event. Even at a distance, its scale leaves Caleb staring. He guesses the width at a hundred feet and its height off the ground at maybe fifteen. The steel framework of a wall rises another seventy or eighty feet over the platform. A crane is hoisting another monitor into the gridwork being mounted to this so that Caleb understands that a giant screen will broadcast Tawana and Noel Osterhaus to the farthest reaches of the crowd. Haruto looks away.

"My walks keep taking me here."

"Do they really need that big a television?"

Haruto ignores the question to ask his own. "How's the prep coming?"

Caleb sighs as he tries to find a truthful response. "I don't know how she has the stamina and the, I guess, constancy. The sessions are . . . ."

The old man is frowning and when Caleb falters, he suggests, "Intense?"

THE PROPHET OF CENTRAL PARK

Caleb shakes off the word. "This self-interrogation, it'd be easy to get lost. It shows up all the holes, all the contradictions in what I believe. But Tawana doesn't let . . . she doesn't tell me what to believe but when I'm floundering she says the one thing that helps me find my bearings. She's . . . ."

"A visionary," this as a terrible label from Haruto.

"Yes, but why say it like that?"

"America's not always kind to its visionaries. Especially when they're black."

P C Burhenne

Friday: Day Before the Event on the Great Lawn

Police Plaza One Communique

The large number of people staking out spots for tomorrow's Crusade for Understanding event made early deployment of undercover personnel necessary. Please notify Park officials and commanders of adjacent districts that embedded officers are in place wearing Saturday's color of the day.

Tawana answers Caleb's knock after a second, her usual smile just taking over her mouth.

"Everyone's waiting for you. Dinner's on the table. We **did** agree to take the evening off, didn't we?"

"Yes, yes," and she steps aside so he comes in. The guitarist pushes the door to the jamb without closing it. She holds onto the knob as she says, "I've been asking, seeking, reaching out."

"Is everything all right?"

When she looks up, despair routs the happy face that she put on. "I'm frightened."

Day of the Event

News One

All roads into Central Park are closed to traffic today as are Fifth Avenue and Central Park West from 59th to 110th Streets. Any vehicles parked on those throughways will be towed.

When Caleb peeks from behind the stack of speakers, the only grass visible on the Great Lawn is in the pathways dividing the cordoned squares like the green mullions of a window sash. Below he can see the torsos of men and women jostling against each other but further out the masses become speckled surfaces reaching into the trees at the far end of the field. For the past hour voices from the crowd have been coalescing around competing hymns. Now the traditionalists are singing "I Lift My Eyes" while Tawana's followers answer with her song to the Virgin Mary. National Guardspeople stand with weapons at the corners of the penned-off sections and protect the technicians manning the AV center one hundred feet out from the stage, but Caleb spots other assault rifles bristling up among the spectators and he wishes desperately that he could call off the show.

Sidney comes up beside him. "This is a lot more than I thought it would be."

Caleb doesn't see the need to answer.

Mr. Osterhaus's voice carries from behind them. When Tawana introduced the preacher earlier, Caleb recognized the easy cadence from the man's broadcasts. Now, however, an anxious weight hampers these words. "We've kept everyone waiting long enough."

Like never before, the guitarist is the center of everything about her. She refused the show's make-up artists for Wilma and the director has heightened her searching gaze with a thin application of eyeliner. She has drawn Tawana's lips with a shade of red that adds moisture without being garish, and softened the natural sheen of Tawana's skin without muting its radiance. In white slacks and a purple blouse the guitarist is simple elegance. The preacher is taller than Caleb thought he would be—six, two

P C Burhenne

at a guess—but despite his height and expertly tailored grey suit, he seems to be at Tawana's side rather than the other way around.

"We'll start as we agreed?" Mr. Osterhaus asks her.

In answer she touches his forearm. "This is a wonderful thing you've brought together here."

Tawana and the man both put on and adjust their headsets so the microphones hover like large insects before their mouths. She smiles over at Caleb and Sidney and points to her guitar that Sidney holds, meaning for the roommate to be ready when she motions for it.

She and the preacher walk out to center stage.

The roar is so loud that Caleb looks to see if trees are bending away. Then the preacher Noel takes Tawana's hand and a murmuring disrupts the cheers. "We thank you all for being with us today, those who've come in person, some from very far away, and those who are tuning in from your homes." He lets go of her hand and turns to her.

"Noel and I do not spread the same message but we both hear in the other the Divine Spirit striving to soothe and bring peace," she says.

A collective "Aah" rises from the crowd and Caleb knows that, even through the speakers, Tawana's praeternatural ability to reach out is causing each person who hears her feel that she is addressing him or her personally.

"We ask you all now to join us in prayer," Noel says. "Lord, help us to listen. Help us to open our hearts and minds so that You may reconcile our differences. Tawana?"

Without looking up, Tawana adds, "And in so doing, help us realize we are all your children, and therefore, though we may not know the people around us, they are our brothers and sisters."

"Amen!" The word reverberates outward and the buildings bounding the Park echo it back.

Noel steps forward as Tawana takes a step back. "We've decided to introduce ourselves by describing the paths to our vocations. Those who follow me already know that as a young man, I achieved great success in business. In my twenties I had money and was on my way to amassing even greater wealth. I had all the things that money buys. So much more than I needed. I had the company of beautiful women. And it was never enough. Never. It led me to a very dark place where I began to question why I should go on. And that is a very dark place indeed." On the screen backing the stage, Noel's giant likeness contorts with the distress of that terrible time. All about, spectators mutter or shout out in sympathy. "But my parents knew better than I what their son needed. They sent a family friend who was a preacher and this man helped me understand that my hunger was not for material things but was for spiritual nourishment. With this man's help, in my Houston penthouse apartment, I accepted Jesus Christ as my savior and immediately felt the overwhelming grace of God cleanse my soul. That moment changed the course of my life." Throughout the field Noel's believers raise their hands to celebrate the fruits of God's merciful intervention. "I knew I had to help others receive what had been given to me. My bosses, my colleagues, they all thought I had lost my mind when I quit the next day, but my true purpose had become clear. I was to spread His good word so that others could follow me to salvation. And that purpose has brought me, brings me still the greatest joy and satisfaction a man can know."

Noel places a hand over his heart to accept the field's applause. In the ranks below the stage, Caleb sees some people clap politely, others fervently. Two burly men with assault weapons strapped across their backs look to hurt their hands while the old near-skeletal man between them clasps his together. Caleb can read the "Halleluia"s those dried lips speak though the shout does not rise above the general noise. Then Caleb starts at Davey's voice at his ear.

"Our girl's turn next. Oh, sorry. You know what's she's gonna say?"

Sidney waits for Caleb's answer too. From the prep sessions Caleb has heard the several versions she's composed. "I'm not sure what she's decided."

Tawana steps forward to the spot that Noel relinquished. On the stadium screen her face in close-up is still, eyes shut, until the internal search turns to a calm repose and she lifts her chin and looks out again and begins.

"I came to a life in service to God because of the examples of service that rescued me from my own dark and desperate place. As a teenager I became an orphan. My parents were loving protectors but the family left to me was not. I became a ward of the state, in foster homes, group homes then on the street. I became angry, and afraid. Always, always afraid. Never knowing what the person in front of me wanted, what the person behind me would try to do. But kind souls found me in that hard life. The nurse who helped me bear the terrible decision to terminate a pregnancy that I could not survive in my circumstances." Caleb tenses at the admission he was not sure that the guitarist would make and behind him Davey draws a worried breath. A rumble passes through the tens of thousands watching out front, even as Tawana continues without a pause. "The quirky neighborhood artist who spirited me away from the predator threatening violence unless I entered a life of prostitution for him. That artist's amazing aunt who took me in, saw to it that I received an education and introduced me to the Bible." The disturbance in the crowd morphs here and there into catcalls of "murderer" and "whore" that are then answered by Tawana's supporters, "Hypocrites", "Cast your stones." The screen flashes to Noel holding out a hand for his followers to stop, though Tawana rivets his gaze. "Through reading the scriptures, I came to recognize that the Divine had worked through those kind souls to lift me up and I experienced a calling to do for others what they did for me. But above that the Bible challenged me to draw closer to God, to struggle to know Her Will for us, through prayer and meditation, and also through talk with others seeking closeness. Like this extraordinary gathering today."

Tawana gestures outward to the populated plain. Many, though not all, cheer. Noel comes forward again.

"I hope everyone accepts that we have shown ourselves honestly, without pride. Or deception. Well, so much to discuss."

Noel falters a moment so Tawana steps in. "The 'Her Will' references are problematic, huh?" and when "Yes"s fly back from all points, she smiles and points out as if to them all. "Thank you for telling me true," then to her partner on the stage, "May I explain?"

On the screen, Noel smirks in appreciation at her deft defusing of critics and nods. Davey chuckles, Sidney whispers, "Smooth," and Caleb begins to hope the guitarist will survive today's spotlight unscathed.

"I don't believe God identifies with only His sons, that She relates to only Her daughters. I flip back and forth between each as a feeble attempt to address a Presence I cannot comprehend."

People whistle approval. Noel does not falter this time.

THE PROPHET OF CENTRAL PARK

"Let us talk about the person of Christ. Jesus is central to my faith and to the faith of so many of those who've joined us today. You did not speak of His role in your journey. Would you do so now?"

To Noel she says, "Here is where we need God's spirit of reconciliation, of openness." Then to the watching mass, "Some of you hold Christ to be the Son of God and Divine Himself in a manner apart from all other humans. I see him as a child of God as we are all children of God, a man who attained a near perfect communion with the Almighty, one we all can attain, although only through great, great sacrifice. A point that separates us. But I hope we all agree that we should follow the example of his life dedicated to others. And I hope we conclude today that the latter is more important than the former."

On the screen, Noel's face communicates regret overcome with conviction.

"Of course we celebrate Christ's life as the model for our own but that point of separation, as you call it, looms large. The gift of God made man and His willingness to endure crucifixion to pay for our sins are the key to our salvation. God's grace can only be given. Apart from asking for it by accepting Christ as our savior, no act on our parts can earn redemption."

Segments of the crowd cry out, "Testify, testify." Tawana projects rather than raises her voice in that way of hers; this rolls forth to dampen the chant.

"Yes, here we disagree." She looks from the immense congregation to Noel and back. Her own regret is solemn. "I believe our practices in this world make us capable or unable to accept the gift of the next." Over the stage Noel's eyes move about as if he has lost his place on a script. Tawana faces him with a favor. "I wrote something recently that speaks to this. May I?"

Still not back on his cue, the preacher nods and tells his members of the crowd, "Like so many before us, Tawana spreads the good word through song at times." The guitarist motions for her instrument. Sidney mutters, "Changed my mind," but Davey gives him a shove so that the roommate reaches her slowing from a trot. When Sidney returns, Davey leans in to tell him, "Smooth," to which the roommate says, "Shut up, you."

P C Burhenne

After a moment to tweak the tuning, Tawana launches into a mournful dirge. The purity and depth of its gospel-cloaked sound surprises a reaction from the Great Lawn like a cat's purr on an immense scale. She sings:

Was man expelled
or did we break apart
then vanity compelled us leave?

A golden rule
kept strife from paradise
ensured the people's common wealth

Great evil starts with slights
that barely prick the skin
a whisper launched our fall
not us   think you and I

We're self-deceived
expatriates
not refugees

Yes, self-deceived
expatriates
not refugees

Tawana holds out the instrument for Sidney to come take away. The multitudes divide to join either an ovation or a displeased lowing that crystallizes into a jumble of objections. Past the returning roommate, Caleb glimpses the enraged scowl on the haggard face of the emaciated old man. His eyes in their hollows gleam with contempt. When his armed companion on the right speaks an urgent message into his ear, the old man swipes him away. The imperious gesture, the whole haughty attitude troubles Caleb.

"You believe Adam and Eve left Eden by choice?" A hint of mockery inhabits the preacher's question.

THE PROPHET OF CENTRAL PARK

Tawana's giant self holds a finger to the bridge of her nose, breathes deeply and delivers her answer with that finger keeping its meter. "I believe a person steeped in selfish ways will not abide the Heavenly Kingdom."

Noel reaches his arms to the sky to announce the good news. "But after death God the Father will cleanse the souls of all who wished to be saved so we may live in harmony at His side in heaven."

The preacher's followers roar approval. This rebuttal stirs the starved, head-shaved figure to shake a fist at Tawana. Caleb cannot look away from his mouth twisted about some damning curse. Noel pauses to accept the praise but when he turns back, Tawana gives him a sad shake of her head as she answers.

"I do not understand that God who in the afterlife transforms certain of his children, souls you've already said in no way earned this gift, into selfless beings so they may live in peace together, but He will not bless His children thus in this world which is beset by all the forms of misery that selfishness breeds."

The cadaverous figure can only stare back at Tawana's reply. His lips work against each other but bring forth no words. Caleb expects his rage would have him turn away if the press of people allowed it. Those eyes shouting what the mouth can not.

"It's him!" Caleb exclaims. "It's him, it's him, it's him." This as Noel says, "It's not for us to know the entirety of God's plan but He has revealed what we need to know in the Bible."

Davey pulls Caleb back, challenges him through a cross frown, "What the hell are you on about?"

"My father's out there! In front of the stage."

The sculptor rears back, then looks out as if to find the man, though from where they stand now, the bank of speakers blocks most of the crowd. Sidney is there too. "Are you sure?"

"I just spent four days with him in my face. He shaved his beard and head but, yeah, it's him and he's not here to celebrate. I've got to find police."

The steps are at the back of the platform. The tent for the support staff gives out only a muffled word or two now that the crusade is underway. Two officers guard the break in the barricade surrounding the rear area, one a wiry Asian man bulked up by his vest and equipment belt and the other taller, truly stout and pink-faced. Both move a hand nearer their guns as Caleb hurries toward them so that he shows his own empty hands and stops a few feet away.

"I need your help, please, officers. My name is Caleb Ellison. I've been in the news a lot the past few weeks." Caleb is relieved to see recognition light in each of their faces. "I'm on stage and I saw my father in the crowd. He's wanted by you guys and the FBI for helping to kidnap me. He's with two men who are armed and he owns a handgun too which I bet he has with him."

The taller officer—his breast tag reads "Dubrowski"--points to his partner, Wong. "Check it out and come back. I'll call it in. What's your father's first name?"

"Alfred."

Officer Wong herds him back on stage. Sidney and the sculptor are jitterbugging in wait for them. A dispatcher broadcasts the possible sighting on the radio pinned to the policeman's chest. The officer almost steps to the edge of the speaker bank, saying, "Okay, show me--" then stops himself. "I might spook him if it is your dad." Wong removes and activates his phone. "Act like you're panning the crowd and take a picture of him."

Caleb holds the phone out and watching the view screen at an angle so he himself is hidden, snaps a photo of Alfred Sr. Snatching back the phone, Officer Wong scuttles away, pressing his chin aside to speak into the radio. "Notify action commander, I have an image of the subject."

Tawana's calm tone aggravates Caleb's sense that danger encircles her. "I hold the Bible to be a magnificent and inspired attempt to understand God's Will, undertaken by a group hungry for that connection, but as a product of humans, it is flawed as all our efforts must be."

"Are you absolutely fucking sure," Davey demands at Caleb's side so that the breath from this spews into his ear.

When Caleb peeks out again, Alfred Sr. trembles at the blasphemy bandied about in front of him. Both companions are whispering at Caleb's father, their bobbing heads suggesting calls to action. Nearby spectators are shuffling restively, aware now of a disturbance.

"Yes, absolutely."

THE PROPHET OF CENTRAL PARK

Noel responds, "As you said, the Scriptures are inspired. Almighty God overcame our frailties to deliver to us His unadulterated Word. As Matthew tells us, 'With man this is impossible, but with God all things are possible'."

"Then we've gotta get her off there, get her somewhere safe," Davey says. Caleb agrees yet he stays put, constrained by the weight of attention that a step forward will drop upon him. And if he's wrong . . . . The others stay frozen too.

Tawana actually chuckles and smiles. "As you said before, so much to discuss." Then she considers a moment before going on, "Scholarly and historical questions aside, I don't believe God's unadulterated word could fail to convince, let alone engender so much disagreement among people who claim it as Gospel." She holds up a hand to stanch the upset bubbling behind the preacher's sudden frown. "I know you believe unconditionally," then she moves that hand to include the immense field. "As do so many of you present today. But different sects of Christians interpret the Bible differently. And around the world different societies of loving and humble people find the message of the Divine more clearly accessible in teachings other than the Scriptures."

Caleb looks for movement from the authorities stationed about the green pathways. He knows guards must be posted below the grandstand but they are out of sight.

Noel says, "Obviously the fault lies with us, not God. Our arrogance leads us to dissect His Word for minor inconsistencies to impugn it when we would be so much better off opening our minds and hearts to the rewards Jesus promises us."

Alfred Sr. nods to his compatriots with a resigned scowl that leaves Caleb praying silently for Wong to hurry.

Tawana is nodding too, laughing now as she gestures to herself. "By the arrogant, you mean me. And it's true, I cannot ignore the contradiction between gospels. The Jesus of Matthew who preaches of the coming of God but never speaks of himself as divine and refuses to perform miracles as a demonstration, and the Christ of John who constantly proclaims his divinity and performs miracle after miracle as proof. But in the spirit of this day, I hope we can focus on what we do agree upon—the benefits that you mentioned and that I see too in following the teachings and examples of Christ."

P C Burhenne

Alfred Sr. has his head bowed. Caleb sees he is mouthing a prayer.

Noel's voice is solemn in asking, "First, tell me, if you reject the absolute authority of the Bible, what then is the rock upon which your moral life is built? What is the foundation for the decisions you make about right and wrong?"

Tawana answers him at once, "Yes, Noel, yes. That is the heart of the matter, isn't it. I've dwelt on that question for many hours. I've asked Her guidance and I always return to Christ's life and his golden rule."

Police officers are now moving along the paths but Alfred Sr. is focused on something blocked from view yet in his grip. His companions have moved forward to screen his actions. Caleb cries, "Oh, no, they're not going to get to him!"

"Why, what's happening?" Davey is looking out over Caleb's shoulder.

Tawana continues, "And I've found a rock in that command to do unto others as I would have others do unto me. I've tried to consider all the emotions that drive me, good and bad. Jealousy and admiration, anger and sympathy, the full gambit and each of them arise from one of two basic forces. Fear and love. Concern for myself over us, or concern for us over myself. When I am guided by the latter, I feel myself in keeping with that golden rule. When I am guided by the latter, I believe I serve God's Will."

The police spot Alfred Sr., are closing in but he is raising his gun and they will not reach him in time. Tawana's fans are shouting their agreement, thousands upon thousands of throats overwhelming Caleb's scream of "Watch out!", the buzz of a bee disturbing the guitarist's concentration for a second only. Caleb bolts toward her, with no more thought to the spectacle he makes. The movement catches Tawana's eye, and the preacher's, and they turn to him. It catches the attention of Alfred Sr. who instinctively swings the gun to the new threat and Caleb freezes at his father's Smith & Wesson trained on him. The two companions are urging Alfred Sr. to hurry, the surrounding crowd are now shouting in alarm and Caleb sees clearly the progression across his father's face from shock at Caleb's sudden appearance to betrayal to hatred that spreads like a dark shadow falling over the man. Then the muzzle becomes a point of brilliance that in an instant wraps Caleb in a blinding white shroud.

* * *

THE PROPHET OF CENTRAL PARK

Yahoo news flash

Moments ago a gunman opened fire at the Salvation in the Park event in New York's Central Park. Initial reports indicate two people have been shot, a member of the crowd and a participant on stage. Bystanders quickly subdued the assailant. Updates on the condition of the gunshot victims will be forthcoming.

Caleb gazes down at his own body sprawled upon the stage floor, legs straight and apart, arms flung to the sides, eyes staring up bewildered at the specter of his self departing. Kneeling at his side, Tawana presses a palm to the bullet wound, the muscles of her forearm flexed as if this effort will stop the flow of blood. Davey, Sidney and the preacher stand at his feet, facing the crowd as a shield to protect him. The sculptor is ashen, the other two are gone the color of Davey's marble. Tawana tells them, tells the plain of witnesses, "Please, pray with me." The sobs she strains to hold off nevertheless seep through as vibrato troubling the words. "Please, if it's possible, Lord, please let Caleb stay with us. Please, do not take him." A babble of pleas for his preservation rise from the mass and he wants so much to return but a summons turns him to the Great Lawn too. At the farthest reaches of the gathering, too distant to see yet clear to him, a figure beckons. He walks, he moves, he goes over top the people. Over his father and the two accomplices pinned to the ground by a scrum of concerned citizens and law enforcement, Alfred Sr. shouting, "It's the burden of Abraham." Caleb moves on and the field of wavering heads and shoulders goes still and silent except for the androgynous conductor standing on a cardboard square at its rear, disheveled but no longer filthy in the dingy grey sweater and jeans out of which all blue has leached. The vagrant welcomes Caleb to sit on the placemat and does so too. Caleb tries again but cannot make the figure's features conform to one gender.

"You gave your life for hers. You gave her a reprieve."

Caleb is too disoriented to speak at first. Feels too small. Until the final remark. "Why just a reprieve?

"Every day is a reprieve," then the vagrant leans his/her head aside to add, "It's true, though, those like Tawana who answer my call unconditionally pay the highest price." The vagrant straightens. "Tough month, huh?"

The flippant remark surprises a chuckle from Caleb, though with a longing finish. "Well, I guess it's over now."

"Maybe." This with a pensive lift of the eyebrows.

The seat suddenly feels precarious under Caleb. "What does that . . . what happens now?"

The vagrant's voice takes on a huskier timber. "I don't know yet."

The other watches then, not unkindly. Caleb remembers his manners. "Thank you for staying with me in the cellar."

The vagrant accepts this with a nod then in the most serious manner yet asks, "If you could change it all, go back to the square and this time stand by while those men attacked the volunteers' table, would you?"

Phantom memories of an alternative month flash by: no new circle of friends and William just a long-deceased uncle he missed the opportunity to know, his totems a hobby and Tawana a fascinating character with whom he avoids eye contact on the subway, but his body whole, a future at the auction house still bright and his family intact if estranged. The relish of those tourist soldiers for the harm they were about to do tips the balance.

"I would do the same."

"Always the fighter." An answer showing that the vagrant followed his thoughts. "I am glad you two came together. For awhile I worried you wouldn't accept Tawana."

"'Accept'?"

The vagrant is still and his gaze claims Caleb's. "I am well-pleased with that girl."

The pronouncement should dismay, but Caleb finds he **has** accepted her.

"What have you learned from Tawana?" and when Caleb gulps like a fish plucked from the water, the vagrant goes on, "She is a teacher in everything she says and does."

Caleb grasps that this is a test. He reviews his time with the guitarist, watching her spread her message to others and having her gently prod him with questions. "She engages people." The vagrant attends Caleb with the weight of silence and stern patience of a judge. "Whether they like her or are angry with her, she engages."

THE PROPHET OF CENTRAL PARK

This last decides the vagrant to continue. "Your father shot to kill you, his son, a terrible act, but in many ways his father did the same to him. Over many years. The poor man never stopped being the boy who wet the bed again after his William left."

Caleb sees Alfred Sr. not as the figure commanding the dinner table at which Caleb grew up but as that traumatized youth. "Why didn't you help him?"

"I ask myself that question countless times a day." The vagrant's eyes blaze and Caleb trembles. "Your father struggled all his adult life not to become the brutal man who raised him but violence begets violence. It takes an extraordinary effort to break that chain."

Sympathy for the childhood that Alfred Sr. never fully escaped pushes at the weight of betrayal inside Caleb and he almost announces that he will forgive the man. Perhaps not at that moment but at some point in the stretch of eternity. In the next instance, the reference to the chain seizes his attention and with it, the label of him as the fighter. Caleb gasps as if this place had air and it had suddenly been sucked away and he clutches at his chest where a wound should be, all at the realization of the link he has been forming in his family's hateful tapestry.

The vagrant does not smile as much as exude satisfaction at the epiphany so that the waystation they are in brightens, and he or she puts a hand over Caleb's chest. Warmth passes through Caleb's body that is uncomfortable in its intensity. Then with a flick of the fingers the vagrant sends him away, hurtling through the brilliant white shroud and the burning sensation becomes a pain as if a horse kicked him in his ribcage. He flickers his eyes open to a trio of shapes that are blocking out the blue of the sky.

"Wait! Lady, what did you do? I got something," a voice says.

Another answers, "How is this fucking guy alive?"

Then Tawana, "Oh, thank you, God. Thank you for sending him back."

P C Burhenne

Epilogue: April 5

Maynardsville Picayune
  Native son Caleb Ellison has filed permit requests with town authorities to open the William Ellison Crisis Intervention and Cultural Center in the vacated building on Front Street that once housed Mercurio's Supermarket. The stated purpose of the center is support for the region's LGBTQ community and for women and families dealing with pregnancy concerns along with sponsorship of events to increase dialogue over divisive social issues. Community opposition to the project is already forming and some town officials have gone on record against the petitions. When reached for comment, the center's creator said he expects legal action to be part of the way forward. Readers will recall that Mr. Ellison recently returned to Maynardsville after recovering from a life-threatening gunshot wound at the hands of his father, local auctioneer Alfred Ellison Sr., suffered during last fall's well-publicized Salvation in the Park crusade.

"Yeah, Sidney and Davey are coming over for dinner tonight," Haruto confirms.

Caleb looks about his living quarters with the large patches of wall opened for new wiring. "Tell them both I miss them."

"You should be here with us."

There is a pause that the honk-heavy soundtrack of Manhattan fills. Caleb can imagine the old man's embarrassed duck of the head at letting the last slip out and a heartburn from homesickness makes Caleb wince himself. "I wish I was coming too but I am where I'm supposed to be. Is Sidney still happy with his new roommate?"

"They seem to be getting along. Anyway he's got Davey. Tell me how your sculpture's coming. They'll both want to know. As will Agnes."

Caleb swivels about to the studio portion of the room. The figure with an enigmatic welcome and tattered clothes sits in Buddha fashion on the worktable. "Why don't I send pictures and you can critique it over dessert?"

"Yes, do. We'd all love that."

THE PROPHET OF CENTRAL PARK

"Talked to Tawana today," Caleb says. "She's making her way to my neck of the woods. She's in central PA right now."

"Someplace called Altoona. One of her disciples found her a place to 'engage with people' for a few days."

"They're volunteers, Haruto, not disciples."

"Tomato, tomahto. But I am happy she's not alone on her Magic Mystery God tour," and with a dramatic sense of timing, the old man says, "I just turned over another batch of hate mail to the FBI."

Tawana and the few with her are driving a converted school bus, not a tie-dyed VW minibus, but Caleb lets it go. Haruto never understood her choice of the vagabond preacher's life instead of Noel Osterhaus's offer to partner with him on a nationally broadcast program and Caleb knows that it falls to the old man to cull out the vile death threats from the letters people send. "Well, I'm hoping I get to see her in a couple weeks."

A sigh comes through the cell then. "Give her a hug for me." Caleb barely has a chance to say, "Will do," before Haruto hurries on, "Elliot got in to see your father this week. He passed on your letter. I can only imagine what you put in there. Besides William's letter." Knowing what he wrote, Caleb waits. "Elliot said at first he thought your father was going to attack him. The guard actually rushed in. Your father was screaming, 'How could he know that.' In the next second, he was slumped over the letter crying his eyes out."

"What does Elliot think?"

"Your father will not live long enough to get out of prison."

After the call, the refuge-in-progress reinforces how much work he needs to do to recreate a home for the one he has sacrificed. If that is even possible in a town so angry at his return. With a bracing breath, he says, "This should have been here for you, Annaliese."

Caleb goes for a short walk; a friend of Mr. Tompkins is coming in an hour to look over the job of repairing the sheetrock. The snout of the wolf's head that his Pop Pop carved for the cane juts out ready to snarl between Caleb's middle and index fingers. A light grey canopy traps the town and the cool day is raw with the moisture from the river. This evening's dinner with Carolyne's family, and hopefully their mother, preoccupies Caleb so that he doesn't pay attention to the figure walking toward him on the sidewalk until the man stops Caleb with a rough hand to the chest.

"So you came back to open up a homo store. I always knew you were a faggot."

Caleb has just enough time to recognize his assailant as a classmate with whom he fought over the same type of taunt in high school before the man spits in Caleb's face.

The electricity of rage displaces his convalescence's weariness and his palm squeezes the oaken head so that the wolf would yelp if it was alive. The man sneers, daring retaliation. He is an inch taller than Caleb and though farmwork is wearing away the definition of his athletic past, he is still an imposing figure in his orange and green flannel shirt. However, Caleb stops himself raising the club.

"Didn't think so," and the man's grin is another spit in the face as he goes past.

"Wait, Teddy?" Caleb says as he wipes away the mucus with his forearm.

"You should go with your first instinct and watch me walk away."

Teddy has swung back ready to fight. Instead Caleb laughs. "What, are we still two knotheads in the schoolyard? You obviously have something you want to say to me. Say it." Caleb starts past the stumped Teddy back towards the storefront. "Come on. I'll make you a cup of coffee. You can tell me all the things I'm doing wrong."

Teddy pivots with Caleb but instead of moving, he stammers out, "What, whatta you doing?"

Caleb holds out both hands as if to indicate, "Table, coffee, talk," then at the unease that the invitation is raising in the man, Caleb says, "Look, I'm not gay and even if I was, you're not my type."

Teddy continues to hesitate, uncertain what the manly response is.

"I know you go to service, Teddy, at least you used to. We both believe in God, not the same things, but we're both believers. God wants us to talk, even if we're angry with each other, She wants us to talk."

"She!" Teddy bursts out, his face taking on its face-spitting expression again.

"There. Something else you can yell at me about. And I promise I'll listen, Teddy, but please, give me the same courtesy." Again Caleb holds out his hands. "Table, coffee, talk. And the coffee is really good. A friend sends the beans to me from New York. So what do you say?"

THE PROPHET OF CENTRAL PARK

The End

P C Burhenne

Acknowledgments

I owe many thanks to the members of the Tuesday Night workshop whose criticisms over two decades sharpened my writing skills. Michael Brennan's encouragement helped me sustain my determination to see this book published. Barry Dougherty and Jeffrey Goldberg both provided invaluable advice on how to draw readers like you to these pages. Sally Arteseros worked diligently to ensure that I told this story in as professional a manner as I am capable of. I feel a special debt of gratitude to Gerry Jonas who read each draft and suggested the solution to a persistent problem with the opening. My daughter Clare constantly assured me that I was up to the task of self-publishing. Above all I thank Eve who has not only been an honest but stalwart supporter of my literary dreams but who also allowed me the time and resources to see this project through to completion. I love you always.

www.ingramcontent.com/pod-product-compliance
Lightning Source LLC
Chambersburg PA
CBHW071552110726
47908CB00007B/2074